Rosie Goodwin has worked in social services for many years. She has children, and lives in Nuneaton with her husband Trevor and their four dogs.

Praise for Rosie Goodwin:

'A heart-throbber of a story' *Northern Echo*

'A touching and tender story . . . tremendously uplifting and life-affirming. A feel-good read that tugs at the heart strings' *Historical Novels Review*

'A gifted writer . . . Not only is Goodwin's characterisation and dialogue compelling, but her descriptive writing is a joy' *Nottingham Evening Post*

'Rosie is the real thing – a writer who has something to say and knows how to say it' Gilda O'Neill

'Goodwin is a born author' *Lancashire Evening Telegraph*

'Goodwin is a fabulous writer . . . she reels the reader in surprisingly quickly and her style involves lots of twists and turns that are in no way predictable' *Worcester Evening News*

'Rosie is a born storyteller – she'll make you cry, she'll make you laugh, but most of all you'll care for her characters and lose yourself in her story' Jeannie Johnson

'Her stories are now eagerly awaited by readers the length and breadth of the country' *Heartland Evening News*

By Rosie Goodwin and available from Headline

ROSIE GOODWIN

The Misfit

headline

First published in Great Britain in 2012
by HEADLINE PUBLISHING GROUP

First published in paperback in 2012
by HEADLINE PUBLISHING GROUP

1

Cataloguing in Publication Data is available from the British Library

ISBN 978 0 7553 8573 7

Typeset in Calisto MT by Palimpsest Book Production Ltd,
Falkirk, Stirlingshire

Printed and bound in Great Britain by Clays Ltd, St Ives plc

Headline's policy is to use papers that are natural, renewable and recyclable
products and made from wood grown in sustainable forests. The logging and
manufacturing processes are expected to conform to the environmental
regulations of the country of origin.

HEADLINE PUBLISHING GROUP
An Hachette UK Company
338 Euston Road
London NW1 3BH

www.headline.co.uk
www.hachette.co.uk

For Trev . . . as always. x

Acknowledgements

Many thanks to everyone at the circus in Lincolnshire for talking to me and giving me such a good insight into circus life.

Loneliness and the feeling of being unwanted is the most terrible poverty.

– Mother Teresa

PART ONE

Abandoned

Chapter One

4 August 1988

'We'd better make this snappy, otherwise Sister will have our guts for garters. We've only got ten minutes before we're due back on the ward.' Jackie Bell grinned at her partner in crime and fumbled in her handbag for her cigarettes and lighter as they stepped out into the warm sunshine.

Her friend, Lilli, took the cigarette Jackie was offering, lit it and inhaled. They were in the bin area behind the huge hospital in Coventry where she and Jackie were trainee nurses. The place was strictly out of bounds to all members of staff, apart from the porters who delivered the rubbish there. But Jackie and Lilli were not above flouting the odd rule or two, especially when it meant sneaking a crafty fag. The two girls had become close in the time they had worked together, although they made an unlikely pair. Jackie was plump and extrovert, with huge brown eyes that always seemed to be sparkling with mischief. Her mop of wild dark hair invariably managed to escape the band she tied it back in, no matter how much lacquer she used. By contrast, Lilli Cooper was petite, fair and softly spoken.

'Shame we've got to go back to work on such a lovely afternoon, ain't it?' Jackie turned her face up to the cloudless blue sky above them.

'Well, at least we've got a whole weekend off to look

forward to,' Lilli pointed out, puffing furiously on her cigarette. 'Only two more shifts to go now.'

They stood there enjoying the sun's warmth on their skin and trying to ignore the stench that was issuing from the huge industrial bins. The pong was always far worse when it was warm, but they were both more than willing to put up with that if it meant snatching a little time out.

Behind them they could hear the sounds of the busy hospital: trolleys being rolled across tiled floors, phones ringing and the distant hum of numerous voices.

And then came an unfamiliar sound, which made them prick up their ears.

'Did you hear that?' Dropping her cigarette stub, Jackie ground it out with the heel of her flat black shoe as she looked around nervously.

Lilli nodded, her eyes darting amongst the bins. 'Yes, I did. It sounded like a kitten, didn't it?'

Moving tentatively forward, the girls looked this way and that around the enormous metal containers. The sound was louder now and they split up to search separately, aware that they should really be on their way back to the ward.

Seconds later, Jackie almost collided with Lilli, who was standing behind one of the largest bins staring down.

'What's wrong?' As Jackie's eyes dropped to the bundle close to Lilli's feet, she gasped. 'My God! It's a baby,' she uttered in disbelief. A sturdy cardboard box was propped up on a pair of old crates, with a handwritten notice Sellotaped to the side. 'PLEASE TAKE CARE OF ME' was written on it, in large shaky letters. And that was all.

Lilli bent down and scooped the child into her arms. The baby, wrapped in a pink blanket and dressed in a faded blue Babygro, was red in the face with crying.

'She looks as if she's only just been born,' Lilli whispered. 'But who would just leave her here like this?'

'I don't know,' Jackie gulped. 'But what do we do with her now?'

'Well, we can't just leave her here, can we?' Lilli said. 'We'll have to take her inside.'

They both stared at the baby for a moment as Lilli rocked her soothingly. She wasn't the prettiest of babies. She had a shock of downy hair and her face was wrinkled like that of a very old woman. Her small hands were clenched into fists as if she was protesting at her treatment, but her saving grace was her eyes; they were the colour of bluebells.

'How will we explain how we found her?' Jackie asked anxiously. 'We shouldn't even *be* here.'

'We'll have to cross that bridge when we come to it. She might need medical attention, so at least she's been left in the right place. Come on, we'd better go and get this over with.'

Jackie nodded before meekly following her friend through the double swing doors that would take them back into the hospital.

The next morning, Jackie was waiting for Lilli at the entrance to the hospital when the latter arrived waving a newspaper in the air.

'Have you seen this?' She pushed the paper towards her. 'The lass has made the headlines.' Lilli took it from her and quickly began to scan the page.

Newborn Baby Girl Found Amongst Bins at Hospital

A newborn baby girl was found yesterday amongst the rubbish bins at the back of the Wellsgrave Hospital in Coventry. The child is reported to be doing well but police are concerned that the mother may be in need of urgent medical attention and are urging her to come forward. The child is presently being cared for by nurses at the hospital who have named her Lilli after the young nurse who found her. Anyone who can help to establish the child's identity is being asked to contact their nearest police station as soon as possible.

'Phew!' Folding the newspaper, Lilli took a deep breath as she and Jackie went through the huge revolving doors and headed for the children's ward. She had barely slept a wink the night before for thinking of the child, and she and Jackie had arranged to come to work half an hour early so that they could visit her.

They were shown into a side-ward, where they found the baby contentedly lying in a small cot. A middle-aged social worker was in there speaking to the Ward Sister, who smiled at them as they entered.

'This is Lilli, the young lady who found the baby,' she informed the woman as Lilli hung over the baby's cot.

After a while, Lilli raised her head to ask, 'What will happen to her now?'

The social worker pursed her thin lips. 'That all depends on whether we manage to trace the mother or not,' she answered truthfully. 'The best scenario would be if the mother came forward and we could reunite her with her daughter. But if she doesn't, the baby will go to a foster-carer in a few days' time and then possibly for adoption.'

'Oh.' Lilli's eyes filled with tears as she looked down at the baby again. It was so sad to think that she had no one. Or at least no one who cared enough to want her. But then she had done her bit and all she could do now was leave the baby in the capable hands of the Social Services.

'Goodbye, little Lilli – and good luck.' Tucking the pink

teddy bear she had bought for the child into the cot, she bent to kiss her soft cheek. As she walked away, she had a dreadful premonition that the poor little mite would need all the luck she could get in the days and years ahead.

Chapter Two

'It seems the police have traced the child's mother,' Jean Beckham told her colleague three days later in the Social Services office where they worked in Coventry.

'Really?' Lindsay Bent took a large bite of her apple as she stared at Jean. The two women had shared an office for six months now, ever since Lindsay had started there fresh from university – and despite the difference in their ages, they got along very well.

'Yes, I had a call just before you got in. I'm going along to the police station to see the mother shortly, although now I know who it is I have very little hope that she'll want the baby back.'

'Why is that then?' Lindsay raised a carefully plucked eyebrow as she slid off the desk and ran her hands down the sides of her tight jeans.

'Because the mother – in fact, the whole family – has been known to the Department for some time now. They live in Radford, and little Lilli's mother has been seen working the streets. The last I heard, her husband was in nick. She has three children already and she's only about twenty-three, if I remember correctly. The other kids have only just managed to avoid coming into care on more than one occasion.'

'Christ!' Lindsay whistled through her teeth. 'Rather you than me then.' Lifting a heavy folder, she headed for the door, saying, 'Good luck. I'll look forward to hearing how it goes, but I've got to shoot off now. I'm on a course in Warwick today and I'm late already. Bye!'

Jean grinned wryly as the door slammed. Lindsay was a character, to say the least, but there was never a dull moment when she was around. Jean knew there were a lot worse she could have been landed with. Glancing at the clock, she realised it was time she was going too. The police intended to detain the baby's mother until she got there, so she'd better go and get it over with – although she didn't relish the prospect. What normal, caring woman could abandon her newborn baby?

When she returned two hours later, she blinked with surprise to see Lindsay sitting at her desk.

'I bombed along the motorway, only to find the course had been called off when I got there,' the young woman grumbled. 'The trainer is away sick apparently, but never mind that for now – how did you get on?'

'Not well,' Jean said wearily as she slung her bag onto her desk. 'The mother told me in no uncertain terms that she can have nothing to do with the child, although she's clearly very upset about it. She says it would be more than her life was worth if her old man came home to find another baby in the house. He's been in nick for eighteen months, so I dare say it would take some explaining, wouldn't it? Somehow she'd managed to keep her pregnancy a secret from everyone, helped no doubt by the fact that she is more than a little well-rounded – and that's putting it kindly. I suppose she dumped the baby out of sheer desperation when she was born. *And* she'd delivered her all on her own! Can you believe that?' Jean sighed before going on, 'The only good thing to come out of it is the fact that she's agreed the child can have her surname until she goes for adoption – and she's also quite happy for her to keep the name Lilli, which is what the hospital named her. Between you and me, I felt a little sorry for her, and I can understand why she's done what she's done – up to a point. Her hubby has got a criminal record as long as your arm, and she and the other children have already had to be put in a refuge for their own safety more than once. She lives in mortal fear of him, from what I can see of it, and I reckon she'd have been happier if they'd just locked him up and thrown away the key.'

Lindsay frowned as she flicked her long brown hair back across her shoulder. 'So what happens now then? It doesn't sound as if she's going to change her mind.'

'No, it doesn't,' Jean agreed regretfully. 'Although I have to say, in some ways it will probably be better for the baby in the long run. She'd no doubt have ended up in care sooner or later if her mother *had* taken her home. Even though she's agreed for the baby to go for adoption, I shall still have to give her some more time to think about it, just in case she changes her mind. Truthfully, she's so scared of her husband that I think that's about as likely as a snowball's chance in hell, but procedures have to be followed. In the meantime, I've already got a foster-carer lined up for Lilli and I shall be fetching her from the hospital and taking her there tomorrow.'

'The poor little sod,' Lindsay said with feeling, as tears clogged her throat. 'Fancy your own mum not even wanting to see you. The woman must have a heart like a swinging brick.'

'I think it's more a case of she daren't see her,' Jean said sadly. 'You're still very new to this game, love, but believe me, in time you'll have cases that will break your heart. It's all part of the job.'

Lindsay nodded solemnly before turning her attention back to the pile of paperwork teetering on the edge of her desk.

There was obviously going to be a lot more to being a social worker than she had anticipated, and she just hoped that she would be able to handle it.

Later that afternoon, Jean arrived at the hospital armed with a baby car seat and headed for the children's ward. All the nurses flocked around Lilli's cot the second Jean appeared, and she saw that the tiny scrap had become a favourite with them.

'We shall miss her,' the Ward Sister told Jean as she stroked the baby's hand. 'She's a placid little soul. I hope she's going to a good home?'

'Oh, she will, I assure you,' Jean responded. 'We have a waiting list a mile long of couples waiting to adopt babies. But until then I've arranged for her to stay with foster-carers.' She was touched when a young nurse then proceeded to pack some baby clothes into a bag. All the nurses had chipped together to supply them so that Lilli would not leave with nothing. Jean smiled at them gratefully before plucking the baby from her crib and strapping her securely into her car seat.

'Right then, I'll be off,' she told them. 'Thank you all for everything you've done, and rest assured she will be fine.' Many of the young nurses had tears in their eyes as they kissed the infant goodbye, and Jean Beckham beat a hasty retreat in case she started crying too. She was a soft soul at heart.

Half an hour later she placed the sleeping infant into the arms of Sue Mitchell, a foster-carer who lived in Radford. Sue was used to caring for pre-adoption babies, although lately more and more single mums seemed to be keeping their babies, so she wasn't quite so much in demand any more. A great Amazon of a woman, with a kindly face and three grown-up children of her own, who had all long since flown the nest, Sue had soft blue eyes and hair that was greying at the temples – and children were attracted to her like bees to honey.

'She'll be absolutely fine,' she assured Jean with a twinkle in her eye. 'I have done this before, you know – more times than I care to remember, if I'm to be honest.'

'I know you have,' Jean agreed, distractedly running her hand through her thick brown hair. 'It's just . . . I don't know – I feel so sorry for the poor little thing.'

'Well, the way you have to look at it is that she's going to make some childless couple very happy in the not too distant future. Now you get back to your job and let me get on with mine, eh? No doubt Madam here will be screaming for a feed soon and I have to establish some sort of routine for her. I have everything ready for her, so you needn't worry.'

'Thanks, Sue.' Jean inched reluctantly towards the door with one eye still firmly fixed on the baby. 'I'll keep you informed of what's going on.'

'You do that.' Sue followed her to the door with the infant still tucked into the crook of her arm and seconds later, Jean was marching down the path leaving baby Lilli to spend her first night in her temporary new home.

Chapter Three

'So that's all the court cases out of the way. The adoption papers are signed and all I have to do now is contact the new adoptive parents to see if they are still happy to go ahead with it.' Jean smiled as she sipped at the mug of tea that Glenis, Lilli's latest foster-carer, had made for her. Sadly, Sue Mitchell had only kept the baby for two months before handing her back because of an illness in the family, which meant that Lilli had already had two homes, poor little mite.

At the moment, Lilli sat propped against cushions on the floor, surveying the two women solemnly. She was almost six months old now and had proved to be very little trouble in the time that Glenis had cared for her. She seldom cried and ate everything that Glenis put in front of her. The woman had been weaning her for almost four weeks now, and Lilli had already progressed from Farley's rusks to baby rice. She slept through the night and to all intents and purposes was a model baby, so Glenis wondered why she wasn't more sorry to hear that she would be moving to her new home shortly. Normally she grew very attached to the babies she cared for, but for some reason she had found it difficult to form a bond with Lilli. In fairness, the child could by no stretch of the imagination be termed as a pretty baby. But it was more than that. It was something to do with her eyes. They were the bluest eyes Glenis had ever seen, by far her best feature, and yet when the woman looked into them she always felt very uncomfortable. True, they were a beautiful colour – but dull and soulless, as though baby Lilli had given up all hope before her life had even started.

'Are you still thinking of the couple in Nottingham?' she asked, dragging her attention away from Lilli.

'Yes,' Jean nodded. 'I reckon they'd be perfect for her. They adopted a little boy three years ago. Joshua is four now and they're desperate for a little girl to complete their family.'

'Then she will be perfect for them,' Glenis agreed. 'And I doubt she will have any problems settling. She's a very placid child. In fact, I sometimes think she's *too* placid.'

'What? Do you think there might be something wrong with her?' Jean asked in alarm.

'Oh no, no, nothing like that,' Glenis hastened to assure her. 'She's had all her medical checks and seems to be fit as a fiddle. It's just . . . Oh, I don't know. She doesn't laugh much as you'd expect babies her age to do. And when I go into her room first thing in the morning, I don't even get a smile. She's just such a *solemn* little girl.'

Jean chuckled. 'I wish *my* brood had been a little more that way. They were all holy terrors until they got to school,' she recalled. Then, glancing at the clock, she rose swiftly and said, 'I really ought to be going now. I'm due in a team meeting in half an hour, and if I hit the traffic in the city centre I shall be late. I'll ring the Nielsons and give them the good news, and then arrange for them to come and meet Lilli, if that's all right with you?'

'Of course it is.' Glenis saw her to the door before rushing away to prepare Lilli's next bottle.

The following week, Glenis answered a knock on the door to find an attractive young couple standing there. The woman was clutching the hand of a smartly dressed little boy and she flashed Glenis a friendly smile as she said, 'Hello, I believe you are expecting us. I'm Fay Nielson and this is my husband Gordon and our son Joshua. We've come to meet Lilli.'

'Of course.' Glenis held the door wide as she ushered them inside, thinking what a handsome family they were. Fay Nielson was dainty, blonde and immaculately dressed in a smart navy-blue suit and high-heeled shoes. Her husband was dark and towered above her. He was also smartly turned out in an expensive-looking grey suit and a crisp white shirt, with a blue tie that exactly matched the colour of his eyes. Jean had told Glenis that he was a solicitor, so she had half-expected him to come well dressed. This family weren't short of a bob or two either, if what Jean had told her was anything to go by. If they took Lilli, she would probably never want for anything, least of all love. According to their notes they had tried for a baby of their own for years before finally adopting Joshua, and now all they wanted was a little girl to complete their family. As Gordon took his wife's elbow protectively, Glenis could see that they were a close couple. Their son looked remarkably like his father, and knowing that he too had been adopted, Glenis found it somewhat surprising as she bent to smile at him. He grinned shyly back and snuggled into his mother's skirts as she thought what a beautiful child he was.

But what would they think of Lilli? Glenis had dressed her in a pretty pink dress with matching bootees, but all her best efforts had failed to make her look any prettier. It was a sad fact that Lilli was as plain as a pikestaff, and no amount of frilly dresses was going to change that.

Still, Glenis consoled herself as she led them towards the lounge where the baby was sleeping in her pram, they say beauty is in the eye of the beholder so they might look at her differently from me.

'She's in here,' she trilled cheerfully. 'She's fast asleep at the moment but she's due for a feed in half an hour so she should be awake soon. I'll leave you with her whilst I go and make you a nice cup of tea, shall I?'

Glenis could see the excitement in the younger woman's eyes as she approached the pram, and waited for her reaction as she peered down at the sleeping baby.

'Oh.' Fay glanced towards her husband. 'She's er . . . a big baby, isn't she?' For the moment it was all she could think of to say. She had yearned for a beautiful little doll that she could dress up and show off, but Lilli was not what she had been expecting.

'She loves her bottle and her food,' Glenis agreed, 'and a more placid child you couldn't wish for. She only cries if she's hungry or needs changing, and she sleeps all through the night.' Even as she spoke, Lilli's eyes suddenly snapped open and she stared up at the strangers staring down at her as if it was an everyday occurrence.

'Hello, little one.' Gordon Nielson leaned into the pram and tickled beneath her chin, but she merely gazed back at him with no flicker of emotion.

'She can be a solemn little thing,' Glenis said apologetically. 'And I have to admit she isn't the prettiest baby in the world. But then they reckon it's the ugly ducklings that turn into swans, don't they?'

Fay bristled as all her maternal instincts suddenly rushed to the surface. 'I think her face is full of character,' she said, and after glancing at Glenis for permission she then lifted Lilli from the pram and cradled her in her arms as Glenis shot off to make them all a drink.

By the time she got back with a tray laden with tea, biscuits, some milk for Joshua and a bottle for Lilli, the Neilsons were all huddled together on the sofa playing with the baby, who was looking back at them with no interest whatsoever.

'I did warn you that she could be solemn,' Glenis muttered, and now she came to think of it she realised with a jolt that she could not remember ever seeing the infant laugh.

'May I feed her?' Fay asked, and Glenis immediately handed her the bottle and watched as Lilli began to suck hungrily at the milk whilst Joshua watched, intrigued.

When she had finished her feed, Fay then changed her nappy, laughing at the baby's fat little bottom, and Glenis could tell that after her initial reaction, Fay had already bonded with her. Gordon seemed more reserved, but then Glenis supposed that being a man he wouldn't show his feelings as openly as his wife.

'So, what do you think of her then?' Glenis asked after an hour had passed.

Fay stared across at her with stars in her eyes as she told her breathlessly, 'I think she's just *perfect* for us and I'd like to call her Rebecca.' Then as an afterthought, she asked Glenis, 'We will be allowed to change her name, won't we?'

'Oh yes, I believe so, once the adoption is final.'

'Then I shall ring Mrs Beckham the minute we get home and tell her that we'll take the baby as soon as we possibly can. Is that all right with you, darling?'

Seeing the bright hope in his wife's eyes as she looked towards him, Gordon nodded, but then Glenis, who was very astute at judging people, had already formed the impression that this man would have done anything to please his wife. He certainly didn't seem as keen on the idea of taking Lilli as she did, but then things had a habit of turning out for the best, and Glenis could only hope for Lilli's sake that they would this time too.

Chapter Four

December 1993

'Rebecca, will you *please* stop wriggling about!' Fay pleaded as she squeezed the child into her costume for the Nativity play. They were due at the school in half an hour's time, and Fay was beginning to panic as Gordon looked on with an indulgent smile playing about his lips.

'It's er . . . not the most flattering of costumes, is it?' he ventured as Fay tied the striped tea towel around their daughter's head.

Fay, who was still stinging because Rebecca had been chosen to be one of the three shepherds rather than the Virgin Mary, glowered at him.

'Well, at least she isn't just in the chorus.'

'That's true,' he said hastily. He could never understand why the mums made so much of these things. The way Fay had been going on for the last two weeks, Rebecca might have landed a part in a West End musical. The night before, they had been to see Joshua in his play – and at one stage Gordon had thought Fay was going to burst with pride, although Rebecca clearly hadn't enjoyed the evening that much. She had fidgeted in her seat from the second they arrived until Fay's nerves were stretched to breaking-point. But then it was nothing unusual. Rebecca hated Joshua getting Fay's attention and would go to any lengths to prevent it. Thankfully, Josh was a placid kid for most of the time and able to ignore his younger sister's tantrums, although there had been times when he had snapped and they'd come to fisticuffs and had had to be separated. Even so, he was fiercely protective of her, which Gordon found very endearing.

The fact that Rebecca was so jealous of her brother worried Gordon, but whenever he commented on it, Fay would jump to the girl's defence, insisting that sibling rivalry was normal.

Gordon wasn't so sure, and worried about how obsessed his wife seemed to be with the little girl. He had lost count of the money she had spent on pretty clothes for her over the past four years she had lived with them – not that it had done much good, from where he was standing. As his mother had been fond of saying: 'You can't make a silk purse out of a sow's ear.'

Rebecca was a plump little thing with a shock of mousy brown hair who already stood a good head taller than the other children in her class. Her appearance was not enhanced by the glasses she was now forced to wear, which Gordon considered to be a shame since Rebecca's eyes were in fact her best feature – a striking shade of blue.

Now as he stared down at her dull brown costume he chucked her under the chin and told her kindly, 'You look great, baby. Mum and I are going to be really proud of you tonight and I'm going to take lots of photos of you.'

Rebecca gazed up at him blankly as Fay snatched up her handbag and tried to tidy her hair in the mirror above the mantelpiece all at the same time.

'Come on then, let's get going.' She ushered the two children towards the front door.

Rebecca glared at Josh before taking a firm grip on Fay's

19

hand and placing herself between them. The act was not lost on Gordon but he remained tight-lipped and merely winked at the boy as he took his car keys from the hall table.

'Oh, wasn't she just *wonderful?*' Fay gushed two hours later as Gordon drove them all home. 'I still can't understand why they picked Lucy Grey to be the Virgin Mary above our Rebecca. Lucy didn't even make a particularly good Mary, especially when she tripped over at the end. Rebecca could have done it so much better.'

Ever the peacemaker, Gordon nodded, although in truth all Rebecca had had to do was stand there, and as for Lucy falling over . . . Well, Fay had obviously not noticed that Rebecca had stuck her foot out and tripped her up – either that or she had chosen to ignore the fact. Not that he would dare point that out to Fay, who wouldn't have a wrong word said against the child. It concerned him when he saw how Fay always took Rebecca's side against Josh. But thankfully, Josh had an entirely different nature to his sister. He was very laidback and took it all in his stride most of the time. After all, as Fay regularly pointed out to him, his sister was much younger than him so he must *never* slap her back if she hit him.

Gordon didn't altogether agree with this theory, but once again held his tongue for the sake of peace.

The fact that he had never really bonded with Rebecca worried him too. It had been totally different with Joshua. The very first time he had set eyes on him, all his paternal feelings had risen to the fore and he had somehow known that he could take the child and love him as if he was his own, which he did, unconditionally. But then Josh was so different from Rebecca in looks as well as nature. Even so, he tried his best with her for Fay's sake. He knew that she loved the little girl and was thankful that the terrible years when they had been desperately trying for a child of their own were over. He could still remember Fay crying broken-heartedly each month when her period started, and then had followed the countless tests and trips to the hospital. But thankfully Rebecca's arrival had ended all that. Fay considered that she had her little family now, and she was content, so who was he to argue?

To all intents and purposes they were very lucky. They had a beautiful detached four-bedroomed house in Sherwood, a better part of the town. He had a good job – he was a partner in a solicitor's firm, and this enabled him to make sure that his family wanted for nothing. Both of the children attended private schools, and although the fees were inordinately high, both he and Fay considered it was worth it, to give their children the best possible education. All in all, everything was going well, except . . . he pushed the disturbing thoughts away as he glanced at Rebecca in the rear mirror. She was still wearing her shepherd's costume and, strapped into the back of the car, was gazing back at him from those soulless blue eyes. He quickly turned his attention back to the road again as he listened to Fay prattling on, but he wasn't really taking in what she was saying. He was thinking of Rebecca's beginnings. On a few occasions lately he had suggested that they should be honest with the children, and tell them that they had been adopted – when they were old enough to cope with the information – but Fay was fiercely against it.

'How would Rebecca feel, knowing that her birth mother valued her so little that she abandoned her shortly after she was born – and that she had already had two homes before she came to us?' she had retorted hotly. 'Just imagine what that could do to a child's confidence! No – it's better that neither of them knows – ever. We are their real parents, to all intents and purposes, and that's the way I want it to stay.'

'But Josh might remember that he didn't always live with us. He was a little older than Rebecca when we adopted him,' Gordon pointed out.

'He was only one, so it's highly unlikely, and I think the best thing we can do is face that if and when it ever comes to it,' Fay had snapped back, her pretty face set in grim lines.

After her tirade, Gordon had shrugged and the subject had not been raised again for some time. He could understand what Fay meant, in all fairness. After all, it wasn't Rebecca's fault that she had been born; fathered by accident by one of her mother's clients when she had been working on the streets.

They didn't even know who her birth father was, and probably never would. But there was something about this child that made it difficult for Gordon to fully take to her. He felt sad for her, admittedly, and found it hard to believe that any woman could abandon her own flesh and blood as Rebecca's true mother had done, but then he supposed that everyone was different; it took all sorts to make a world. He himself would most certainly be out of a job if everyone was the same. Rebecca might just surprise him and make them all proud of her one day, and until then he would play the part of a doting dad to the best of his ability.

Josh's beginnings had been very different from his sister's. His young unmarried mother had come from a very upper-class family in London. As soon as her family had discovered that she was pregnant, the poor girl had been banished to an elderly aunt where Josh had been born, and it was she who had cared for him until ill-health had prevented her from doing so any longer. Rather than face the shame of having an illegitimate grandchild, the girl's parents had then placed the little boy up for adoption, and as far as Gordon was concerned, their loss had been his and Fay's gain. Now Gordon wondered if the difference in the children was down to genes.

'*Ouch!* What did you do that for?' Josh's yell brought Gordon's thoughts firmly back to the present.

'What's the matter now?' Fay demanded with a martyred expression.

Josh rubbed at his arm, his brown eyes swimming with tears. 'Rebecca pinched me again . . . for *nothing!*' he answered indignantly.

Even in the gloomy car interior Fay could already see the beginnings of a bruise forming. 'Now, Rebecca,' she scolded softly, 'be a good girl. We're almost home now.' And then to Josh, 'She didn't mean it, darling. She's just tired.'

Gordon gritted his teeth. If it was left up to him, Rebecca would have had her hand slapped. She might not be so keen to do it again if she was chastised occasionally, but as usual he said nothing. Instead he just concentrated on getting them all home safe and sound.

Two hours later, when the children had been bathed and tucked into bed, Gordon poured himself and Fay a large glass of wine each and collapsed onto the settee as he loosened his tie and kicked off his shoes with a sigh. It had been a long day.

'What did Mrs Granger want you for this evening?' he asked then, as he suddenly remembered the Headmistress pulling his wife to one side after the Nativity play.

'Oh, it was nothing really,' Fay said guardedly as she joined him on the settee and curled her legs up beneath her. 'Just some silly argument Rebecca and another little girl got into in the playground at dinnertime, apparently. The girl fell over and accused our Rebecca of pushing her, but I'm sure she didn't. I think the girl was just trying to get her into trouble.'

'Hmm. It's a shame she hasn't made any friends, isn't it?' Gordon said tentatively. And just as he'd expected, Fay was instantly on the defensive again.

'Well, she's only been at the school for a few months,' she said. 'We've got to give her a chance, haven't we?'

'I suppose we have, but the other little girls at the school seem to get on well enough.'

Fay sniffed. 'Yes, but Rebecca is shy. It will probably take her a little longer to settle in than them.'

Gordon could feel the tension building and quickly changed the subject, knowing when he was beaten.

Upstairs in her pretty bedroom, Rebecca lay watching the shadows on the ceiling with a grin on her face as she remembered the way Lucy Grey had sprawled across the stage when she had tripped her up. But it served her right. Rebecca had been sick of Lucy bragging about the fact that she had been chosen to be Mary in the play. She didn't like Lucy, or the circle of friends that the little girl played with each breaktime. They never let her join in and they called her horrible names and teased her. Or at least, they had; they didn't do it so much now since she had started to lash out at them. They simply kept their distance and didn't talk to her, which suited her just fine. They were sissies, just like Josh. He was a big cry-baby too, but it didn't matter because their mum loved her *much* more than Josh. Rebecca made sure of that and was constantly getting him into trouble. Not that it stopped him following her about all the time.

She snuggled up to her pink teddy. She loved her teddy more than any of the other toys she had. Her mum had told her once that someone special had bought it for her when she was just a baby, and she wouldn't go to bed without it.

Her teddy was her best friend – her *only* friend if it came to that – except for her mum, of course.

Rebecca hoped that when she grew up, she would be pretty too, like her mum. The other girls might not laugh at her then and call her names; horrible names like 'four eyes' and 'fatty'.

She sighed as her eyes grew heavy and eventually she slept.

Chapter Five

'Anyway, you're just a nasty bully!' Lucy Grey taunted as she and Rebecca circled each other in the playground. 'And you're ugly too. Everyone says so. You don't look anything like anyone else in your family an' my mum says that's 'cos you were *adopted*.'

Rebecca scowled. What did adopted mean? she wondered. But then her thoughts returned to the girl in front of her. Rebecca was six years old now and had still made no friends at school. It was no wonder really. Despite all her best efforts, the other children still picked on her and now she had put up a barrier to protect herself from further hurt. She tended to keep herself very much to herself unless she was causing trouble, which she did with monotonous regularity, much to the chagrin of the longsuffering Headmistress. Barely a week went by when Mrs Granger didn't have to ring Fay over some misdemeanour, and she was beginning to despair of the child now. She was a complete misfit – a fact that never failed to surprise the woman as Rebecca's parents seemed to be such a lovely couple.

Now, as Lucy bent to rub her grazed knee, Miss Clark, who was on playground duty, bore down on them like an avenging angel.

'Now then, what's going on here?' she barked.

'I was going to see my friends over there, and as I passed Rebecca she tripped me up.' Lucy waved her hands vaguely in the direction of her friends as tears spilled convincingly down her cheeks.

Miss Clark glared at the culprit. Whenever there was trouble, Rebecca Nielson always seemed to be involved.

'I did not,' Rebecca spat before the teacher could say another word. 'She fell over all on her own. I was nowhere near her.' But she knew that she was wasting her breath. No one ever listened to her and now she had almost given up trying to tell them.

'She *was* so,' one of Lucy's little friends piped up. 'We were all standing over there and we saw Rebecca trip Lucy up as she passed by her.'

'Right, well, you all go back to play,' the woman told the child as she took Lucy's trembling hand. 'And you, Lucy, come with me. We need to clean that knee up. You can go and sit outside the Headmistress's office, Rebecca. I shall get her to deal with you after the lunch-break.'

Rebecca stormed off, her face contorted with rage as a ripple of giggles passed through the little crowd that had assembled. Soon she was seated on the hardbacked chair outside the Headmistress's office, swinging her legs. And when Miss Clark appeared some ten minutes later and swept into the room without giving her so much as a glance, her face darkened.

Shortly afterwards, the door opened again and Miss Clark beckoned her inside. Rebecca felt very small as she peered up at Mrs Granger who was watching her from her seat at a high desk.

'You *again*, Rebecca,' she sighed. 'You do realise that what you did was very naughty and spiteful, don't you? I'm afraid this is going to mean another call to your mother, and for the rest of the week you will miss your breaks. You can sit in the hall and practise your letters while the other children go out to play.'

The girl glared at her resentfully before turning on her heel and leaving the room without a word. She knew better than to argue with a teacher. They never listened to what she told them.

Fay was waiting for her at the gates of the school as she always was when the bell sounded that afternoon, and as Rebecca walked towards her she could see that her mother wasn't happy.

'Oh, *what* am I going to do with you?' Fay groaned quietly as Rebecca joined her. 'I've had another phone call from Mrs Granger saying that you hurt Lucy again. Is it true?'

With tears pricking at the back of her eyes, Rebecca shrugged as her mother took her hand and led her towards the car, and the journey home passed in silence.

The subject was not raised again until later that evening when the family were seated around the table at dinner.

'So . . .' Gordon said as he tucked into the pork chops and new potatoes Fay had cooked for them all, 'your mum tells me you've been naughty at school again, Rebecca. Would you like to tell me why?'

'It was 'cos Lucy was being horrible to *me*,' Rebecca muttered, spearing a pea onto her fork.

'Oh yes? What did she do to you then?'

Hearing the note of resigned disbelief in her father's voice, Rebecca's temper flared.

'She's *always* horrible to me!' she declared petulantly. 'An' the other girls are too. Today she told me I was adopted. She said her mum reckons I don't look like anyone in our family. What does adopted mean?'

As Fay almost choked on the potato she was eating, Rebecca saw her mother and father exchange a glance and an unsettled silence settled on the room. Then suddenly Fay rose and began to hurriedly stack the unfinished meals onto a tray as her father told her, 'We'll discuss this later, when your mother and I have had a little time to talk things over.'

'But what about our pudding?' This was from Josh, who was looking confused. His parents seemed to be totally flummoxed, although from where he was standing he felt sure they should be used to Rebecca being in trouble now.

'I er . . . I'll fetch yours and Rebecca's in,' his mother said as she scuttled from the room, closely followed by his father. Josh shrugged. Adults could be very hard to understand. But he was a typical growing boy, never happier than when he was eating, and the minute his mother placed a steaming dish of sticky toffee pudding in front of him he forgot about everything else and dug into it as if he hadn't eaten for a month.

In the kitchen Fay was leaning heavily on the sink, every vestige of colour drained from her face.

'What are we going to do?' she asked as she gazed distractedly from the kitchen window. She had always dreaded this happening and now that it had, she had no idea at all how to deal with it.

Gordon plonked himself down at the kitchen table and told her softly, 'We're going to have to tell her the truth, love. In fact, we're going to have to tell them both. I've always thought this might happen. People hereabouts know that the children were adopted, which was why I told you that we should tell them ourselves rather than let them hear it from someone else.'

Fay came to join him and flopped down on the next chair, her face a picture of misery.

'B . . . but how will they take it?'

'Absolutely fine, if we go about it the right way,' he assured her. 'Let's stick to our normal routine for now and go and help them with their homework, and then when they've had their baths we'll sit them both down and explain.'

29

Fay nodded numbly in agreement. She didn't have much choice, the way she saw it.

Two hours later, with both children bathed and in their nightclothes, the family settled down in the living room. This was the time that Fay usually loved best. Quality time with her family before the children went to bed, but tonight she was trembling.

'Aren't we having the telly on?' Josh asked as he looked at his parents' strained faces.

'Not yet, son.' Gordon patted his knee affectionately. 'There's something me and your mum need to talk to you about first.'

Rebecca looked from one to the other of them, sensing that it was going to be something important as Gordon ran his tongue across his dry lips.

'The thing is . . . we need to talk about what Lucy said to Rebecca at school today – about her being adopted.'

Josh frowned. 'But she isn't adopted, is she? She's my sister!'

'Actually, son . . . she is. And so are you.'

Josh shook his head, growing agitated. 'But we *can't* be. We've always lived here!'

'Well, yes, you have – at least you have since you were both very tiny,' Gordon soothed.

'Really?' Josh's eyes popped wide with surprise. At ten years old he vaguely understood what adoption meant, and whilst he had always wondered why he and Rebecca looked nothing alike, he'd had no idea that they'd been adopted.

'So does that mean that I have another mum an' dad somewhere?' he now asked, showing no signs of distress whatsoever, much to Fay's relief.

'Yes, you have,' Gordon answered truthfully.

'Then why didn't they want me?'

'It isn't always a case of not wanting a child,' Gordon explained as best he could. 'Sometimes there are reasons why people can't keep their children.'

'Oh.' Josh gazed pensively up at the chandelier as he tried to digest what Gordon had just told him.

'And when that happens,' Gordon went on gently, 'people like me and your mum get the chance to adopt them.'

'So will my *real* mum and dad come back for me one day?' Josh asked innocently, and Fay felt as if her heart was being torn from her chest.

Gordon shook his head. 'No, son. It doesn't always work like that. You see, your mum and I went to court and had your name changed to ours. Nielson. That means *we* are your real mum and dad, now and for always.'

A look of relief flitted across Josh's face, but now Rebecca, who had so far kept quiet, piped up, 'But I still don't understand what adoption means. Why didn't you just have some babies of your own? The sort that grow in your tummy like Lucy's mum did, instead of taking us away from our real mum? Lucy has a baby brother *and* a sister, and her mum didn't give *them* away.'

Seeing that Gordon was out of his depth, Fay stepped in swiftly.

'Sadly, some ladies – like me – can't grow their own babies in their tummy, so they have to grow them in their heart until it's time to fetch them from Mummies who can't keep them.'

'Oh.' Rebecca concentrated on her hands for a moment before asking, 'And will my *real* mummy come for me one day?'

'No, darling. Like Joshua, you are ours now,' Fay told her, but when she reached out to stroke the child's face, Rebecca flinched away from her. Now she understood why she wasn't pretty like her mum. It was because Fay *wasn't* her real mum. Her real mum must have been ugly like she was, and that was why the children at school made fun of her, because she was large and clumsy. It all made sense now, and a wave of resentment flooded through her. That must be why her real mum had given her away – because she wasn't dainty and pretty like Lucy Grey.

Much later that night, after Fay had read her a story and tucked her into bed, Rebecca lay brooding on what she had learned.

Even at six years old, certain things were beginning to make sense now. She had once heard her Aunt Alison, who was her mum's sister, jokingly remark, 'Well, I must say you keep Rebecca lovely – but I'm afraid all the fancy clothes in the world aren't going to make any difference to her looks, poor lass.'

They had been in the kitchen at the time on one of the couple's infrequent visits and Rebecca had been hovering unnoticed by the back door while Josh played football with his eight-year-old cousin, Casey, in the field behind the house. Amber, his sister, was almost thirteen and she was happily watching *Father Ted* on the TV in the living room.

Deeply indignant, Fay had snapped back, 'Well, for what it's worth *I* think Rebecca is gorgeous. At least, I'm sure she will be when she gets a little older and loses some of her puppy fat.'

'Puppy fat?' Aunt Alison had snorted derisively. 'Oh, come on, Fay, admit it – the kid's built like a brick shithouse!'

Her dad had entered the kitchen then and glared at Aunt Alison. He wasn't too keen on his wife's older sister, and even less so on her husband, Ken, and it often showed, although he did try to be polite.

'That's our daughter you are talking about,' he had told her tightly, and Aunt Alison had chortled with laughter.

'Yeah, OK, if you say so, love. Though I don't know why you couldn't have waited till a prettier one came along.'

Rebecca had slunk away then, unable to listen to any more, and she had gone into the shed and cried until her bluebell-blue eyes were red and swollen, which she knew only made her look uglier still.

That evening, she had overheard her dad telling her mum that he thought her sister and her family were common, but Rebecca didn't really understand what that meant. However, she did understand what Aunt Alison had meant when she said they should have waited for a prettier one – and it cut deep, especially as Amber, her cousin, was so nice to look at.

She then began to wonder what her real mum and dad were like, and resentment started to bubble inside her. *One day*, she vowed, *I'll find them and they'll be sorry they gave me away*. And on that thought she drifted into an uneasy sleep.

It was two weeks later when Fay received yet another phone call from Mrs Granger, this time asking if Fay would call into the school to see her.

Fay sighed as she lifted the car keys and headed for the door, wondering what her daughter had done this time.

She didn't have to wait long to find out. Once at the school she was shown into the Headmistress's office, where the woman was waiting grim-faced to see her.

'Do sit down, Mrs Nielson,' she said, and Fay obediently perched on the edge of a hard-backed chair to face the music.

'So, Mrs Granger, do we have a problem?' Fay asked politely.

'I'm rather afraid we do.' The woman cleared her throat, obviously uncomfortable. 'The thing is . . . Well, there's no easy way to say this. Rebecca has never been the easiest of children, but over the last couple of weeks her behaviour has become intolerable and now I am receiving complaints from the parents of children she has bullied.'

Deep down, Fay knew that what Mrs Granger was saying was probably true, because Rebecca's behaviour had worsened at home too – ever since the night she and Gordon had been forced to tell their children that they were adopted. But even so she was not going to sit here and listen to the woman slate her daughter.

Standing, she drew herself up to her full height before hissing, 'We *are* talking about a six-year-old child here, aren't we, Mrs Granger, and not a serial killer? Goodness me . . . with the fees that we pay for Rebecca to attend this school, I expect better.'

Mrs Granger had the good grace to flush, but even so she was still determined to go through with this to the bitter end.

'I am very sorry, Mrs Neilson, but under the circumstances I have no choice but to ask you to find another school for your daughter.'

'You *what*? You're expelling a six year old?' Fay thought she must be hearing things but Mrs Granger nodded regretfully.

'I'm afraid that's exactly what I'm doing,' she agreed, and without another word Fay turned on her heel and stormed out of the room. *You can stick your damn school where the sun doesn't shine*, she fumed to herself, and then she marched out to her car without a backward glance.

Chapter Six

'Oh, do we really have to have them all here for the whole afternoon?' Gordon groaned one evening in late July as he helped Fay with the dirty dinner dishes.

She grinned at him as she hovered over the sink. 'Don't be such a grump. They *are* family, and we can hardly not invite them to Rebecca's birthday party, can we?'

'I suppose not,' he mumbled as he dried a plate. As far as he was concerned, even fleeting visits from Fay's sister were enough to cope with, without being saddled with the rest of the family for the whole afternoon.

'I don't know what Alison ever saw in that useless good-for-nothing, Ken,' he commented. 'No wonder your parents, God rest their souls, were so disgruntled when she took up with him. They told her she was making a mistake – and weren't they proved to be right?'

'That all depends on how you look at it,' Fay replied. 'I suppose you could say that they haven't got much, apart from a council house. But then they could hardly afford a mortgage with Ken being on the dole, could they? And Alison seems happy enough.'

'Huh! He could get a job if he really wanted one,' Gordon quipped. 'He's just bone idle, if you were to ask me.'

'Each to their own.' Fay pulled the plug out of the sink,

35

and as the water gurgled away, she grinned at him. 'Not everyone is a workaholic like you.'

'Mm, well, it's working hard that's got us this place, *and* pays for our children to have private education,' he pointed out, flapping the tea towel around the kitchen of their neat detached house. 'Speaking of which, you'll need to be buying Rebecca a new uniform for when she starts her new school after the holidays, won't you?'

'It's all ordered,' Fay assured him, and then she added, 'I just hope she settles better in this place than she did in the last one.'

'Time will tell.' Gordon folded the towel before heading off to his study, where he had a pile of paperwork to plough through before the next day. Fay moved to the kitchen window that overlooked the huge garden and saw Joshua kicking a football about. Rebecca was no doubt closeted in her room looking at comics or listening to one of her Madonna albums. It was a habit she had adopted of late and Fay wasn't at all happy about it. Not that there was much she could do about it. Rebecca was a law unto herself lately, even though she was not quite seven years old. Walking through the spacious lounge, Fay straightened the cushions on the settee as she headed for the stairs. She might as well go and get Rebecca bathed early. It was obvious that she wasn't going to coax her outside even though it was a beautiful evening, and she herself was feeling tired and in need of an early night.

Once upstairs she ran the bath before heading off to Rebecca's room. Just as she had thought, the child had her head buried in a comic, and when Fay asked her to come for a bath she glared at her resentfully.

'Do I *have* to?'

'Yes, you do, Madam. Now come along, chop, chop!'

Rebecca slammed her comic down and slouched along the

landing, and soon she was in the bath as Fay hovered over her, washing her hair and chatting away.

'Are you looking forward to starting your new school?' she asked brightly as she worked the child's mousy-coloured hair into a lather.

Rebecca shrugged and Fay had to swallow the hasty comment that sprang to her lips. She'd had a devil of a job finding another school that was as highly recommended as the last one. Or more to the point, one that would take her, and she thought that Rebecca could at least have pretended to be looking forward to starting at Rosedale. The fees at the new school were even higher than the previous ones, and she just hoped that this time it would be worth it.

'And are you looking forward to your birthday?' she asked next, thinking of the shiny new bicycle that Gordon had hidden in the garage. Surely that would put a smile on her daughter's face . . .

Again, Rebecca shrugged and Fay felt despair sweep through her. Ever since their daughter had learned that she had been adopted, she seemed to have shut herself off from them, even from Fay, whom she had previously adored, and Fay didn't quite know what to do about it. 'Aunt Alison and Uncle Ken will be coming and bringing Amber and Casey,' she prattled on. 'And they'll be delivering your cake tomorrow. That will be nice, won't it? We can have the party in the garden if the weather stays fine. You'll like that, won't you?'

'Mm,' Rebecca muttered absently at she swiped at the bubbles in the bath, and too tired to try any more, Fay became silent.

Rebecca's birthday dawned bright and clear and Fay spent most of the morning getting all the food ready for the party while the little girl rode up and down outside on the pavement on her new bicycle.

She had shown very little emotion when Fay and Gordon gave it to her before her dad left for work that morning, but then they were getting used to her sulky ways by now.

Alison, Ken and their family arrived at two o'clock, and from then on Fay was rushed off her feet, scurrying here and there making sure that they all had plenty to eat.

At last everyone had eaten their fill, and while the children entertained themselves, Fay began to carry the dirty pots into the kitchen helped by Alison, who kept glancing at her out of the corner of her eye.

'I have to say, sis, you're looking a bit peaky,' Alison commented after a while.

'Oh, I'm fine. Just a bit tired, that's all.' Fay pushed her hair behind her ears as she eyed Alison's outfit. She was dressed in leggings and an oversized T-shirt that would have looked far better on a teenager. But then Alison had always been the unconventional one of the family, much to their parents' distress. Even now Fay could well remember the terrible rows they had had over her sister's rebelliousness. Alison had always been a law unto herself and it was doubtful that she would change now.

'I reckon you've lost a bit of weight as well.' Alison wasn't ready to drop the subject of her sister's health just yet.

'Well, I have been feeling a bit under the weather. You know – a bit sicky,' Fay admitted grudgingly. 'If it will make you feel any better, I'll go and see the doctor for a check-up when the kids go back to school. I doubt I'll get a chance before then.'

Alison grinned. '*Sicky*, eh? You don't think you're pregnant, do you?'

'There's hardly much chance of that, is there?' Fay snapped before she could stop herself.

Alison instantly felt guilty. 'Sorry, love. I didn't think.' She could have bitten her tongue out. She of all people knew how much Fay had longed for a baby of her own before adopting Joshua and Rebecca, and now here she was rubbing salt into the wound.

'It's all right.' Fay squeezed her hand affectionately. 'To be honest, Gordon has been nagging me to go to the doctor's too. But now I will – I promise.'

Fay nodded and the conversation turned to other things, much to her relief.

Alison had bought Rebecca a new Robbie Williams album for her birthday and now they could hear it throbbing away in the girl's bedroom.

Alison grinned. 'Sounds like Her Ladyship approves of my choice of music,' she commented.

'She loves Robbie Williams and Madonna,' Fay told her. 'I've no doubt we'll get sick of hearing it now.'

It was then that Gordon strode in looking very smart in a dark suit and tie. He had taken a few hours off work to attend Rebecca's party and he greeted Alison politely as he placed his briefcase down on a chair and loosened his tie.

'Where's the birthday girl?' he asked, and Fay pointed towards the ceiling. As the music wafted down to him he suppressed a sigh. It was a beautiful day and he had expected to find his daughter outside on her new bike. But then he didn't want to upset Fay by saying anything. Rebecca could do no wrong in her eyes, as he had discovered long ago.

'I'll go and have a chat to Ken then. Is he in the front room?'

When Fay nodded he headed in that direction and found Ken lounging on the settee with a can of lager in one hand and a cigarette dangling from the other. The chap was dressed in combat trousers and an army top, and Gordon felt he would have looked more in place on a parade ground than in someone's front room, but of course he was too polite to say so.

39

'All right, Ken?' he asked amiably and the man grunted in acknowledgment as Gordon took off his jacket and hung it neatly across the back of the chair. All the time he was keeping a wary eye on the cigarette ash that was threatening to fall onto his new Axminster carpet at any second. Very discreetly he inched the ash tray beneath it before asking, 'So how are things? Any sign of a job cropping up yet?'

'Nah,' Ken muttered. 'Nothin' doin' at the mo, mate. But then it's like I say to Ali, somethin'll turn up.'

'Hm.' Gordon managed to keep the note of amusement from his voice. Ken had never done a day's work in all the years he had known him, so it was unlikely he would want to start a job now.

'I reckon your Fay 'as got a few more of these in the fridge if yer fancy one,' Ken told him now but Gordon shook his head.

'No, thank you. It's a bit early in the day for me. But I might go and cadge a cup of tea off her.'

Ken snorted. ''T'ain't never too early in the day fer a lager. But I s'ppose it's each to his own.'

It took all Gordon's willpower not to kick the idle layabout up the backside, but instead he went back to the kitchen where the women were putting the candles on Rebecca's cake. Fay had deliberately waited until he got home. Now all she had to do was try to prise the girl out of her room. Once she had gone, Alison immediately whispered to Gordon, 'I was just saying to Fay that she looks a bit run down. She's promised to get herself off to the doctor's.'

He nodded. 'Good. I've been telling her the same. She pushes herself too hard, what with one thing or another. She's either cleaning the house, running around after the children or involved in some charity do or another. But then I don't need to tell you that, do I? You know what she's like.' As he glanced at the blousy-looking woman in front of him, it struck him afresh just how very different the sisters were. They were like chalk and cheese in looks as well as natures, and he always complimented himself on being married to the best one. Even so, Fay loved her sister and Gordon tried hard to make Alison and her family welcome when they visited, although he had to admit that it went sorely against the grain.

'An' how is that little madam upstairs behavin' now?' Alison asked.

Gordon flushed and once again the woman got the impression that perhaps Gordon wasn't quite so enamoured of his daughter as Fay was.

'Well, Fay has got her into a new school, where she'll start after the summer holidays. We can only hope that she'll settle better there than she did at the last one.'

'If you were to ask me, I'd have to say what that little devil is lackin' is a bloody good hidin'. Now Josh – he's a different kettle o' fish altogether. He's a lovely little chap – but *her* . . .' Alison said bluntly.

Thankfully, Gordon was saved from having to reply when Fay re-entered the room holding the birthday girl's hand.

'Here she is,' Fay said brightly. 'Now let's get everyone all together to sing "Happy Birthday" while you blow your candles out, shall we, darling? Gordon, will you fetch Josh and Casey in from the garden and see where Amber is, please? And would you get Ken for me, Ali?'

Soon they were all assembled in the spacious kitchen and Rebecca stood uncomfortably shuffling from foot to foot while they all sang 'Happy Birthday' to her. Then she blew out the candles on the cake. The second it was over, she scuttled off to her room again.

'Ungrateful little bugger,' Alison tutted. 'All the trouble you've gone to, Fay. You'd have thought she'd at least *pretend* to be enjoying herself!'

'She is just shy,' Fay retorted defensively.

'Bloody spoiled rotten, more like,' Alison muttered under her breath.

Fay chose to ignore the quip as she concentrated on cutting the cake. The rest of the afternoon passed slowly until at last Alison gathered her family together.

'I've got Bingo tonight up at the Grand,' she told her sister. 'So we'd better be off.'

Gordon glanced towards the stack of empty lager cans on the coffee-table. 'Are you sure Ken will be all right to drive? He's had a lot to drink.'

'He'll be fine,' Alison giggled. 'My Ken can hold his booze along with the rest of 'em an' it don't affect him at all.'

'Well, if you say so.' Gordon followed them out to their battered Ford Cortina. It was so old that it looked as if it was only the rust holding it together, but he didn't comment even when he noticed the absence of a tax disc in the front window. He very much doubted whether Ken would have bothered to insure it either, but then at the end of the day it was none of his business.

He and Fay waved them off until the car turned a bend in the smart tree-lined avenue and then Gordon draped his arm about his wife's shoulders as he let out a sigh of relief.

'Phew, thank God that's over. Come on, we'll go and have a quiet cuppa now. You look all in.'

Fay was secretly pleased that it was over too but she merely smiled as she followed her husband back inside. She doubted that Rebecca had enjoyed the party at all. In fact, she had spent most of the day locked away in her room, but then, that was nothing unusual – and at least Fay had the peace of mind of knowing that she had *tried* to make it a special day for her.

*   *   *

'Stuck-up pair o' buggers,' Ken said as the car swerved away from the kerb, and Alison laughed softly. Gordon and Ken were as different as two men could be, and she sometimes wondered how her sister put up with Gordon. He was such a snob, but then she supposed it wouldn't do if they were all to want the same. Her Ken might have his faults but he suited her. And for all Gordon's pompous attitude, little Josh was a sweetheart. Her smile vanished as her thoughts moved on to Rebecca. There was something about the little girl that she had never been able to take to from the day Fay and Gordon had brought her home – and it was nothing to do with her looks, although she was never going to win any beauty contests, that was for sure. No, it was her eyes. They were guarded, and the bright blue orbs seemed to be able to bore right through you. As a scuffle between Amber and Casey broke out in the back seats she turned to reprimand them, and for now her niece was forgotten.

Chapter Seven

Rebecca pressed her ear closer to the door, but all she could hear was muttered words and the sound of an occasional muffled sob coming from her mother.

She frowned as her eyes settled on the twinkling lights on the Christmas tree in the hallway. It was early December, and usually the house was a happy place in the build-up to Christmas, but it certainly hadn't been so this year. Normally her mum would be rushing off, only to return with arms full of bags that she would quickly whisk away with a huge smile on her face. But now Fay rarely left the house, apart from when Gordon took her on one of the frequent trips to the hospital. Sometimes Mrs Middleworth, the elderly grey-haired lady who looked like everyone's favourite granny, came from next door to babysit for her and Josh. And then when he came home, her dad would be sad and quiet and would put them to bed without so much as a cuddle. Then when her mum was sent home again, she would look frail and old, although she still gave them a kiss. Rebecca had been shocked to notice that her mum was losing her hair, and one day she had dared to ask her why it was happening.

Her mum had glanced at Gordon and squeezed his hand very tightly before trying to explain. 'The thing is, sweetheart, I er . . . I've been a little bit poorly and I'm having this treatment called chemotherapy that makes my hair fall out. But when I get better it will all grow back again, I'm sure, so don't get worrying about it.'

Rebecca had gazed into her mum's eyes and felt afraid. She'd done a lot of eavesdropping of late and sometimes she had heard the words 'cancer' and 'aggressive' whispered, although she had no idea what they meant. Perhaps they were something to do with the illness her mum was suffering from?

Dad had employed a lady from an agency to come in and clean the house each day for them, and it was he who now dropped Josh and herself off at school every morning before going off to work. Aunt Alison came a lot more regularly now too, and only last week Rebecca had barged into the kitchen to find her dad crying in Aunt Alison's arms. It had affected her deeply. She had never seen her dad cry before, but when she had asked him what was wrong, Gordon had pulled away from her aunt and mumbled that he wasn't crying; he simply had something in his eye. Rebecca hadn't believed him for a single second but she didn't ask any more questions. She somehow knew it would be a waste of time.

She frowned as she went to sit on the bottom step of the stairs. Her mum spent a lot of time lying in bed or on the settee now, and Rebecca missed some of the things that she had always taken for granted, like Fay reading her a story at bedtime, for example, or keeping her bedroom tidy for her. Mrs Middleworth made her do it herself.

'You are quite old enough to put your own things away now,' the woman would tell her, and Rebecca would grudgingly do as she was told.

Her dad was strict with her too, and if she made any demands on her mum he would usher her away and tell her to be 'a good girl'.

Gordon entered the hall at that moment, and seeing her sitting there he told her, 'Go up and have your bath, Rebecca.'

'Will Mum come and wash my hair for me?' she asked hopefully.

He shook his head. 'Your mum is having a rest,' he told her in a voice that brooked no argument. 'And you are quite big enough to do it yourself now. Just make sure that you wash all the soap out, there's a good girl, and when you come down I'll have your supper ready.'

Rebecca scowled. Supper when Dad got it would probably mean opening a tin of soup or something equally as boring. Mum hardly ever cooked for them any more. She stamped off to do as she was told, passing Josh who had just come out of his room.

'Dad's making supper again,' she grumbled, and he narrowed his eyes at her.

'Well, you could hardly expect Mum to, could you?' he retorted. 'She only came home from hospital this morning.' Seeing his little sister's downcast expression, his face softened. 'Look, I'll tell you what, when you've had your bath and we've eaten we'll have a game of snakes and ladders, if you like.' He still looked out for Rebecca, and she took full advantage of this. Only the day before, she had persuaded him to tidy her room – not that he had got any thanks for it. Rebecca was used to being waited on hand and foot and it went sorely against the grain to have to do anything for herself or anyone else. Josh, on the other hand, was only too happy to run errands and fetch and carry for his mum if she was having a bad day.

Now she sailed past him without giving him an answer and slammed the bathroom door resoundingly. Shaking his head, Josh hurried downstairs to help his dad. His sister was only seven years old and so he always made excuses for her selfish behaviour. She was only a kid, after all. He, however, felt very grown up at almost twelve and was happy to help as much as he could.

Rebecca arrived in the kitchen sometime later to find a mess of congealing beans on toast waiting for her on the kitchen table.

'It might have gone a bit cold now,' her father informed her. 'I didn't realise you'd be so long in the bathroom but I dare say it's still eatable.'

'I don't like beans on toast,' she muttered sulkily.

'Then I'm afraid that's tough luck,' her father told her, uncharacteristically sharply. 'I've never professed to be a master chef so just think yourself lucky you've got that. There are starving children who would be glad of it, and it's not my fault if you decided to spend so long having a bath. I do have other things to do than run around after you, you know.'

Josh shot her a warning glance as Rebecca picked up her knife and fork and began to push the food around her plate. Her mum would have made her something else if she'd told her that she didn't like it, and Rebecca just hoped that Fay would get better soon so that things could get back to normal.

But things *didn't* get back to normal, and the following week when she got home from school, she found Mrs Middleworth waiting for her. One of the neighbours had picked Rebecca up from school, which was unusual in itself.

'I'm afraid your mum has had to go back into hospital, dear,' the kindly neighbour told her, dabbing at her eyes. 'Your dad is there with her now, but don't worry, I've got you some dinner ready. I've done you a nice chicken casserole.'

Rebecca frowned. 'Will Mum be home tonight?' she asked and Mrs Middleworth shook her head.

'It's highly unlikely, dear. But come along and have this dinner while it's nice and hot. Josh has already had his and I'm sure your dad will be back as soon as he can.'

Rebecca sat down at the table feeling very disgruntled.

Tomorrow was the last day of term before they broke up for the Christmas holidays and her mum was supposed to have come and seen her in the school play. She was only in the crowd scenes of the Nativity play this year, admittedly, but it was very thoughtless of her mum to clear off back to hospital like that.

She had just finished her meal, which was actually quite nice, when the back door flew open and her Aunt Alison appeared, closely followed by her Uncle Ken.

'What's happened?' Alison asked, and then seeing Rebecca still sitting at the table she flapped her hand at her and told her, 'Go off into the lounge and watch the telly for a while, there's a good kid. I need to speak to Mrs Middleworth.'

Rebecca reluctantly did as she was told. She hovered in the hallway for as long as she dared, trying to listen to what the adults were saying, but all she heard was Mrs Middleworth say something about her mum going into a place called a 'hospice'. She wondered what a hospice was as she trudged away. It seemed that no one told her what was going on any more.

Her mum didn't come home that day or the next, and it was Saturday when Aunt Alison turned up yet again and told her, 'You and Josh are coming to stay with me for a few days. Let's go and pack you some clothes, shall we?'

'B . . . but it's Christmas next week,' Rebecca objected, wondering why her Aunt Alison's eyes were all swollen and red. She hadn't seen her dad for two whole days now. Mrs Middleworth said he was at the hospice with Mum, and Rebecca was feeling totally confused. And she certainly wasn't happy about going to stay with Aunt Alison. She lived in a place a long way away called Bedworth, in a very small house with a tiny garden, and she didn't feel there would be enough room for them all there. Even so she quietly followed her aunt up the stairs and stood by while she rammed some clothes into a bag.

'On the way I'm going to take you and Josh to see your mum,' her aunt informed her, and Rebecca perked up a bit at that. At least she would be able to ask her mum when she was coming home.

In no time at all she and Josh were crammed into the back of her uncle's dirty old car, and sometime later they pulled up at the hospice. Rebecca couldn't see much because it was dark, but it looked a bit like a hospital although it was surrounded by a very large garden.

'You go in first, love,' Uncle Ken said to his wife. 'I'll keep the kids here with me.'

Rebecca sighed. She couldn't see any reason why they couldn't have all gone in together but she knew there would be no point in saying so. After what seemed a long time, Aunt Alison came out again. Rebecca saw immediately that she had been crying again but even so she ushered the children ahead of her into a long corridor. At the end of it, Rebecca saw her father waiting for them and she raced towards him.

'Aunt Alison says we have to go home with her,' she told him breathlessly. 'Why is that, Dad? Why can't we stay at home with you till Mum comes back?'

'Because . . .' He took a deep breath. 'Mum is very poorly. And I . . . I don't know when she will be coming home. But let's go and see her now, shall we? She's longing to see you both.'

He nudged Josh and Rebecca into a room where they saw their mum lying in a bed, looking very white. She held her hands out to them and they both rushed towards her.

'It's good to see you,' she mumbled as she stroked the hair back from Rebecca's face. 'I want you both to remember that

I love you very, very much. And I want you to be good for your dad . . . Can you both do that for me?'

'You missed seeing me in the Nativity play,' Rebecca told her accusingly, ignoring her question.

'I . . . I know I did, pet, and I'm sorry. I would have loved to have been there,' Fay whispered. She looked very tired and tearful, and now their dad was ushering them towards the door again.

'All right, kids, that's enough,' he told them in a choked voice as he gently pushed them both in the direction of their aunt who was waiting for them near the door. 'I'll fetch you home again just as soon as I can, I promise. In the meantime I want you both to be on your best behaviour for Aunt Alison.' And with that he disappeared back into the room without another word.

The journey to their aunt's home was made in silence, and by the time they arrived, Rebecca's eyes were drooping with tiredness.

'Come on, you two,' Aunt Alison said in a no-nonsense sort of voice. 'Let's get you both to bed.'

The children trooped wearily after her, and in no time at all Rebecca found herself in the bottom bunk in Amber's room. There was no sign of her cousin, but she was too tired to ask where she was, and before she knew it she was fast asleep, despite being in unfamiliar surroundings.

The sound of her father's voice woke her early the next morning, and struggling out of the bed she shot off down the stairs.

She stopped in the doorway of the poky little lounge to see her dad sitting on Aunt Alison's rather grubby settee with his head in his hands.

'Have you come to take us home?' she asked abruptly, without bothering to give him a word of welcome.

'Yes, he has,' Aunt Alison answered for him. 'But first I need to talk to you and Josh. Go and fetch him, would you? He's sleeping in Casey's room. The second door on the left along the landing.'

Rebecca slouched away, disgruntled. It seemed that someone was always telling her what to do just lately. Soon, she and Josh were standing in the kitchen with their aunt. There was no sign of their uncle and Rebecca could only assume that he was still in bed.

'Right then, kids.' Alison lit a cigarette and puffed on it furiously as she stared at them through a haze of smoke. 'I'm afraid I have some bad news for you.' She hesitated as if she was searching for the right words before going on, 'The thing is . . . well, your mum has gone to heaven. Do you understand what that means?'

'Doesn't that mean that she's died?' Josh asked fearfully as tears sprang to his eyes.

Alison nodded. 'Yes, it does.' She saw no point in lying to the child, but Rebecca looked totally bewildered.

'So when will she come back from heaven?' she asked innocently.

'You *can't* come back once you're dead,' Josh informed her scathingly.

'Oh. So who will cook us our Christmas dinner then?'

Josh glared at her. He loved his sister dearly, but there were times when her selfishness shocked even him.

'We'll have to help Dad cook it,' he told her. She was only seven years old, after all, and he realised that she might not fully understand the finality of death, so he was willing to give her the benefit of the doubt.

'Why don't you both go upstairs and get your things?' Aunt Alison asked them now. 'I know your dad is worn out and keen to get home.'

51

Both children turned to do as they were told, and it was as they mounted the stairs that it hit Rebecca: her mum was gone and life as she had known it was never going to be the same again. It was a very frightening thought.

Chapter Eight

Fay Nielson was laid to rest three days after New Year's Day. It had been the worst Christmas that either of the children had ever spent.

Their father was so locked in grief that he had barely seemed to know that they were there, and if it hadn't been for the kindly ministrations of their elderly neighbour they wouldn't even have had a Christmas dinner. Piles of dirty washing were beginning to mount up on the bathroom floor, and the curtains remained firmly shut as if their dad was trying to lock the world out.

Mrs Middleworth arrived shortly after breakfast and shooed Gordon away to the bathroom. 'Go on,' she told him sternly. 'Make yourself respectable. You can't go to your wife's funeral looking like a rag bag. And get a shave too, young man. You look like a tramp. The children will be perfectly all right here with me, and while you've gone they can help me have a bit of a tidy-up. The place certainly looks as if it could do with it.' She looked about at the piles of discarded newspapers and dirty pots. Fay had always kept the place as neat as a new pin, and Mrs Middleworth knew that she would have died of shame if she could have seen it now. Gordon rose from the settee and shambled off to do as he was told like an automaton.

Meanwhile Rebecca put her hands on her hips and pouted. 'Why can't me and Josh go to Mum's funeral?'

'Because funerals are no place for children,' Mrs Middleworth informed her shortly. She knew that she should try to have a little more patience with the child, especially today of all days. But for some reason, Rebecca had always managed to rub her up the wrong way, although she had all the time in the world for Josh, who was a pleasant-natured, likeable young chap.

'Now,' she said, clapping her hands. 'Let's try and get some sort of order back in here, shall we?' And then much to Rebecca's disgust she began to bark out a list of little jobs for them to do.

At eleven o'clock they heard a car pull up outside, and before Mrs Middleworth could stop her, Rebecca ran to the curtains and peeked through them to see a shining black hearse parked there.

'Is that Mum in that big box?' she asked solemnly. Josh had come to stand at the side of her and he started to cry as he slid his arm about her shoulders and nodded numbly.

Rebecca frowned but then piped up, 'Ah well, she wasn't our *real* mum, was she, 'cos we're adopted. Our *real* mums are still out there somewhere, and one day I'm going to find mine.'

Mrs Middleworth thought what a hard-hearted little miss she was as she crossed to place her hand on Josh's shoulder. She could have no idea how bewildered the child was feeling. They could see their father walking away down the drive and his shoulders were stooped with sorrow. Aunt Alison and Uncle Ken were in another shiny black car that was parked behind the hearse, and once their father had got into it to join them, Mrs Middleworth drew the children away from the window.

'Come along now,' she choked. 'Let's go and make a nice cake for when your father gets home, shall we?'

* * *

54

By the time Gordon got back, the house was spick and span. Mrs Middleworth had kept the children busy all day and Rebecca was none too happy about it. From the day her mum had brought her home she had been cosseted and pampered, and she didn't like having to do menial jobs that she had always had done for her.

Josh was quiet and withdrawn, nothing like his usual cheery self, and Rebecca knew that he was missing their mum. She was too, although she would never have admitted it. Fay was the only person who had ever shown her any genuine affection, and now she felt very alone and frightened. The children at school had always picked on her because she was bigger than them, but Fay had never shown her anything but kindness. Who would care about her now?

Ever since the day she had been told she was adopted, Rebecca had tried to push the knowledge to the back of her mind. It was just too confusing to think about. But now she would have to accept that Fay and Gordon had never been her 'real' parents, and she just longed to be old enough to go in search of her birth family. Surely they would love her? But even so, the thought of never seeing her adopted mum again was hard to take in. She kept imagining that Fay was going to walk through the door at any minute – and when she didn't, her loss would hit the little girl afresh.

That night, she lay in bed trying to picture what her real parents were like and what she would say to them when she found them. And she *would* find them. She was determined to, more than ever now that her other mum was gone.

Gordon seemed to be in a trance when he came home. Mrs Middleworth ushered him to the table and placed a hot meal in front of him. She had been shopping and had stocked the food cupboard up for them, but as he stared down at the steaming roast beef dinner with all the trimmings, he might have been looking at a plateful of poison.

'I'm sorry, I can see you've gone to a lot of trouble and it looks wonderful,' he muttered. 'But I'm really not hungry, Mrs Middleworth.'

'I'll have it,' Rebecca piped up, greedily dragging the plate towards her. She and Josh had eaten their dinner some time ago but she was hungry again now, and this was the first decent meal they had had for days.

Gordon sent them both to bed early that night, saying he needed some quiet time, and Rebecca simmered with resentment. Gordon had always been kind to her, but it was Fay who had pandered to her every whim and she was feeling sorely neglected. Still, she consoled herself, she and Josh would be back at school next week, and then things might get back to normal.

But things didn't get back to normal. The day after Fay's funeral, Mrs Middleworth came down with a heavy cold and was confined to bed, so the bereaved family were left to fend for themselves.

Josh would raid the cupboards and prepare makeshift meals for himself and Rebecca with anything he could find, whilst Gordon sat in the lounge staring off into space as the world went on around him. He hardly seemed to know the children were even there, despite Josh's best efforts to pull him out of his depression. He would make his father a cup of tea but it would stay where he placed it on the small table at the side of the sofa to go cold until Josh took it away again.

The following week, Aunt Alison and Uncle Ken arrived mid-afternoon and Josh ushered them into the lounge hoping they would be able to get his dad to talk. By then he and Rebecca were wearing whatever clothes they could get their hands on that were still clean. Josh was doing his best with the housework, but using the washing machine was beyond him.

'So,' Alison said as she sat down in the chair opposite Gordon and lit a cigarette. She would never have dared to do that while Fay was there, but things were different now. 'Don't you think it's time you tried to snap yourself out of this, Gordon? I know it's hard but you do still have two kids to care for.'

Gordon stared at her from watery eyes before saying quietly, 'I am aware of that, but I don't seem to be able to motivate myself to do anything.'

Alison exchanged a glance with Ken before saying tentatively, 'Actually, me and Ken have come up with an idea that might help you. For a while at least . . .'

Gordon stared dully back at her, so she rushed on. 'The thing is, we thought you might be glad of a bit of space, so we wondered how you'd feel about us taking the kids to stay with us for a while. We er . . . we'd need you to pay us – just for their keep, of course. What do you think?'

'You're not taking Josh,' Gordon said instantly. 'But you can take Rebecca if you like.'

Rebecca, who was standing in the doorway, scowled, but before she could object, Alison smiled.

'That won't be a problem. She can stay with us for as long as you like. I can get her into the school up the road from us for now. But I'd need . . . shall we say fifty quid a week for her keep?'

'I can look after Rebecca,' Josh said hotly. He had come to stand by his sister and was appalled at the thought of her being shipped off to their aunt's.

'No, Josh, you and I can muddle along,' Gordon told him gently. 'But it's different for a girl. She needs a woman about the place. This will be for the best and it will only be for a while.'

'Right, that's sorted then.' Alison sighed with relief. 'I'll just go and grab some of her stuff. An' er . . . do you reckon you could let me have a couple of weeks' board for her up front?'

Without a word, Gordon took his wallet out and peeled off a number of notes, which he handed to Alison as Rebecca looked on in shocked horror. She felt as if she was being sold.

'I'm not going anywhere,' she declared, crossing her arms with a mutinous expression on her face.

'Oh, don't be so silly. It's only for a little while till your dad gets back on his feet, and you'll be fine with us,' Alison told her encouragingly, then she swept past her and up the stairs, where she began to collect up some of the dirty clothes that were scattered about the floor and put them into a carrier bag.

Josh looked on helplessly but there was nothing he could do. His father had said that it was only going to be for a short time, which was something at least.

In no time at all Alison was ready to go, with the money Gordon had given her burning a hole in her purse. She would be able to go to Bingo again tonight now and stock the fridge up with lager for Ken. It would almost be worth having to put up with Rebecca.

'Come on,' she told the girl, tossing her coat at her. 'You'd best put that on. It's freezing out there and we want to get back before the frost settles on the roads.'

Rebecca cast an imploring glance in Gordon's direction but he was staring off into space again and so she followed her aunt and uncle out to their car with dragging footsteps.

Josh stood waving at the door with tears in his eyes, but Rebecca ignored him. Their dad had chosen to keep Josh with him, which just went to show that Gordon didn't want her at all.

She clambered into the back of the old car, swiping the empty chocolate and crisp wrappers onto the floor. Her only consolation was that her dad had said it would only be for a short time. But how long was that? A week? A month?

It was not yet four o'clock in the afternoon but already the light had gone from the day, and by the time they drove into the council estate in Bedworth where her aunt and uncle lived, it was dark.

They parked on the road outside the house. There was no drive here and her aunt told her abruptly, 'Bring your bag.'

Neither she nor her uncle had uttered so much as one word to her for the whole of the journey and Rebecca was feeling tearful by now although she was determined not to let them see her crying.

Lugging her bag, she followed them through the rickety gate and along the path overgrown with weeds to the front door. The paint was peeling off it just as she remembered. The house she had just left was as big as the whole terrace of four houses here and she wondered how they all managed to fit into such a poky place.

'You can take your stuff up to Amber's room,' her aunt told her when they were inside the tiny hallway and Rebecca quietly went to do as she was told. Once in Amber's room she clicked the bare light bulb on and looked about her. The bunk beds were unmade, and tubes of open make-up were strewn all across the scratched dressing-table that stood opposite them. This was the only furniture in the room, apart from a wobbly chest of drawers. There was no room for a wardrobe where she could hang her clothes. The wallpaper was faded and peeling away in places, and the carpet she stood on was so old and threadbare that the colour was now indistinguishable. Rebecca thought of her own pretty bedroom back at home and her resentment towards her dad intensified. How *could* he have sent her to such an awful place? And why hadn't he let Josh come with her? It wouldn't have been so bad if her brother had been there too, but as things stood she felt totally abandoned.

Blinking, Rebecca managed to hold back the stinging tears that were threatening to fall. She had never been a child that cried often. In fact, now that she came to think of it, she could scarcely remember crying at all. She had had little in her life to cry over up until now, apart from the cruel taunts of her schoolmates. Since her adopted mother's death her overriding emotion had been one of anger. Why had her mum gone and died like that? Why had she left her? Now other emotions crept in as she thought back to their life together. Fay had always told Rebecca that she loved her . . . and the girl began to remember happier times.

The east coast was less than two hours away from their comfortable home in Nottingham, and often during the summer her mum would pack up a picnic hamper and her dad would drive them to the beach for the day. She could remember the donkey rides and the sticky, delicious candyfloss and toffee apples they would buy for her and Josh. And then at the end of the day when she was feeling comfortably sleepy, her mum would tuck her down in the back of the car beneath a cosy blanket, and she would nap until they got home. Then her dad would carry her upstairs while her mum fussed over her and got her ready for bed.

She thought of the Christmases, so very different to the one she had just spent, when she would wake to find piles of presents beneath the Christmas tree and the family would all sit down together to a wonderful Christmas dinner: a large turkey cooked to perfection with all the trimmings, followed by trifle and mince pies and an enormous Christmas pudding. But there would never be another Christmas like that now. Mrs Middleworth had told her gently that her mum was gone forever, and that sounded like an awfully long time to a seven-year-old girl.

'Rebecca! What are you doin' up there? Get your arse down here this minute if you want something to eat.' Her aunt's voice echoed up the stairs and Rebecca started as she gripped her teddy bear tighter to her. Then turning slowly she made her way downstairs.

Chapter Nine

Rebecca had been staying with her aunt for three days when she got her first slap – and it came as a shock to her.

They had all just finished a rather unappetising meal of fish and chips that her uncle had fetched from the chip shop. They were almost cold and greasy by the time he got them home, no doubt after calling into the pub in Collycroft for a swift pint, and Rebecca pushed the food about the greaseproof paper with a sulky expression on her face.

'So what's up with your dinner then?' her aunt snapped.

'It's disgusting, that's what's up with it,' Rebecca snapped back, and without warning her aunt leaned across the table and clouted her firmly about the head.

'We'll have less of your lip, my girl,' she threatened. 'Just who the bloody hell do you think you are anyway? I reckon you've been thoroughly spoiled, that's the problem.'

Rebecca recoiled in shock. No one had ever slapped her before and she was fuming. 'I don't like chips!' she spat.

Her aunt laughed. 'Well, *tough*! You'll just have to bloody go hungry then, won't you? Don't think I'm going to pander to you like our Fay did. Spare the rod an' spoil the child – that's what I say, and if I have any more of your mouth you'll get another clout!'

Rebecca scraped her chair back from the table and stumbled away up the stairs to the small bedroom she shared with Amber. Her cousin found her there a few minutes later. She had thrown herself across the bottom bunk and was thumping the grimy pillow as she sobbed bitterly.

'Are you all right, kid?' Amber whispered.

Rebecca stared up at her, her glasses all askew as she choked, 'She hit me!'

'Huh! That was only a tap,' Amber said, as she perched next to her and swiped the damp hair from her brow. 'You should see her when she really gets going. Me and our Casey have had some right good hidings in our time.'

Rebecca sniffed loudly and wiped her nose on the sleeve of her cardigan as Amber smiled at her sympathetically. Strangely enough, for all her brash front she had found an ally in Amber. The older girl felt sorry for her and quite liked her, although she would never have admitted it.

'Why don't you get into your jamas and have an early night?' Amber suggested now, but Rebecca shook her head.

'I . . . I don't want to. I want to go home.'

'I dare say you do, but I don't think your dad is ready to cope just yet. Look, I'll tell you what, I'll sneak you some biscuits up later if you like, an' if you don't want to go to bed yet, why don't you come down an' watch telly for a bit wi' me? *EastEnders* is on soon.'

Rebecca swung her legs to the end of the bed and watched as Amber began to slap on some make-up haphazardly.

'I've got a date tonight.' She winked at Rebecca in the mirror. 'But don't get tellin' me mam an' dad, will yer?'

Rebecca shook her head solemnly before asking, 'Aren't you a bit young to have a boyfriend?'

Amber giggled, 'No, o' course I ain't. I was fourteen last week. You sound like them pair downstairs. Now shoot, while I get meself ready, there's a good kid.'

The child reluctantly did as she was told. She didn't really have much option, and once in the lounge she saw her aunt pulling her coat on.

'I'm poppin' out for a game of Bingo,' she informed her. 'Your Uncle Ken's gone up the Liberal Club but our Amber will keep her eye on you an' Casey till I get back.'

Rebecca chewed on her lip. She knew that Amber was planning to go out but she said nothing, although the thought of staying in the house without an adult was a little scary. Things were so different here to what they had been at home, and she wondered again how long it would be before her dad came to take her back. She had been there for three days but they felt like three years, and once again she felt the urge to cry as she thought of all she had lost.

It was much later when Rebecca, who had fallen into a doze on the settee, was wakened by someone tenderly stroking her cheek. Her eyes flew open to find her Uncle Ken hovering over her with a smile on his face.

'Come on, little 'un. Let's get you up to bed, eh?' It was the first time he had spoken to her since she had been there and Rebecca was confused at his sudden show of kindness.

'What time is it?' she asked as she sat up and knuckled the sleep from her eyes.

'Oh, it's not that late. Yer aunt ain't even back yet, so let's get you settled down.'

He placed his arm about her shoulders and as he led her towards the stairs she glanced around for a sign of Casey, but he was nowhere to be seen. She supposed he had already gone to bed and meekly followed her uncle upstairs. He clicked the bedroom light on and as he advanced on her, she shrank back against the wall.

'Let's get you into your pyjamas then, shall we?' he suggested, and now she shook her head vigorously.

'N-no, it's all right. I'm a big girl now and I can undress myself.'

'Rubbish,' he chuckled, taking a firm hold of her arm. 'If you let me help yer, we can have yer tucked up in no time.' And before Rebecca could object further, he tugged her jumper over her head and went to do the same to her vest.

'I like to keep my vest on,' she told him, snatching her pyjamas from the bed and backing towards the door with her arms crossed tightly against her chest.

For a moment she thought he was going to take it off anyway but then he stood up and smiled before asking, 'Your aunt didn't hurt yer when she clocked yer one earlier on, did she?'

Rebecca nodded numbly, feeling very vulnerable and humiliated.

'Good. That's good, but what yer need to remember is, if you're a good girl for me I can make things a lot easier here fer you. Do you understand me?'

Rebecca nodded again although she didn't really understand what he meant. She just wanted him to leave her room.

'Right.' He licked his lips and bent to plant a wet kiss on her cheek as she flinched away. She could smell his beery breath and just wanted him to be gone now.

It was then that the front door opened and they heard Amber pounding up the stairs. Her uncle hurried towards the door, growling, 'And where the bloody 'ell 'ave you been then, miss? I thought yer mam told yer to look after the little 'uns tonight?'

'Oh, I have been,' Amber told him breathlessly. 'I just popped round to Kim's to get a CD she'd borrowed. I've only been gone for five minutes.' As she winked at Rebecca the girl lowered her head.

'Right. Well 'appen it's time you were gettin' yourself to

bed now, as I was just sayin' to the young 'un here. Goodnight, both.' And much to Rebecca's relief he left the room then, closing the door behind him.

She was woken the next morning by someone banging on the front door, and after creeping out of bed she peeped out of her curtains to see a man with a huge bag standing on the doorstep. Minutes later her uncle let the man in and Rebecca tiptoed out onto the landing to hear what was going on in the hall way below.

'So how many did yer get this trip then?' she heard her uncle ask.

'There's twelve thousand in there,' the visitor replied and as she peeped through the banisters she saw him unload a large number of long packets of cigarettes onto the hall floor. Her uncle took a wad of money from his pocket, counted through it, and handed it to the man, who quietly slipped away after telling him, 'Pete will be round later wi' the booze.'

Frowning, Rebecca went back to her room to find Amber waiting for her.

'Dad just got a delivery, did he?' she asked, yawning.

'A . . . a man just brought lots of cigarettes,' Rebecca whispered.

'Good. Once the old man has flogged a few I might be able to tap him up fer a bit o' pocket money then.'

When Rebecca stood there looking totally confused, Amber explained: 'Dad has young blokes who go over to France on the ferry for him an' bring him back fags an' booze. Dad slips 'em a few quid for goin' and then makes a profit when he sells the stuff on to his mates in the pubs. But that ain't all he dabbles in. He ain't averse to passin' on stolen goods neither. Most of what goes missing hereabouts ends up in the cupboard under the stairs till Dad sells it on.' Seeing that Rebecca didn't have a clue what she was on about, Amber sighed. Rebecca was such a big girl for her age and so solemn that Amber sometimes forgot that she was only seven years old. 'Come on,' she said, holding her hand out. 'Let's go an' see if there's anythin' in the cupboard fer us breakfast, eh? I reckon we've got some cereal but I ain't sure if there's any milk till me mam sends our Casey up the shop. Never mind, we can always make do wi' a bit of dry toast, can't we?'

It didn't sound at all appetising but Rebecca took her hand and went downstairs with her all the same.

The following week, Amber and Casey returned to their schools after the Christmas break and Aunt Alison went marching off to try and get Rebecca into the local infants' school, leaving her with her Uncle Ken. He had barely spoken to her since the night he had put her to bed, but now he patted his knee and suggested smarmily, 'Why don't you come an' sit on Uncle Ken's lap an' give me a cuddle, eh?'

Rebecca regarded him warily as she slowly shook her head.

'Aw, come on. Don't be so mean,' he said encouragingly. 'Everyone needs a cuddle now an' then.'

Before she could stop him he reached out and caught her arm, then, lifting her as if she weighed no more than a feather, he plonked her on his lap.

She squirmed uncomfortably as he began to gently caress her back. 'Now that's nice, ain't it?' he crooned. 'Didn't I say yer old Uncle Ken would be good to you if you was nice to him?'

Before Rebecca could answer he took a handful of coins from his pocket and pressed them into her hand. 'There you go,' he grinned. 'There's a bit o' pocket money fer you to be goin' on with.'

As she stared down at the coins he began to stroke her leg just above the knee.

'Yer know, people say yer a plain little thing but I reckon yer a pretty little gel. Here, let's see what yer look like without yer specs on, eh?' After slipping her glasses off he nodded approvingly. 'Just as I thought. Pretty as a picture.'

Rebecca blushed. No one but her mum had ever told her she was pretty before, and she quite liked how it made her feel, although she wasn't so keen on Uncle Ken stroking her leg. It made her feel all funny inside and she wished that he would stop.

And stop he did when the back door was suddenly flung open and Pat Blair, a friend of Alison's, marched into the room.

'So where is she then?' She stopped abruptly when she saw Rebecca perched on Ken's lap. 'Christ, Ken, don't tell me you've gone all paternal at last?' she chortled as he hastily slid the girl onto the seat at the side of him.

'Ali's gone up the school to see if she can get the little 'un 'ere a place there,' he explained, looking slightly uncomfortable. 'An' me an' young Rebecca was just havin' a little chat.'

'Oh.' Pat was vaguely surprised. In the five years that she had lived in the street she had never seen Ken show so much as a flicker of interest in either of his own children, so why he should start now with this little girl was a puzzle.

Rebecca was inching away from him as Pat looked at her.

'This is Rebecca, she's our niece,' Ken introduced her.

Pat already knew all about their little lodger from Alison but she smiled at the girl as she asked, 'And how are you settlin' in, love?'

'Oh, I'm not here to stay,' Rebecca said hastily. 'My mum . . . died . . . and my dad needed a little break.'

'I'm sorry to hear that.' Pat studied her. Just as Alison had said, the child was no beauty, but she *was* beautifully spoken, even if she did sound rather out of place in her present surroundings. Alison was never going to get an award for housekeeping, that was for sure. She also suspected that her friend was being paid to take the kid for a while. As much as Pat liked Alison, she knew her well enough to know that she certainly wouldn't have done it out of the goodness of her heart.

Ken lumbered out of the chair and grinned sheepishly at her. 'Actually, seein' as yer here, Pat, could you keep yer eye on this one for me till the missus gets back? I could do with nippin' out.'

Pat rightly guessed that his 'nipping out' would mean going to the pub to take orders for his latest delivery of fags and booze. She sometimes wondered how Ken had managed to keep out of prison, with all the 'beer runs' he organised. In the time she had lived near him, the house had been raided by the coppers more often than she cared to remember, but each time Ken had managed to talk his way out of it. But then he was clever, was Ken. He never kept all his ill-gotten gains in one place. Most of the fags and booze was distributed out to friends' and neighbours' houses shortly after it was delivered until he sold it on. And then what was kept in the house he could always claim was for his own use, which was just as well, as rumour had it that another raid was on the cards any day now. It was one of the reasons she had called round – to warn him. He was certainly a different kettle of fish from her own husband, who hadn't got the sense he was born with. He had spent half of their married life in and out of nick. But that was all in the past now. The last time he had been sent down, two years ago, he had been sentenced to twenty years for armed robbery, with a recommendation from the judge that he serve his whole term. Pat could still remember sitting in the courtroom on the day the sentence had been passed, and the flood of relief that had flowed through her. It was over – *finally* over.

Sometimes now when she looked back, Pat wondered how she had ever put up with the way her husband had treated her. A violent man, he had put her in hospital more times than she cared to remember. And more than once she had been forced to do things she was not proud of, just to put food on the table for the kids while he squandered away all his ill-gotten gains on gambling, fags and booze. She had left him so many times, only to go limping back when he promised things would be different. But they never were. Now she was trying to build a new life for herself. She had two girls and two boys, but only the youngest boy was at home now. The older ones had all flown the nest some time ago. She had actually given birth to five. She tried hard not to think of the two that were absent from her life, particularly the eldest boy who had been such a clone of his old man that his behaviour had become intolerable and she had been forced to place him into care. She doubted the youngest – who had been yet another mistake shortly after Mick had come out of prison some years ago – would want to have anything to do with his dad when he came out of jail this time. The lad had seen too much. And truthfully, she knew that this would really be no bad thing.

Shortly after meeting Alison, she could remember Ali asking her why she had put up with Mick's cruel behaviour for all those years, and for the first time Pat had been forced to admit that she had suffered from what she termed 'the battered wife syndrome'. She couldn't live with him, yet she couldn't live without him. There were hundreds of women she knew of and whom she had met in various refuges, who had been exactly the same. But that would all change now. Mick would be gone for a very long time – and now she could finally try to get her life back on track.

Ken was heading for the door, and as he passed her, Pat

wrinkled her nose in distaste. His long greasy hair was straggling over the neck of his collar, and he hadn't shaved for days. Nor had he bathed, judging by the stale smell that was emanating from him. But there was nothing new there.

As she looked back at Rebecca who was standing with her head bent, shuffling from foot to foot, a surge of sympathy rushed through her. Poor little sod, she certainly didn't have a lot going for her.

'Go on then,' she told Ken, taking pity on the child. 'I dare say as I haven't got anythin' that needs doin' as won't wait for a while. I've got nothin' spoilin'.'

Ken quickly made his escape while the going was good and Pat looked back at Rebecca.

'An' now how's about you an' me go an' make ourselves a nice cuppa, eh, while we wait for yer aunt?'

Rebecca stared at the woman for a moment. She was very well built with bleached blonde hair that was frizzed and backcombed into a halo about her head. Thick rimmed glasses were perched on the end of her nose and her clothes were too tight, but for all that she was clean and had a kind face. Rebecca nodded as she quietly followed her into the kitchen. The way she saw it, anything was better than being left on her own with her Uncle Ken. He had shown her nothing but kindness, and yet for no reason that she could explain, he made her feel uneasy.

Chapter Ten

The following Sunday morning, Rebecca was woken by the sound of someone hammering on the front door, followed by a loud crash as the door imploded into the hallway. She heard her uncle thump down the stairs, cursing loudly as he went – followed by the sound of men shouting.

'Wh-what's happening?' she asked, terrified, as Amber groaned and slid down out of the top bunk.

'It's another raid, by the sound of it,' her cousin yawned, and when Rebecca looked confused, she explained, 'It's the coppers. They'll turn the house upside down now before they leave, you just see if they don't.'

Just as she'd said, two policemen barged into the room only seconds later. 'Could we have you two girls out on the landing please, while we search your room,' the older of the two men asked. Rebecca was shaking by then as she clambered out of her bunk and shrank into Amber's side.

'Oh, why don't you just sod off,' Amber hissed. 'Yer won't find nothin' in 'ere.'

'Then you won't mind us having a look about, will you?' the officer retorted.

Rebecca's eyes were on stalks as Amber dragged her out onto the small landing. They had to press themselves against the wall as there seemed to be police crawling all over the place.

'W-will we be arrested?' she asked fearfully.

'Will we 'eck as like,' Amber snorted. 'It ain't us they're after, it's me dad.' They could hear him downstairs shouting loudly enough to waken the dead, but the police simply ignored him as they systematically searched the place room by room.

One of the younger officers crowed with delight when he found some sleeves of cigarettes in the cupboard beneath the stairs, but Ken just grinned back at him confidently when the young man waved them in his face.

'There's only a couple o' thousand there. An' they're fer me own use. You just try an' prove otherwise.'

'All right, girls, you can go back to bed now. Sorry for disturbing you,' a young Constable said now as he came back out of their room. Rebecca shot past him like a bullet from a gun, and after leaping back into bed she pulled the covers over her head and lay there trembling for what seemed like a very long time. There was no way she was going to be able to go back to sleep.

Eventually the house became quiet again, and she ventured downstairs where she found her aunt slouched in a chair in her dressing-gown puffing on a cigarette.

'Where's Uncle Ken?' she asked as she looked around. Casey and Amber were there but there was no sign of him.

'The rozzers have taken him down the nick to ask him some questions,' her aunt said baldly, and seeing the look of horror on Rebecca's face she added, 'But don't get worryin', they can't pin nowt on him. He'll probably be back for dinnertime.'

To Rebecca, this was like another world, and more than ever she wished that she could go home.

Pat came to see them shortly afterwards, and spotting Rebecca's sombre face, she smiled at her before telling her aunt, 'Didn't I tell you I'd got wind that this was on the cards? Had Ken got rid of everythin'?'

Her aunt nodded glumly. 'Yes, everythin' apart from a car stereo that one o' the lads turned up with late last night, but luckily they didn't find that. Ken had hidden it in the washin' machine.'

Car stereos in washing machines? Rebecca didn't have a clue what they were on about, but wisely didn't ask for enlightenment.

The day had got off to a really bad start but hopefully it would get better. It was Sunday, and had she been at home with her mum, she would have been looking forward to a really nice roast dinner. Her mum had always cooked them a lovely meal on Sunday but she thought there would be little chance of that here.

As the morning advanced she knew that she had been right. One neighbour after another trooped in and out, keen to know what was going on, and Casey and his friends noisily took over the living room. There was no escape upstairs either, as Amber was in their room with her music throbbing away, and so Rebecca sat on the stairs hugging her knees feeling totally miserable and out of place.

Uncle Ken came home at three o'clock in the afternoon.

'The bastards couldn't pin a thing on me,' he told his wife gleefully. 'An' I put the fear o' God up 'em when I told 'em I was goin' to sue 'em for wrongful arrest.'

'If you fell in the cut you'd come out with a pocket full of fish,' Rebecca heard her Aunt Alison say, although she hadn't a clue what the strange statement meant.

Aunt Alison eventually gave her a slice of pizza that tasted like cardboard for her lunch, but by then she was so hungry that she would have eaten almost anything and she cleared her plate. As she'd quickly discovered, in this house you ate *what* was put in front of you *when* it was put in front of you – or you went without. It seemed like a lifetime away now since her mum had plied her with different meals until she came upon one that Rebecca was willing to eat.

Again she felt a sharp stab of homesickness but she didn't say anything. She knew now that it would be a waste of time and she would just be told in no uncertain terms to 'shut up!'

Late in the afternoon her aunt led her to the bathroom and told her, 'Get yourself washed. You start at your new school tomorrow and we want you looking half-decent, don't we?'

'But we haven't been shopping for my new uniform,' Rebecca objected.

'*New uniform!*' Her aunt snorted with derision. 'Do you think I'm made o' money? You'll make do with our Amber's old one. It's been stuck in the cupboard for years an' I dare say it will be a bit big on you. Still, it'll do for now. Till I can tap your dad up for the money for a new one, that is.'

Rebecca finally went to bed with a feeling of dread as she thought of the day ahead. Would the school be an all-girls school like the private one her mum and dad had sent her to? Would she be accepted there? She certainly hadn't been popular at the other two schools she'd attended. But then why should things be different now? She certainly wasn't any prettier, so no doubt she would just be picked on again, especially in the ill-fitting uniform that her aunt was insisting she should wear. Questions floated round and round in her head until at last she slipped into an exhausted sleep.

Her aunt roughly shook her awake the following morning.

'Come on,' she ordered. 'It's time to get you to school. But don't go thinkin' I'll be walkin' you there every day. You're quite old enough to get yourself up of a mornin' and get yourself off.'

'B-but I don't know the way,' Rebecca stammered.

'Well, that's why I'm takin' you today, ain't it? So as you

do know. Now get your skates on an' then I can get back an' pinch another couple of hours in bed.'

Rebecca struggled into the school uniform that her aunt had thrown onto the bed. The sweatshirt was badly faded and the skirt reached down to mid-calf, but she rolled the waistband up until it was a more acceptable length then went down to join her aunt in the kitchen. It was bitterly cold in there and she shivered as her aunt slapped a bowl of cereal in front of her.

There was hardly any milk left in the bottle and it looked very unappetising, but she cleared the dish all the same and then it was time for them to go.

Once outside, Rebecca clung to her aunt's hand. The pavements were white over with frost and her teeth were chattering with cold. Rebecca had no idea where they were going or even whereabouts in Bedworth they were, apart from when she had heard Pat call it 'the Jocks Estate'.

Eventually they turned into a road and she saw some children streaming through a pair of gates further up the path.

'That's the school,' her aunt informed her.

Rebecca frowned. She had never seen so many children all in one place and all at the same time in her whole life.

'But there are boys going in there!'

'Well, of course there are. This is a mixed school.' Her aunt chuckled.

'Are they in separate classes to the girls?' Rebecca asked. They were almost at the gates now and her heart was pounding.

'Of course they ain't. Why would they do that?' Her aunt drew her to a halt and passed her a brown paper bag, saying, 'You'll find some sandwiches in there for your lunch.'

'B-but I always had a cooked dinner at my other schools,' Rebecca stammered.

'Yes, well, that was then and this is now – and if you think I'm payin' the prices they charge for school dinners you've got another think comin'.' It was obvious that Alison was losing patience with her now and Rebecca began to panic as she pushed her through the gates.

'Aren't you coming in with me? I don't know where to go!'

Her aunt sighed in exasperation. 'You just go in them doors there, look, an' tell 'em your name. They're expectin' you an' then they'll show you what classroom to go to. Come on – look lively. It'll be time to come home if you dither about much longer.' And with that she turned on her heel and left Rebecca standing there feeling more terrified than she had ever felt in her whole life.

Eventually she plucked up enough courage to cross the playground, painfully aware of the many eyes that were following her progress. Once at the doors she pushed them open and found herself in a large entrance hall with an office to one side. She crossed to it and a lady sitting on the other side of a glass window looked through it to ask, 'Yes?'

'I . . . I'm Rebecca Nielson,' the child muttered, hoping she would be heard above the din of the children swarming through the corridors on their way to their classrooms. 'It's my first day here and my aunt said you would be expecting me.'

'Oh yes, of course. Sit down there, Rebecca, and I'll deal with you in a moment.'

Rebecca did as she was told. Slowly the corridors emptied and became silent and then she heard the sound of high heels tapping towards her. She looked up to see a young woman smiling in her direction.

'You must be Rebecca?'

The girl nodded as the woman beckoned her to follow, saying, 'Then come this way, Rebecca, I'll show you where the cloakroom is before I take you to your classroom. I'm Miss Baxter, by the way.'

With her heart in her mouth Rebecca followed behind her and soon she found herself in a long narrow room where rows of coat hooks hung above low wooden benches.

'This can be your hook here,' the woman told her. 'The last but one. Look, I've put your name above it all ready for you.'

After sliding her arms out of her coat, Rebecca hastily hung it up, very conscious of the shabby uniform she was wearing beneath it. In contrast, Miss Baxter looked very smart in black trousers and a crisp white blouse with a pretty frill running all down the front of it. She was quite tall and had lovely shoulder-length blonde hair, and Rebecca didn't think she looked at all like a teacher.

'Right, now let's show you where the classroom is.' The kindly young woman could sense the child's nervousness and was doing her best to put her at ease, although she didn't seem to be doing a very good job of it if Rebecca's pale face was anything to go by.

Rebecca was soon lost in a myriad of corridors and she wondered how she was ever going to find her way about. The interior of the school was much larger than it looked from the outside. At last Miss Baxter paused outside one of the many doors and told her, 'This will be your classroom, dear. You'll be in Mrs Jennings's class and I'm sure you'll like her. She's very nice.'

Through the door Rebecca could hear the hum of children's voices but the instant Miss Baxter opened the door it became silent and a sea of faces looked towards her.

Rebecca felt completely overwhelmed. In her last school there had only been eighty pupils in total, but in this one classroom alone there looked to be at least half that many children.

She wished that the ground would open up and swallow her as Miss Baxter led her to the front of the class and whispered something in Mrs Jennings's ear.

Mrs Jennings nodded as she smiled at Rebecca, and then when the younger teacher took her leave she addressed the class.

'Children, this is Rebecca Nielson who will be joining us. I hope you will all make her feel welcome.' And then to Rebecca, 'You can share that desk with Charlotte over there, dear.'

Rebecca moved forward and sank onto the hard wooden seat and within minutes the lesson recommenced. Her teacher seemed pleasant enough, so she supposed that was something to be thankful for at least. The woman was middle-aged, plump and had greying hair that curled around her head like a halo. Rebecca's first day at her new school had well and truly begun, whether she liked it or not, and she had no choice but to get on with it. And perhaps, just *perhaps*, if she tried to be a little friendlier the other children might like her this time? With a new resolve she smiled shyly at the girl sitting next to her, who was eyeing her curiously.

At break-time a bell sounded and the children began to swarm towards the playground, paying Rebecca no heed at all. She tagged onto the back of them, collecting her coat on the way, and soon found herself outside. Boys were kicking a football about and girls stood in little groups chatting and pointing towards her as she hovered uncertainly in the doorway.

'Come along, girl. Don't get blocking everyone's way,' the teacher who was on playground duty barked, and Rebecca quickly stepped out.

'Sure they've put yer in the right class, are yer?' one girl taunted callously. 'Lookin' at the size o' yer, I'd have thought yer were ready fer the next school.'

Rebecca felt colour rise in her pale cheeks as the other girls began to titter.

'An' where did yer get that uniform from? A second-'and shop, were it? Pity they didn't 'ave one that fitted yer.'

A little crowd had gathered now and they were all watching her, adding to her humiliation. And there and then her resolve to make friends dissolved like mist. What was the point in trying? The only person who had ever loved her was gone forever.

'Leave me alone,' she ground out threateningly, causing a fresh gale of laughter to break out.

'*Ooh*, just 'ark at 'er,' one of the girls quipped. 'Little Miss 'Oity-Toity, eh?'

Rebecca marched away with as much dignity as she could muster. It seemed that things would be no better here than they had been in her previous schools – but who needed friends anyway?

Chapter Eleven

It had now been two whole weeks since Rebecca had gone to stay with her aunt, but to her it felt like forever.

She was aware that her Aunt Alison had phoned her dad, no doubt to ask him for more money. But whether he would come to see her or fetch her home was debatable. She was missing the life she had led far more than she could have ever imagined, although she was surprised to find that she didn't miss Josh. It was quite pleasant not to have him following her about all the time as he was prone to do. Even so, every day she wished that things could just go back to the way they had been. But of course, she knew that this could never happen now. Her mum had gone to that place called heaven and could never come back. Sometimes, Rebecca longed to be there with her. At least then she would feel wanted again, which she certainly didn't at her aunt's. Admittedly, her uncle was kind to her – but that was only on the rare occasions when she found herself alone with him. He ignored her for the rest of the time.

Amber was kind too, not that she saw much of her. She was out and about with her friends for most of the time, as was Casey – and they only seemed to come home to eat and sleep. The night before, Amber's boyfriend had taken her to the cinema to see *Braveheart* and she had told Rebecca all about it as they lay in their room that night. There had been a terrible row before she went out because Amber had gone into town in the afternoon and come back with her belly-button pierced. It was the latest craze and her aunt didn't approve of it at all.

'You'll be sorry if you get an infection in there,' Aunt Alison had warned, but Amber had just shrugged.

Even though she didn't like living there, Rebecca was getting used to it now. She'd become adept at keeping out of the way, which usually meant spending long lonely hours sitting on the bottom step in the hallway.

At least she could see all the comings and goings from there. Men were constantly knocking on the door for Uncle Ken with stolen goods, which Ken would then pass on to some unsuspecting soul for a profit. He and Aunt Alison had had a terrible argument the week before when he had taken possession of a load of jewellery. Aunt Alison had selected a rather pretty sapphire and diamond ring and said that she *must* keep it. But Uncle Ken had forbidden it.

'Don't be so stupid, woman! What if the coppers come an' see it on yer finger? I'll be up the Swanee good an' proper then,' he had stormed.

Aunt Alison had reluctantly handed it back and he had disappeared off to the pub with his ill-gotten gains while she sulked at home.

Today was Sunday. A good day as far as Rebecca was concerned because at least she didn't have to go to school. She didn't like it there although Charlotte, the little girl she sat next to, was nice to her. The other children had wasted no time at all in nicknaming her 'Fatty' and 'Four Eyes' and Rebecca hated them with a vengeance.

She'd had a dish of lukewarm tinned chicken soup slapped down in front of her for her Sunday dinner, which was a far cry from the delicious meals her adoptive mum used to cook for her. But she was even getting used to that too now. She knew that she must have lost some weight because her clothes were loose on her now. But she didn't mind that. Perhaps children at school would be kinder to her if she wasn't so fat.

It was as she was sitting there feeling very sorry for herself that the front door swung open and Casey barged in. 'Uncle Gordon's just pulled up,' he informed them all breathlessly, and instantly, Rebecca's heart soared. Her dad must have come to take her home!

Rushing to the door, which Casey had left swinging open, she stood in the icy draught watching as her dad climbed out of his car and Josh got out of the passenger seat. Her heart was thudding with joy and anticipation as a small crowd of children gathered to admire the shining Bentley, which was her dad's pride and joy.

'Here, Casey.' She saw her dad hand Casey, who had skipped back outside again, some money. 'Guard the car with your life, will you? I don't want to come out and find it with no wheels.'

'Right you are, Uncle Gordon.' Casey's chest swelled with importance as he glared threateningly at the assembled children. And then her dad and Josh were walking down the path, and unable to stop herself, Rebecca ran to him and threw her arms around her father.

Looking very embarrassed, Gordon gently stepped away from her and patted her head before striding on down the path.

Once they were inside, her dad marched into the front room to see her Aunt Alison. Josh hurried over to Rebecca.

'Are you all right?' he asked anxiously.

Rebecca's eyes welled with tears. 'I don't like it here,' she whimpered. 'Have you come to take me home?'

'I don't know. I don't think so . . . not just yet,' Josh admitted in a small voice.

They turned and walked into the front room, just in time to see their dad hand another wad of notes to Aunt Alison. The woman flicked through them quickly before saying sweetly, 'An' what about the money fer her school uniform, Gord? The poor little lamb's havin' to wear our Amber's old one, an' it's years old, an' at least three sizes too big for her.'

Rebecca watched her dad's lips tighten into a hard line. He hated it when her aunt shortened his name, but even so he merely peeled off some more notes and handed them to her.

Rebecca's heart sank into her shoes. If her dad was giving her aunt more money it must mean that he hadn't come to take her home. Instantly, all the good feelings she had experienced only seconds before fled and she asked him tearfully, 'Haven't you come to take me home?'

Avoiding her eyes and looking very guilty, her dad shook his head. 'Not just yet, pet. I need a little more time.'

'How *much* more time?' Rebecca thrust her chin out resentfully. It all seemed so unfair. Josh was still at home, so why couldn't she be there too?

'Oh, I shouldn't think it will be long now,' her dad said vaguely. 'And now we really ought to be off.'

'But you've only just come! I haven't had time to speak to Josh properly yet,' the child objected.

Gordon sighed. 'Very well, I'll have a cup of tea and give you both ten minutes.'

Rebecca glared at him as the injustice of it all slapped her in the face afresh. Even so, ten minutes was better than nothing, so while Aunt Alison went to put the kettle on she took Josh's hand and dragged him upstairs to her room. Even though she didn't really love him, he was about the only link she had with home right now. Luckily Amber was out so at least they could talk in private.

After a cursory glance around, Josh sat down on the end

of her bunk and asked, 'So how are you *really*?' Rebecca looked pale and unhappy and he was concerned about her.

'I hate it here.' Rebecca's small hands bunched into fists as she stood at the window gazing down into the neglected garden at the back of the house. 'The food is horrible, I don't like the school I'm going to as the children there make fun of me, and this place is *dirty*!'

'Hm.' Josh had to agree with that. The sheets on his sister's bed looked as if they hadn't been changed for months, and Rebecca herself looked none too clean either, if it came to that.

'Well, things aren't that much better at home,' he told her. 'Dad still hasn't gone back to work and he hardly goes out at all, unless it's to go to the shop or the off-licence. He's drinking a lot,' he confided worriedly.

'Why?'

Josh shrugged. 'I suppose it's 'cos he misses Mum. And *I* miss her too,' he said with a catch in his voice. But then with a supreme effort he forced a smile to his face. 'Never mind though, eh? Things can only get better and I've no doubt the next time we come, it will be to take you home.'

'Do you really think so?' Rebecca asked hopefully.

Josh nodded; there was nothing else he could say to make her feel any better. 'Now . . . tell me all about this new school you've started at,' he said. And so for the next ten minutes Rebecca did just that, although he noticed that she didn't have anything complimentary to say about it.

All too soon, their dad's voice echoed up the stairs and Rebecca looked bereft as she grabbed Josh's hand.

'Please will you talk to Dad and tell him I want to come home?' she begged.

'Josh, can you hear me? It's time we were going!'

Josh felt as if he was being ripped in two as he rose and

headed for the door. 'Of course I will, and we'll be back before you know it,' he promised, not knowing what else to say – then he was clattering away down the stairs and Rebecca felt her whole world fall apart all over again. She heard the front door slam as Josh and her father left, and loneliness coursed through her veins. Her dad hadn't even bothered to say goodbye to her, which just went to show how much he loved her. She sat there for a long time staring off into space. Perhaps she could run away? Her dad would realise just how much she wanted to go home then and he might take her back. She was plotting how best to go about it when she heard her uncle come in, closely followed by a horrified shriek from her aunt.

'What the bloody 'ell is *that*?' Rebecca heard her say, and curious, she dried her eyes and went back down the stairs only to see her uncle standing in the doorway of the front room holding a very bedraggled pup by the length of rope about its neck.

'This 'ere is Casper,' her uncle answered. 'Old Mick up the pub were goin' to drown him, 'cos he's eatin' him out of house an' home, so I thought I'd fetch him back for the kids. As a pet, like.'

'A *pet*!' Aunt Alison gasped. 'Why, it's the mangiest, ugliest dog I've ever seen. No wonder Mick wanted to drown it. What arsehole in their right mind could take to *that*? What breed is it supposed to be, anyway?'

'I were told he were a Staffie.' Her uncle dropped the makeshift lead and the poor mutt dropped onto its belly.

'A *Staffie*? Huh! You could have fooled me. He looks like a right Heinz fifty-seven. An' I don't know about eatin' him out of house an' home. The poor little bugger looks starved to me,' Aunt Alison commented.

Rebecca inched closer, forgetting her own misery for the moment. Just as her aunt had said, the dog looked like a right little mongrel – but then he turned to stare at her appealingly as if he was pleading with her to like him.

'I think he's nice,' she said cautiously, and both her aunt and uncle looked at her in amazement. Rebecca rarely said anything apart from when she was spoken to, and then only if she absolutely had to.

'An' will *you* be prepared to clean up after him an' take him for walks if we keep him?' Her aunt's voice was caustic.

Rebecca nodded enthusiastically.

'All right then,' Alison said eventually. 'He can stay. But only on a trial, mind. If he starts chewin' everythin' in sight he'll be out of the door with me foot up his arse.'

Rebecca felt a surge of pleasure as she bent to stroke the little dog's dirty coat. Just like her, he wasn't the prettiest of creatures, which she supposed was why she had felt an instant affinity with him. Neither of them was wanted either, not really, but from now on they would be the best of friends, she just knew it. She studied him solemnly as he gazed back at her. He was a tan sort of colour with pointy ears and a short tail, and his body was quite long, like that of a sausage dog. To make things even worse he had short stumpy legs and a squashed little face, but somehow his huge, soulful brown eyes seemed to make up for the rest of his appearance.

'Here.' Her aunt opened her purse and handed her some loose change. 'If he's stayin' you'd better get up the shop an' buy a couple o' tins of dog food. Not the dear stuff, mind! An' you can take that mutt with you. The shop on the corner should still be open if you get a shufty on.'

Without even stopping to fetch her coat, Rebecca bounded towards the door with Casper close on her heels. Outside, the street-lights had just come on as the afternoon darkened, but with Casper close beside her on his makeshift lead, she didn't feel frightened. Once at the shop she tied him to the lamp-post while she hurried inside to get his food, and when she came back out he strained on his lead to get to her as he wagged his tail furiously.

'That's a good boy,' she cooed as she bent to stroke him. 'We'll get you home and feed you, then give you a nice bath, eh? I have to say you don't smell very nice. And I'll have to ask Aunt Alison for a blanket for you to sleep on too. There are some cardboard boxes in Uncle Ken's shed so we'll make you a bed out of one of those. She might even let you sleep in my room with me and Amber if you're really good.'

As she spoke, Casper lifted his leg and urinated up the lamp-post. Rebecca giggled. The more she looked at him, the handsomer he seemed to become, and already she couldn't think why she had thought he looked peculiar when she had first seen him.

Suddenly she didn't feel quite so alone.

Chapter Twelve

'Come on, Casper. It's time for your walk.' Rebecca attached the new lead Uncle Ken had bought for her to the dog's collar.

'You'll not be goin' far in this.' Her aunt gestured towards the window. It had been snowing non-stop for three days now and the weather was causing chaos on the roads, particularly the motorways. The pavements were treacherous and Alison was refusing to venture out; she had battened down the hatches.

'Casper likes the snow,' Rebecca informed her brightly, heading for the door. 'And we won't be long.'

Alison sniffed. As far as she was concerned, the kid could be gone all night for all she cared. Gordon was overdue his board money for her keep and when she had phoned him at the weekend to tell him she needed it, he had used the weather as an excuse for not coming. To add insult to injury, he had sounded as if he was pissed, and since then hadn't even been bothering to answer the phone. Still, she consoled herself, he can't ignore me forever. I'll try again in a minute when the kid is safely out of the way.

Rebecca had barely reached the front gate with Casper frolicking along at the side of her when Alison did just that.

For a while the phone just rang and she began to think he was going to ignore it again when suddenly her nephew's voice wafted along the line to her.

'Hello.'

'Is that you, Josh?'

'Yes.'

'It's Aunt Alison. Is your dad there?'

A pause from the other end, then, 'He er . . . can't come to the phone at the minute.'

'Why not?' She was fast losing patience now.

'He's umm . . . asleep.'

'*Asleep?* But it's only five o'clock in the afternoon. Has he still not gone back to work?'

'No,' Josh admitted in a small voice.

Alison wanted to rant and rave but stopped herself at the last minute. It wasn't Josh's fault that his dad was turning into a raving piss head, after all.

'Well, when he does wake up, could you tell him I need to speak to him – urgently. I ain't a bleedin' charity, and if he wants me to keep his kid here he needs to get off his arse and get some money to me double quick.'

'I'll tell him,' Josh muttered, sounding acutely embarrassed.

Alison placed the phone down with her lips set in a grim line. It had been several weeks since Fay had died, but instead of getting a little better, Gordon seemed to be getting worse. Not that there was much she could do about it.

One thing was for sure though – if he still hadn't paid her a visit by the weekend, *she* would visit *him*. Fay had had some nice designer gear and he'd probably be glad for her to sort through it for him. There was no point leaving her clothes hanging in the wardrobe and they'd fetch a nice few bob if she brought them all home and sold them to her mates on the estate. Sadly, there was no way they would fit her. Fay had been at least three or four sizes smaller. There was her jewellery too. Fay's diamond engagement ring alone must have been worth a King's ransom, and the way Alison saw it, as Fay's only sister she was entitled to it. It didn't occur to her that Gordon might want to keep it to pass on to Rebecca when she was older.

Glancing through the hall window, she shuddered. The snow was coming down in a thick white sheet and she was almost out of fags. Ken had sold his last assignment and the weather had prevented the blokes from doing another run for him so far this week.

'Casey!' Her voice echoed up the stairs. 'Get your arse down here! I need you to go to the shop for me.'

She was feeling very hard done by, as she should have been going to Bingo tonight with Cynth from three doors away and Pat from just up the road. She hoped that there was something good on the telly this evening. There was no way she was venturing out, that was for sure.

As Rebecca came to the small park at the end of the estate she let Casper off his lead and he bounded comically through the snow, his short stubby legs flying in all directions. She smiled. Things had got better since her Uncle Ken had brought Casper home and the two were inseparable now. Up until now Rebecca had never had to worry about anyone but herself. But she was fast discovering that it was quite nice to have Casper reliant on her. He would be sitting by the door waiting for her when she came home from school each afternoon with his tail wagging expectantly, and suddenly living with Aunt Alison didn't seem quite so bad – especially as her aunt was flatly refusing to set a foot out of the door right now. It meant that she never had to be on her own with Uncle Ken; when they were alone he was very touchy-feely and Rebecca didn't like it at all.

Casper came bounding back to her now, and bending, she giggled as his wet tongue washed her cheeks.

Uncle Ken and Aunt Alison tended to ignore him,

although they did buy his dog food, which Rebecca fed to him every afternoon. He slept beneath her bed and luckily Amber had stopped complaining about it since Rebecca had bathed him. He actually smelled quite nice now, a fact Rebecca was proud of. The only thing that did worry her was what was going to happen to him when her dad came to take her home. It appeared that neither her aunt nor her uncle really wanted him, so she was hoping that she would be able to persuade her dad to let her take him with them. She had no doubt that Josh would love him just as much as she did.

As she thought of her brother now, a wave of homesickness swept through her and the happy mood dissolved. Josh had always looked out for her and she found that she missed him. It was bitterly cold and she wished that her Aunt Alison had brought her warm scarf and gloves with them. They were still at home, tucked neatly in her drawer where her mum had kept them. She would never have let Rebecca go out without being properly wrapped up in the cold, but Aunt Alison didn't seem to care much what she wore.

Rebecca was still hoping that her aunt would soon buy her a new school uniform that fitted her properly, with the money that her dad had given her expressly for that purpose. As yet it hadn't materialised and Rebecca was beginning to wonder if her aunt hadn't spent it on something else. Money seemed to slip through her fingers like water, most of it on going out to enjoy herself.

The snow had soaked into her socks now, and so calling Casper to her, the girl turned in the direction of home again, hoping that her aunt had had the immersion heater on so that she could have a nice warm bath.

It was as she was leaving the park that she saw a tall fair-haired boy walking towards her and realised that it was Pat's youngest son, Joe. He glimpsed her at the same time and his face broke into a broad smile.

'How you doing, little 'un?' he asked pleasantly.

Rebecca's stomach did a somersault. Joe was really handsome. She had only met him twice before. He was always nice to her and never called her names as some of the other children on the estate and at school did. Nothing had changed there. It seemed she was destined to be as much of a misfit here as she had been at home in Nottingham.

'I'm fine,' she replied shyly as he bent to stroke Casper.

'Nice dog,' he commented and she flushed with pleasure. 'But it's a bit cold for a little 'un like you to be out though, ain't it?'

'I had to bring Casper out for his walk,' she explained, almost tripping over the words.

'I'd have thought your Uncle Ken would have done that. You ain't old enough to be out after dark.'

Joe was fourteen years old and seemed very grown-up to Rebecca as she fell into step with him and they moved on in silence until they came to Comen Road.

'Right, I'm off to get some dinner,' he told her as they approached his mother's house.

'Be seeing you.' And with that he was gone, leaving a warm glow in the pit of Rebecca's stomach.

On the following Saturday afternoon, Amber took Rebecca into town with her to do some shopping. She pointed out the old almshouses that had now been converted into flats for the elderly, and they strolled around the market as Rebecca looked about with interest. She was quite enjoying herself, but then anything was better than being stuck in with Aunt Alison. The snow still showed no signs of ceasing as yet and her aunt was still flatly refusing to leave the house. Instead she was walking about like a bear with a sore head, snapping at everyone who got in her way.

It was late afternoon by the time they got back, and instantly they heard her aunt and uncle having a heated debate in the kitchen. When Amber walked in and raised a curious eyebrow, her aunt told her, 'I've just had a call from that neighbour of our Fay's, Mrs Middleworth. She was all of a tizzy and told me she thinks I ought to get over to see our Gordon. He's going from bad to worse, by all accounts, and won't shift his arse out of the chair.'

Rebecca's stomach flipped over as she listened silently. Did this mean her dad was ill? And if he was – what would happen to her and Josh?

'We'll have to go tomorrow now,' her aunt said irritably, glancing towards the appalling weather conditions beyond the window. 'Ken's only just got back from the Cricketer's Arms and he's had so much to drink he can barely walk a straight line, let alone drive.'

'W-will I be allowed to come?' Rebecca asked tentatively.

'Well, I'm hardly bloody going to leave you here on your own, am I, unless our Amber can look after you, that is!'

'Sorry, I've already made plans,' Amber said hastily.

Her aunt scowled and quickly lit a cigarette then stormed away into the front room as a million different emotions raced through Rebecca. She was going home – but would her dad allow her to stay? And if he did, what would happen to Casper? He had come to mean the world to her, but she doubted that her aunt and uncle would look after him properly if she wasn't there.

Still, at least she would get to see her home again, if only for a short while, and she would worry about Casper later.

They set off at ten o'clock the next morning, but the weather conditions on the road were diabolical and it was almost lunchtime before they pulled onto the drive of the neat detached house in Nottingham. Instantly Rebecca saw that all the curtains on the front of the house were drawn tight and she frowned. Surely her dad and Josh weren't still in bed?

Aunt Alison had grumbled all the way there and she didn't seem any happier now that they had arrived. Picking her way carefully through the snow on the drive until she got to the front door, she rapped on it loudly, shivering.

Josh answered it almost immediately and when he looked beyond his aunt to Rebecca he smiled.

'Hello, Aunt Alison,' his aunt said sarcastically as she elbowed past him into the hall where she shook the snow from her coat, then, 'Where's your dad?'

Josh cocked his thumb towards the lounge door. 'He's in there. He doesn't come out much now.'

'Then it's about bloody well time he did. Wallowing in self-pity ain't going to make things any better.' His aunt slung her coat over the hall chair and marched purposefully towards the lounge as Rebecca slunk towards Josh and stood beside him.

'So what's all this then?' the two children heard her shout as she saw Gordon slumped disconsolately in a chair. The room reeked of stale whisky, and a number of empty glasses and bottles were strewn across the coffee-table. A lump formed in Alison's throat as she wondered what her sister would have thought of it, if she could see it now. Fay had always kept the house so immaculate and had taken such a pride in it. Were she still alive, she would be rushing about putting the kettle on and plying them with biscuits or home-made cakes, but of course that would never happen again now. Alison blinked back tears. The house felt so empty without her, but this wasn't the time for sentiment – so, marching towards the window, she threw the curtains open. As the cold light spilled into the room, Gordon blinked blearily.

'Whash up?' he slurred.

Alison glared at him with contempt. Gordon had always been such a smart man, but this wreck in front of her was filthy. The front of his shirt was covered in stains and he looked as if he hadn't shaved or combed his hair for weeks. He even managed to make her Ken look smart – and that was saying something.

'Just what the bloody hell do you think you're playing at?' Alison rapped out in her usual forthright way. 'Look at the *state* of you, man! Ain't it about time you started to pull yourself together?'

Tears of self-pity stung Gordon's eyes as he sat forward and buried his head in his hands.

'I haven't got anything to live for any more,' he muttered miserably.

Alison snorted. '*Rubbish!* You've got two kids who need you, a smashin' home and a good job to go to. Though I doubt that will be there much longer if you don't snap yourself out of it.'

Josh, who was standing just inside the doorway, watched in consternation. He felt as if he didn't know his dad any more – this man was a stranger and he didn't know what to do about it. Perhaps Aunt Alison would be able to talk some sense into him, although he was forced to acknowledge that she was a rather unlikely ally. As usual she was dressed in clothes that looked as if she had stepped into the first things she laid her hand on, but desperate causes called for desperate measures.

'Right, Josh, do you know how to make coffee?' When her nephew nodded, she went on, 'Good, then go and make him a mug, and make it strong, I mean strong enough to stand the spoon in it. And you, Ken, help me shift some of this lot.'

As she waved in the direction of the discarded whisky bottles on the table, Ken leaped to do as he was told. There was still some left in a few of them. He would pour it all into one bottle and take it home with him, he decided. No sense in wasting it.

While everyone was busy, Rebecca sneaked away to her room. Once inside, she stared around. She had forgotten how nice it was and realised again how lucky she had been. There were bright pictures on the walls, and her feet sank into the thick pink wall-to-wall carpet beneath her feet. Clean curtains hung at the window and a thick duvet covered the bed. She wondered why she had never valued it before as she thought of the poky room and the cheap rickety bunk beds back at her aunt's.

As young as she was, she had already understood that there was very little chance of her staying here today. From the look of her dad, he could barely take care of himself and Josh. In fact, she had a funny feeling that Josh had been looking after *him*, so she doubted whether he would let her come back home just yet.

Sinking onto the edge of the bed, she let her mind wander back to happier times with her mum.

Chapter Thirteen

'Right – now that the place is fit to be seen I'm going to go and look at what state your bedroom is in,' Alison informed Gordon bossily.

'*No*. It's all right in there,' Gordon shot back, grimacing as he took another swig of the black coffee in his hand.

'Well, I just thought while I was tidying it up I might sort through a few of our Fay's things,' she told him cagily. 'It can't be doing you any good having to look at all her stuff lying about, every time you open your eyes in the morning. So I'll pack some of them up and drop them off to the charity shop for you, shall I?'

'*No!* I want everything left exactly as it is!'

'All right, all right. Keep your hair on,' she snapped back. 'I'm only trying to help.' She was deeply disappointed at not being allowed to rifle through her late sister's things. After all, they were no good to Fay now, were they? She stomped off to the kitchen where she saw Gordon's wallet lying on the table. Opening it, she extracted fifty pounds for Rebecca's board and then another twenty for luck. Gordon was so out of it she doubted he would even notice it was gone, and she had to cover the cost of Ken's petrol, didn't she? It was while she was standing there that there was a tap on the back door and as it inched open, an elderly lady peeped round it at her.

'Hello, dear. I'm Mrs Middleworth from next door,' she introduced herself, eyeing Alison's garish outfit curiously. 'I'm so sorry I had to ring you, but I didn't know what else to do.' She clicked the door shut and stood there wringing her hands together nervously.

'You did right,' Alison assured her and the woman seemed to visibly relax.

'The thing is – someone from Joshua's school called around on Friday. They wanted to know why he hadn't been attending, but Gordon was in no fit state to talk to them. Luckily I was here. But they did insist on seeing Gordon and when they had, they told me that if things don't improve soon, they'll have no choice but to inform Social Services.'

'Christ all bleedin' *mighty*,' Alison groaned as Mrs Middleworth's eyes almost started from head. 'That's *all* we bloody need on top of everything else.'

Mrs Middleworth's lips set in a disapproving line. 'Yes . . . well, hopefully it won't come to that. How is the dear man today? He's taken your poor sister's death very badly.'

'The *dear man* was as pissed as a newt when we got here,' Alison said nastily, staring at the row of pearls around the older woman's scraggy neck. They looked expensive and she guessed that the old dear was worth a bob or two.

'Oh, I see. Then now that you are here I'll leave him in your capable hands, shall I?' Mrs Middleworth shot back through the door like a startled rabbit as Alison lit a cigarette and dragged on it wearily.

Silly old cow, she thought, before wandering back into the lounge.

'Right, I dare say we ought to be going now else we might not get back in this lot.' Alison glanced towards the window as she ground her cigarette out in the nearest plant pot. 'Where's Rebecca?'

'She's upstairs in her bedroom,' Josh told her.

'Well, go and get her then, there's a good lad. No – on

second thoughts, don't bother. I'll go. She could do with a few more clothes, so I'll pop up and help her pack a few. Have you got a carrier bag?'

Josh nodded before sloping off to the kitchen to return seconds later with a Marks & Spencer's bag.

Alison took it off him and headed towards the stairs. She doubted if there would be an Asda or Tesco bag in the place. Fay had been fussy about where she shopped.

Once upstairs, she tossed the bag to Rebecca and told her to pack a few more clothes before going off to her late sister's bedroom. Once inside, she clicked on the light and glanced about the room – then, crossing to the dressing-table she slipped a couple of bottles of expensive French perfume into her pocket before quickly rearranging the ones that were left so that Gordon wouldn't notice they were missing. Not that there was much chance of that. The state he was in at present, a bloody steam train could run through the front room and she doubted he'd notice it.

Patting her pocket, she grinned as she clicked the light back off and headed for the stairs again.

Josh looked tearful as Rebecca came to join them but Alison ignored his sad expression as best she could.

'If you need us, just give us a ring,' she told him, avoiding his eyes. 'And be a good lad for your dad, eh?'

He nodded miserably as Alison opened the front door and ushered Rebecca and Ken ahead of her, telling him, 'We have to go now or we'll never get home with the roads being as bad as they are.'

Rebecca went without a word, sensing that it would do no good to cause a scene and tell them that she wanted to stay. Her father hadn't uttered so much as a single word to her during the whole time they had been there, and if it hadn't been for Josh she wouldn't particularly have wanted to go home. Her dad didn't seem to care about her at all, and now that her mum wasn't there to keep it spick and span, her lovely house was in almost as bad a state as Aunt Alison's.

The journey back was painfully slow as they skidded about on the roads, and her aunt swore constantly. Her uncle didn't seem much happier either.

'Fancy havin' to go all that bloody way just to sober the drunken sod up!'

'Huh! Hark at the pot calling the kettle black,' Aunt Alison retorted. ''Cos you never get drunk, do you?' Taking the little wad of notes from her pocket she waved them in front of him before hastily tucking them back. 'It weren't *entirely* a wasted journey – look. I helped meself to some board for Rebecca. I mean, there were no point in asking him for it, was there? He was off with the fairies. And it ain't as if I'm taking anything I ain't entitled to. He can't expect us to keep the kid for sweet Fanny Adam, can he?'

Tucked in the back of the car, Rebecca sighed in the darkness. It was more than obvious that her aunt and uncle didn't really want her either. But at least she had Casper now and he made up for a lot.

When they finally pulled into Comen Road, Rebecca's feet were so cold she could scarcely feel them, but she forgot all about her discomfort when she saw the lights of a police car blazing into the night. It seemed to be parked outside her aunt and uncle's house.

'Oh *shit*!' Uncle Ken slammed the heel of his palm onto the steering wheel. 'It looks like we're being busted again.'

Alison looked genuinely frightened as she glanced towards him. 'B-but you had a delivery this morning, didn't you – off the shoplifters? Did you have time to get the stuff out of the house?'

'Did I hell as like,' he ground out. 'I was going to get rid of

101

it this afternoon, weren't I? But instead I had to go harin' off to Nottingham.'

'What are we going to do?'

'Ain't much we *can* do, is there, apart from go an' brazen it out? But leave the talking to me.'

Alison nodded numbly as he pulled the car into the kerb and stepped out into the thick falling snow. 'Get her round to Pat's and keep her out of the way,' he told his wife, jerking his thumb at Rebecca, and while Alison struggled out of the car he strode towards the front door which was swinging open. As Alison ushered Rebecca past, the child saw that every light in the house was blazing and the place was teeming with uniformed policemen.

'What's happening?' she asked fearfully, but Alison ignored her and hauled her along until they came to Pat's house. She thrust her into the kitchen without knocking and Pat, who was sitting at the table reading a magazine, looked up in surprise.

'Keep her here for a while, would you? Our place is swarmin' with pigs.'

'Christ.' Pat looked worried. 'There ain't nowt in there, is there?'

'Yeah, there is. The shoplifters brought Ken a load of gear round this morning and he's got a stash of jewellery that one of the lads dropped off last night. It's that bleedin' hot it'll burn their fingers if they find it. And it ain't cheap stuff neither. I'm telling you, Ken's not gonna talk his way out of this one.'

'Well, you get round there and leave the little 'un with me. She can stay as long as it takes, so don't get worrying about her.'

Alison disappeared back the way she had come as Pat smiled at Rebecca.

'Come on through to me lounge, love, and sit here by the fire,' she encouraged kindly. 'You look frozen through. I'll

102

make you a nice hot drink, shall I, and then you can watch a bit of telly, eh?'

Completely bemused, Rebecca sank into the comfy chair at the side of the fireplace. What had her aunt meant when she told Pat that there was 'hot' jewellery in the house? How could jewellery be hot?

But then she looked around and forgot all about the drama going on in her aunt's home. She liked it here and it was nice to be spoiled for a while. Pat's house was nothing like as grand as the one she had been brought up in, but it was much cleaner than her aunt's and it was warm in here too, so she might as well make the most of it. There were chairs at either side of the fireplace, and thick red curtains blocked out the cold night. There was a blue carpet on the floor too, and although it didn't match the curtains, it had been hoovered and was clean at least. Ornaments were dotted along the shelf of the mantel-piece and a warm fire was burning in the grate. But Rebecca thought it was a shame that Joe wasn't there. She liked Joe.

Pat made her a plateful of hot buttered toast and a mug of hot chocolate, and once she had placed them in front of her she asked, 'So how was your dad, luvvie?'

'Not very well,' Rebecca told her as she crammed the delicious treat into her mouth. 'Aunt Alison said he was drunk.'

'Oh.' Pat looked at her sympathetically. 'Happen he's missing your mum, and having a drink is his way of dealing with it,' she said for want of something to say.

'She wasn't my *real* mum,' Rebecca answered matter-of-factly. 'She told me and Josh that we had been adopted. That means we belonged to someone else but they didn't want us.'

'Oh!' Pat looked shocked but tried her best to hide it. 'Well, even so I'm sure she loved you both very much. And perhaps there were good reasons why your other mum couldn't keep you.'

'She did love us, you're right. And she loved me the best, more than Josh. But I don't think my dad loves me.'

'Of course he does,' Pat said quickly, as her heart went out to the child.

'Then why has he let Josh stay at home with him and sent me away?' Rebecca asked with the logic of a child.

Feeling totally out of her depth, Pat cleared her throat. 'Well, you're a girl, aren't you? and he probably thought you needed a woman to look after you for the time being.' The excuse sounded pathetic even to Pat but it was the only one she could offer for now.

Rebecca shrugged. 'At least I've got Casper now.' And then as a terrifying thought occurred to her, 'The police won't hurt him, will they?'

'Oh, goodness me no,' Pat hastily assured her. 'Casper will be fine. I've been round to check on him two or three times. I let him out into the garden and fed him too. Now eat that up and I'll put the telly on for you. Just one thing . . . when is your birthday?'

Rebecca thought this was a rather strange thing to ask but all the same she answered, 'I was born on August the fourth, 1988.'

'Oh!'

Rebecca frowned as Pat raised her hand to her mouth, but then she was smiling again as she bustled away to wash the pots in the sink.

It was some time later when Rebecca stirred in the chair, woken by the sound of lowered voices. She had been so comfortable, full and warm, that she must have dozed off, but now she could hear her aunt and Pat whispering at the small table in the corner of the room.

'So how long do you think they'll keep him?'

'Christ knows,' she heard her aunt reply in a worried voice.

'I'm telling you, Pat – I reckon they'll throw the book at him this time. If he don't go away, I'll eat my hat.'

Rebecca wondered where her uncle might be going to but stayed very still so that she could continue to listen to the conversation.

'Apparently that jewellery was from a robbery in Nicholas Park in Nuneaton. Worth a bleedin' fortune accordin' to the coppers, and *my* stupid husband got caught red-handed with the whole bloody lot of it. On top of that, they took all the gear that the shoplifters brought round. All designer stuff and worth a packet.'

'Phew . . . then he is in trouble,' Pat said. 'Where have they taken him?'

'He's at the copshop in Bedworth and there's no chance of him getting out tonight. They reckon they can't even get him a solicitor until tomorrow morning, and Ken won't say a word without one present. He knows his rights, which is something. Not that I think a solicitor will do him much good this time. I reckon he'll need a miracle. I just hope he gets bail, that's all.'

'I'm sure he will,' Pat tried to comfort her. 'You've got to try and think positive.'

It was then that she glanced towards the chair, and seeing that Rebecca was awake she nudged Alison hastily before saying, 'Hello, sleepy-head. Had a nice nap, did you? Your aunt is here now to take you home.'

Alison looked towards the child resentfully before snapping, 'Come on then. Get your shoes and your coat on. It's way past your bedtime.'

Rebecca wished that she could have stayed with Pat for a little longer but did as she was told all the same. As she had discovered, to disobey Aunt Alison meant a clip round the ear, and at least she would get to see Casper again, so things weren't all bad.

When they entered her aunt's house some minutes later, Rebecca gazed around in amazement. The place was never tidy, but now it looked as if a hurricane had swept through it. Furniture was overturned, and dirty ashtrays, broken pots and old newspapers littered the floor. It looked as if the police had almost torn the house apart this time.

'Oh dear,' she murmured.

'Just go and get your pyjamas on and get yourself off to bed,' her aunt said sharply.

Rebecca was only too happy to do just that, especially as she could see Casper lying at the top of the stairs waiting for her with his tail wagging furiously.

She entered the room she shared with her cousin to find Amber tidying up. Or at least she was stuffing everything that had been pulled out of the drawers back into them in a higgledy-piggledy fashion.

Amber snorted when she saw her standing there. 'Another bleedin' police raid,' she groaned. 'An' I reckon me dad will go down for sure this time.'

'Down where?' Rebecca asked innocently.

'Never you mind. Just get yourself into bed, eh?'

Rebecca sighed. No one ever told her anything. But then she was getting used to that by now.

Chapter Fourteen

Uncle Ken was back when Rebecca arrived home from school the following afternoon and he looked none too happy. In fact, he was in a towering rage and appeared to be more than a little drunk.

'They got me bang to rights this time, the lousy bastards,' she heard him say as she took her coat off and bent to stroke Casper. Her uncle was sitting at the kitchen table with Aunt Alison, a can of lager clutched in his hand. Just one of many, if the overflowing rubbish bin was anything to go by, and Aunt Alison was crying.

'But there must be *something* your solicitor can do,' her aunt wept.

'Not unless she can work fuckin' miracles,' he grunted. 'Apparently they'd been investigatin' me for months, an' someone has grassed me up about the booze runs. Just let me find out who it was and I'll break their bleedin' neck with me bare hands.' He took another long slurp from the can and as Rebecca entered the room, he sneered, 'And you'd best tell that ruddy useless git Gordon that he'll need to take his kid back an' all. You'll not be able to keep her once I've gone down.'

There it was again – that strange expression – but Rebecca knew better than to ask what it meant. The last thing she wanted was yet another cuff around the ear from her aunt.

'You can go round the chip shop in a minute,' her aunt

told her with barely a glance in her direction. 'But for now, me and your Uncle Ken have things to talk about, so get yourself into the front room and watch the telly for a bit.'

Rebecca trailed away only to find Casey with two of his friends gawping at the television. Taking Casper's collar she led him upstairs to her room and perched on the edge of the bunk bed.

'Grown-ups are strange, aren't they?' she whispered, and he wagged his tail as if in agreement. Rebecca shivered as she rubbed her hands together to try and warm them. As usual it was cold upstairs, and beyond the bedroom window she could see the snow coming down in thick white flakes. But at least it had made the overgrown garden look pretty, and everywhere looked clean and bright.

'Did you hear what Uncle Ken said?' she asked Casper now as he licked her leg with his warm tongue. 'He says that Aunt Alison is going to have to ask my dad to take me home. But don't worry. I'll take you with me and Josh and I will look after you then. You'll like it at my house. It's warm and clean, or at least it was while my mum was there.' She thought back to the state of the place when she had paid her last visit there with her aunt and uncle. Her dad had been drunk, just as her Uncle Ken was now, but surely he would have had time to get over that by now? She had never seen him drunk before, and she hoped that she never would again.

Shortly afterwards, her aunt came up the stairs.

'Our Casey has gone for some chips so get yourself downstairs if you want some,' she said irritably. 'And then later on I'm going out with Pat for a game of Bingo. I'm sick of being stuck in the house, so mind you behave.'

Rebecca slid off the bed and sidled past her aunt. After her meal she helped to clear the table while her uncle settled himself in the fireside chair with yet more cans of lager.

'Amber won't be back till late,' her aunt informed Ken some time later as she applied her lipstick in the nicotine-stained mirror hanging above the fireplace. 'She's gone to her mate's straight from school and Casey's gone out sledging with his pals, so you've only got Rebecca to keep an eye on and she should be in bed soon.'

Ken nodded morosely, obviously feeling very sorry for himself as Aunt Alison shrugged her coat on.

'Right, I'm off then. See you later,' she shouted across her shoulder and seconds later Rebecca heard the front door slam.

Feeling the child's eyes on him, Ken rounded on her. 'And what are *you* standing there staring at? Go and get a bath.'

Glad of a chance to escape, Rebecca shot off upstairs and was heartened when she turned the taps on to see hot water spurting into the bath. Aunt Alison must have had the immersion heater on and Rebecca was happy to take advantage of the fact. All she got usually was a wash in cold water, so this would be an unexpected treat. Fastening the rickety latch, she undressed quickly as the bathroom filled with steam, and seconds later slid into the bath with a sigh of contentment.

She had been lying there for some minutes when the door suddenly burst open and Uncle Ken appeared with a smarmy smile on his face.

'Need a hand to wash your back, do you?'

Rebecca hastily shook her head as her cheeks flooded with colour and she tried to cover herself.

'N-no. I'm fine thanks,' she stuttered.

'Of course you do,' he said cajolingly as he approached the side of the bath. 'Now just sit forward and give me that sponge.'

Rebecca tried to rise but he placed his large hand on her shoulder and forced her back down with a thud that had the water slopping over the side of the bath. He then soaped the sponge and as Rebecca squirmed with embarrassment he began to wash her all over, lingering over her undeveloped breasts.

'You'll have a nice little pair o' tits on you in a few years' time,' he murmured thickly, much to Rebecca's mortification. 'There now . . . that's nice, ain't it?'

Rebecca wanted to scream at him that no, it wasn't – but she was so terrified that she sat rigid as he continued to rub her.

'Did your dad used to bath you like this?' he asked.

Rebecca nervously shook her head. 'N-no. Mum used to help me, but Dad never came into the bathroom while I was there.'

'Well, that surprises me, 'cos all dads should help their little girls. But never mind, I'll help you now. Get out and come into my bedroom, and I'll show you what else dads do for little girls.'

Rebecca's stomach turned over with fear as her head wagged from side to side. 'I . . . I don't want to.'

Uncle Ken's face became stern now as he ground out, 'It ain't a matter of what *you* want, miss. Now put this on and do as you're told if you know what's good for you.'

Trembling, Rebecca stepped out onto the dirty lino clutching her nightdress to her as her uncle turned and staggered off in the direction of his room. He was very drunk, so drunk that he couldn't even walk in a straight line, so Rebecca hoped that once he had lain down he would forget all about ordering her to join him. She heard the bedsprings squeal in protest as he collapsed onto them and she stood there as still as a statue. Then she pulled on her nightie and a clean pair of pants, but after a moment she nearly jumped out of her skin when he barked, 'Come on, then – I'm waiting!'

Gulping deep in her throat, she tentatively crossed the

110

landing to see her Uncle Ken lying beneath the grimy bedcovers. His clothes were in an untidy heap on the floor at the side of the bed and the room was in darkness save for the light that was shining through the window from the street-lamp outside.

'Get here *now*, otherwise I'll come and fetch you.'

Cautiously she approached the bed and suddenly his hand lashed out and he caught her arm in a cruel grip.

'Now come on and don't be frightened,' he cooed. 'I'm going to show you something nice, and it's cosy and warm in here.'

Before Rebecca had time to think, he had dragged her in to lie at the side of him, and then his hands began to wander across her shaking body.

'That's nice, isn't it?' he whispered huskily as his hand began to stroke her inner thigh. 'I'm going to show you what to do so that when you meet a boy you like, you'll be all ready for him.'

'I . . . don't like boys,' Rebecca gasped as tears stung the back of her eyes. 'And I want to go to my own room.'

'Don't be silly.' He chuckled. 'Of course this is what you've been wanting. I've seen the way you look at me. Now just lie still and enjoy it.'

His foul-smelling breath was fanning her cheek now, and panic set in as his hand fondled her most private place. Rebecca began to struggle but that only seemed to excite him all the more, and as she lay there with tears gushing from her eyes, she wished that she could have died and gone to heaven with her mum.

An hour later, when Uncle Ken's snores were echoing about the chilly room, Rebecca crept from the bed, snatched up her torn clothes and limped across the landing to the bathroom.

The water in the bath was cold now but she climbed into it and began to scour herself with the sponge, sure that she would never feel clean again. She felt as if she had been rent in two and wondered if this terrible pain would ever go away. And as she lay there, his words played over and over in her mind. *Don't ever tell anyone what's happened tonight or they'll lock you away for being so wicked. You made me do it.*

Tears spilled down her cheeks. Uncle Ken must be telling the truth; that must be why her first mum hadn't wanted her. Why she never seemed to have any friends. Why her dad didn't love her. Because she was bad, wicked.

If you tell anyone, your aunt will kick you out and your dad will never let you go home. You'll have nowhere to live. No one to care.

Rebecca clapped her hands over her ears to try to drown out the words he had said, but they played over and over in her head and she had to bite down hard on her lip to stop her sobs from escaping. If Uncle Ken heard her, he might come and take her back into his bed and do *it* again, and she knew that she wouldn't be able to bear it.

Eventually she climbed out of the bath as quietly as she could and pulled her nightdress over her head. It was torn all the way down the front now, as were her knickers, and she would have to throw them away before Aunt Alison saw them. The woman would never notice. But she wouldn't think about that for now. She had more pressing things to worry about.

Creeping onto the landing, she stood for a moment until the sounds of Uncle Ken's snoring reached her. Then quiet as a mouse she fled to her room where she lifted Casper onto her bed and cuddled him to her as she cried as if her heart would break.

Chapter Fifteen

'What the bleedin' hell do you mean, you don't want to go to school?' Aunt Alison demanded the next morning.

'I've got tummy ache,' Rebecca whimpered from beneath the crumpled covers.

'Oh great! As if I ain't got enough on me plate to worry about,' her aunt said unsympathetically. 'Well, you can just stay there then. Don't think you can wag a day off school to sit down downstairs watching telly and having me waiting on you hand and bloody foot.'

As she left the room, slamming the door resoundingly behind her, Rebecca sighed with relief. She had lain awake for most of the night, too afraid to go to sleep, and now she was so tired that she could barely keep her eyes open. She lay in bed for two days, blissful days when she didn't have to set eyes on her uncle, but eventually her aunt forced her out of bed and on the third day she went back to school.

It was as the class broke up for the morning break that Mrs Jennings asked, 'Could you stay behind for a moment, please, Rebecca?'

The girl hung her head as the other children sidled past, sending curious looks in her direction. Once they were alone the woman smiled at her and said quietly, 'I believe you've been unwell, dear. Are you feeling better now?'

Avoiding her eyes, Rebecca nodded sullenly. The griping

pains in her stomach had subsided to a dull ache now but she still felt dirty and confused.

'Are you quite sure you feel well enough to be back at school?' Rebecca had never been exactly the life and soul of the party since joining her class, but today she seemed positively withdrawn.

Again Rebecca nodded, but thankfully Mrs Jennings was stopped from asking any more questions when Miss Baxter stuck her head round the door. 'There's a cup of tea ready for you in the staff room,' she said brightly, and then spotting Rebecca, she smiled apologetically. 'Sorry, I didn't realise you were talking to someone.'

'It's all right. You can go and join the other children now, dear,' Mrs Jennings said. As Rebecca crept away like a wounded animal, the woman sighed. 'Poor little devil,' she muttered, as much to herself as the younger teacher. 'That child just seems to be so unhappy all the time. Although after recently losing her mum and being carted off to her aunt's I suppose it's understandable.'

Kerry Baxter nodded in agreement. 'It is a shame,' she agreed. 'But I have to say Rebecca doesn't make it easy on herself. She makes no effort to fit in with the other children, and when you try to be nice to her she can be downright rude. It's as if she's put a guard up. But never mind that for now, come and get your drink otherwise break will be over.'

Mrs Jennings nodded and pottered off to do as she was told, determined to speak to Rebecca again at a more opportune moment.

On the way home from school that afternoon, Rebecca's feet dragged across the slushy pavements. Since Sunday she had managed to avoid seeing her uncle, but she doubted if she would be able to do that this evening, and the thought of it filled her with dread. What if her aunt decided to go out to Bingo again and left her alone with him? Would it happen again? She shuddered at the thought of his great ham hands brutally pinching and nipping her private parts, and as she remembered the feel of his wet sloppy kisses she had to swallow the vomit that rose in her throat. But what could she do about it? If she told anyone, her uncle had said she would be locked away for being wicked. And who was there to tell? No one cared about her, not even her dad; he had made that crystal clear.

As she neared the house, the feeling of dread intensified and for a minute she considered running away. But then she thought of Casper and forced herself to move on. The novelty of having a pet had soon worn off for her aunt and uncle, and if she didn't go home there would be nobody to look after him. Steeling herself, she pushed open the rickety gate and within seconds was in the hallway. The sound of raised voices greeted her, issuing from the kitchen. Her aunt and uncle were rowing – again! It seemed to be all they had done over the last couple of days, so it didn't really surprise her any more. Her aunt gave her a cursory glance before turning her attention back to her husband.

'You're bloody gut selfish, that's what you are!' she screeched. 'What's going to happen to me and the kids when you get sent down? What are we supposed to live on? Bloody fresh air?'

'You could get off your fat lazy arse and find a job,' Ken shot back sarcastically and this seemed to have a sobering effect on Alison, who gazed at him open-mouthed.

'B-but I *do* work – here.' She spread her hands to encompass the organised chaos in the kitchen. 'I work me fingers to the bone looking after you and the kids and keeping this place going.'

The man snorted with derision. 'Huh! You could 'ave fooled

me. The place is a tip. Why, you don't even get your arse out of bed till midday, half the time. And furthermore, I've never heard you moan about what I do before, 'specially when I hand you a wad. You don't worry about where it came from then, do you?'

Her aunt suddenly caught sight of Rebecca, who was listening at the door.

'And what are *you* gawping at, standing there earwigging,' she barked. 'Get that bloody mutt on his lead and take him out for a walk. He's pissed all over the kitchen floor twice today already, and if he don't pack it in soon he'll be having his marching orders.'

Rebecca almost stumbled in her haste to grab Casper's lead and in no time at all she had dragged him outside, where she let out a long breath.

Joe was passing the gate and he paused to smile when he saw her. 'How are things in there then, little 'un?' he asked, thumbing towards the house.

Rebecca walked to the gate to join him. 'Not very good,' she said. 'Aunt Alison and Uncle Ken are having another row.'

'Well, I dare say they're worrying about what will happen when your uncle goes to court,' he commented.

'Oh, he's not going to court,' Rebecca informed him innocently. 'He's going *down*. But what does that mean, Joe? *Down* where?'

Joe pursed his lips. She obviously didn't grasp what was going on, poor kid.

'The thing is,' he began, 'when the police raided the house, they found things that shouldn't have been there – stolen things. Your uncle shouldn't have had them. And going down means going to prison.'

Rebecca's eyes stretched wide. '*What?* You mean they might lock my uncle away in jail?'

116

'That's about the long and the short of it,' he admitted.

To his amazement, Rebecca grinned and Joe was momentarily lost for words. He had expected her to get upset, but instead here she was, her blue eyes sparkling, beaming like a Cheshire cat. It was as if she was pleased to hear that her uncle was going away! She was a funny little kid, there was no doubt about it.

'Be seeing you,' he said casually, and Rebecca stood and watched him walk away until he disappeared around the corner.

'Did you hear that, boy?' She bent to stroke Casper, who was staring up at her adoringly. 'At least if Uncle gets sent to jail I won't have to worry about him doing the bad thing to me again.'

As she pushed her hand into her coat pocket it came into contact with something soft and she realised with a little start that it was the pair of knickers her uncle had torn off her the night he abused her. She had wiped herself with them after he had finished with her, and had been horrified to see that there was blood on them! Convinced that he had done something bad to her insides, she had hidden them in her coat pocket until she could dispose of them in secret, in case her aunt found them and started asking questions. Now she quickly lifted the lid of a dustbin she was passing and buried them beneath the rubbish inside as her cheeks flamed with shame and humiliation. If he was sent to prison he would never be able to do it again. That was something at least.

Thankfully, Rebecca was not left on her own again for another whole week, but one evening as they sat eating their customary chip meal her aunt announced, 'I might go to the pictures with Pat tonight. There's a James Bond film on, *GoldenEye*, and it's supposed to be good.'

'Huh!' Ken scoffed. 'You must want something to spend your money on if you're going to watch that rubbish. The Beatles film *A Hard Day's Night* is on the telly and you could watch that for nothing.'

'So *you* watch it then,' Alison retorted. 'Pierce Brosnan wins for me every time. Phoar! I wouldn't kick *him* out of bed, I don't mind telling you.'

Ken raised his eyebrows. 'Chance would be a fine thing,' he muttered sarcastically before returning his attention to the paper that was propped up against a milk bottle on the table. Rebecca had always wondered how he could eat and read the paper at the same time, but her uncle certainly seemed to have perfected the art, if the chips disappearing down his throat at an alarming rate were anything to go by.

Now her stomach lurched and suddenly she wasn't hungry any more. She laid her fork down. What if Casey went out too? Amber had already gone and she couldn't bear the thought of being alone with her uncle again. But what could she do about it? Strangely enough, since the night he had abused her, he had carried on as if nothing had ever happened, and sometimes Rebecca wondered if she had dreamed it. But then the memories would flood back and she knew that she hadn't. He was just the same as ever, ignoring her as if she wasn't even there. But would he do that when they were alone again? It seemed that she was about to find out, and the thought made her tingle with fear.

Now, oblivious to her terror, her uncle stabbed his finger at the paper. 'There's a bit in about Larry Grayson here,' he told Alison. The comedian, who had lived in nearby Nuneaton, had died a year ago, and her uncle had been a great fan of his.

Alison rose from the table, clearly more interested in getting ready to go out than listening to her husband. 'That's nice,' she murmured, and seconds later she disappeared off into the hall and Rebecca heard her clattering up the uncarpeted stairs. She slid off her seat and quickly followed her, and once upstairs she shut her bedroom door and lifted Casper onto the unmade bunk bed with her.

She hugged him fiercely as tears pricked at the back of her eyes, and then she waited.

Eventually she heard her aunt go downstairs again and then the sound of the front door closing behind her. Holding her breath, she listened for her uncle's footsteps coming up the stairs – but thankfully all she could hear was the drone of the TV from the front room. 'Perhaps if I'm very quiet he'll forget that I'm here,' she whispered hopefully to Casper, and curling into a ball she shut her eyes tight and eventually nodded off into an uneasy doze.

It was some time later when her bedroom door squeaked open, which brought her springing upright in bed to see her uncle standing in the doorway.

'Hello, sweetheart,' he said in a sickly-sweet voice. 'How about coming into my room and being nice to me, eh? It ain't too often you and I get the chance to be alone, is it?'

Rebecca's mouth was so dry that she couldn't get any words out, so instead she shook her head vehemently.

He chuckled, a low growling sound deep in his throat that turned Rebecca's blood to water and swiped Casper off the bed. She slid across the bed as far away from him as she could get, and plastered her back against the wall. But he was already advancing on her and she knew that she would be no match for his strength. As his hand snaked towards her, desperation took over: sinking her teeth into the back of his hand, she bit down as hard as she could. He yelped with pain and she was gratified to see blood spurt from the wound as he waved his hand wildly in the air.

'Why, you little cow! You'll fuckin' pay for that!' Turning on his heel, he hurried towards the bathroom as Rebecca began to cry. She could hear the sound of the tap running and knew it was only a matter of minutes before he was back.

Flinging herself off the bed, she took to her heels. She had no idea where she was going, but knew that she couldn't stay there. She practically flew down the stairs and was just inches away from the front door when a heavy hand closed across her shoulder. She screamed for all she was worth. Her uncle's hand was roughly wrapped in a threadbare towel, but strangely his voice was soft again now as he clamped his other hand across her mouth.

'Now then.' As he swung her round to face him, her glasses flew off the end of her nose. 'I know you didn't mean to do that, so let's go back upstairs and make friends, eh?'

He lifted her easily, and as he turned she heard her glasses crunch beneath his feet. But they were the last thing on her mind at present. As he carted her back the way she had just come, she went limp in his arms. There would be no sense in trying to fight him.

After carrying her into his room he laid her gently on the bed then began to undress with a wide smile on his face. Rebecca knew that the nightmare was about to start all over again and she closed her eyes tight and prayed for it to be over quickly.

Chapter Sixteen

During the next two weeks Rebecca found that she could actually manage quite well without her glasses. She had told her aunt that she had trodden on them accidentally, but as yet her aunt hadn't made her an appointment at the optician's and Rebecca doubted that she would. Even so, apart from when she had to read a lot she got by and so she said nothing. There was no point in upsetting her aunt any more than she already was. There had been no word from her dad and Alison was desperate for some money from him again now.

'We'll have to go and see him, that's all,' she grumbled to Ken. 'Now we've got the date for your court case in March it's more important than ever.'

But they never got the chance to see him again because the very next day, shortly after Rebecca got in from school, there was a knock on the door and Alison answered it to find a social worker standing there.

The young woman was fashionably dressed and quite pretty with blue eyes and long brunette hair.

'Hello, I'm Miss James,' she introduced herself as Alison stared back at her blankly. 'I'm a social worker and I was wondering if I might have a word with you in private.'

Suddenly nervous, Alison nodded as she held the door wide. 'You'd better come into the front room,' she said, wondering why the young woman might be there. Had someone called the Department and complained that she wasn't looking after Rebecca properly? She wouldn't be surprised at some of the nosy cows thereabouts. Too interested in everybody else's business by half they were, but she'd hear the woman out before she said anything. And it would be God help them when she found out who had grassed her up.

'If you're here about Rebecca she's upstairs—'

Miss James held her hand up and stopped her mid-flow. 'No, Mrs Lambert, it isn't about Rebecca I'm here. At least not directly, for now.'

'Oh.' Alison went down like a balloon as she gestured towards the settee which was strewn with newspapers.

Miss James tactfully moved them to one side before sitting down as Alison asked bluntly, 'So why are you here then?'

'I'm afraid I've come about your nephew, Joshua. I'm sorry to have to tell you this but we have had no choice but to take him into care. He's with foster-carers in Leamington at present, but Mrs Middleworth, his father's neighbour, informed us that you were temporarily caring for Rebecca at present so we were wondering if you might possibly be able to take Joshua too?'

'*What?*' Alison blustered. 'But why? What's up with Gordon?'

'He's er . . .' Miss James chose her words carefully. 'Well, the thing is – it appears that since the death of your sister he has developed a drink problem. He's certainly in no fit state to care for a child, and after numerous phone calls from various concerned people we had to go and investigate. When we saw what state the house was in, we got Mr Neilson to allow Joshua to come into voluntary care whilst we make further investigations and get him some help.'

Alison sighed. 'I've seen this coming,' she said. 'He was as drunk as a lord the last time we went to see him. But I thought he'd snap himself out of it.'

Miss James was silent for some minutes whilst she allowed

what she had just told Alison to sink in, then she asked, 'So do you think you might be able to take Joshua? It's always so much better when we can keep children within their own family units.'

'I ain't a bloody charity, you know!' Alison grumbled as she realised that there would be no more money forthcoming from Gordon. 'Rebecca eats us out of house and home as it is.' In actual fact Rebecca had lost a considerable amount of weight since going to live with her aunt, but Alison didn't tell the woman that, of course. As far as she was concerned, social workers were a nosy lot of buggers and the less they knew and the fewer dealings she had with them the better.

'Would we get paid for taking Josh and keeping Rebecca?' she asked as the possibility occurred to her.

Miss James shook her head. 'As things stand at present, no. But we could run health and police checks on yourself and your husband. And if you were prepared to attend some courses and become approved carers, there is a possibility that we could pay you then.'

Alison blanched at the thought. She'd never been one for wanting to better herself, but even if she had been, she knew that as soon as they ran the police checks on Ken, the likelihood of ever becoming approved would fly right out of the window.

'No, I don't really want to go down that route,' she said firmly. 'So p'raps Josh is best to stay where he is for now till our Gordon sorts himself out.'

Could she have known it, Miss James was breathing a sigh of relief. After seeing the state of the house she was balking at the thought of placing another child in there.

'Very well. I hope you appreciate that I had to ask,' she said pleasantly. 'And of course you are under no obligation, but perhaps I could see Rebecca before I go?'

'Why do you want to see her?' Alison demanded suspiciously.

'Oh, it's just routine really,' Miss James assured her.

Reluctantly Alison went to the foot of the stairs and shouted to Rebecca, and seconds later the girl came down and appeared in the doorway, eyeing the social worker warily.

'Hi, Rebecca.' The young woman smiled widely, all the while taking in Rebecca's grubby oversized uniform and her sullen expression. She certainly didn't appear to be the happiest of children and she looked rather neglected into the bargain, although she was pleased to note there was no sign of physical abuse.

'So how are you settling in here with your aunt and uncle?'

Rebecca shrugged as she dragged the toe of her shoe across the threadbare carpet and studiously avoided the woman's eyes.

'She's a bit shy,' Alison butted in quickly. 'Ain't you, ducks?'

Rebecca nodded, and seeing that she wasn't going to say anything, Miss James rose.

'So how long will our Josh have to stay in care for?' Alison asked, and now it was the social worker's turn to shrug.

'It all depends really,' she told her honestly. 'We have offered counselling and help to your brother-in-law, but if he doesn't choose to co-operate, well . . .'

When her voice trailed away, Alison scowled. 'Well what?'

'Then we shall have no choice but to go to court and get a care order on Josh, and he will probably go into a long-term fostering placement. But let's hope it won't come to that.'

'Hmm.' Alison was deeply concerned. Not about Josh but about the fact that she might get saddled with Rebecca for good. This had been meant to be a short-term arrangement, after all, and if she wasn't going to be paid . . . Her thoughts were racing ahead but they were brought sharply back to the present when Miss James told her, 'I should be going now,

Mrs Lambert. Thank you for your time and I'll keep you updated of developments. Goodbye.' Flashing a final smile in Rebecca's direction she left and instantly Alison lit a cigarette and inhaled deeply. As luck would have it, Ken was at the police station. Because he was on bail he had to report there once a week until his case went to court, but she knew he'd have something to say about this latest news when he got in.

The way she saw it, they should visit Gordon as soon as possible. Tonight, if need be, to get some more money out of him. If he was as out of his head on drink as the social worker had said, he probably wouldn't even know they were there, and with a bit of luck she'd be able to help herself. After all, the way she saw it, she was owed! She was looking after his kid, wasn't she? And half of what Gordon owned had belonged to Fay. In truth, she was still a bit miffed that Fay hadn't left her anything, but then in fairness she probably hadn't expected to pop her clogs at such a young age.

When Ken came back shortly after and she told him of Miss James's visit, he agreed with her about going to see Gordon. He was in a black mood and it was becoming worse with every day that grew closer to the court case.

'Stupid drunken sot!' he raged.

Alison pursed her lips. She'd lost count of the number of times Ken had come home so drunk he'd collapsed on the bathroom floor and stayed there till morning. But now didn't seem like the most opportune time to point it out. He had enough on his plate. She was more worried about herself and how she was going to manage at the moment. And their Amber was neither use nor ornament at present. Little cow. She'd got herself a boyfriend and was so moody and pre-occupied these days that she'd bite your head off soon as look at you.

'Well, if we're going we may as well go now,' she said philosophically. 'There ain't no point in putting it off.'

Luckily the snow had finally stopped and the big thaw had set in, although it was still bitterly cold and the roads were icy.

Amber and Casey had already gone out, so they bundled Rebecca into the back of the car and set off. Thankfully the worst of the rush-hour traffic was over but the journey still took longer than it should have because of the weather conditions. Ken grumbled all the way while Alison lit one cigarette after another and held her tongue. She'd hoped to go to Bingo with Pat tonight, but then she supposed if she came away from Gordon's with a wad of cash, which she had every intention of doing, it would be worth missing it for one night.

The heater in the car had packed up, and by the time they drew onto the drive of the Nielsons' smart detached home in Nottingham, they were all shivering.

The house was in darkness and Ken scowled. 'I hope we ain't come all this way for nothing.'

'He's probably in the kitchen.' Alison got out of the car and rang the doorbell, but there was no answer. She began to bang on it and it was then that Mrs Middleworth's head appeared over the neat hedge that divided the gardens.

'Oh, hello, dears.' Her wrinkled face was full of concern. 'They've taken young Joshua away, you know?'

'I already know that. That's why we're here, but do you know if Gordon is in?' Alison asked. 'I've been hammering on the door loudly enough to waken the dead but he ain't answering.'

'I haven't seen him go out,' the old lady replied. 'But don't worry – I have a key. Fay gave it to me when they went on holiday once so that I could water the plants for her before she . . . Well, anyway I kept it and I've used it a few times whilst I was trying to help out. Just hold on and I'll go and get it for you.' She disappeared as Alison stood there stamping her feet to try and get warm. The frost was already thick on the ground and she was worrying about the journey home.

Some minutes later Mrs Middleworth's head popped over the fence again and she held a key out to Alison.

'That's the one,' she said. 'I always meant to give it back, but with all that's happened it's a good job I didn't.'

Alison inserted it in the lock and sighed with relief when the door clicked open.

'Thanks,' she said shortly, and after ushering Ken and Rebecca ahead of her into the spacious hallway, she slammed the door resoundingly without another word. 'Now where's the bloody light switch?' she cursed as her hand searched across the dark wall at the side of the door. Rebecca clicked it on and the place was suddenly flooded with light.

'That's better.' Alison stood and bawled, '*Gordon!*'

When there was no answer, she strode purposefully towards the lounge. That too was in darkness, but after switching the light on in there they saw that this room was empty too.

'Where *is* the man?' Alison muttered as she headed for the kitchen. Again, there was no sign of him in there, nor in the dining room or the conservatory.

'He must be upstairs if he's in,' she commented now.

Ken nodded in agreement. 'Do you want me to go up and have a look?'

She shook her head. 'No, you go into the kitchen and see if you can rustle us a warm drink up. I'm bloody frozen through.'

He trotted off in that direction as Alison took the stairs two at a time with Rebecca close on her heels.

'I'll check the bathroom, you check his bedroom,' she ordered and Rebecca obediently headed off to do as she was told.

It felt strange to be walking into her mum and dad's bedroom again, but once inside she clicked on the light and as her eyes settled on the bed she froze. She was still there some moments later when Alison joined her.

'Well, what you standing there like a bleedin' stuffed dummy for? Is he there?' When her eyes followed Rebecca's she froze momentarily before screaming at the top of her lungs. '*KEN!*'

Almost immediately they heard him lumbering up the stairs towards them and then he too stopped in his tracks as he saw Gordon, who was stretched out across the bed, his eyes staring sightlessly up at the ceiling.

'Christ Almighty!' He gulped deep in his throat before hustling the child and Alison from the room. 'Go an' phone for an ambulance an' the cops, an' tell 'em to make it quick.'

Dragging Rebecca behind her, Alison rushed away to do as she was told, but she knew it was a waste of time. She was no doctor, but it was obvious that Gordon was dead.

Back in the bedroom, Ken cautiously approached the bed and looked down on his brother-in-law, the sickly smell of blood in his nostrils making him want to retch.

Gordon had cut his wrists, neatly and efficiently, and the sharp kitchen knife was still clutched in one hand. Ken shook his head in disbelief. Gordon had been such a clever man, a man with everything to live for. Surely he hadn't done this because of losing Fay? Ken just couldn't envisage loving *anyone* enough to die for, even Alison, but then he and Gordon had been two different breeds. Ken had always known that, and deep down had envied him. Well, he certainly didn't envy the poor bastard now. Backing away, he stood against the wall as he waited for the police and the ambulance to arrive.

Chapter Seventeen

The ambulance was the first to arrive within a matter of minutes, closely followed by a police car that screeched to a halt with its sirens blaring.

A policeman ushered them all into the kitchen whilst two paramedics rushed upstairs. Rebecca was wide-eyed and clearly in shock as Alison pushed the child roughly ahead of her. She plonked her down none too gently on the first chair they came to then hastily lit a cigarette as she stared at the police officer.

'He's dead, ain't he?' she said abruptly through a cloud of smoke.

'We'll know more when the paramedics have examined him,' the officer replied. 'But now why don't you tell me exactly what's happened?'

Alison took a deep breath and then blurted out the whole sorry story as another policeman scribbled away furiously in a notebook. She had just finished the tale when one of the paramedics stuck his head round the door. The officer quickly excused himself and stepped into the hall to join him.

When he re-entered the room, his face was grim. 'I'm afraid you were right, Mrs Lambert.' He kept one eye on Rebecca, wondering how the poor kid was going to cope with this latest tragedy, then said kindly, 'Why don't you pop into the lounge, love?'

It was unthinkable that she should have to deal with losing

her dad so soon after losing her mum, and he didn't want to have to say too much in front of her.

Once the child had gone, her shoulders slumped, he told Alison, 'The paramedic has just confirmed that your brother-in-law is dead and has been so for some hours, apparently.'

'So what happens now then?'

'Well, obviously until we are sure that this was suicide we will have to investigate to rule out foul play.'

'Foul play?' Alison's eyes were bulging. 'Ain't it more than obvious that he topped himself? The knife is still in his hand, for heaven's sake!'

'Even so, we have to be completely sure.' His voice was placating. 'Now how about you tell me everything again from the beginning.'

And so begrudgingly she did, and all the time in the lounge Rebecca sat there staring at a spot on the ceiling, oblivious to everything that was going on around her. The house seemed to be swarming with police now, and people were moving up and down the stairs as if it was a thoroughfare.

All Rebecca could see was the image of her dad lying on the blood-soaked bed. She supposed she should be crying but she just felt dead inside. She had no one now. Uncle Ken must be right. She was bad, otherwise things like this wouldn't be happening to her, would they? And what would happen to her now? She'd always thought she would return home, bringing Casper with her one day, but that would never come about now. And Aunt Alison didn't really want her; she made that more than obvious. She suddenly became aware of the policeman crouching in front of her, smiling kindly.

'Rebecca, there is a doctor here. Perhaps we should get him to take a look at you, eh?' he said gently. 'You've had a terrible shock finding your dad like that, and he might be able to give you something to make you feel a bit better.'

'Don't want anything,' she muttered sullenly.

'Oh. Well, I think I'd like him to look at you all the same.'

Knowing better than to try and argue with adults, Rebecca scowled as her uncle entered the room and said hastily, 'She's all right. She just said so, didn't she? We'll get our own doctor to see her when we get home, if need be. I think she's had quite enough to deal with for one day, without having a stranger interrogating her.'

The Inspector shrugged resignedly. He'd only been trying to help, but he accepted that her extended family knew the child a lot better than he did. After what the poor kid had just witnessed he had no doubt she'd be in need of some counselling. But if they were willing to organise it then he supposed he shouldn't interfere.

By now they had fetched Mrs Middleworth from next door to confirm their time of arrival and to verify that she had given them the key, and they could hear her muffled sobs coming from the direction of the kitchen where a policewoman was questioning her.

'I er . . . I'll make us all a hot drink, shall I?' Alison asked nervously for want of something to do, and the Inspector strode from the room after giving a cursory nod.

Almost an hour later, Gordon's body was removed from the house in a body bag, and as it passed the kitchen door Alison shuddered. Seconds later the Inspector came back into the room and told them, 'I think that's about it for now. You may all go if you wish but I'll be in touch if there's anything else I need to speak to you about. I've contacted Social Services for the address of where Joshua is, and someone will be going out to inform him shortly of what's happened – unless you would rather do it, of course?'

Alison shook her head hastily, and tight-lipped he nodded. It would have been better for the poor kid to hear of his father's death from family, but then he supposed his aunt had had a lot to contend with, what with coming in and finding the body like that so soon after losing her sister. He was actually feeling quite sorry for her until she piped up, 'Before we go, can I get a few bits together?'

'What sort of bits?'

'Well, me sister's jewellery for a start-off. She won't be needing it now, will she? An' she had some nice stuff.'

He eyed her impassively, thinking what a hard-hearted bitch she must be. 'I'm afraid that won't be possible,' he informed her in a voice colder than the frost outside. 'While investigations are under way, everything must remain exactly as it is.'

'Huh! Well, it'll all come to me anyway, now our Gordon's gone,' she said huffily.

'That may well be the case, but as I said – for now, nothing must be touched.'

Alison snatched up her bag as anger flared in her eyes. 'We might as well get off then. Good night, Inspector.'

He watched as she pushed Rebecca towards the door and bit back the retort on his lips. How could *anyone* think of their own gain when they had just discovered that a member of the family had died in such a tragic way? And what was she thinking of, talking like that in front of a little girl who had just lost her dad? He'd noticed that not once had either the man or the woman asked the child how she was, or offered her an ounce of comfort. Poor little sod. But then it took all sorts to make a world, he supposed. He waited until he heard the door close behind them then hurried away to join the other officers who were still upstairs searching the bedroom for signs that might suggest Mr Nielson's death had been anything other than a suicide.

'Well, that was a turn-up for the books, weren't it?' Alison said once they were in the car and on their way home. 'You do realise what this means, don't you? Like I said back there, we were Fay and Gordon's only living relatives so we should cop for the bloody lot. The house an' all.'

Ken whistled through his teeth. The fact hadn't occurred to him but she did have a point. They'd be rolling in it. The house alone must be worth at least three hundred grand. And just when he was about to be locked up an' all. It was sod's law.

'How long do you reckon it will be before we can get our mitts on it?' he asked now.

Alison shrugged. 'I shouldn't think it will be anytime soon. I dare say solicitors and that will be involved, and you know how longwinded they are. But at least we know it's coming. Where else would it go?'

Both of them were smiling, and in the back of the car, Rebecca listened to them with a sick feeling in the pit of her stomach. She would never be able to go home now, and if she had to stay where she was, her Uncle Ken would do the bad things to her every time her aunt went out. Amber was hardly ever in these days so she was being left with him more and more. The thought was even more terrifying than her father's death and she began to cry softly, not that either of the people in the front seats noticed – they were too busy planning what they were going to do with her dad's house and money.

They got home to find Pat had just arrived and Alison immediately sent Rebecca off to bed.

'You'll never guess what's happened, not in a month of Sundays,' she told her as she fetched a bottle of sherry from the cupboard under the sink. She then began to tell Pat all about what had happened as the other woman listened wide-eyed.

'Poor bugger. The bloke must have been feeling low, to top himself like that,' she remarked. 'And how has Rebecca taken it?'

Alison waved her hand dismissively as she poured generous measures of sherry into two mugs. 'Oh, *she'll* be all right,' she said airily. 'I mean, it ain't as if they were her *real* mum and dad, is it?'

'No. I don't suppose it is,' Pat muttered. 'But they were all she'll remember.'

'I have to say Josh is a nice enough kid,' Alison said as she took a long slurp of her drink. 'But the day they fetched Rebecca . . . well, she were such an ugly baby! She ain't much better now, if truth be told but our Fay idolised her.'

'So Josh and Rebecca aren't related then? By blood, I mean?' Pat knew deep down that the children weren't related but she wanted it confirmed.

'Oh no,' Alison said airily. 'Josh came from a very posh family in Kenilworth. The daughter got pregnant and her mum and dad made her give Josh up for adoption. Rebecca's mother was . . . well, between you and me, our Fay once confided that the girl's mum was a prostitute. She dumped the kid in the bin area of the Wellsgrave Hospital on the day she were born. Two young nurses found her and then she were fostered out till our Fay adopted her.'

Pat had gone quite pale. 'How *awful* for the poor little mite. Did Fay ever get to meet her real mum?'

'Oh no. That wouldn't have been allowed, but Social Services do have to inform the adopters where the babies come from.'

Pat chewed on her lip as she tried to take it all in, then finishing her drink, she stood up. 'I'm going to get off,' she said. 'What with what you've told me about Gordon and

Rebecca, I'm shook to the roots so I can only imagine how you must be feeling.'

'It ain't all doom and gloom,' Alison said casually. 'I'm the only living relative, so guess who should cop for the lot? Me! I'm gonna be rich, Pat. What do you think o' that, eh?'

Pat frowned. 'But wouldn't the children be classed as their closest relatives?' she questioned.

'Huh, they're just kids, ain't they? What could they do with a house an' all that dosh? No, I'm certain it'll come to me.'

'Then I wish you luck. But it's a shame your sister and brother-in-law had to die for you to get it, ain't it?' And with that Pat quietly left the kitchen.

Alison scowled as she poured herself another drink. She'd expected her mate to be pleased for her. But then it was probably just a touch of the green-eyed monster raising its head. For the first time in her life she and Ken were going to have money, and already she was thinking of ways they could spend it, so sod what Pat thought of her. If things went to plan she wouldn't be living around here for much longer. Perhaps they could start with a nice holiday abroad? She'd never been abroad before . . . Her mind raced as she thought of the wonderful life ahead. Admittedly, Ken might not be there to share her good fortune straight away if he had to do a stretch, but she'd make it up to him when he got out.

Smiling dreamily, Alison Lambert began to plan her future.

Chapter Eighteen

The inquest into Gordon's death was held in the first week of March 1996 and a verdict of suicide was passed.

Pat went along with Alison to the court in Warwick as Ken had had to attend Bedworth police station as part of his bail conditions.

'Well, that was a waste of time, weren't it?' Alison said grumpily as they made their way back to the bus station. 'A blind man on a galloping donkey could see that Gordon had done himself in.'

'I suppose they have to be sure,' Pat stated sensibly, picking her way through the deep puddles on the pavement.

'Hmm, now we have to see what the solicitor says tomorrow,' Alison said on a brighter note. The letter requesting that she and Ken attend the offices of Orme, Ladro & Staples Solicitors in Rugby had arrived by post the day before, and ever since opening it, Alison had been bursting with excitement.

'Now the inquest is over, the police have no excuse to keep us out of his house,' Alison bubbled on. 'Though I reckon me and Ken are going to sell it and buy us somewhere a bit closer to home. Of course we've got to get the funeral over first, now the police have released his body for burial, so I dare say we'll have to shell out for that. What do you think? Should we bury him or go for cremation?'

Pat shuddered as she listened to Alison speaking so

heartlessly. 'I reckon you should give him the sort of funeral he would have wanted. Did he ever say what his preference was?'

'Not to me, but I dare say he would have said in his will. The police found it in the safe at the house, but they handed it to the solicitor unopened so I won't know until tomorrow. I'll give him a decent send-off though. It's the least I can do, ain't it?'

Pat said nothing. Over the last two weeks Alison had filled the house with new furniture, all on the never-never, and she just hoped her friend wasn't riding for a fall. She would have no way of paying for the stuff if anything went wrong, but she was already spending as if money was going out of fashion. Not that she would dare to say anything, Alison would just think she was jealous if she did, and that was far from the case. Pat might be poor, but unlike Alison she put her family above anything and couldn't bear the thought of losing any of them, even if by doing so she could be a millionaire. To her, some things were more important than money. She had learned that long ago.

For most of the way home on the bus, Alison chattered nonstop about the impending visit to the solicitor's until Pat's head was bursting.

'I'll tell you what,' she said eventually, hoping to change the subject, 'I'll have Rebecca round at my house for tea tonight, if you like. You and Ken will have a lot to talk about after the inquest and it might be as well if Rebecca doesn't hear too much about it. You know what they say – little pigs have big ears.'

Alison readily agreed. Pat had been a real godsend over the last couple of weeks, taking Rebecca for hours at a time and keeping the kid out of her hair, which suited her down to the ground. Not that she intended to get rid of her now.

How could she, when she and Ken were about to inherit all her father's money?

'That'd be a great help,' she responded immediately. Ken was due in court the following week and she was trying to spend some time with him, although the thought of him being locked up wasn't quite so daunting now. She'd be too busy spending all Gordon's lovely dosh. She smiled smugly as she stared from the window and lapsed into silence, much to Pat's relief.

Rebecca was quite pleased when she got home from school and was instantly sent round to Pat's. The woman's house was always warm, and it was much more comfortable than her aunt and uncle's place, even with all their posh new furniture. She always got to have a nice dinner there too, which made a welcome change from chips. When she had lived with her mum, chips had been a rare treat, but now she felt as if they were coming out of her ears and she was sick of them. Pat had been really kind to her and was Rebecca's favourite person now. Sometimes she would take her out for a treat with Joe, and a couple of times, when her aunt had wanted her out of the way on a weekend, they'd gone to visit some of Pat's friends who always made a fuss of her.

'How's that suit yer then, luvvie?' Pat asked as she ladled a portion of steaming cottage pie onto her plate. The noise of the television in the background was loud but Rebecca quite enjoyed it. It was homely and she felt safe here. Her happy mood disappeared, however, when Pat told her, 'Me and your auntie are off out tomorrow night, but you can come here for your tea before we go, if you want?'

Rebecca suddenly lost her appetite as her blood turned to water. That would mean she would be alone with her uncle again and that could only lead to one thing – the bad thing. She tried not to think about it as she pushed the food about her plate until Pat asked, 'What's wrong? Don't you like cottage pie?'

'Y-yes . . . but can't I stay round here tomorrow night until you and Auntie Alison get home?' The words were out before Rebecca could stop them.

'Why would you want to do that?' Pat asked with a puzzled frown. 'Your Uncle Ken will be there to look out for you.' And then as a terrible thought occurred to her, she leaned in closer to the child and asked in a low voice, 'Your uncle hasn't done anything to upset you, has he?'

Terrified now, Rebecca hastily shook her head and tried to raise a smile. Then, lifting her knife and fork she pretended to attack her food as Pat watched her musingly.

The next morning, Rebecca was packed off to school and Alison began to get ready for her appointment at the solicitor's.

'Just make sure you put your suit on . . . Oh, and there's a clean shirt hanging on the wardrobe,' she yelled up the stairs to Ken.

He sighed. He couldn't even remember the last time he had worn his one and only suit, and wasn't even sure that he'd still fit into it now. She'd ordered him to have a bath too.

Ten minutes later, Alison found him in the bedroom struggling to do up his trousers.

'These have shrunk,' he grumbled. 'I can't wear them – they'll cut me in half.'

'It's not the trousers that have shrunk, it's your damn beer belly that's grown – and you bloody well *will* wear them,' she warned. 'I'm not having you turn up at the solicitor's looking like the poor relation. Do the buttons on your jacket up. No one will notice your trousers are too tight then and we'll get you a new suit as soon as we've got the money.'

It turned out that the jacket was now as ill-fitting as the trousers and the buttons strained across his beer belly, but Ken did as he was told all the same. He knew better than to argue with Alison when she was in this mood. While he fiddled with his tie she slipped into the new dress she'd treated herself to out of the rent money. The way she saw it, she needed to look smart and the rent man wasn't due until next week, by which time she was convinced Gordon's money would be safely deposited in her bank account.

After coiling her hair onto the top of her head, she slipped her feet into high-heeled shoes then snatching up her bag she glanced at the cheap alarm clock on the bedside table.

'Come on,' she said, unable to keep the excitement from her voice. 'Let's go and do it, eh? I just hope that old banger of ours gets us there on time. That's one of the first things on my list, a brand new car. Perhaps a Jag, eh? That'll give the neighbours something to gossip about, won't it?'

When they eventually pulled up outside the offices of Orme, Ladro & Staples in Fawsley Road in Rugby, Ken gulped.

'Bloody Nora! This looks a bit posh, don't it?'

Alison giggled nervously. 'Well, very soon now we'll be posh too, so don't let it get to you. Just remember, we're as good as they are.' And so saying she got out of the car, straightened her skirt and strode into the office, closely followed by Ken who could barely breathe in his too-tight clothing.

'Mr and Mrs Lambert to see Mr Staples,' Alison told the glamorous receptionist imperiously.

The young woman ran a scarlet fingernail down the list in the appointment book. 'Take a seat and I'll inform Mr

Staples you are here,' she told her pleasantly. 'I believe he is ready for you.'

Alison perched primly on one of the elegant low leather chairs in the waiting room whilst Ken chose to stand. He was too afraid of his trousers splitting if he sat down, so instead he pretended to study one of the pot plants that were scattered about.

'Mr Staples will see you now,' the young woman informed them seconds later. 'Would you come this way, please?'

Nose in the air, Alison sailed past a desk where another young woman sat busily typing as Ken hurried to keep up with her. God, he would be glad when this was over. This bloody suit was so uncomfortable he could scarcely wait to get it off.

The girl showed them into a large airy office. An enormous leather-topped desk was placed in the centre of the room, and behind it sat a handsome middle-aged man with thick dark hair and strikingly blue eyes. For some reason Alison had expected someone much older, so she was agreeably surprised.

'Ah, Mrs and Mrs Lambert. It was good of you to come.' He rose and extended his hand then told them, 'Do sit down.'

They each took a seat as he opened a sealed envelope that lay on the desk before him.

'May I say before we begin how sorry I am for the loss of your brother-in-law and your sister, Mrs Lambert. I knew them both personally, especially Gordon. I worked with him from time to time in a professional capacity and we also used to play golf together. They will both be sorely missed.'

'Thank you,' Alison simpered, trying her best to look suitably subdued.

'And now, I suppose we should get down to the matter at hand – the reading of the will. I personally drew this up with Mr Nielson shortly after the death of his wife, and it has

141

remained in the safe here ever since. Are you ready to proceed?'

Ken and Alison nodded in unison and so the solicitor solemnly began.

Unable to contain her excitement for a second longer, Alison leaned forward in her seat, her hands clasped in her lap.

'This is the last will and testament of Gordon Matthew Nielson, made this day . . .'

His voice droned on as Alison's impatience grew, but within five minutes her mouth was gaping open and she was staring at the solicitor in disbelief.

'B-but there must be some mistake,' she stuttered. 'I am Fay's only living relative!'

'Apart from her children,' Mr Staples corrected her gently.

'But they *ain't* her children – not really! They were both adopted.'

'Even so, in the eyes of the law they are classed as her next-of-kin, and both she and Mr Nielson were in agreement that the children should inherit their estate should anything happen to them before the children reached adulthood. As I have just explained, Mr Nielson has left a sum of money that should cover the cost of his funeral and any expenses incurred in the selling of the house and contents. The rest of the money will then be put in a trust fund until the children both reach the age of twenty-one, when they will each be able to access their inheritance.'

'But why has he left a measly ten grand to Rebecca and the main part of it all to Josh?' Alison exploded.

'That I cannot say,' the solicitor told her ruefully. 'All I can do is abide by my client's last wishes.'

'Why it's . . . it's bloody outrageous!' Alison ranted as her dreams of becoming rich slipped away like water down a plughole. 'He must have been out of his mind when he made that will. I'll contest it!'

'Of course, you could do that if you so wish,' Mr Staples told her patiently. 'But I have to warn you that to go down that route would cost an awful lot of money and the chances of any judge overriding Mr Nielson's will are very slim.'

'And what are the kids supposed to live on until they grow up?'

Mr Staples spread his hands. 'I understand that Joshua is already in care and that Rebecca is living with you, so Mr Nielson obviously presumed that the children would be provided for.'

'That's bloody typical of him!' Alison stormed. 'And what did he think we are – a ruddy charity? It costs money to bring kids up and that's something we are rather short of.'

'I'm very sorry if you are disappointed with Mr Nielson's decisions,' the man said, 'but I'm afraid there is nothing I can do about it.'

'Well, you ain't heard the last of this yet!' Alison rose from her seat, her eyes blazing. 'Come on, Ken. I reckon it's time we got some legal advice from someone who don't talk out of their arse!' And with that she stormed out of the office like a ship in full sail.

Once in the car, her anger gave way to tears. 'What we going to do?' she said fearfully. 'I've put us in debt up to the neck, thinking we were going to get that money. How could Gordon do this to us? And you're in court next week so you won't be able to help.'

Ken undid the button on his trousers and the top button of his shirt, his face dark.

'Well, perhaps if you'd waited for the readin' o' the will before going out spending money like you'd won the pools we wouldn't be in this mess,' he accused.

'Oh, that's right, blame *me*!' Alison shouted. 'How was I to know this was gonna happen?'

Ken started the car and it sputtered away from the kerb. So much for going out and buying a new one. As things stood, he couldn't even afford to get this one repaired.

The journey home was made in stony silence as Alison fumed and Ken fretted. They were up the creek without a paddle now, the way he saw it.

Pat was hovering in their window when they drew up at home, with the bottle of champagne Alison had bought in anticipation cooling in the fridge. One look at Alison's face, however, warned her that things might not have gone as her friend had expected.

'What's wrong?' she asked the second Alison set foot through the door.

'What's wrong?' Alison shrieked, slinging her bag down onto the settee. 'The lousy bastard ain't left us so much as a brass farthing – *that's* what's wrong!'

'Oh.' Pat didn't know what to say as Alison lit a cigarette and puffed on it furiously.

'He's left the whole lot tied up for the kids till they come of age. Most of it went to Josh,' Alison fumed. 'We get a lousy few grand to bury the bastard and that's it! So it turns out you were right.'

'Oh!' Pat said again, still lost for words. Then: 'But what about all the new stuff you've been buying?' She nodded towards the new leather-look three-piece suite and the new television set. 'How you gonna pay for it all now?'

Alison glared at her. '*That*,' she said, 'is the leading question. How *am* I gonna pay for it?'

'Perhaps the shops would come and take all the stuff back if you asked 'em,' Pat suggested tentatively.

'Huh! And pigs might fuckin' fly.'

Ken had disappeared off upstairs but now he reappeared dressed in his customary jeans and a grubby T-shirt.

'That's better,' he sighed. 'I felt as if I'd been trussed up like a turkey ready for the oven in that bloody suit.'

'I'm glad that's all you've had to worry about,' Alison spat resentfully.

Ken took a can of lager from the fridge, studiously avoiding the bottle of champagne. That had cost an arm and a leg an' all, and for what? They certainly didn't have anything to celebrate now!

'Look, I reckon I'm gonna shoot off,' Pat said tactfully. 'You two need a bit of time on your own.' She disappeared through the door as Alison sank wearily down onto the nearest chair. One thing was for sure, if Gordon hadn't already been dead she'd have done the job for him!

It was later that night as they were heading for Bingo that Pat said tentatively, 'Rebecca were sayin' yesterday that she didn't like stayin' in with your Ken on her own.' She had been worrying all day about whether she should speak out, but she felt that something was seriously wrong and couldn't stop herself.

'So?' Alison was still stinging from the trip to the solicitor's, but as she pondered on Pat's words her face darkened. 'She's a spoiled little bitch an' probably thinks I should be there panderin' to her an' all,' she muttered, but the seed of doubt had been planted and she determined to have a word with Ken the instant she got home.

The row that ensued later that night brought Rebecca springing awake.

'If I find out you've been messin' about with that kid I'll cut your balls off an' stuff 'em up your arse,' she heard her aunt bellow. 'An' don't look so wide-eyed an' innocent. I've seen that stash o' bluies yer keep hidden under the floorboards in our room. They're all child-porn, an' if the police 'ad found 'em, you'd be on another charge an' all!'

'Why would I mess wi' that little trollop?' her uncle shouted back indignantly.

'So why did she tell Pat she didn't want to stay in on her own with you? *Eh*?'

Rebecca jammed the pillow over her head to block out the sounds of their voices. Thankfully, Casey had stayed in that night, so her uncle had left her alone. But would this make things worse for her now? She doubted it. Things really couldn't get much worse than they already were.

Chapter Nineteen

A week later, Pat once again stood at Alison's lounge window staring up and down the road with a worried frown on her face.

Alison and Ken had left for the courts at eight o'clock that morning, but there was no knowing what time Ken's case would be heard and so Pat had volunteered to be there for when the kids were due home from school.

Just then, a taxi appeared around the corner and drew up outside. Seconds later, Alison got out looking very despondent.

'Well?' Pat demanded as Alison walked through the front door.

'He got five years.' The woman wearily took her coat off and threw it across a chair. 'It was awful, Pat. The buggers had got him for things he'd handled months ago. They've been watching him apparently, and just biding their time until they'd got him bang to rights. He'll do at least two and a half years, even with good behaviour. They're sending him to Winson Green.'

'Oh.' Pat hastily went into the kitchen, filled the kettle and put it on to boil, although judging by the look on Alison's face she needed something a little stronger than tea.

'You'll be surprised how quickly the time will go,' she said inadequately, as Alison came and sat at the table. What else could she say? They'd all known that it would be nothing short of a miracle if Ken didn't go down, but none of them had expected the sentence to be so severe.

'When will you be able to go and see him?' she asked now as she spooned sugar into two mugs. While she'd been waiting she'd had a quick tidy-up and the house looked cleaner than it had for years.

'They'll send me a Visiting Order.' Alison's voice was dull. 'That'll be something to look forward to, won't it?' she croaked sarcastically.

It was whilst they were sitting at the kitchen table nursing the mugs of scalding tea that Rebecca appeared. Sensing instantly that something was wrong, she glanced nervously from one to the other.

'Your uncle's . . . well, he's had to go away for a time,' Pat told her tactfully. The kid deserved to know, after all.

Rebecca suddenly felt as if a great weight had been lifted off her shoulders and it took her all her time not to show her relief. Somehow she knew that this wouldn't have gone down too well. Alison had been particularly irritable with her since the night she and her uncle had rowed, and she feared that things might get even worse now.

'Your aunt is feeling a bit stressed today and I thought perhaps you could come round to my place for tea?' Pat suggested now. 'Joe is going out with his chums so I'm getting the bus into Coventry a bit later on to see me mum. Do you fancy coming?'

Rebecca nodded, trying not to appear too eager. She had been to see Pat's mum Caroline – or Caz, as she was known – a few times now and always enjoyed going there.

'Is that all right with you?' Pat asked.

Alison waved her hand dismissively. She could take the brat for good, for all she cared. She had more pressing things on her mind. Ken's sentence had come as a shock and then there was Gordon's funeral to get through tomorrow. It was going to be a very low-key affair. Alison had ordered the cheapest coffin she could find. There would be a short service at the church and then the grave where Fay had been buried only months before would be reopened and he would be buried in there with her. She hadn't even bothered putting funeral notices in the newspapers. The way she saw it, he was dead and nothing was going to bring him back, so why waste good money? Because she had been so frugal there would be quite a few hundred pounds left over from the funeral allowance, not that it would go far towards paying what she owed. The shop where she had bought all the new furniture had been most unhelpful. They had told her that it was impossible for them to take it back as it was now second-hand, and that if she didn't keep up the repayments on it they would send the bailiffs in.

'Please yourself,' Alison had stormed as she strode out of the shop.

Now she saw Rebecca going to the cupboard and immediately snapped, 'What are you doing? I thought you were going out with Pat.'

'I am, but I just want to feed Casper first.'

'Huh! There's no way we can afford to keep that greedy bloody mutt now,' Alison said peevishly. 'He eats for England, he does. We'll have to find him a new home.'

Rebecca's face crumpled. 'But . . . he could share my dinners,' she ventured. Casper was all she had left in the world, and the thought of losing him was unbearable.

'Come on, pet,' Pat coaxed. She could see that Alison was about to explode and hoped to avoid an argument. 'We can talk about this later.'

She waited until the child had emptied the contents of a tin of dog food into Casper's bowl then took her hand firmly.

'I'll have her back for bedtime,' she told Alison, who huffed irritably, as if she couldn't see the back of them quickly enough.

It was as they were walking towards her house that Pat studied Rebecca out of the corner of her eye. The child had never been pretty, although the loss of her glasses and a considerable weight-loss had gone some way towards improving her appearance, but Pat had always been impressed with her personal hygiene – until a few weeks ago, that was. Now Rebecca looked like a little waif. Her clothes were grubby and creased, and her hair was lank and greasy. It was as if the child didn't care about how she looked any more – but then, who could blame her? From the second she had walked through their door, Ken and Alison had made it blatantly clear that the poor kid was only there on sufferance, and she must be feeling terribly lonely. Casper was the only one who showed her any affection, apart from Pat herself, so it was no wonder she thought so much of the little dog – and now she was at risk of losing him too. Pat's kindly heart went out to her.

'I've got a nice bit of pork and some baked spuds cooking in the oven,' she told her now in a cheery voice. 'We'll have some of that and then catch the bus to see me mum, shall we?' She was hoping to cheer the little girl up, but her words didn't seem to be having much impact. She rightly guessed that Rebecca was worrying about whether Casper would still be at home when she got back. Now that Alison had decided to get rid of him, she could do just that at any minute. Pat and Alison mucked along very well for most of the time, but Ali could be a heartless cow sometimes.

She ushered Rebecca ahead of her into the warmth of her cosy kitchen before serving their meal. Joe had already eaten and gone out, but there was still plenty left.

'There, that'll warm you up,' she said encouragingly, putting a plate down in front of her. 'Get it down you and then we'll be off, eh?'

Rebecca stared down at the steaming food in front of her. A home-cooked meal was a rare treat nowadays, but she was so worried about Casper she wondered if she would be able to eat it.

Pat watched her push the meal around for a while before suggesting, 'Why don't you leave that until we get back? I can always pop it in the oven and warm it up for you again, and we ought to be going really.'

Rebecca slid off the chair without a word and soon they were heading for the bus that would take them to Caz's house in Coventry.

Once they got off the bus they seemed to walk for a long way past rows of terraced houses that all looked the same, until a block of highrise flats loomed into view.

'Here we are then,' Pat wheezed. 'I hope that damn lift is working tonight. Me legs feel like they're dropping off.'

Rebecca hadn't said a single word on the bus and Pat was really worried about her. There was a gang of youths congregated in the entrance hall, drinking cans of lager, smoking joints and being very noisy.

''Ere granny, 'ave yer got any spare fags on yer?' one of them asked cheekily.

Not intimidated in the least, Pat glared at him. She'd dealt with far harder cases than him in her time.

'No, I ain't,' she retorted. 'And even if I had, I wouldn't be giving them to you. Now shift out o' me way before you feel me foot up your arse.'

The youth was so astonished that he did as he was told without a word as Rebecca looked up at Pat admiringly.

Pat winked at her. 'You have to show the cheeky young

buggers round here who's boss,' she told her. 'If they think you're scared of 'em you stand *no* chance.'

They were at the doors to the lift now and as they slid open, Pat sighed with relief. 'Thank God fer that. I didn't fancy climbin' all those stairs tonight. I don't know how me mam manages it.'

The lift began to rise, and seconds later stopped on the fifth-floor landing where Pat ushered Rebecca out. The smell of stale urine was overpowering and the walls were covered in graffiti. Some of the doors to the flats were hanging off the hinges where they had been kicked in, and Rebecca eyed them warily as they hurried past. Caz's flat was the last one on the landing, next to a huge window which gave them a panoramic view of Coventry.

'Nice view, ain't it?' Pat commented once she had rung the doorbell. 'It's just a shame this place is such a shithole.'

She had no chance to say more because the door was inched open then and Caz peered out at them. Her face broke into a smile when she saw who it was and she opened the door wider.

'Come on in. This is a nice surprise. I weren't expectin' no company tonight.'

Pat gently nudged Rebecca ahead of her, and as always, the child felt as if she was stepping into another world. A dark blue wall-to-wall carpet stretched along the hallway and there were pretty pictures on the walls. In the small lounge, a gas fire with fake logs was gently flickering, making everything seem cosy and inviting, and the curtains were tightly drawn against the cold, windy evening.

A settee was positioned in front of the fire and in the corner was a small television set which Caz had obviously been watching.

'You sit yourself down, pet, and make yourself comfy while

I go and get you a nice drink of lemonade,' she said to the child. 'And while I'm at it, I'll make me and Pat a nice cuppa. Do you fancy a biscuit with it?'

Rebecca shook her head as the two women turned and pottered away.

Once in the privacy of the small kitchen, Caz immediately asked, 'So how did Ken get on in court?'

'He got five years, Mam.'

'Five years?' Caz repeated incredulously. 'Christ Almighty, how's Alison taken that?'

'Not well, as you can imagine. And she's got Gordon's funeral tomorrow.'

'An' is the little 'un going?'

Pat snorted. 'Huh, I doubt it. You know what Alison's like. As long as the kid is out of the way at school she's happy. Between you and me, I can't see her keeping her for much longer, now that Gordon isn't here to pay for her keep. Alison might be a mate, but I think we both know she don't do nothing out of the goodness of her heart.'

Caz's face crumpled with sympathy. 'But what will happen to the poor little mite? Where will she go?'

'I ain't got a clue. Into care, I suppose – the same as her adopted brother. But don't go getting any ideas about *you* taking her. You'd stand no more chance than me, with your track record with Social Services.'

'I know – I know! But she's just lost her mum and dad an' all.' Caz sighed heavily as she poured lemonade into a glass.

Rebecca took it politely when the woman carried it into the lounge to her. She was watching *Coronation Street* and seemed perfectly content with her own company.

'Me an' Pat are just havin' a bit of chat in the kitchen an' then we'll be in to join you. All right, love?'

Rebecca nodded as Caz slipped away again before turning

her attention to the photos on the mantelpiece above the gasfire. There were pictures of three children, one of whom was Pat, at various ages, and one of a much younger Caz smiling up at a man who had his arm around her shoulders. Rebecca guessed that this must be her late husband. Pat had told her that her dad had died a few years ago. Rebecca thought that Caz must get very lonely, stuck up here all on her own. She had no idea how old the woman might be – very old though, probably fifty at least. She was pretty in the photo, but the hard life she had led had taken its toll on her, and now she looked much older than she actually was. She was kind though, and on the few occasions when Rebecca had visited her with Pat, she had always made her feel sort of . . . special. It was a nice feeling, the sort of feeling that she had used to have sometimes when her mum was alive.

Sighing, the little girl snuggled further down into the chair. It was warm and cosy here, and before she knew it she had fallen fast asleep – and Pat left her there until it was time to go home.

Chapter Twenty

Alison spent a miserable evening feeling thoroughly sorry for herself. She was still reeling with shock at the severity of the sentence the court had passed on Ken, and was worrying about how she and the kids were going to survive. She would have to pay a visit to the DSS tomorrow afternoon, once she'd got Gordon's funeral out of the way, and see what benefits she was entitled to. What other option was open to her? It never occurred to her that she might try to get a job. Alison had never done a day's work in her life and had no intention of starting now. The way she saw it, the state owed her a living if they were locking her chap away.

Thinking of the funeral she would have to attend tomorrow, she ground her teeth. She wouldn't have been in this mess if that lousy brother-in-law of hers hadn't cut her out of his will. If she could have got her hands on his money she would be sitting pretty now. But then she had never seemed to have any luck, unlike Fay, who had always had everything. From as far back as Alison could remember, Fay had been their parents' blue-eyed girl, whilst they had looked upon her as a rebel. She snorted as she remembered. A right pair of Holy Joes, her mum and dad had been. Church every Sunday and tea served from china cups. They had almost had a dickey fit when she'd met Ken at just sixteen, and then disowned her when she got pregnant within months with Amber.

Three years later, her dad had died of a massive heart-attack and her mother had blamed her for it, saying she had broken his heart. Silly old cow! Alison had felt no sorrow at all when her mum then died eight months later from cancer. And just as she had expected, she had found herself left out of that will too. The whole lot went to Fay, as if *she* had needed it! She had hooked up with Gordon by then and her future had looked rosy. Now they were both dead too. It was funny how life turned out, when you came to think of it.

The slam of the door brought her thoughts sharply back to the present and she heard Amber stamp up the stairs.

The girl had been in a funny mood lately and Alison was none too pleased with her. Some months ago, word had reached her and Ken that Amber was seeing one of the biggest rogues on the estate. He had his fingers into all sorts of pies – drugs, burglary, the lot – and added to that he was in his early twenties, far too old to be going out with a fourteen-year-old girl. Not that Amber would listen to her or Ken when they tried to talk to her about it. Amber was very like her mother and stubborn as a mule, so all they could do was hope that the fling would soon fizzle out. Thankfully, there was every chance of that happening. Lee Bradford was a right Jack the lad, by all accounts, and Amber was a hot-arsed little madam, so the chances of it lasting were slim, which was something at least. Alison heard Amber dash into the bathroom and lock the door as she poured herself another generous glass of wine. She was already on her second bottle – she needed it tonight.

Ten minutes later, she realised her fag packet was empty. Thankfully, there was another full sleeve upstairs in her room that the cops had missed when they raided the house. She was heading up the stairs to fetch them just as Amber emerged from the bathroom, wrapped in a grubby bath-sheet.

For an instant, her daughter was illuminated in the doorway

from the bathroom light behind her, and Alison froze. And then she suddenly covered the distance between them with a speed that would have done justice to a sprinter, and before Amber could stop her, she had whipped the towel away leaving the girl to cover herself as best she could.

''Ere, Mam, what the bleedin' hell do you think you're doing?' she objected.

'What the *fuck* is that?' Alison stabbed her finger towards Amber's swollen stomach with a look of horror on her face.

'I . . . I was going to tell you,' the girl murmured, shame-faced. 'But what with all this going on with Dad and that, I couldn't seem to find the right time.'

'Oh, you were just gonna wait till it popped out, were you? How far gone are you?'

'About four months.' Amber snatched the towel back and wrapped herself up again as Alison sagged against the wall in disbelief.

'You *stupid* little mare! You'll probably be too far gone to get rid of it now.'

'I don't *want* to get rid of it,' Amber said defiantly. 'It's *my* baby – mine and Lee's.'

'Oh yes, and what does he say about it?'

'Well, I ain't actually told him yet,' Amber admitted in a small voice.

'And you mean to tell me he ain't even *noticed*? Why, he must have shit in his eye. He'll drop you like a hot brick when he finds out.'

'No, he won't.' Amber's chin jutted with defiance. 'Lee *loves* me. He said so. And *I* love him. And anyway, why are you being such a hypocrite? You weren't that much older than I am now when you got pregnant with me.'

'I was sixteen and left school, which is a world away from fourteen,' Alison raved, slamming her fist into the wall. 'And this on top of everything else . . . your bloody timing is perfect! Of course he said he loves you – *all* blokes will say that if it means getting their end away.'

'Well, you should know,' Amber sneered. Before she knew it, her mother's hand snaked out and caught her a blow on the cheek that threw her against the wall.

'*You cow!*' the girl screeched as she straightened and reeled away.

Alison was ashamed. 'I'm sorry, love – it were just the shock, that's all. I didn't mean to hit you.' But her words were lost as Amber slammed her bedroom door so resoundingly that a lump of plaster fell off the wall in a cloud of dust. Alison stood there feeling as if her whole world was falling apart and wondering what else life had in store for her. Surely things couldn't get any worse, she thought self-pityingly.

Pat had hoped that a bit of time alone would put Alison in a slightly better frame of mind, but when she returned Rebecca a couple of hours later she found her in an even worse mood.

'Get upstairs to bed,' she barked at Rebecca the second they walked through the door. Only too happy to oblige, once she saw that Casper was still there safe and sound, the child rushed off to do as she was told with her pet close behind her.

However, curiosity got the better of her when she was halfway up the stairs and she paused to eavesdrop.

'You ain't gonna believe what's happened now!' she heard her aunt wail as Pat joined her at the kitchen table. 'That stupid bloody daughter o' mine has only gone and got herself in the club.'

'You're joking!' Rebecca heard the shock in Pat's voice and guessed that this club Amber was in must not be a very nice one.

'Why would I joke about something like that?' Alison whined, as if it was all Pat's fault.

'So what's she gonna do about it? Is she going to get rid of it?'

'Huh! Judging by the size of her, she's left it too late for that. And anyway, she's saying she wants to keep it. I can't believe I didn't notice before,' Alison fumed. 'I don't know what she's thinking of – a baby at her age when she's still only a kid herself.'

'Well, she won't be the first on this estate,' Pat pointed out. 'Half the teenagers round here are pushing prams before they've left school. But what about her boyfriend – will he stick by her?'

'I doubt that very much, if his reputation is anything to go by. He's had half the girls within a three-mile radius, by all accounts, so God knows why our Amber thinks she's something special. He'll probably dump her the second he finds out, and then it will be left to me to keep her *and* a baby. That's all I need on top of everything else that's happened, ain't it? And I've got Gordon's bloody funeral to get through tomorrow an' all.'

Shock surged through Rebecca as she crouched there with her arm about Casper, who was licking her face with his warm wet tongue as if he hadn't seen her for a month. *A baby!* Amber was going to have a baby! She knew now how babies were made, having overheard some girls talking about it in the playground at school. You had to do the 'bad thing' like Uncle Ken had done to her, and then a baby started to grow inside you. Terror coursed through her as a thought occurred. What if *she* was growing a baby? What would happen to her then? Too afraid to stay there any longer in case she was discovered listening, she scuttled off to her room, and after hastily undressing, she slid into the cold bed. Amber was already asleep in the bunk bed above her, and her soft snores echoed around the small room as Rebecca lay shivering. Then her thoughts moved on to the other thing her aunt had said. *And I've got Gordon's bloody funeral to get through tomorrow an' all.*

They must be burying her dad tomorrow. But why hadn't her aunt told her? Surely she would be going to the funeral too? She wasn't really all that bothered about saying goodbye to her dad, but she somehow knew that Josh would be going. She didn't even know where he was now, apart from the fact that he was living with foster-carers somewhere. Nobody ever told her anything!

Pulling the covers up to her chin, she rolled herself into a ball and eventually she slept.

Aunt Alison was up early the next morning, which was surprising. Rebecca had grown accustomed to getting herself up and off to school, but today her aunt was applying her make-up in the mirror above the mantelpiece dressed in a smart pair of black trousers, which looked new, and a black jacket.

She gave Rebecca a cursory glance as she entered the room before snapping, 'Get yourself some cereal if there is any left, and then take yourself off to school.'

Rebecca hovered for an instant, waiting for her aunt to tell her where she was going, but when she didn't she moved into the kitchen just in time to see Casey disappearing out of the door. He had left an empty cereal packet and an empty milk bottle on the table next to his dish, so Rebecca guessed that there would be no breakfast again. Still, at least there was some rather stale bread left in the bread bin, so she hastily made herself a couple of bread and marge sandwiches for her lunch and after stroking Casper she sneaked away.

*   *   *

160

The funeral was a dismal affair. The only people who attended were Alison, Mrs Middleworth, Josh and his foster-mum, and the solicitor.

When Mr Staples saw the cheap coffin, he said nothing although Alison could sense the disapproval coming off him in waves as they stood through the short service. There was no music, no hymns and no flowers, apart from one wreath of red and white carnations from Mrs Middleworth. It truly was a budget send-off.

Following the service in the small church the vicar led the way to the opened grave and Gordon was laid to rest with Fay.

Glad to leave, Alison headed for the lych-gate without a backward glance. It was a case of good riddance to bad rubbish as far as she was concerned, and now she could get on with other things.

She caught the bus back to Bedworth and headed for the DSS office where she tearfully told them of the position she was in, playing heavily on the fact that she was caring for her dear departed sister's child as well as her own two children. They were the first tears she had shed all day but the person dealing with her simply stared back at her dispassionately.

'And then on top of everything else I've just found out that my fourteen-year-old daughter is pregnant!' Alison dabbed at her eyes for effect.

Ten minutes later, she stormed out of the offices in a towering rage. Just who the hell did that trumped-up woman think she was anyway? Alison had expected a bit of sympathy for the circumstances she found herself in but instead the woman had been cutting.

'You are young and healthy. You'll just have to go out and find yourself a job,' she had told her unfeelingly.

Alison was fuming. A job indeed! The woman had spoken

as if they grew on trees. Alison had no qualifications what-soever, so what chance of finding a job did she have? Admittedly, the woman had granted a few benefits to tide her over while she looked for work, but she'd made it more than clear that it was only a temporary solution, and then what was she going to do when the benefits were stopped?

There was nothing else for it. She would have to contact Social Services for a start and have Rebecca put into care. There was no way she could afford to keep her for nothing now. If truth be told, she didn't want to anyway. With her mind made up on that score, she stamped towards home.

Chapter Twenty-One

Alison didn't have to contact Social Service because two days later, shortly after Casey and Rebecca had left for school, someone rapped on the front door.

Alison was still in bed with a terrible hangover from the night before and she groaned as she pulled the pillow over her head, hoping that they would go away.

They didn't, and the knocking grew louder. Cursing Amber, who was also still in bed, Pat dragged her old dressing-gown on and padded downstairs, cursing.

'All right, all right! Keep your bleedin' hair on. I'm coming, ain't I?'

Still grumbling, she flung the front door open and blinked with surprise when she saw Miss James standing there.

'So where's the bloody fire then?' she quipped sarcastically, quickly regaining her composure. Leaving the door hanging open she then padded off into the kitchen where she lit a cigarette and waited for the social worker to join her.

Miss James stood in the doorway, looking round at the mess before saying, 'I'm sorry to disturb you, Mrs Lambert, but I need to speak to you rather urgently.'

Alison eyed her curiously, sensing the younger woman's discomfort. 'Oh yeah? What about?'

'It's about Rebecca actually.'

'What about her?'

'Well . . .' Miss James paused, choosing her words carefully.

'It's been brought to our attention that your husband has been sent to prison. Is that correct?'

Alison smirked. 'Seeing as it was plastered all across the front of last night's local paper it's hardly any secret, is it? But I've no doubt it was that interfering solicitor Staples who informed you.'

'I'm not at liberty to divulge that information,' Miss James said primly. 'But unfortunately this does cast a different light on your caring for Rebecca. You see—'

'Stop right there!' Alison held her hand up, a grim expression on her face. 'If you've come to tell me that I ain't a fit parent 'cos of what Ken's done, you can save your breath. Fact of the matter is, I was gonna get in touch with you anyway. Now that Ken's in nick and I've no money coming in, I can't afford to keep Rebecca here any longer, so you can move her to wherever you like as soon as you like. The sooner the better for me, in fact.'

'Oh!' Miss James was so taken aback at the apparent lack of care that she was momentarily rendered speechless. 'So you will have no objection if we place Rebecca with approved foster-carers then?'

'That's what I just said, ain't it?' Alison lit another Benson & Hedges and glared at the young woman. 'Got somewhere in mind for her, have you?'

'As a matter of fact I have.' Miss James refrained from saying exactly where. 'And I was wondering if I might come and move her this afternoon as soon as she gets in from school?'

'Suits me.' Alison shrugged nonchalantly. 'I'll have her stuff packed ready. See you about four-ish, shall I?'

Miss James was so nonplussed she scarcely knew what to say, so she merely nodded as she backed towards the door and made her escape. Once seated in her car, which had already attracted a large number of truants, who were eyeing her shiny wheelcaps greedily, she sighed. She had come expecting tears and pleas for the child to be allowed to stay. How wrong could she have been? It was evident that Alison couldn't see the back of the poor kid quickly enough. But how was Rebecca going to cope with yet another major change in her life, so soon after losing both her adoptive parents? Starting the car, she drove away with a heavy heart. This was fast becoming one of the saddest cases she had ever had to deal with.

When Rebecca arrived home from school that afternoon, the first thing she did when she opened the door was shout to Casper. Usually he was there waiting for her, but today there was no sign of him.

Barging into the kitchen, she asked, 'Where's Casper? He wasn't—' Her voice stopped abruptly when she saw Miss James sitting at the kitchen table and she glanced towards her aunt for an explanation.

'Casper's gone,' Alison informed her unfeelingly. 'Old Wilf from up the club took him earlier. I did tell you I couldn't afford to keep him any more. And Miss James here . . . well, she's come to take you to a foster home.'

Rebecca paled to the colour of putty. This double shock was just too much to take in, all in one go. Strangely enough she felt nothing at the thought of being taken from her aunt, but the prospect of never seeing Casper again was more than she could bear.

Meanwhile, Miss James cringed at the callous way Rebecca's aunt had told her she was leaving. Surely she could have tried to soften the blow a little?

'Don't worry, Rebecca,' she said with a kindly smile. 'I'm taking you to stay with lovely people. I'm sure you'll like it there.'

Rebecca ignored her, keeping her eyes trained tight on her aunt who was at last beginning to look slightly uncomfortable.

'You gave my dog away. He was the only friend I had,' she ground out accusingly with her small hands bunched into fists and tears trembling on her lashes.

'Well, what were I supposed to do? I can barely afford to feed meself now, let alone a dog!'

Appalled at the way Alison was handling the situation, Miss James began to gather up the Tesco carrier bags containing Rebecca's belongings. Her aunt hadn't even cared enough to find her a suitcase and let the child leave with a little dignity.

'Come on, love. Let's go,' she said quietly, and turning on her heel, Rebecca walked out of the house ahead of her without even looking back once.

It was whilst Miss James was placing the bags on the back seat of her car that Pat came haring down the road towards them.

'Oh sweetheart, I can't believe it's come to this.' Clearly distressed, she caught Rebecca to her and hugged her tight. 'Your aunt told me what was happening this morning after this young lady here had left, and I gave her a right earful, I don't mind telling you. You won't catch me crossing her doorstep again, the unfeeling bitch!'

Miss James looked on in amazement, although she was genuinely pleased to see that there seemed to be at least one person in the world who cared about Rebecca.

'I'm Pat from just up the road.' Pat thrust a piece of paper into the astonished young woman's hand. 'That's my address. You will let me know how she goes on, won't you? And perhaps I could go to see her from time to time?'

'Well, I . . .' Miss James looked towards Rebecca, who nodded, before saying, 'I'll certainly do my best if that's what Rebecca wants.'

Pat then bent to Rebecca's level and looked deep into her scared blue eyes. 'You look after yourself now, do you hear me? And if ever you need anything, I'll be right here.'

Rebecca sniffed and swallowed the enormous lump in her throat before clambering into the back of Miss James's car. And then Miss James drove away and as Rebecca looked through the rear window she saw Pat standing there waving. A pain tore through her. She was about to lose yet another person she had cared about, and it seemed so unfair. There was no one left to trust and yet another chapter of her life was about to begin. But one day she determined she would find the people who had started it all – the parents who had deserted her at birth – and somehow she would make them pay.

'We're going to a place in Nuneaton,' Miss James informed her conversationally as they passed the George Eliot Hospital a short while later. 'The Browns, who you'll be staying with, are ever so nice and they have two children of their own too. One of them is about your age, so hopefully you'll make a new friend.'

Rebecca stared numbly from the car window. All she could think about was Casper. She didn't much care what was going to happen to her any more. Would this Wilf feed him and take him for walks? Would he let him sleep in his bedroom so that Casper didn't get frightened in the night? She had no way of knowing, and could only pray that he would be well cared for.

'I thought when you get settled in it might be nice if we arranged a visit with Josh for you,' Miss James remarked. 'Would you like that?'

Again only silence answered her, so eventually she gave up and concentrated on the road which was busy with rush-hour traffic.

'That's Lamp Hill up there – look,' she tried again after a time. 'That's where the Browns live. This is the Stockingford area of the town.'

Rebecca looked ahead with no interest whatsoever as Miss James smiled at her in the mirror. Lamp Hill appeared to be a huge estate and Rebecca wondered how anyone could ever find their way around it.

'All the streets and roads up here are named after trees, and you'll be staying in Cedar Tree Road.'

Soon after, she pulled up in front of a neat semi-detached house. The lawns were trimmed and a profusion of flowers grew in the borders. As they walked up the path, a plump, middle-aged woman with a kindly smile came to the door.

'Why, you must be Rebecca,' she said. 'Come on in, love, and meet the family. We've been expecting you. We've waited tea for you as well. I hope you like pork chops.'

Her friendly nature brought no glimmer of a reaction from Rebecca, who simply stared blankly ahead. She didn't trust adults any more. Her real mum had abandoned her. Her second mum and dad had died, and her aunt had made it very obvious that she had never wanted her from the second Rebecca set foot through her door. Her uncle had done terrible things to her, and the social worker appeared to think she could just move her at the drop of a hat as if she was a parcel. Well, this woman could be as nice as she liked. From now on, Rebecca was determined never to trust anyone again. The shutters were up!

PART TWO

Chasing Rainbows

Chapter Twenty-Two

September 2000

'So basically what you're saying is – this is the end of the road?'

Mary Brown twisted her hands together, avoiding Miss James's eyes.

'I'm afraid it is – I'm so sorry,' she muttered guiltily. 'But it's become unbearable now. God knows, both Mick and I have done our best to make her feel a part of the family, but it's as if she doesn't care for anything or anyone. It's worse for our Katie. I thought with her and Rebecca being the same age, Katie would be able to bring her out of her shell, but she makes Katie's life hell and I can't put the poor kid through any more. The school holidays were a complete nightmare. She'd go off out and I never knew when she might come back in or what she was up to. I thought once they got back to school things would improve, but if anything they've got worse.'

'Don't feel guilty,' Miss James said gently, reaching out to squeeze Mary's hand. 'I know you've done your best. In fact, off the record, I think you've done really well to keep it going as long as you have. I know Rebecca isn't an easy child, but I'd hoped with a bit of stability in her life she'd change.'

Mary shook her head, feeling an absolute failure. She

was a very experienced carer and hated to give up on a child, but Rebecca's behaviour was affecting the whole family now and she knew that she had to put her own children first.

'She went off into town straight from school the other day,' Mary confided now. 'And within an hour I had a policeman knocking on the door. She'd been shoplifting again, from Boots this time. But why does she do it? I don't deny her anything she asks for, within reason. Her wardrobe is bulging with clothes she refuses to wear. Instead she walks around in baggy jumpers, and getting her to have a bath or a shower is a nightmare. I'm just at the end of my tether. But what will happen to her now?'

'Don't you get worrying about that,' Miss James soothed. 'Another carer I know in Hill Top has a vacancy, so as soon as I get back to the office I'll give her a ring and see if she's willing to take her.'

'I'm so sorry.' Mary looked devastated as Miss James rose to leave. Rebecca was twelve years old now, and during the time Mary had cared for her, the child had given her hell. Shoplifting, going off until late at night, bullying at school. Most of the children in her class at school were terrified of her.

'Do you think I should prepare her for the move?' Mary asked as Miss James made for the door.

'That's entirely up to you. I'm quite happy to do it if you feel you can't.'

'No, it's my decision she goes, so I should at least have the guts to tell her,' Mary said stoically. 'But I will try to do it sensitively.'

'Very well, meantime I'll ring you as soon as I've spoken to the other carer. I'll try to arrange the move for as soon as possible. Today, if she's able to take her, so perhaps you could start some of her packing?'

Mary nodded, and once she had closed the door on the social worker, she had a little cry before going about her day-to-day business.

Miss James phoned her an hour later as promised to inform her that she would be there to move Rebecca to her new placement after school that day. Mary put the phone down with a heavy heart. For herself she felt relief, but she was worried about how Rebecca would take the news. It would be yet another rejection, the way she saw it, after all.

As it turned out she needn't have worried. Once Rebecca was home from school she sat her down on the settee and began tentatively, 'I'm afraid I have something to tell you, love, and I hope it won't come as a shock but—'

'You're getting rid of me,' Rebecca stated flatly.

Mary's mouth gaped and just for an instant she thought she saw a wounded look flash in Rebecca's eyes but it was gone so quickly she might have imagined it.

'I wouldn't put it quite like that, but you are moving to another placement, yes.'

Rebecca shrugged, implying that she didn't give a damn, as if all the time she had lived with Mary counted for nothing.

'So when am I going? And where?'

'You're going this evening to another carer who lives in Hill Top. But it will only be a short-term placement until they can find you something that's just right for you.'

Another shrug before she began to get out of the chair.

'I'm so sorry,' Mary said regretfully. 'But it's got to the stage where I don't feel I can't help you any more.'

'No one can help me,' Rebecca replied darkly. 'I'm a reject. A misfit. No one has ever wanted me, not even my own mother, and no one ever will.' With that she walked quietly from the room as Mary hung her head.

The house that Miss James pulled up in front of some time later was very different from Mary's. There were bicycles thrown down on the front garden and the sound of Robbie Williams singing 'Angels' was throbbing out of an open bedroom window. Rebecca had walked away from Mary without a backward glance and Miss James had felt sorry for the woman after all she had tried to do for the girl. But then she was getting used to Rebecca's blunt ways by now.

'I think you'll find the lifestyle here with Lynne and Rob rather different to Mary's,' she told Rebecca as she lifted her smart suitcase from the boot. At least she wasn't moving with her belongings in carrier bags this time. 'They have two other placements – Justin is sixteen and Kelly is nine. Their own children have left home now but they like having youngsters about the place. However, it will only be temporary, until we can find somewhere more permanent for you.'

Rebecca sniffed. It didn't really matter to her. Some time ago she had decided that she didn't even want to see Josh any more, despite the fact that he wanted to see her, and she had stuck to it. As far as she was concerned, this place would be just somewhere to sleep until she was old enough to get her own home and start searching for her real mum and dad. Nothing much mattered to her but finding them – and it would be God help them when she did. She would make them pay for the heartless way they had abandoned her.

Miss James glanced at her, but as usual Rebecca's face was devoid of any expression. Still, she consoled herself, this placement had a lot more chance of working than the last one. Lynne was used to caring for more difficult children. Children who had suffered abuse, or who had behavioural problems.

Truthfully, Rebecca's behaviour hadn't been too bad until the year before when she had got in with a gang of kids from Lamp Hill, well-known troublemakers. Rebecca had been attracted to them like a bee to honey because they didn't make fun of her or taunt her as most kids her own age did. They had accepted her into their gang and it had been downhill all the way then for Mary. Now at just twelve years old, Rebecca was already an adept shoplifter. She had taken to clearing off after school – when she went to school, that was – and finding her way into town all by herself, which Miss James knew was unacceptable. She was far too young to be doing things like that, but then Rebecca did not behave or act like an average twelve year old. Miss James had seen it happen too many times before. The puppy fat had melted away and Rebecca was tall for her age, making her appear much older than she actually was. She seemed to have no regard for anyone, apart from Pat, her aunt's neighbour, who had kept in constant touch with her since she had left Alison's home. Through Pat, Miss James had discovered that Rebecca's uncle was now out of prison, although he hadn't returned to the family home for some reason. She also knew that Amber, Rebecca's cousin, now had a little boy with another baby on the way. It didn't really surprise Miss James. She had seen it all before.

Her biggest regret was that Rebecca had point blank refused to ever see her adopted brother, Joshua, who was very keen to see her. Thankfully he was still with the same carers and doing well by all accounts, which was something to be grateful for at least. Now she hoisted Rebecca's case up and picked her way through the bicycles strewn across the garden to the front door. It was opened by a woman fashionably dressed in jogging bottoms and a pastel coloured T-shirt that showed off her slim figure. Her straight blonde hair was tied back into a ponytail and Rebecca briefly thought she didn't look old enough to have a grown-up family. She was certainly a far cry from the homely-looking carer she had just left.

'Aw, you're here then. Come on in.' She held the door wide as Miss James and Rebecca stepped into a small hallway. Coats were slung across the banister post, and two fat cats were curled up fast asleep on the bottom two steps of the stairs. 'They're Starsky and Hutch,' she told Rebecca when she saw the girl looking towards them. Rebecca didn't comment as she and Miss James followed Lynne into a surprisingly spacious lounge. A little girl was sitting on the couch in there with her eyes glued to *Buffy the Vampire Slayer* which was blaring out on the television set.

'Turn that down a bit, there's a love,' Lynne encouraged. 'We can't hear ourselves think.'

The girl gave an exaggerated sigh but did as she was told, briefly glancing at Rebecca before her attention returned to the screen again.

'Do you want to come through to the kitchen while Miss James and me get all the paperwork done out of the way – or would you rather stay in here?' Lynne asked.

Rebecca sagged onto the nearest chair without replying and Lynne shrugged as she led Miss James towards the kitchen.

'She's a barrel of laughs, ain't she?' Lynne commented once the kitchen door was closed behind them. 'I'm going to have me work cut out with this one.'

'I'm rather afraid you will,' Miss James replied honestly, then she quickly launched into a brief account of Rebecca's history.

When she had finished, Lynne whistled through her teeth. 'No wonder the poor little sod is so po-faced. What she's been through is enough to make anyone lose their sense of humour, ain't it?'

Miss James nodded in agreement as she watched Lynne fill the kettle and put it on to boil. 'She has had it tough, but the trouble is, Rebecca's got a chip on her shoulder the size of a house brick and she won't let anyone get close to her. The only one she's got any time at all for is a neighbour of her aunt and uncle who befriended her while she lived with them.'

'So why don't you let her live with this neighbour then?'

'Because her track record with Social Services when her own kids were little isn't great,' Miss James said sadly. 'Admittedly she seems to be genuine with Rebecca, and she seems to have changed, but I'd be laughed out of court if I suggested putting her there.'

'Hm, that's a shame then. But I can give it my best shot. You know me – firm but fair, so let's see how she settles.'

Miss James thoughtfully spooned sugar into the coffee Lynne had handed her. 'I'm not sure how she'll be with Rob,' she admitted to Lynne tentatively. 'She doesn't seem to get on with men very well at all.'

'Has she been abused at some time?'

Miss James shook her head. 'She shows all the classic signs of sexual abuse, but she has never disclosed anything to me. You know, wearing baggy clothes, not washing, no self-esteem, et cetera. I set up some counselling for her at one stage but that fell as flat as a pancake. She never opened her mouth once during the whole session, so it's had to be put on hold. But I haven't given up on it and I'm hoping that she'll agree to it at some stage. She certainly won't open up to me and I've tried everything, believe me. I just feel that Rebecca isn't a bad girl deep down, she's just had a rotten time of it from day one and I think that's why she behaves as she does to cover the hurt.'

'Aw well, I dare say she'll shout up if and when she's ready for it,' Lynne said philosophically and the two women then went on to talk of Rebecca's bedtime and what she did and didn't like to eat, and so on.

In the lounge, Rebecca was sitting with her arms tightly folded and a deep frown on her face. Every now and then the little girl, who Rebecca guessed must be Kelly, would glance at her, but one dark stare from Rebecca had her eyes quickly focusing on the TV again. The noise from the television and the music from upstairs seemed to be competing against each other, but suddenly the noise overhead stopped abruptly and seconds later she heard heavy footsteps pounding down the stairs. The lounge door opened and a tall gangly-looking lad with protruding teeth appeared. He was dressed in an Adidas track-suit and had a baseball cap pulled down low over his forehead.

He eyed Rebecca. 'Oh, so you're the new inmate, are yer?' he drawled as if Rebecca were being admitted to a prison. If he had hoped to frighten her he was disappointed, for she merely stared back at him coldly.

'I'm Justin, but everyone calls me Legs,' he went on. 'An' as long as you remember that I'm top dog here, you an' me will get along just fine . . . *understand*?'

Again she merely stared at him contemptuously. She could well see where he had got his nickname from – he appeared to be all arms and legs – but if he thought his hard talk was going to frighten her, he had another think coming. She hadn't knocked around with the most notorious gang of kids in Lamp Hill without learning a thing or two. Legs was at a loss what to say. Normally any new recruits to the house knew within minutes that he was not one to be crossed and respected that he was the boss, but this cocky little mare was staring back at him as if she didn't give a toss. She'd have to be taught a lesson and brought into line – at the opportune time, of course. He looked her up and down as if she was something nasty stuck to the bottom of his shoe, but still he got no reaction. She wasn't the prettiest of creatures, he found himself thinking, as he wondered how old she was. Probably about thirteen, he judged. And certainly not girlfriend material. Crossing to Lynne's handbag, which was on the dining-room table, he glanced towards the kitchen door before hurriedly opening it and helping himself to a couple of quid.

'Not a word to Lynne,' he breathed. 'Else I'll tell her *you* took it.'

As Rebecca sneered, he felt hot colour flood into his cheeks but he had no chance to wipe the smirk from her face because at that moment the door opened and Lynne and Miss James appeared.

Hastily pocketing the money, he smiled angelically. 'Oh, I was just coming to tell you I'm off to the youth club. Is that all right, Lynne? I won't be late back.'

'Of course it is.' She smiled at him. 'And I gather you've introduced yourself to Rebecca? She's going to be staying with us for a while.'

'Yes, I have – and that's nice,' he replied as if butter wouldn't melt in his mouth.

'Good lad, Justin. You get off now then. We don't want you to be late.'

She watched him leave before muttering to Miss James, 'You know, I think I'm finally getting somewhere with him. He was a right little tearaway when he arrived a few months ago, but he seems to be calming down nicely now.'

Rebecca wondered if she would still think so, if she were to tell the woman that he had just nicked money from her purse, but she didn't say anything. She already had something over him, and at the first opportunity she would use it to her advantage.

Miss James left with assurances that she would inform Pat of her new address and Lynne then showed her to her bedroom. It was small but pleasant enough. There was a single bed and a pine wardrobe with a matching chest of drawers.

'The bathroom is just along there.' Lynne pointed to a door along the landing. 'Now – house rules. You will be expected to keep your own room tidy and be in on time if you go out. You clean the bath out ready for the next person when you've used it, and you make sure you're in for mealtimes otherwise you go hungry. Do you think you can manage that?'

Rebecca shrugged as Lynne left her to unpack, quietly closing the door behind her. The silly cow could spout house rules for as long as she liked as far as Rebecca was concerned. She had already sussed that she probably wasn't going to like it there and had no intentions of staying for long anyway.

Chapter Twenty-Three

Within a week, Rebecca's first expectations of living with Lynne were confirmed. Lynne had tried her best admittedly to earn her trust, but Rebecca didn't trust anyone any more and she simply ignored all Lynne's best efforts to be kind. She hated it there and hated Legs even more. He was clearly Lynne's blue-eyed boy and took full advantage of the fact. Kelly was no problem. She was a timid kid and Rebecca forgot she was there half the time. Rob, Lynne's husband, was all right too. Very quiet and laid-back, he was happy to leave the running of the household and the care of the kids to Lynne. But Rebecca still didn't trust him. After what had happened with her Uncle Ken, she no longer trusted any male and avoided him like the plague. On the other hand, Legs was seriously getting on her pip now. She'd had a lot to contend with in the short time she'd been there – starting at yet another new school being part of it. But his continual hassle was just the final straw. In front of Lynne he was all sweetness and light, but as soon as she was out of earshot the taunting would begin.

'What's it like to have a face like the back of a bus then, kid? Cor, ain't it time you took a bath? You smell like rottin' meat! I bet *you* ain't got the lads queuin' up for a date!'

Up to now Rebecca had managed to control her temper, but now she was out for revenge and she had worked out exactly how to get it.

She had seen Legs dip into Lynne's purse on at least four more occasions over the week, but had noted he was always careful never to take enough to be missed. Just tonight she'd seen another one pound fifty disappear into his pocket before he left for the youth club in town. Now, once she was sure that he would be well on his way, she chose her moment and crossed to Lynne's purse. A quick glance around to make sure that she was alone, and then two ten-pound notes were quickly tucked away into her pocket.

It was the following morning before Lynne realised the money was missing and she kicked off bigtime.

'Some sticky-fingered little sod has been in my purse,' she snapped when she opened it to dole out their dinner-money for school.

Legs instantly looked towards Rebecca, his face a picture of innocence. 'Well, I don't want to be a grass, but I thought I saw her hovering round your bag just before I went out last night.'

Lynne whirled round to Rebecca, her eyes blazing. It must have been the new girl who had taken it. Justin and Kelly had never stolen off her before, so who else could it be?

'Empty out your pockets,' she ordered.

Looking her straight in the eye, Rebecca did as she was told. Nothing!

Lynne glared at her. 'Well, we ain't got time to argue about it now else you'll be late for school. But don't you worry – I'll find it if I have to tip your bedroom inside out. I don't put up with stealing!'

Rebecca sauntered away with a defiant look in her eye, pausing only to grin at Legs, who suddenly felt uneasy. He certainly hadn't risked taking that much money from Lynne's purse at one time, so it *had* to be her – but why was she grinning at him like that? Deciding that there wasn't much he could do about it for now, he snatched up his bag and flounced away as Rebecca watched him go with an amused twinkle in her eye. Now she'd show him who was boss!

Once all the children had left for school, Lynne fumed her way through two cups of coffee before going upstairs to tackle the bedrooms. It was her day for changing the beds and whilst she was about it she fully intended to search every inch of that little minx's room. She had tried really hard with her, even more so since hearing what a bad time the poor kid had had of it. But all her attempts to get close to her were flung back in her face and she was getting frustrated, although she was experienced enough to know that it was still very early days. If Rebecca had had the money, then Lynne was determined to find it even if she had to tear her room apart. She'd had quite a few foster-kids now and was wise to all their little hiding places.

She tackled Kelly's room first as this was always the easiest, and while she was at it she had a cursory peek in all her drawers, just in case. As she'd expected she found no sign of the money, so she moved on to Justin's room. She would leave Rebecca's until last, guessing that she would need to spend more time in there. First she stripped the sheets from his bed and remade it with fresh ones, then she began a quick search through his drawers, not that she expected to find anything but it wouldn't hurt to look. As she had thought, the search turned up nothing. Stooping to gather up the dirty laundry, she turned to leave and it was then that she spotted a book on his bedside table. But what was that poking out of the top of it? Dumping the laundry onto the floor again she crossed to the book and opened it, and as she did so two ten-pound notes were revealed. Lynne gasped with shock. So Rebecca was not the thief, after all! It just went to show how wrong she could be, although she would never have suspected Justin of robbing her.

White rage bubbled through her veins. He'd feel the length of her tongue when he got home, all right – and he could bloody well apologise to Rebecca as well.

Rebecca felt as if she was walking into World War Three when she got home that afternoon. Justin and Lynne were in the kitchen and she could hear their raised voices from the hallway.

'How *dare* you steal from me?' Lynne ranted. 'And then to try and blame the new kid . . . it's unforgivable.'

Rebecca smirked as she hung her coat up. She'd just had time to sneak into Justin's room that morning and hide the money in his book when he went down to breakfast. But it had been a close thing and she couldn't be sure that Kelly hadn't caught her coming out of his room. Still, if she said she had seen her, Rebecca would just deny it and brazen it out: she was good at that now.

As she walked into the kitchen looking the picture of innocence, Lynne instantly told Justin, 'Now you just apologise to Rebecca for accusing her of stealing my money – *go on*!'

'I bloody well won't!' he stormed, his hands clenched into fists. 'She must have gone into my room and planted the money there.'

'Oh yes, *of course* she did, and there's a purple pig flying past the window – look!' Lynne clearly didn't believe him and that seemed to incense him all the more.

'I didn't take it!' he bellowed, red in the face with rage. He was furious at the false accusation.

Rebecca cast her eyes down, looking suitably upset as Lynne went on, 'I don't believe a word of it, so save your breath, young man, and consider yourself grounded until further notice!'

He seemed to swell to twice his size. 'That ain't fair! I never took it, I tell you! And there's no way I'm saying sorry to her for sommat I didn't do.'

'Suit yourself,' Lynne huffed, equally as determined as he was. 'But be warned, until you do you'll not set foot out of that door again, apart from going to school. Now get to your room and think about what you've done!'

Legs stormed away, casting a venomous glance at Rebecca as he passed her.

'Look, love, I'm sorry I assumed it was you that had taken the money,' Lynne said, once he had stamped away to his room. 'It was unfair of me. Can we start again?'

Rebecca nodded before heading for the lounge where she sat with a wide satisfied smile on her face. And this was only the beginning. She had barely even started with Legs yet, but by the time she'd done with him, he'd wish he'd never set eyes on her.

The atmosphere between Rebecca and Legs was somewhat strained to say the least for the next two weeks. Legs longed to smack the smug smile off Rebecca's face every time she silently taunted him, but he knew that would only make things worse. Lynne had decided he was guilty and nothing would change her mind now. He'd learned that some time ago. The bitch had even called his social worker in to 'chastise him'. She was a prim-faced, rounded little woman who always looked as if she was sucking a wasp, and Legs had nicknamed her Mother Teresa – not that he was brave enough to call her that to her face, of course.

'I am *most* disappointed in you, Justin,' she had told him righteously as she balanced her china cup on her saucer.

Legs had been forced to look away rather than give her a mouthful.

'Stealing is a heinous sin,' she'd gone on. 'Especially from Lynne, who has been so *very* kind to you.'

Legs stifled the urge to tell the pompous old bint to 'piss off'. He was sick of being grounded now and just wanted to get out and about again. He'd bide his time before he paid Rebecca back, but when he did she'd bloody well know about it, he was determined about that.

And now at last the curfew was lifted and he could hardly wait to gollop his tea down and get out with his mates again. At school earlier in the day they'd arranged to go joy-riding – if they could hotwire a decent car, that was.

Unknown to him, Rebecca had overheard them and had every intention of going along if there was half a chance. It shouldn't be that difficult to get out. Her school did a disco each week for the First Years, and Lynne had been encouraging her to go, saying that it would do her good to make some friends her own age. She could sod that! Girls her age held no attraction for Rebecca at all. They were a lot of sissies. All they could talk about was boys and make-up, which she found utterly boring. She didn't like Legs and made no secret of the fact, but she did miss being part of a gang, and if she could get in with his then she was prepared to be a little nicer to him.

Lynne was delighted when Rebecca mentioned over tea that she might just give the disco a go and hurried away to Rebecca's room to choose something suitable for her to wear.

Rebecca cringed when she saw the outfit that Lynne had chosen. A skirt and top that would make her look about seven years old. She put it on all the same. She could hardly say she was going in her uniform, after all.

She waited impatiently while Lynne fussed over her hair, insisting that she should wear it loose. Legs had been gone for a good five minutes already and if Rebecca didn't get a move on she knew that she would have no chance of following him. But then at last, Lynne was satisfied and she turned Rebecca around to look in the dressing-table mirror.

'See how pretty you are when you make a bit of an effort,' she cooed like a mother hen. 'Now do you want Rob to run you there?'

'Oh no, I'll be fine,' Rebecca assured her hastily. 'I don't want him to miss the Olympics highlights.' He had commandeered the TV for the whole of the last week from the moment he got in from work.

'Well, if you're sure you'll be all right,' Lynne said uncertainly. 'Off you go then and have a lovely time. But mind you're not late home.'

Rebecca bombed away, yanking the stupid slides out of her hair as she went, and didn't stop until she had turned the corner into Marner Road. And there he was up ahead of her, his hands in his pockets, whistling merrily as he sauntered along.

'Here, Legs, hold up!'

He turned to see who was calling him and when he spotted her, his lip curled.

'What do *you* want?'

'Well, I got to thinking that if we've got to live in the same house we ought to try and get along,' Rebecca said breathlessly. 'And I'm sorry about getting you into trouble about the money, but I was fed up with you calling me names all the time.'

'Is that so?' He leaned down until his face was dangerously close to hers. 'Problem is, I don't *wanna* be mates with a little geek like you. Me mates would laugh me off the planet if I turned up with you in tow. So *piss off* and leave me alone if you know what's good for you!'

Rebecca's lips set into a grim line as he turned and strode away from her. So . . . he didn't want her in his gang, eh? Even after she'd apologised and given him the chance to be friends instead of enemies. Well, now he'd be sorry.

Keeping close to the hedges and fences that bordered the gardens, she followed him through the estate until the fields that led to Bermuda Village came into view. A gang of youths and girls of various ages had congregated on the fence there and when they saw Legs they called out to him. One was swigging from a large bottle of cider, which he then passed around, and another of the boys had his tongue down the throat of a girl who was wearing the shortest mini-skirt Rebecca had ever seen. She crouched behind a tree until they moved off across the fields. Then, after biding her time, she crept after them. Eventually the group split up and Rebecca continued to tail Legs and two other boys as they headed towards Bermuda Village. It was getting dark now, which made it slightly easier. Once they came to the village she saw them approach a man who was standing beneath a lamp-post. He was dressed in denim jeans with a hoodie pulled low over his face, and after a few moments' conversation one of the lads handed him some money in exchange for what appeared to be some small plastic bags.

Rebecca grinned. So Legs and Co were into drugs, were they? She had recognised the wraps instantly as the same that the gang she had associated with in Lamp Hill had used. All she had to do now was bide her time and she could get Legs into yet more trouble. He'd regret refusing her entry into his gang before she was finished with him. But now she knew that the time must be getting on, and if she didn't get herself home she too would be in trouble. Melting into the darkness, she hurried back the way she had come.

Chapter Twenty-Four

'Off to the disco again tonight, are you, love?' Lynne asked pleasantly a week later as she loaded two fat lamb chops onto Rebecca's plate at dinner.

Avoiding Legs's eyes, Rebecca nodded. Lynne wouldn't allow her to wander the streets, but if she thought she was going to the disco with other girls from the estate along well-lit roads, she would have no objection to her going out.

Rebecca once again reluctantly succumbed to Lynne's attempts at making her pretty before escaping as quickly as she could. A few days ago she had crept into Legs's bedroom, and after a scout around had managed to find one of the wraps he had bought off the drug dealer the week before, hidden in his sock drawer. It was in a safe place now, and one day soon she might use it against him – but not until the time was right and not until she'd given him another chance to have a change of heart. She still missed being part of a gang. When she had knocked about with the Lamp Hill gang she had felt a sense of power. With them she was no longer the spotty-faced kid that everyone made fun of, but someone to fear. Now she wanted to feel that thrill again, but Legs was standing in her way. She would ask him just once more to allow her to join his gang and if he still refused, he would have to be punished.

Speeding along the street, she saw him up ahead and making no effort to hide this time she yelled, 'Legs – wait!'

She skidded breathlessly up to him. 'Look, how about we start again?' she began. 'I really want to be part of your gang, OK? It could be great, you know.'

'Fuck off!' he said, looking her up and down with hostility. 'Why, we wouldn't let a skanky little kid like you in our gang for anythin' – so like I said before, piss off, unless you want a good hidin'.'

Rebecca's nostrils flared with anger. 'You'll be sorry for this,' she said threateningly.

Legs threw back his head and laughed aloud. 'Yeah, right. I'm fuckin' terrified.' With that he swaggered away, leaving Rebecca feeling utterly humiliated. Until the anger set in again, that was, and then her eyes glittered dangerously. 'Right, meladdo, you asked for this,' she muttered, and set off after him, once more keeping a safe distance.

This time he met his group on Coventry Road, and she followed them down the Griff Hollows. It was easy to stay out of sight as the lane was tree-lined. At the bottom of the Hollows a car was parked, no doubt by someone who had chosen to go fishing, and Legs and his followers descended on it like a plague of locusts.

'Christ, we've hit the jackpot here,' she heard Legs mutter gleefully. 'It's one o' them new Mondeos. Kyle, get a brick or sommat. We'll smash the window and hotwire it before the owner comes back.'

Rebecca turned and raced back the way she had come. Now was the time for Legs to get his comeuppance, if she had anything to do about it. Halfway up the hill was a red phone box; she snatched the door open and hastily dialled 999. Seconds later, she left the box and hid behind a tree to wait. Sure enough, within a couple of minutes the sound of sirens pierced the air and she saw a police car speed past. Running now, she got back down the hill just in time to see a police officer bundle Legs and one of his cronies into the back of the police car. The rest of the gang had done a runner and were probably halfway to Bedworth by now, but she didn't care about them. All she cared about was getting her revenge on Legs – and she'd done that all right.

'You're early, aren't you?' Lynne said when she arrived home soon after.

'Oh, I had a bit of a headache so I thought I'd come back early,' Rebecca said sweetly.

Lynne frowned. She wasn't too happy about Rebecca walking home alone, but then she had been honest, so she decided she'd let it go this time.

'Well, you go up and get tucked in then,' she said kindly. 'I'll bring you a nice cup of cocoa up in a bit.'

Rebecca nodded and went without a murmur. As she passed the lounge she saw that Rob was glued to the TV again. He'd be off to the copshop soon to bail Rob out, if everything went to plan.

Once upstairs she hastily changed into her nightie before going to keep watch from the bedroom window – and sure enough, within no time at all a police car drew up outside.

Hopping into bed she lay and listened to the sharp rap on the door and then Lynne's shout of anger as the officer explained what had happened. Shortly afterwards, Rob went off to the station with the police and she heard Lynne banging about downstairs. Rebecca gloated. She didn't mind betting Legs wouldn't be feeling so clever now; she wouldn't have wanted to be in his shoes.

It was gone ten o'clock when Rob and Legs finally got home. Rebecca had dozed off but the sound of raised voices echoing from downstairs woke her up. Lynne was giving Legs a right roasting by the sounds of it but it served him right.

Now all she had to do was put the icing on the cake the following morning.

Legs was very subdued at breakfast. Rob had left for work over an hour ago and Lynne was banging about the kitchen, obviously in a vile mood.

'Why aren't you in your school uniform?' Rebecca asked innocently.

'He won't be going in today, his social worker is coming in to see him first thing,' Lynne told her shortly. 'I'm wondering now why I ever talked him into staying on for another year,' she ranted on. 'The way he's heading, he'll end up in a remand centre instead of a good job.'

'Well, I'd better get off, else I'll be late,' Rebecca said, standing up – and then, as if it was an afterthought, she added, 'Oh, and by the way – you dropped this on the landing this morning, Justin.'

Making sure that Lynne was watching, she flashed him an angelic smile as she pushed the wrap she had found in his room into the middle of the table.

Lynne seemed to freeze for a second before leaping on it and waving it in the air. 'This is drugs!' she screeched. '*DRUGS!* As if you ain't in enough trouble trying to steal a car! Well, this is the end of the line here for you, young man. I'll put up with most things but I'll not have drugs in my house, not with two young innocent girls here.'

Rebecca batted her eyelashes as if she didn't have a clue what Lynne was on about as Legs glared at her menacingly. *The little bitch.* She must have stolen that from his room. He'd wondered where it had gone. And he wouldn't be surprised if it wasn't her who had called the police and dobbed him in the night before, either. They had told him they'd had a tip-off from an anonymous caller, and he didn't have to be the Brain of Britain to put two and two together!

Lynne was ushering Kelly and Rebecca out of the room as if she couldn't bear them to be in the same room as him any more, and Rebecca went meekly although she couldn't resist one last peep over her shoulder at him.

His hands were bunched into fists and the girl felt a thrill of satisfaction. She'd taught him a lesson he wouldn't forget in a hurry.

She arrived at school to find it was alive with gossip. News of Legs's arrest the night before had spread quickly. Usually all the kids ignored her, but suddenly she was everyone's best friend and they all wanted to talk to her. She lived in the same house as Legs, after all, and they knew she would be able to inform them about what was happening first-hand.

'Is it true then?' asked a youth with the worst case of acne she had ever seen. 'Did Legs really get arrested last night for tryin' to nick a car?'

Basking in the attention, Rebecca nodded affirmatively.

'Is he still at the copshop?'

A crowd was gathering now as Rebecca swelled with importance.

'No, they let him come home with Rob last night.'

'So what's gonna happen to him now?'

Rebecca shrugged indifferently.

'An' is it true that Kyle Harris got arrested an' all?'

Again she nodded, mindful of a teacher striding towards them.

'What's going on here?' Mr Briggs bellowed and instantly the crowd began to disperse.

'We were just chatting, sir,' Rebecca told him innocently

before turning and making her way into the school. She was confident that the interrogation would begin again as soon as the bell for break sounded and was looking forward to it immensely. It was true what they said – revenge *was* sweet.

The day proved to be the best Rebecca had ever spent at school. Kids approached her, repeatedly asking questions and hanging on every word she said. Until the afternoon break, that was, when one boy in particular singled her out in the playground. Rebecca recognised him instantly as Brad, one of the boys from Legs's gang who had done a runner the night before and left Kyle and Legs to face the music.

'Word's all round school that you know what happened last night,' Brad said to her.

Rebecca nodded, a wide smile on her face.

'So how come *you're* so genned up on what went on then?' he asked suspiciously.

Rebecca faltered for a second as she realised her mistake before bluffing, 'Well, I heard Lynne going on about it at breakfast this morning. And I heard them talking to him when he got home from the police station with Rob last night.'

'Hmm!' Well aware that she knew he was part of the gang, his eyes narrowed to slits as he studied her. 'It's funny how someone called the cops on us, ain't it? There weren't a soul about in the Hollows, an' Legs had just mentioned that he'd told you to piss off . . . It weren't *you* that grassed us up, were it?'

'Of course it wasn't!' Rebecca denied hotly, but he'd seen the look of triumph in her eyes and didn't believe a word of it.

Leaning in close, he muttered, 'I'd watch me back if I was you, little 'un, and don't even *think* o' mentionin' my name to the cops, 'cos I shall be havin' a word wi' Legs the first chance I get, an' I can safely say he ain't goin' to be none too pleased wi' what I tell him.'

'Suit yourself,' Rebecca put her nose in the air and walked

away in a huff, none too happy at the sudden turn of events. It had been quite nice to be the centre of attention for a change, instead of having to skulk in corners and keep out of everyone's way. But the experience had been very short-lived, and if Brad put the word about now, she knew that her life wouldn't be worth living. Still, what else was new? Rebecca was used to being the outcast now; the misfit whom no one wanted to know, so no change there.

There was a review going on back at Lynne's that afternoon when Rebecca got home. Lynne instantly ushered her into the kitchen to join Kelly, who was drinking a glass of milk at the table. But not before Rebecca had glimpsed a policeman and Legs's social worker in the lounge as well as a number of people she didn't recognise.

'We have called an emergency case conference for tomorrow,' Rebecca heard the social worker say before Lynne closed the kitchen door behind her.

'What's going on?' she asked, all wide-eyed innocence as Lynne poured milk into another glass.

'I dare say you may as well know,' the woman said resignedly. 'No doubt it will be all around the estate in no time anyway. Legs tried to steal a car last night and got caught by the police – and that packet you found on the landing this morning contained drugs.'

'Oh,' Rebecca said, pretending to be shocked. 'What will happen now? Will he go to prison?'

'He could get sent to a remand centre,' Lynne answered, her voice heavy with concern, 'but no one knows for sure until he goes to court. What we do know is he's in serious trouble. But it's nothing for you to worry about. We'll sort it.'

Rebecca sipped at her milk primly, all sweetness and light, as Lynne turned to go back into the meeting asking, 'Would you just keep your eye on Kelly for me until the meeting's over?'

'Of course,' Rebecca said obligingly. Once Lynne had disappeared back into the lounge, Rebecca licked her milky moustache and grinned. Perhaps things weren't going to be as bad as she'd thought. After all, no one could prove that it was she who had rung the police, could they?

The mood in the house was subdued once all the visitors had left, although if looks could have killed, Rebecca would have dropped down dead each time Legs glanced in her direction. She didn't much care. What could he do anyway? He would be far too scared to drop himself into yet more trouble, and she intended to milk the situation for all it was worth.

Brad Johnson called round for him after dinner, but when Lynne answered the door she told him frostily that Legs was grounded until further notice.

'Can't I just have a word?' Brad asked persuasively.

Lynne faltered, then told him, 'All right – but make it quick.'

Seconds later, Legs was down at the door with him, their heads bent close together.

Rebecca had an awful feeling that this might not go in her favour, and when Legs re-entered the room she knew that her instincts had been right. Legs looked like he was about to explode with rage, although of course he had more sense than to say anything in front of his carers. He had suspected that it was Rebecca who had dobbed him in, but now he was sure of it – and somehow he would make the little cow pay for what she'd done!

Chapter Twenty-Five

Two weeks later, Pat landed on Lynne's doorstep to pay her customary monthly visit to Rebecca.

Lynne didn't wholly approve of Pat, but as this woman was the only person in the world for whom Rebecca appeared to have any feelings, she allowed the visits to go ahead.

Pat found Rebecca a little subdued. As she warmed her frozen hands at the gas fire she asked, 'What's up, pet? You've got a face on yer like a wet weekend.'

Rebecca glanced towards the kitchen door where she could hear Lynne clattering about, making the visitor a cup of tea.

'Oh, Legs has gone and got himself into trouble and the atmosphere here isn't very nice at the minute.'

'What's he done then?' Pat shrugged her coat off and settled herself into one of the comfortable armchairs as Rebecca told her all about it. When she was done, Pat whistled through her teeth.

'Silly young bugger, him. But why should what he's done affect you?'

'Everyone at school thinks I'm the one that grassed him up to the police,' Rebecca told her, being very careful to play the innocent party. 'And . . . well, there are a lot of threats being thrown around.'

Pat's chest puffed with indignation. 'And have you told Lynne about this?'

Rebecca nodded miserably. 'Yes, but she says to just keep my head down and it will all blow over.'

'Happen she's right,' Pat said wisely. 'That is, unless there's anythin' in what they're sayin'?'

'Of course there isn't!' Rebecca felt colour flood into her cheeks but set her chin stubbornly as Lynne came back into the room balancing a cup of tea and a plate of biscuits on a tray.

'She's told you what's going on with Justin then?' Lynne enquired as she saw Rebecca's downcast expression.

'Yes, she has – an' she's told me she's bein' bullied an' all. What are you doing about it?'

'Look, perhaps it would be better if we had a little chat in the kitchen?' Lynne suggested tactfully, glancing towards Kelly who was hanging on their every word.

Rebecca folded her arms across her chest with a dark expression on her face as the two women sidled away. Kelly turned her attention back to the TV now that there was no one to earwig, so Rebecca went and placed herself strategically on the chair next to the kitchen door.

Making a great play of examining her nails she strained to hear what was being said beyond the door.

'So?' Pat was the first to start the conversation. 'What's going on then?'

'I'm afraid I'm not too sure that Rebecca is as innocent in all this as she says she is,' Lynne confided. 'And as for the bullying – well, I've spoken to the school but they say that nine times out of ten it's Rebecca herself that does the bullying. She's a tough little cookie, ain't she? What I mean is, I've done my best to make her feel welcome since she's been here, but it's as if she doesn't trust anyone, myself included. I know she had a hard time at her aunt's, but surely she should be over that by now?'

'Huh! Livin' with her aunt was only the tip of the iceberg,' Pat snorted. 'Poor little sod has had it rough since the day she was born, one way and another. But then you'd already have been told that, no doubt.'

Pat lowered her voice considerably but Rebecca discovered that if she inched the chair a little closer to the door she could still hear what she was saying. She didn't care that Kelly was watching her now, quite aware of what she was doing. If they were talking about her then she had every right to listen!

'On the day Rebecca was found, her mam had left her at the back o' the Wellsgrave Hospital,' Pat said quietly and Lynne nodded.

'Yes, I already know that. Her mother was a prostitute, wasn't she?'

Pat lowered her eyes and shrugged. 'Who is to say? Maybe she had to do that, to feed her family. From what I heard, she dropped for Rebecca while her husband was in nick. Well, it stood to reason that the poor bugger couldn't keep her, didn't it? I mean, her husband were a thug by all accounts and he'd have battered the living daylights out of her if he'd come out to find her with another sprog he hadn't fathered. Two young nurses found the baby apparently, and then she were shipped off to different foster-homes for a while. When she was a few months old, Fay – that was her aunt's sister, and her husband, Gordon – adopted her, so you might say Rebecca had landed on her feet. They were well off, see? But it didn't quite work out like that. From what Alison told me, Rebecca was an ugly little cuss when she was a baby. I find that hard to believe meself 'cos I've always thought Rebecca could be a bonny girl if she had a bit o' confidence in herself. But anyway, it seems Fay doted on her but not for the right reasons. Fay were a lovely-looking girl, see, and I think she spent most of the time tryin' to turn Rebecca into a little

Barbie doll. Not that she succeeded. Alison reckons she were always a bit of a disappointment to her and that she only took her because she were so desperate to have a little girl. And then Fay got cancer, so Alison took Rebecca to help out. Well, that's what she says, but between you an' me I know she only took her because Gordon was slipping her back-handers to keep the kid. Sadly, Fay died and Gordon went to pieces. Rebecca has an adopted brother, as you probably know. Joshua, his name is, and it must have hurt the poor girl when her adopted dad chose to keep him at home with him and not her. Then Gordon goes and tops himself, don't he? Alison were spittin' feathers 'cos she thought her and Ken would cop for the inheritance. Trouble was, he left most of it in trust for Josh when he comes of age. And the rest you know. You're the second set of foster-carers she's had since they died, but she's never really had any stability in her life, so it's no wonder she's put up barriers.'

Rebecca heard Lynne's sharp intake of breath. 'But she seems to look forward to seeing *you*,' she pointed out.

'Aw well, that's probably 'cos when she was livin' with her aunt an' uncle I was the only one who ever took the time to show her a bit of decent kindness. Now I ain't professin' to be no saint, but every kid needs *someone* to care about 'em, don't they?'

'I suppose they do.' Lynne suddenly wished that she'd tried harder with Rebecca after hearing such a sad story. Of course the social worker had given her basic information, but somehow hearing Pat expand on it made it all the more heart-breaking. It was no wonder the girl was the way she was.

In the lounge the colour had drained from Rebecca's face. Her real mum had been a *prostitute*! She knew what that word meant now because she had heard some of the girls at school talking about it. They were bad women – dirty women – who let men do the horrible things her uncle had done to her for money. Her mother hadn't wanted her, and neither had Fay – not really, if what Pat was saying was true. Thinking back, she believed it. Her adoptive mum had never really loved her. Rebecca had been a disappointment to her because she wasn't pretty, and Fay had been more obsessed with trying to turn her into the little girl she wanted her to be rather than loving her for herself. The truth cut deep. And truthfully, although he had always been kind to her, she had always known deep down that her adoptive dad had never really bonded with her. Josh had always been his favourite and he had just tolerated her. And then there was Aunt Alison and Uncle Ken . . . Suddenly she remembered what her aunt had said to her mum on that long-ago birthday, *Couldn't you have waited for a prettier one?*

Even they had never liked her, not really, and now she understood why they had taken her in. It wasn't out of the goodness of their hearts, it was for money, and when her dad died and the money dried up, her aunt had shoved her into foster-care.

She could feel a big choking lump swelling in her throat as she dashed blindly from the room. Once upstairs, she flung herself onto her bed and there she did what she rarely allowed herself to do. She cried as if her heart would break.

If Rebecca had seemed somewhat stand-offish in the lead-up to that night, over the following weeks she distanced herself even further from everyone. Lynne noticed but was so taken up in preparing Legs for court that she didn't have time to do anything about it.

Rebecca came home from school one blustery day to find Lynne and Rob in the kitchen. There was no sign of Legs but she knew that they had gone to court with him that day.

'Justin has been sent away to a residential unit,' Lynne informed her.

'Is that like a prison?' Rebecca asked.

Lynne glanced at Rob for support. 'Well, not a prison exactly. It's more like a home for bad lads.'

Funnily enough, Rebecca almost felt sorry for him now. After all, Legs had had a bad beginning like her. No one had cared about him either, but there was nothing she could do about it now. Nodding, she slipped away to her room to think about it.

It was on her way home from school the following day that Brad and his gang appeared as if by magic as she passed the Jubilee Sports Centre in Greenmoor Road.

'Psst, come here,' he urged from the shelter of some trees in the surrounding playing-fields.

Rebecca's steps faltered and that was her undoing. Before she knew it, two of Brad's cronies had dragged her into the bushes.

'What do you want?' she asked, showing no flicker of fear although her insides had turned to jelly.

'Proud of yerself, are yer?' Brad ground out. 'Legs has been sent away an' it's all 'cos of you.'

Rebecca stuck her chin defiantly in the air and made to walk away, but two of the bigger lads had a firm hold of her arms and her strength was nothing compared to theirs. Brad had produced a large length of wood, and now he brandished it at her threateningly.

'We reckon you need to be taught a little lesson,' he told her, and that was when Rebecca began to struggle – not that it did much good.

The first blow caught her full in the stomach and knocked the wind out of her, and as she sank to her knees the boys all joined in, kicking and punching her. She curled up into a ball and tried to protect herself as best she could as tears of humiliation poured down her cheeks. The tops of her legs were warm and sticky, and her shame increased as she realised that she had wet herself.

Eventually she heard a voice say, 'That's enough now, Brad. You'll kill her at this rate.'

She felt someone drag him off her as vomit rose in her throat, and then his nose was pressed against hers and he told her, 'Breathe a word to anyone about this, an' I'll finish you off proper next time. Do you understand?'

'Y-yes,' Rebecca croaked. Her lips were swelling and one eye was shutting already.

Giving her one last hefty kick in the guts for good luck, Brad walked away with his mates swaggering closely behind as Rebecca lay there trembling. She felt as if she had been run over by a steamroller and wondered how she was going to get home. She wasn't even sure that she could get up, but fear of lying there in the dark made her drag herself to her knees and when the dizziness passed she slowly hauled herself to her feet.

The trip home seemed to take forever and the second she walked through the door, Lynne flew into a panic.

'Good God above!' She raced to Rebecca's side and put her arm round her. 'What the hell has happened to you? Who did this to you?'

'No one,' Rebecca said sullenly through swollen lips as she gingerly lowered herself into a chair.

'What do you mean – no one!' Lynne said angrily. 'You'd better tell me right now before I phone the police.'

'No! Don't do that!' Rebecca caught Lynne's arm. 'I don't want the police. I . . . I had a fight.'

Lynne stared at her incredulously. 'You had a fight? Who with? The Incredible Hulk! Look at the state of you. We need to get you to a hospital and get you checked out. There could be something broken.'

'There isn't,' Rebecca told her dully. 'I'm just sore, that's all.'

'Well, I'm still taking you to the hospital anyway,' Lynne said adamantly, snatching up her car keys, then shouting through to the lounge to Rob she asked him, 'Would you keep your eye on Kelly? I'm taking Rebecca to the hospital. She says she's been in a fight.'

He instantly appeared in the door and gawped when he saw the state of her. 'Christ, you poor kid.' He looked really horrified but Rebecca ignored him as she allowed Lynne to lead her upstairs to get washed and changed, then out to the car. She didn't want to go to the hospital but at least she'd managed to put Lynne off getting the police involved – for now anyway.

Two hours later she walked back out of the A & E Department with her wounds cleaned and dressed, and with assurances that nothing was broken.

'I suppose that's something,' Lynne grumbled as she drove them home. 'But I think you've got some explaining to do, young lady.'

Rebecca shrank down in her seat. 'It was just an argument, that's all,' she mumbled resentfully.

'Who with?' Lynne was like a dog with a bone and clearly not ready to let this go without some explanation.

'Just some girl I bumped into on the way home,' Rebecca lied. 'She started calling me names and the next thing I knew we were brawling.'

'Would you recognise her again?'

Rebecca immediately shook her head. 'No, it all happened so quickly. I can't even remember what colour hair she had. I'd never seen her before.'

'Hmm!' Lynne didn't believe her and wondered if this had something to do with Justin being sent away. She was no fool and knew that Justin had been convinced that it was Rebecca who had called the police on the night he had tried to steal the car. Could it be that his mates had taken justice into their own hands? This was the most likely answer – but what could she do if Rebecca refused to tell her about it? And if she pursued it, would she be making things worse? The doctor had established that Rebecca wasn't badly injured, after all. It was mainly cuts, bruises and a large dose of dented pride. She would have to give this serious thought before she decided which course of action to take. For now she simply asked, 'How are you feeling?'

'I'm fine.'

She's a gutsy little sod, I have to give her that, Lynne thought, and she then lapsed into silence for the rest of the way home. Rebecca clearly wasn't in the mood for conversation.

Chapter Twenty-Six

Rebecca managed to wangle the next two days off school, pleading that she was sore, but on the third day, Lynne put her foot down and insisted that she should be well enough to go back by now.

Rebecca scowled her way through breakfast and left the house without uttering a word, but she didn't head for school. Instead she made her way to the woods at the bottom of the Griff Hollows, fully intending to make herself scarce for the day. There was little chance of anyone discovering her there and there were plenty of places to hide should anyone come looking for her. She spent the morning sheltering beneath an enormous oak tree but then she got bored so she came back out of the woods onto Coventry Road and headed for the Pingles Fields. She'd heard the kids at school say that there was a circus arriving there today, and as it was midday there would be little chance of bumping into anyone she knew. She took the short cut through Coton churchyard, pausing every now and again to read the inscriptions on the gravestones. And then she dashed across the main road and stood admiring the Big Top. It was enormous, but apart from some men who were sprinkling fresh sawdust onto the floor inside the ring, it was deserted. They gave her a cursory glance but then went back to what they were doing, clearly not interested in a spotty-faced kid with a black eye who was doubtless playing hookey from school.

Across the field was a line of trailers and caravans, and outside one of them, a tall attractive lady with striking blonde hair was training a number of small Papillon dogs. On the side of her van *Madam Gina and her Dancing Butterfly Dogs* was painted in large, brightly-coloured letters. Rebecca watched from a distance as the woman put the dogs through their paces.

'Come on, Honey,' she cooed to a small rust- and white-coloured dog. Rebecca grinned as the animal leaped through the hoop the woman was holding waist-high.

'Good girl.' The woman fed the tiny dog a treat from the pocket of her tracksuit bottoms before turning her attention to another two. 'Now Tinkerbell and Tilly, it's your turn,' she encouraged.

Rebecca stood there for some time utterly entranced until the woman suddenly spotted her from the corner of her eye. 'Shouldn't you be at school, pet?' she called in a broad Yorkshire accent.

Rebecca flushed. 'No!' she lied.

The woman shrugged. 'That's enough for now,' she told her little pack, and began to usher them into a large trailer without even glancing in Rebecca's direction.

The girl kicked at a stone before wandering off to watch the men erecting the stalls and the rides that surrounded the Big Top. Everywhere was hustle and bustle and she found herself thinking how exciting it must be, to be a part of it all. But there was little chance of her ever belonging to a circus, even when she was old enough. Everyone here seemed to be good-looking, so where could *she* ever fit in? She was plain; she only had to look into a mirror to confirm that, even if everyone wasn't always telling her.

Guessing that the time must be moving on now, she headed back to Lynne's house with a heavy heart, praying that Lynne wouldn't have already found out that she had wagged another day off school.

The second that she set foot through the door she knew that her prayer had gone unanswered. Lynne's face was straight and unsmiling, and her social worker was there looking equally angry.

'So where have you been, miss?' Lynne demanded. 'And don't get telling me any more of your lies and saying you've been to school because I know you haven't. The Headmaster rang earlier on to ask how you were and I had to tell him that you should be there.'

Bitter resentment rose in Rebecca's throat.

'I didn't feel like going,' she replied cockily. 'So I didn't.'

Lynne looked towards Miss James and spread her hands in a helpless gesture as if to say, *see what I mean?*

Miss James sighed heavily before asking, 'So where have you been, Rebecca?'

'Here and there.' Rebecca slung her bag down and crossed her arms defiantly.

The two women exchanged a glance and then looking vaguely uncomfortable, Miss James began, 'Look, dear, I know you've had a lot of upheavals in your life, but the thing is, Lynne doesn't feel that this placement is working and so . . . well, the long and the short of it is I'm going to be looking for another home for you.'

Rebecca felt as if someone had thumped her in the stomach. 'But I haven't been here long,' she gasped before she could stop herself. She was going to be on the move again? But then no one ever wanted her for long, so why should Lynne and Rob be any different?

'Well, you know this was never intended to be a long-term arrangement,' Miss James explained.

'When will I be going and where?' she asked as Lynne guiltily averted her eyes.

'I'm afraid I can't answer either of those questions yet,' Miss James said. 'But as soon as I've located another suitable placement I'll be in touch. It shouldn't be long though – probably within the week, although I can't promise that you'll be staying in this area. You could possibly go to Warwick, Kenilworth or Leamington.'

She might have been talking about the other side of the world. Rebecca had no idea where any of those places were. It would mean yet another new school, another set of kids to make fun of her. Her stomach churned with apprehension, but her face showed no sign of emotion. She was good at hiding her feelings now.

'Fine,' she snapped, and walked back out of the house without so much as another word.

'Rebecca, come back here!' she heard Lynne shout, but she completely ignored her and in no time at all found herself back in the Pingles Fields, and once more in front of the big caravan where she had seen the woman putting her dogs through their paces. It was dusk now and lights were beginning to go on, giving everything a magical air as everyone prepared for the first performance. An enormous man in a clown's costume walked past her as if she was invisible, and when she peeped into the Big Top she saw the trapeze artists practising their show high up under the roof.

Rebecca was totally fascinated by it all, and her eyes shone as she stuck to the shadows and watched everything from a distance. Soon some men entered the ring and began to juggle, whilst a midget dressed in another clown's costume waddled around the ring checking that all the seats were in the correct places. It seemed that everyone had their jobs to do, even the performers who were now in costume, and they did them quickly and efficiently.

Soon, hordes of people began to form a queue at the box office where one of the girls who had been practising earlier on the trapeze was busily selling tickets with a loose dress thrown over her elaborate sparkling costume.

Rebecca stayed as long as she dared whilst a small band practised in the side of the enormous tent, and then she slunk away to hide in the trees. She ached to go inside and watch the show but she had no money and she knew that she stood no chance of getting in without a ticket. Two burly men were standing on either side of the entrance now, taking the tickets from people as they entered the Big Top. She listened enviously to the show begin, and heard the huge round of applause as the band struck up the opening chorus. It was all so exciting and glamorous, and more than ever she wished that she could be part of it. But the doors were firmly closed now and so she dawdled back to Lynne's to face the music. She had nowhere else to go.

Lynne was waiting for her in the kitchen and instead of shouting at her as Rebecca had expected, she smiled at her sadly. 'I'm so sorry you have to move again, love. It's not all your fault really. It's just . . . Well, to tell the truth, after what's happened with Justin, Rob and I have decided to stick to younger children. I can manage them more easily. I don't think I'm cut out to care for teenagers, and you did know from the beginning that this wasn't going to be forever.'

'It's no skin off my nose,' Rebecca said in a hard voice, but she felt as if she had been cast aside all over again, even if it was partly her own fault.

Miss James came to see her three days later.

'I've found you a new placement, Rebecca,' she told her

quietly. 'You'll be going to live with the Dickinsons in Stratford, and hopefully it will be a longer-term placement for you.'

Rebecca stared at a spot on the ceiling, seemingly unperturbed by the news although her heart was pounding painfully.

'I thought we could move you next Wednesday,' Miss James went on.

Rebecca sniffed. 'Will I still be able to see Pat?' she asked. The woman had become the only stable person in her life, and although she never showed it, Rebecca had grown fond of her.

'Of course you will. I'll pass your new address on to her as soon as you move,' Miss James promised. Sometimes – just sometimes – she glimpsed the vulnerability that Rebecca hid so well, and she couldn't help but feel sorry for the kid. But Rebecca was a sullen girl and she could well imagine how difficult she must be to live with. Miss James had a horrible feeling that Rebecca was going to become lost in the care system, moved from one foster placement to another because no one could cope with her. She had seen it all before with children who had behavioural problems. Far too many times. But what could she do? If Rebecca wasn't prepared to try, then there was little hope for her.

'Is there anything you'd like to ask me about the Dickinsons?' she enquired now.

Rebecca shook her head. It didn't much matter where they put her, did it. No one really wanted her.

'Well, I'll tell you a little bit about them anyway,' Meg James said with a smile. 'They're an older couple in their sixties and very nice. They live in a small village called Stretton-on-Fosse which is about fifteen minutes from Stratford-on-Avon, and they attend church regularly.'

Rebecca had to stop herself from groaning out loud, since they sounded about as much fun as a bad head cold, but then she did what she was good at. She closed her eyes and let the rest of Meg James's words go right over her head.

During the next few days, Rebecca spent as much time as she could down at the circus. The way she saw it, there was no point in going to school any more and Lynne didn't push it. She knew when she was beaten, and now that the decision had been made to move Rebecca on, she couldn't wait for it to happen. Sadly, she had never taken to the girl and knew that she would be doing her no favours by keeping her. There were some kids that were beyond help – and Rebecca was one of them.

Rebecca would arrive at the Pingles Fields and position herself so that she could watch Gina training her dogs. She never tired of seeing how much patience the woman had with them and was amazed at how clever the little animals were. Harvey Brand's Circus was due to move on to another town on Tuesday, and on Monday night Rebecca finally plucked up the courage to show herself and approach her.

'How old do you have to be, to join the circus?' she enquired in her usual blunt manner.

Gina paused to stare at her. 'You have to be eighteen.'

'Oh!' Rebecca could not keep the disappointment from her voice and now the woman smiled.

'Don't get thinking it's all glamour an' glitz,' she told her. 'The circus is your master when you're a part of it. There's no such thing as a day off, and no matter how rough you're feeling the show has to go on. Your working day begins at five in the morning. Even earlier than that when we move site . . . Does it still sound so attractive?'

Rebecca hung her head, too ashamed to admit that in fact it did. Anything was better than the life she was leading now.

'You from round here, are you?' Gina was curious about the girl despite herself. There was something so sad about her.

'I was born in Coventry,' Rebecca informed her. 'But my real mum didn't want me so then I got adopted and went to live in Rugby.'

'Well, that was nice then.'

'Not really, 'cos my new mum and dad died within months of each other when I was little,' Rebecca told her matter-of-factly. 'Then I went to live with an aunt and uncle for a while.' Her face grew dark as memories flooded back. 'I got put into care then, but my second placement has broken down so I'm being shipped off to another one in a couple of days.'

'I see.' Gina was at a loss what to say. It sounded like the poor kid had really gone through the mill. 'Then good luck, and let's hope you'll be happier in your next home,' she said lamely.

Rebecca nodded before thrusting her hands into her pockets and trudging away. She could hardly believe that she had confided in the woman, seeing as she'd never been able to talk to anyone else about how she felt before. She knew that it would probably be the last time she would ever see Gina and her dancing dogs, and the thought saddened her more than leaving Lynne and Rob. But at least one thing had come out of their meeting; now she knew that one day she would join a circus, even if she had to wait until she was eighteen.

Chapter Twenty-Seven

From the second that Rebecca stepped through the Dickinsons' door she knew that she was going to hate it there. They lived in a small village on the outskirts of Stratford in a cottage that looked like something off the cover of a chocolate box. The inside was all chintz curtains and fussy knick-knacks, and she felt afraid to move in case she knocked something over. There were little ornate tables everywhere, covered in fancy lace cloths, on which stood numerous photos in silver and gilt frames, and both Mr and Mrs Dickinson looked as if they were dressed for church. Mrs Dickinson was wearing a tweed skirt that reached to her calves and a powder-blue twinset that looked as if it might have been in fashion twenty years before. About her throat was a string of pearls, and her greying hair was pulled back into a severe bun at the nape of her neck. Mr Dickinson was dressed in a dark suit and a blue shirt with a darker blue tie, and he reminded Rebecca of one of the older teachers at the last school she had attended.

'Oh, *do* come in, my dears,' Mrs Dickinson gushed, and in no time at all Rebecca found herself perched on the edge of a chair balancing a cup and saucer full of tea on her lap. The china was so fine that she was afraid it might disintegrate in her hands, and the tea slopped over the cup into the saucer. Mrs Dickinson sniffed at this, but wisely made no comment as Miss James went through all the necessary paperwork with her. Oh great, Rebecca thought to herself. Just my luck to get stuck with two old God-botherers.

She sat there for what seemed like hours in the sweltering heat emanating from a roaring fire until at last Meg James said, 'That's all the paperwork out of the way then. Shall we have a look at Rebecca's room now, Mrs Dickinson?'

'Why, of course. Harold, dear, would you mind removing the cups to the kitchen?'

She stood up and after smoothing her skirt she beckoned Meg and Rebecca to follow her up a small dog-leg staircase. '*Do* mind your heads on the ceiling,' she instructed them. 'This cottage is over two hundred years old and I'm afraid they didn't make the ceilings very high in those days. I think people must have been much smaller back then.' She chuckled as if she had just said something highly amusing, but Rebecca remained grim-faced.

'It's absolutely charming,' Meg said quickly. Rebecca secretly thought that it was terribly old-fashioned.

'Oh, thank you, dear.' Mrs Dickinson beamed. 'Of course, the building *is* Listed.' She swelled with pride as she led them along a small narrow landing and flung a door open. 'This will be your room, Rebecca.'

Rebecca looked around glumly. The room was quite small, with a sloping ceiling that followed the roofline, and like the downstairs it was very fussy. There was a flowered eiderdown on a single brass bed, flowered curtains at the small leaded window, which was quite high up, and to top it all there was a flowered carpet that stretched from wall to wall. Rebecca felt as if she was walking into a florist's shop but she managed to raise a smile, knowing that it was expected of her.

'It looks very er . . . comfy,' the social worker said, glancing at Rebecca.

Next to the bed was an oak chest of drawers which looked almost as old as the cottage, and against the other wall was a matching wardrobe. A mirror hung above a small dressing-table and there was also a chair in there.

'So you can sit and admire the view from the window,' Mrs Dickinson explained. 'You can see right across the churchyard from here.'

Rebecca suppressed a shudder. She couldn't think of anything worse than having to look at the graves of dead people and silently promised herself to keep the curtains shut as much as she could.

'Saint Mary's is a beautiful old church,' Mrs Dickinson warbled on as if she had part shares in it. 'And then we have our own little village pub, the Red Duck, *and* a post office. Of course, Harold and I don't use the pub. We don't believe in alcoholic drink.'

Rebecca could well believe it and had to fight the urge to leg it there and then. She felt as if she'd been delivered to the back of beyond and wondered how she was going to bear it.

'Well, everything seems to be in order,' Meg James said in a falsely bright voice, 'so I suppose I should be heading back to the office. Rebecca will be starting her new school on Monday, Mrs Dickinson. Can I rely on you to get her a uniform?'

'Of course. I shall be taking her shopping tomorrow. That will be nice, won't it, dear?' she said, addressing Rebecca now.

The girl smiled weakly. This must be how a rabbit feels when it's caught in a trap, she thought to herself as she followed the two women back down the steep staircase.

Meg James collected her bag and said a hasty goodbye, and then Rebecca was left to Mrs Dickinson's tender ministrations.

As Meg drove away, she frowned. The Dickinsons were still fairly inexperienced carers and up to now had only taken much younger children, for short times. How would they cope with a difficult teenager? But there was nothing she could do about it for now, all she could do was hope that the placement would work.

'Now then, I think we should put your clothes away and

216

then have a little lunch, don't you, dear?' Mrs Dickinson suggested before the social worker's car had even pulled away.

Rebecca nodded and sighed as she lifted her bag and followed the woman back up to the claustrophobic little bedroom.

Mrs Dickinson leaped on her case, and when she opened it she groaned.

'Oh goodness me, this will *never* do!' she exclaimed. 'Every single thing in here needs ironing. We don't want you wearing creased clothes. And some of them look rather grubby too.' She sniffed disapprovingly as she took one of Rebecca's nighties from the case. 'I think we shall have to dispose of at least *half* of these things. Didn't anyone tell your previous carer that cleanliness is next to godliness? I think when we go shopping tomorrow we shall have to start all over again. Some of these things are quite worn.'

Scowling, Rebecca snatched the nightie from her hand. It was her favourite and she had no intention of letting the woman throw it away.

'I like my clothes just the way they are,' she said resentfully and Mrs Dickinson tutted.

'Er . . . very well then. How about we go and get some lunch? We can always do this later when you are feeling a little more settled.'

'I'm perfectly capable of putting my *own* things away,' Rebecca informed her in no uncertain terms. 'And I'd rather you didn't come into my room uninvited.'

'Oh.' The woman looked totally dumbfounded as she hovered like a bird about to take flight. But then she backed towards the door, sensing the hostility that was coming off Rebecca in waves.

'I'll leave you to it then,' she said lamely. 'But don't be too long about it, dear. Lunch will be ready in half an hour.'

As the door closed behind her, Rebecca let out a loud sigh of relief. Silly old cow – there was no way they were going to get along, she knew that already. Even so, she began to cram her clothes into the drawer anyhow. She didn't really feel as if she had much choice at the minute.

The following morning bright and early there was a loud rap on Rebecca's door and she started awake. She lay disorientated for a second wondering where she was and listening to the birdsong outside. It was a far cry from the noise of traffic that she was used to. And then she remembered, and despite promising herself that she didn't give a damn, tears clogged her throat.

'Come along, dear,' Mrs Dickinson trilled. 'I've got a nice boiled egg and bread and butter soldiers all ready for you in the dining room.'

Rebecca groaned – *bread and butter soldiers?* How old did the woman think she was? She hadn't had them since she was at least five!

'Coming,' she called back resignedly, and swinging her legs out of the bed she pulled her comfy old dressing-gown on and padded downstairs.

When Rebecca walked into the dining room seconds later, knuckling the sleep from her eyes, Mrs Dickinson almost choked.

'Oh my goodness,' she declared as if Rebecca had committed a cardinal sin. 'Whatever are you thinking of, dear? Why – you aren't even dressed. You can't come to the table like *that*. Run upstairs and get dressed, there's a good girl.'

Fully awake now, Rebecca blinked. The dining-room table was covered in a crisp white cloth and laid with shining silver cutlery and bone china. Mrs Dickinson was as immaculately dressed as ever, in a different colour twinset today but with her customary pearls about her throat and her hair neatly tied back in a bun. Mr Dickinson was in a suit and tie, and across their laps were clean white linen doilies.

'Is the Queen coming to breakfast?' Rebecca quipped sarcastically.

Mrs Dickinson's thin lips set in a straight line. 'I hardly think there is any call for sarcasm,' she said icily. 'In *this* house we do things properly. Now please go and do as I asked you.'

Rebecca slouched away and once she had gone, Mrs Dickinson said, 'I fear we will have trouble with this one, Harold. The girl has no manners whatsoever and her personal hygiene leaves a lot to be desired too. Still, I have no doubt we'll lick her into shape in due course.'

Her long-suffering husband nodded obediently. He had learned his place long ago and certainly wasn't going to start rocking the boat now. It was so much easier to agree with everything that Mavis said. A smile twitched at the corners of his lips as he thought of Rebecca. He had a funny feeling that Mavis was going to have her work cut out with this one. She seemed like a right little rebel, but it would be fun sitting on the sidelines and watching the battle commence. Lowering his head, he turned his attention back to his boiled egg. At least he had his allotment and the garden to escape to if things got too heated.

Upstairs, Rebecca was banging about as she yanked her clothes from the drawer and got dressed. Mrs Dickinson was just like Mrs Bucket off the telly in *Keeping Up Appearances*, she thought as she pulled a baggy jumper over her head.

Back at Lynne's, breakfast had been a chaotic time, and at her aunt's she had been lucky to even *get* any breakfast. But then perhaps Mrs Dickinson was just trying to impress her? After all, no one lived like this all the time – *did they*? She supposed that only time would tell.

Mr and Mrs Dickinson had almost finished their breakfast by the time Rebecca got downstairs, which was one blessing at least. The older woman ushered her to the table and plied her with food, keeping up a running commentary of what she intended them to do for the rest of the day.

'When I've done my dusting I shall run you into Stratford to get your uniform. And then I thought it would be nice on the way back if I took you into Saint Joseph's, your new school, to meet the staff there. Saint Joseph's is a Catholic school and comes highly recommended.'

'But I'm not a Catholic,' Rebecca pointed out as she spooned runny egg into her mouth.

'Please don't talk with your mouth full, dear. It's *so* ill-mannered. And don't worry about that. You don't have to be a Catholic to attend that school. What religion are you, by the way?'

'Church of England, I suppose,' Rebecca told her. 'Though I don't go to church very often.'

'Oh, how dreadful.' Mrs Dickinson smoothed an imaginary crease in the tablecloth. 'That's another thing we shall have to work on then. From now on you can come with me and Harold. We go every Sunday morning and Wednesday evening.'

Rebecca thought it sounded about as much fun as toothache but refrained from saying so as she concentrated on the rest of her meal.

An hour later, she found herself being whisked into Stratford in Mrs Dickinson's small but immaculate car. As they drove along, Mrs Dickinson pointed out places of interest but Rebecca was only listening to her with half an ear. She was like white noise and Rebecca had switched off over breakfast.

'I really *shall* have to take you into the town centre to see William Shakespeare's birthplace, and you might like to see Anne Hathaway's cottage too,' the woman warbled on. Rebecca was beginning to wonder if she ever stopped to draw breath. 'And then of course there's the River Avon. It's quite beautiful in the summer.'

They were on the outskirts of the town now and Rebecca was relieved when they drew up outside a very posh-looking shop.

'This is where you'll be getting your uniform,' Mrs Dickinson said as she ushered her inside. Twenty minutes later, Rebecca gazed at herself in a full-length mirror in horror.

'I'm not wearing *that* for a start-off,' she said, removing the straw boater from her head and frisbying it across the dressing room.

The shop assistant looked on in alarm as Mrs Dickinson went at a surprising speed to retrieve it. 'But you must wear it,' she scolded, brushing it with her clean white handkerchief.

Rebecca was clad in a demure white blouse topped with a horrendous purple pinafore dress and an equally horrendous blazer with the name of the school emblazoned on the top pocket. Mrs Dickinson had also purchased the appropriate PE kit and half a dozen pairs of white ankle socks as well as a sensible pair of flat black shoes, which would definitely never win any prizes for fashion.

'But it's awful,' Rebecca complained, mortified. 'I look like a freak!' She liked to dress as anonymously as she could, but there would be no chance of that now – she would stand out like a sore thumb! And what sort of a snobby school must St Joseph's be, to make their pupils wear such an awful outfit!

'Rubbish, my dear. You look as smart as a new pin.' Mrs Dickinson eyed her approvingly. 'And you should think yourself very lucky indeed that I managed to secure you a place at Saint Joseph's. It's one of the *very* best schools in the area – unless you go private, of course. Places there are as rare as hen's teeth, I assure you. You'll be mixing with a better class of girl there.'

Rebecca headed back to the changing room then sighed as she saw the assistant bundling all the new clothes into a bag, including the boater. And then it was back into the car and they were on the way home again.

'How long has it been since you had a haircut, dear?' Mrs Dickinson now asked none too tactfully when they had once more reached the leafy green lanes.

Rebecca fingered her long ponytail self-consciously.

'I'm not too sure,' she admitted. 'But I'm not having it all cut off, if that's what you're planning.'

'Oh, no, no. I wasn't intending on making you do that,' the woman said. 'But may I suggest a little trim is long overdue? Perhaps a few inches off, just to tidy it up a little.'

As Rebecca folded her arms and glared through the windscreen, resentment began to bubble inside her. Why was it that people were always trying to order her what to do? Why couldn't everyone just leave her alone? She could hardly wait until she was sixteen. She would leave care then, lie about her age and join the circus. Right now, that was the only dream that kept her going.

Chapter Twenty-Eight

Rebecca's mood lightened somewhat the next day following a phone call to Mrs Dickinson.

'That call was about you, dear,' the woman informed her when she had put the phone down. 'It was your social worker, who tells me you have someone who wishes to visit you. Someone called Pat. Apparently she's coming to see you on Saturday afternoon. Are you happy with that arrangement?'

Rebecca, who felt as if she was dying of boredom, nodded eagerly.

'Very well then, this Pat is going to get a neighbour to drive her here, and I'm told we can expect her around two o'clock.' Mrs Dickinson then continued with her dusting, which had already been done once that day, as Rebecca slouched off to her room.

Once there, she lay on the bed and her thoughts turned to Joe, Pat's son. It had been some time since she had seen him now and she wondered if he would even remember her. She thought of Josh too. It was even longer since she had seen her adopted brother, although she had been offered the opportunity to meet him. Somehow she felt he was better left in the past. He was part of a life she tried not to think of any more. Part of a time when he had been the special child; the child of whom their parents could be proud. More and more of late, when Rebecca thought back to that time, she realised that she had never been what her adoptive mother had hoped for.

She knew she would never be pretty. She knew it every time she looked in the mirror, which was why she was so keen to try the circus life. Not everyone was beautiful there as she had first thought. There were the midgets, cheerful despite their curious little shapes, and the bearded lady, never happier than when she was combing out her long silky beard for an audience. Surely there would be a place for her there? Soon she was lost in daydreams.

Pat arrived bang on time on Saturday and when Mrs Dickinson opened the door to her, she looked her up and down critically. The woman wasn't what she had expected at all. In fact, she looked downright common. She ushered her inside quickly, hoping that none of the neighbours had seen her arrive, and glanced down with dismay at the woman's muddy shoes, which she was about to tramp all over her lovely Axminster carpet.

''Ello, love.' Pat shook herself like a dog before taking her coat off and throwing it over the banister. 'Cor, it's rainin' cats an' dogs out there, I don't mind tellin' yer.'

'Er . . . yes. I suppose it is.' Mrs Dickinson discreetly lifted the coat and hung it on the coat rack before asking, 'Did you come alone, dear?'

'Nah, Matty up the road drove me here but he's cleared off to the pub till it's time for me to go.'

'I see,' Mrs Dickinson said disapprovingly. 'Well . . . do come into the lounge. I gather you aren't a relative of Rebecca's?'

Pat shook her head; she had recently had her hair bleached and it was now a very brassy yellow colour.

'Just a friend, love, who likes to keep me eye on the gel.'

'How kind,' Mrs Dickinson simpered. Rebecca had joined them by now, and once the two of them were seated on the settee, she left them to it, scurrying away to the kitchen to make them some tea.

Pat looked around, impressed. 'Crikey, you've dropped on your feet here, ain't you, pet?' she said. 'It's like sommat you'd see in a magazine.'

'It's dead boring,' Rebecca informed her scathingly then lowering her voice she confided, 'Mrs Dickinson is a real snob – like that Mrs Bucket off the telly. She's so houseproud that you hardly dare to sit down for fear of disturbing the cushions. She gave me a right rollicking yesterday just for lying on my bed and creasing the covers.'

Pat's eyes sparkled with amusement. Then: 'Well, I dare say it's better than having to live in a shithole,' she said bluntly, and although no words were spoken they were both thinking of her aunt and uncle's.

'Yer Aunt Alison an' Uncle Ken ain't together any more,' she went on now.

'Really, so where are they both living?' the girl asked.

'I couldn't rightly say. Young Amber 'as 'ad the baby, o' course, an' is livin' wi' its dad by what I can gather, but yer aunt an' Casey left some time ago. She did a moonlight flit – got herself into debt, see.'

Not really surprised, Rebecca shrugged, then changed the subject. 'I've got to start at another new school on Monday,' she told Pat with a downcast face. 'And you want to see the uniform! I'm going to feel a right ninny in it.'

'Well, the way you have to think of it is that all the others will be dressed the same too, so it won't be so bad,' Pat said kindly. She really felt for Rebecca and wished for the millionth time that she could just take her home with her, but with her track record with Social Services she knew that that was never going to happen.

Mrs Dickinson bustled back in then with a laden hostess

trolley and Pat raised her eyebrows. She wasn't used to this kind of treatment.

'Tea, dear?'

Pat nodded numbly as the woman lifted the fine china tea pot and began to pour the tea into two cups.

'It's Earl Grey,' she informed Pat pompously. 'So much superior, don't you think? And of course you'll have a slice of my jam sponge, won't you? It's fresh out of the oven and Harold always says no one can make a sponge cake like me.'

Pat eyed the china cup and saucer with trepidation, terrified of dropping it. But at last Mrs Dickinson stood back up and smiled at them.

'There then. Do call if you want more hot water. I shall just be in the kitchen.'

Once she'd gone, Pat let out a long breath. 'Phew, I see what yer mean. She's a bit full-on, ain't she? An' I *hate* Earl Grey tea! Superior or not, it always tastes like dishwater to me. Give me a good old English cuppa any day of the week. Though I have to say this sponge ain't half bad.' As she spoke she was spraying crumbs everywhere and Rebecca grinned as she thought how horrified Mrs Dickinson would be if she could see her. But it was so nice to be with Pat. Sometimes Rebecca felt as if she was the only person in the whole world who truly cared about her now.

'How is Joe?' she asked when Pat had gorged her way through half of the sponge.

'He's all right.' Pat chuckled. 'Getting to be a bit of a Casanova, he is – got girls falling over 'emselves to talk to him nowadays. But then he allus was a good-lookin' little bugger. He's got a good job though in a car factory an' he never sees me short, bless him.' She put her plate down and asked on a more serious note, 'But how are you, love?'

Rebecca leaned back in the chair and crossed her arms in

the defensive manner Pat had come to recognise over the years. 'Like I said, it's boring here but I'm OK.'

'Hmm.' Pat narrowed her eyes as she studied the girl. There were dark circles under her eyes and although Rebecca would rather die than admit it, Pat knew that she must have felt the latest rejection by Lynne and Rob. It was just the latest in a long line of rejections, and sometimes she wondered how Rebecca coped. Not that she did anything to help herself. Pat had hoped that as she got older she would start to take a little more pride in her appearance. Most girls her age did – but here she was in her usual baggy jumper with her hair looking as if it hadn't been brushed for days, and it almost broke her heart. Pat suspected her hair could be pretty too if she'd only wear it in a more fashionable style.

Suddenly the concerns she'd been harbouring for some time rose to the surface, and after taking a deep breath she asked tentatively, 'When you lived with your Aunt Alison . . . did your Uncle Ken ever try to . . . *do* anything that he shouldn't to you?'

Colour rose into Rebecca's cheeks. 'What makes you ask that?' she breathed.

'Well . . .' Pat gulped. 'My old man was a right jealous bastard. If he so much as *thought* that another bloke was lookin' at me he'd try to punch me lights out – as if it was all my fault, except when he needed money fer beer, that is, and then . . .' Bad memories were flooding back and she was having a severe case of palpitations. She could have told Rebecca that then he'd been happy for her to drop her drawers for any punter who'd pay the price, but she forced herself to go on. 'So eventually I worked it out that if I didn't make the best of meself, the blokes weren't going to look. I stopped washin' me hair, I took to wearin' baggy clothes.'

'*So?* What's that got to do with me?' Rebecca's eyes were

flashing fire and Pat had a sinking feeling in her stomach. Had she touched a raw nerve?

'I just think that at your age you should be startin' to take a bit more pride in yerself. Unless something *did* happen – and you're afraid to?'

'Nothing happened!' Rebecca snapped, a little too quickly for Pat's liking. 'Now can we talk about something else?'

'Sorry, love.' Pat helped herself to yet another slice of sponge cake and the conversation moved on to other things until it was time for her to leave.

When they were standing at the door some time later, Pat laughed as Matty screeched to a halt outside in his clapped-out Cortina.

'Oh, dear. Looks like he's had a skinful,' she commented as Matty clambered out of the car and waved wildly. 'Let's just hope he gets us home all in one piece, eh?'

Both she and Rebecca were acutely conscious of Mrs Dickinson hovering in the hallway behind them with a shocked expression etched onto her face.

'Should he really be driving, dear? Wouldn't it be best if you got a taxi?' she suggested primly.

Pat snorted. '*Taxi!* Why, it'd cost an arm an' a leg from 'ere, love. I reckon I'll take me chances.'

Turning back to Rebecca, she ruffled her hair. Pat had never been demonstrative when it came to showing affection, and this was about as good as it got. 'Right then, I'd better be off. You take care of yourself an' I'll see you again soon, eh? You know where I am if you should need me, an' good luck with your new school.'

Rebecca nodded, her throat full. Now that Pat was leaving she felt as if she was being abandoned all over again, and she was fighting the urge to beg the woman to take her with her.

She watched her walking away down the path and stood

there until the car screeched away from the kerb, lost in thought.

'Come on in then, dear. You're letting all the cold air in.' Mrs Dickinson's voice sliced into her thoughts like a knife and Rebecca reluctantly did as she was told before scuttling away to her room.

Once there she sank down onto the edge of her bed as she tried to make some sense of the jumbled thoughts that were in her mind. Pat had always been kind to her – but why? She had lived in Coventry before going to live in Bedworth, and once Rebecca had overheard her aunt tell her uncle that Pat had been on the game when her kids were little. She knew what 'being on the game' meant now. It meant that Pat had been a prostitute. Her real mum had been a prostitute and she had lived in Coventry too . . . And then it suddenly hit her like a blow between the eyes and she gasped. But surely that would be too much of a coincidence? Surely Pat couldn't be her mother . . . could she? It was as if the pieces of a jigsaw were falling into place. Why else would Pat have been so kind to her? She must have realised that Rebecca was the daughter she had abandoned when she went to live with her aunt and uncle. And now she was trying to make it up to her. She felt guilty – that must be it.

Rebecca felt as if she had been punched in the stomach, but as always she kept her tears locked inside. *The bitch*, thinking she could con her like that! Well, now that she'd realised who Pat was, she would bide her time, and one day the woman would pay for getting rid of her as if she was only so much garbage. This was the silent promise Rebecca made to herself as she sat on the bed and fumed with anger and hurt.

Chapter Twenty-Nine

'There, dear. I do believe you are all ready to go now – although I do wish you'd taken a little more trouble over your hair. Still, it's too late to worry about it now. Thankfully your hat will cover a multitude of sins.'

Rebecca stood there feeling like a complete idiot as Mrs Dickinson crammed the ridiculous boater hat onto her head. A glance in the hall mirror assured her that not only did she *feel* stupid, she *looked* stupid too, which did nothing at all for her confidence. Not that it was worth complaining. She would just be wasting her breath, as she'd discovered very early on with Mrs Dickinson. She might look like a pushover with her simpering smile and her pearls and her twinsets but she was actually a very strict little woman.

'Oh, and before I forget – I did mention that nuns run Saint Joseph's School, didn't I?' As Mrs Dickinson began to neatly pack her lunch into her bag, Rebecca silently groaned. *Nuns!* That was all she needed.

Happy with her efforts, Mrs Dickinson hooked the brand new satchel over Rebecca's arm and the girl had to stop herself from shuddering. A *satchel* for Christ's sake! Surely they'd gone out of fashion with the Ark? She'd be a laughing stock – until she managed to lose it, that was, which would be sooner rather than later if she had her way.

'Ah, I think I heard the school bus pulling up,' Mrs Dickinson trilled as she glanced towards the window. 'Come along, dear, and don't be nervous. You're sure to make some new friends.'

When she opened the front door, Rebecca saw a mini-bus parked outside the cottage with the name *St Joseph's* emblazoned all along its side. Apparently it did the school run every day, picking up the girls from the outlying villages and delivering them home again each night.

'Have a wonderful time, dear,' Mrs Dickinson told her as if she was embarking on a Mediterranean cruise.

Rebecca shuffled off down the path cursing softly beneath her breath.

The driver smiled at her as she clambered aboard but she merely ignored him as she found a seat. There were three girls already there, and once the bus had set off one of them said, 'Hello, you must be Rebecca. We were told you'd be starting today. I'm Debbie and this is Samantha and Annabelle.'

Rebecca grunted in reply and soon the girls were happily chatting away together again as if she wasn't there, which suited her just fine. She'd never really had any friends before and she certainly wasn't looking for any now.

Staring out of the window, she tried to ignore the whispered comments that she couldn't help but overhear. 'She's not exactly a beauty queen, is she?' Titters were followed by another girl saying, 'No, she isn't, and with an attitude like that she's not going to get into Mother Benedict's good books.'

Rebecca's cheeks were burning as she snatched the sandwiches out of her bag, stuffed them into her pocket and slung the satchel under the seat. At least that was one indignity she could be rid of. Twenty minutes and four more pick-ups later they came to a large old building on the outskirts of Stratford with *St Joseph's School for Girls* written across enormous double gates. The building was approached by a long winding drive, and once the mini-bus pulled up in front of it, Rebecca waited for the other girls to alight before clumsily following them. She had no idea where she should go, but the girl who had been introduced as Debbie approached her after a few minutes and told her, 'If you'd like to come with me I'll take you to Reception and Sister Teresa will tell you where to go.'

Rebecca trailed behind her as they entered the building, glancing this way and that. She found herself in a huge foyer with a large desk set to one side of it. A long hallway stretched for as far as she could see, with numerous rooms – which she rightly assumed were classrooms – leading off it. A nun in a long black habit was seated at the desk and she looked up as Rebecca and Debbie approached.

'This is the new girl, Sister,' Debbie informed her politely and the woman smiled. Rebecca was shocked to see that she was actually quite young and also had a very pretty face. She had always imagined nuns to be wrinkled-up old crones.

'Hello, Rebecca, and welcome,' the nun greeted her in a friendly fashion. 'You are going to be in Sister Agatha's class. It's just along there, the second door on the left, but before you report there we shall have a service in the chapel as we do each morning.'

Girls were streaming past them by now, all curiously glancing in her direction, and Rebecca blushed self-consciously.

'Would you kindly show Rebecca where the chapel is, Debbie, as it's her first day?'

'Of course,' Debbie answered, and beckoning to Rebecca she set off in the same direction as the other girls.

Rebecca shuffled along behind Debbie, forcing her legs to move.

'We have a service in the chapel each morning before we start our lessons,' Debbie explained. 'But it only lasts for about half an hour.'

Half an hour! It sounded like a long time to Rebecca,

although she didn't comment. They seemed to walk along the highly polished wooden floors for ages but at last, Debbie guided her into a room with stained-glass windows dotted about the walls. The weak winter sun was shining through them, reflecting all the colours of the rainbow across the walls, and Rebecca whispered, 'Was this place a church then?'

'No,' Debbie whispered back. 'A very rich family used to live here during the last century, and all the gentry had chapels built into their houses.'

'Oh.' Rebecca took a seat on a hard wooden pew and so the first day at her new school began.

By lunchtime Rebecca was beginning to wonder how she was going to bear it. Apart from Debbie, who was going out of her way to be friendly, the rest of her classmates seemed to be a stuck-up lot and Sister Agatha, her allocated teacher, wasn't much better. She was everything Rebecca had pictured a nun to be. Old and wrinkled. And on top of that she seemed to glide along, as if she had no legs beneath her long black robes. She had an alarming habit of walking amongst the girls and rapping anyone who wasn't concentrating on the knuckles with a ruler. By lunchtime Rebecca's hands were stinging and it was taking all her willpower not to tell the nasty old bag what she thought of her.

'I'll show you where the lunch hall is,' Debbie said when the bell finally sounded, and grateful to escape the watchful eye of the evil old hag who was in charge of her, Rebecca followed her from the classroom.

When all the girls were seated there were yet more prayers before they were allowed to eat their lunch. They then had twenty minutes to file out into the playground for some fresh air before lessons resumed.

Debbie had disappeared by then to be with her friends, so Rebecca slunk off to a corner and watched and listened.

Soon a small group assembled around her and began to eye her up and down as she stared defiantly back at them.

'Don't say much, do you?' one girl jeered.

Rebecca remained obstinately silent.

'Where are you from anyway?'

'None of your business.'

'Ooh, hark at her.' The girl, a tall willowy creature with a mop of dark brown hair, grinned at her friends. 'Thinks she's too good to talk to the likes of us, does she?'

Rebecca made to walk away, but the girl caught her arm and swung her about.

'Let's just get one thing clear. I'm the king pin around here and you'd do well to remember it. If you do as I say, you'll be all right.'

Rebecca snatched her arm away and glared at her. 'I don't do what *anyone* tells me,' she said, and before the girl knew what was happening, she had brought her arm back and socked her soundly round the face.

'Why, you little bitch!' Incensed, the girl lunged at her and in seconds fists were flying and the other girls were shouting encouragement, glad of a distraction.

'Whatever is going on here?' A stern voice suddenly sliced into the excitement and the girls fell silent and melted away as Sister Teresa appeared, her hands tucked into the arms of her long flowing black habit.

'It was the new girl, Sister. She attacked me for no reason.' The girl, who Rebecca had now discovered was called Felicity, piteously swiped the blood from her nose as the nun swept towards them like an avenging angel.

Rebecca could feel her left eye swelling and the pocket was hanging off her new blazer, but she stared back at the nun unblinkingly.

'What disgraceful behaviour! And on your first day too,'

the nun scolded. 'Felicity, go to the sick room and get the nurse to look at your nose, and you, Rebecca, follow me. I'm afraid you will have to go in front of Mother Benedict. She will not tolerate this kind of thing, I can assure you.'

Felicity smirked as she turned away and Rebecca followed the nun back inside, her stomach churning with rage. It was so unfair. She'd just been standing there minding her own business, so why should she take all the flak for what had happened?

Mother Benedict's room was more like a cell than an office, with nothing on the walls at all except for a large crucifix hanging behind her desk. The floor was bare concrete and it was cold in there too. So much so that Rebecca could see her breath hanging on the air in front of her. She wondered how the woman managed to sit in there without freezing her socks off but then the lecture began and her mind shut off, allowing the old woman's words to float over her head. It might be her first day there but she had already decided it would be her last. There was no way she was ever going to set foot in this detestable place again.

'You may go now,' the nun told her at last. Rebecca lurched out of the room driven by white-hot rage. How dare the old bag lecture her like that when it hadn't even been her who'd started the trouble in the first place? Another nun was floating by in the corridor outside and Rebecca was reminded of a big black crow.

'Where are you going, child?' the woman asked as she saw Rebecca stamping towards the front doors.

'As far away from this fuckin' place as I can get!' Rebecca flung across her shoulder, and then she was outside and she stood there gulping in the cold damp air. Realising that they would soon be looking for her, she then headed for a small copse at the side of the playground, and once in the shelter of the trees she sank down with her back against the trunk of a large oak. She would wait there until the mini-bus arrived to take her back to Mrs Dickinson's and then she would tell the old bat just what an awful school it was.

The light was already fading from the day when Rebecca stamped up the path to Mrs Dickinson's front door later that afternoon. The atmosphere on the mini-bus had been icy to say the least, with all the girls ignoring her, but Rebecca was past caring now and just wanted to escape to the privacy of her room. The front door opened before she even reached it and Mr Dickinson stood there looking nervous and worried.

'She's in there, love.' He thumbed towards the lounge door. 'And you'd best be prepared, because if I said she was none too pleased with you, I'd be putting it mildly. She's had a phone call from the school.'

Rebecca sighed. She'd come home intent on telling Mrs Dickinson what had really happened and hoping to find an ally in her, but once again it seemed that no one was going to listen to her side of it. That was the story of her life. Taking a deep breath, she entered the lounge to find Mrs Dickinson waiting for her with her arms crossed and a grim expression on her face.

'I'm just nipping down to the allotments, dear,' Mr Dickinson said, popping his head round the door. He then rapidly made himself scarce, closing the door behind him before his wife could object.

'Right then, young lady. I think you have some explaining to do,' the woman stormed, eyeing Rebecca's ripped blazer angrily. 'I expected better of you, Rebecca. Saint Joseph's is such a wonderful school, and your behaviour there today has lowered the tone.'

'How do *you* know?' Rebecca looked her straight in the

eye. 'You weren't even there and you've only heard what they had to say. What about *my* side of the story?'

'Well . . .' Mrs Dickinson's chin jutted. 'I'm hardly going to doubt the word of a woman of the cloth, am I?'

'Why not? She's only flesh and blood, isn't she?'

'Rebecca, really! I will *not* have you blaspheming in this house.'

Rebecca sneered. 'No, you won't, will you? Nor will you give me a chance. Since the second I arrived it's been "Rebecca, don't do this, Rebecca, don't do that!" I'm almost scared to breathe. You're on my case all the time. Why you foster I'll never know. You don't even seem to *like* children.! It would take a bloody angel to please you!'

'How *dare* you swear in my house!' Mrs Dickinson shouted.

'Oh, I bloody well dare,' Rebecca screamed back, then her lips curled back from her teeth as she surveyed the spotless room. 'Look at this place,' she spat. 'It's not a home, it's a show house. I daren't even sit down in here for fear of disturbing a cushion – and your old man feels the same, the poor sod, that's why he clears off to his allotments so often to get away from your nagging.'

Suddenly extending her arm, she swept her closed fist along the mantelshelf, sending Mrs Dickinson's highly prized Royal Doulton ladies crashing to the floor.

Mrs Dickinson cried out in alarm but Rebecca was past caring now, and raising her foot she kicked out at a small spindle-leg table on which stood an expensive cut-glass rose bowl. As that too shattered, Rebecca smiled with satisfaction as all the hurt and pain she had kept locked inside rose to the surface. Mrs Dickinson was hurtling towards her now, but before she could reach her, Rebecca grabbed the phone and yanked it from the wall.

'Why, you . . . you . . .'

'Go on, *say it*!' Rebecca taunted. 'Say what you really think of me, if you dare!' The façade of the godfearing, perfect foster-mum was gone now and Mrs Dickinson was incensed.

'I *knew* I should never have agreed to have you in my home,' the woman screeched. 'You're nothing but *scum*! Your mother was a whore and you'll end up the same way! You are beyond salvation. You were born bad!'

'My mum *might* have been a whore,' Rebecca spat back, 'but I'll bet she wasn't a stuck-up hypocrite like you. And don't worry – I have no intention of staying in this poxy house a second longer. I've hated being here as much as you've hated having me.' With that she began to stalk from the room, and when Mrs Dickinson put out a hand to stop her, Rebecca slapped it furiously out of the way. 'Don't touch me!'

Mrs Dickinson blanched and backed away from the raw fury sparking from the girl's eyes.

'Y-you can't go anywhere until I've phoned your social worker,' she stuttered.

'Just watch me!'

Rebecca was up the stairs in seconds and stuffing her clothes into a bag as if there was no tomorrow. She'd had enough of being shipped from one place to another as if she was nothing more than a parcel, and she was determined to look after herself from now on. She was back down the stairs in no time, and as she passed the lounge door she saw Mrs Dickinson down on her hands and knees collecting together her treasured china. Typical, she thought angrily. The old bat thought more of a few broken pots than another human being. So much for being a Christian.

It was dark, and once outside she slammed the door behind her so loudly that the sound echoed along the lane and the door danced on its hinges.

She walked blindly on, her anger lending speed to her steps

until suddenly, someone coming towards her asked, 'Is that you, Rebecca?'

She looked up to see Mr Dickinson, armed with a large cabbage.

'Yes, it's me,' she replied dully.

'But where are you going in the dark, love?' As he eyed her bag she shrugged.

'Don't know and don't much care,' she answered miserably. 'Just so long as I get away from that miserable old cow back there.'

Mr Dickinson opened his mouth to protest but promptly clamped it shut again. He of all people knew how difficult his wife could be, and in truth he felt that she'd never really given this girl a fair chance. Instead, she'd tried to mould her into the child she thought she should be, from the second Rebecca had set foot through the door. He could have told her she was wasting her time – if only she would have listened. It would take more than his Mavis to tame this one. The kid had spirit!

'Why don't you come home with me and we'll try and sort things out?' he suggested kindly. 'I promise you can leave tomorrow if that's what you want, but a young girl like you shouldn't be wandering about in the dark all by herself. Where will you go?'

Rebecca sniffed. 'Don't know yet. But don't worry – I can take care of myself.'

Mr Dickinson's kindness was almost her undoing. She could handle people being harsh with her – she was used to it – but kindness was something else entirely.

As she began to walk on he made one last-ditch effort to change her mind. 'Look, if you'll only come home with me I'll ring Social Services tonight, if that's what you want. I can't let you go like this. It isn't safe for you.'

239

Rebecca steeled herself to ignore him as she set off at a trot down the lane again, and soon the lamp-posts were far behind and there was nothing but darkness surrounding her.

Rebecca shuddered and glanced from side to side as the trees swayed in the breeze towards her. The lane looked totally different in the dark and the first flutter of panic began to stir deep inside her. Where would she go? What could she do? She was truly alone now, unless she swallowed her pride and went back to the Dickinsons, but she knew she would never do that. Her pride wouldn't allow her to.

It was just her now – but then hadn't it always been that way?

Chapter Thirty

As Rebecca placed her bag down and leaned against the trunk of a tree, she wondered what time it was. She seemed to have been walking for hours since she had left the lane and set off across the fields. Her hands were scratched from the many bushes she'd forced her way through, and every now and then the sound of a night creature would make her heart leap into her throat. Her eyes felt gritty with tiredness and she knew that she would have to find somewhere to sleep soon. She was so exhausted that she simply couldn't go much further. She was hungry too, and now that she had calmed down a little she wondered how she was going to eat. She hadn't thought to bring any money with her and she doubted that people would give her any out of the kindness of their hearts. But she would worry about that tomorrow; for now, getting some rest was more important.

Pushing herself away from the tree, she forced herself to go on. It had started to rain now – a slow drizzle that soaked through her clothes and trickled down the back of her neck. It was bitterly cold too, and her hands and feet were numb. And then suddenly in the darkness ahead she saw a glimmer of light through the trees and she headed towards it.

Soon she saw it was a farmhouse and she began to skirt around it until she spotted a large barn. If she could get in there she would have some shelter for the night, but first she had to get past a Border Collie dog who was attached to a long chain that was fixed to an enormous kennel.

His ears pricked up as she approached but before he began to bark she began to whisper to him reassuringly.

'It's all right, boy. I'm not going to hurt you, shush now, there's a good dog.'

He put his head to one side as if he was considering what to do, but then thankfully he dropped onto his belly and placed his head on his paws as she edged cautiously around him.

Once she reached the barn door, she inched it open as quietly as she could and slipped inside. It was still cold in there but at least it was dry. As she stood there for a while, letting her eyes adjust to the darkness, something scuttled over her foot. She started, convinced that it was an enormous rat, and then breathed a sigh of relief when she realised that it was a chicken. There were actually a number of them in there hopping across the haybales, and a thought occurred to her. If there were chickens, there just might be eggs.

Dropping her bag, she began to cautiously feel amongst the hay . . . and sure enough, her hand soon settled on the smooth oval shape of an egg. She didn't much fancy raw egg but then she supposed it was better than nothing, so before she could have time to change her mind she quickly broke the shell and tipped the contents into her mouth. It didn't taste very nice and she grimaced into the darkness, but after a further search and three more eggs, at least she didn't feel so hungry. Now she needed to rest. Looking about, she dragged two haybales together and clambered up onto them. The hay stuck into her like needles, but she was so tired that before she knew it she was fast asleep and completely oblivious to her sleeping companions.

The sound of a cockerel crowing in the farmyard woke her

early the next morning and sitting up she hastily knuckled the sleep from her eyes.

She knew that she would have to leave now before someone discovered her there. She briefly thought of searching for some more eggs to take with her for breakfast, but decided against it. Best not push her luck. The last thing she needed was to be found and carted off back to the Dickinsons.

A peep outside showed her that it had stopped raining, so she hastily collected her bag and skirted the farmhouse. There was a light on in the kitchen, and as she tiptoed past, the smell of bacon frying wafted out to her, making her stomach rumble with hunger again. She had almost reached the gate that led into the farmyard when the kitchen door suddenly opened and a man's voice yelled, 'Hey, *you*. What do you think you're doing?'

Not even stopping to look back, Rebecca threw her bag across the gate and scrambled over after it then took to her heels and didn't stop to catch her breath until she had left the farmhouse far behind. Only when she was quite sure that no one was following her did she sink down at the side of a trickling brook. She had a stitch and was shivering in the early morning dew, which was heavy on the grass. But at least the water in the stream looked crystal clear, so she drank her fill before swiping the back of her hand across her mouth. She stood up then and looked about as she tried to get her bearings. It did no good and she had to admit to herself that she was hopelessly lost. She could be two or ten miles away from the Dickinsons' cottage for all she knew.

A picture of Pat swam in front of her eyes but she blinked it away. It was no good thinking of her now. If she really *was* her mum, then Rebecca never wanted to set eyes on her again. Or at least, not until she was in a position to take her revenge on her for abandoning her. But how was she going to survive in the meantime? It had seemed so easy to run away last night, but now reality was setting in. She had nowhere to sleep and no way of getting anything to eat. What was she to do? She washed her face in the stream and dried it as best she could on the sleeve of her damp coat, then set off again. Something would turn up, it was bound to.

By the evening of the third night, Rebecca felt so ill that it was all she could do to put one foot in front of another. She had not been so fortunate since the first night when she had sheltered in the barn and had been forced to sleep under hedges. She had passed through numerous small villages and had managed to steal a bottle of milk from the front step of a cottage, but other than that she had eaten nothing, and now she felt weak. But it was the cold that was the worst and she couldn't seem to stop shivering. She had used up the few dry clothes she had bundled into her bag on the night she left the Dickinsons. Now the ones she was wearing were sodden and clinging to her skin. Despair washed through her. It was dark. So dark that it seemed that something had sucked all the colour from the world leaving everything a drab black or grey, and above a watery moon was peeping over inky clouds, but at least it had stopped raining for now.

Entering a small copse, and too tired to go any further, she curled up into a ball using her bag as a pillow beneath a large tree with overhanging branches. She had never felt so ill in her life and was alternating between shivering uncontrollably and sweating profusely. It came to her that if she was to die there and then, there was no one to miss her. No one to care. Then suddenly it didn't matter. Over the years, she had indoctrinated herself to believe that she needed no one. She had done the job well and now suddenly she saw death as a blessed release. No one could ever call her names or hurt her again if she was dead. It wouldn't matter that she was plain and ungainly because no one would remember her.

Her head felt too heavy for her body now and her eyes were aching – but strangely she didn't feel cold any more. Finally she slept, and her last thought before she closed her eyes was, I hope I don't wake up.

'Come on, luvvie, try and open your eyes, there's a good girl now.'

A voice was coming from a long way away and Rebecca tried to ignore it as she clung on to sleep.

Then there was a hand behind her neck, gently lifting her head, and she felt something cold being trickled into her mouth. The liquid dripped down her chin as she tried to push the hand away but her movements were uncoordinated and instead her hand flapped feebly at the air.

'L-leave me alone.'

'I can't do that. Come on now, just a sip. We don't want you any more dehydrated than you already are,' the gentle voice said.

Rebecca struggled to open her eyes. A face swam slowly into focus and she found herself staring up at a nurse in a blue uniform. There was a tube stuck into her arm and she ached all over as if she had been run over by a steamroller.

'That's better,' the woman said approvingly as she trickled a few more drops of fluid into Rebecca's mouth. For a while the girl continued to try and fight her, but then as the soothing water slid down her throat she began to gulp at it greedily.

'Well done. But just a drop at a time for now. There, that's enough.'

Her head was back on the pillow now and the nurse was writing something on a chart that was clipped to the end of the bed.

'Wh-where am I?' Rebecca asked weakly.

'You're in hospital. But don't worry, you're over the worst – although I have to say, you gave us a scare for a while back there.'

In hospital – but why? Rebecca's mind was a blank – but then suddenly everything came back to her in a blinding flash. She had gone to sleep in the woods, and then . . . nothing!

'How long have I been here?'

'Oh. Let me see.' The nurse was straightening the sheet on her bed now. 'This must be the fourth day.'

'*Four days!*'

'Yes, but it wasn't until yesterday that you started to come back to the land of the living. In actual fact, you've been very lucky. A man walking his dog found you under a tree. You've had pneumonia and if he hadn't found you when he did, well . . .'

Rebecca went limp as she stared up at the clinical white ceiling. So she *had* almost died, then? If only the man hadn't found her, it would all be over now. As it was . . .

'Your social worker has been in to see you every single day,' the nurse went on. 'And what a lovely young woman she is. Miss James, isn't it? I've no doubt she'll be here again today too. It's usually around this time she pops in.'

The door suddenly opened and Miss James appeared as if the nurse mentioning her had somehow miraculously conjured her out of thin air.

'What did I tell you, eh?' The nurse smiled. 'I'll leave you two to have a chat, shall I?' And with that she swept from the room, her flat thick-soled shoes making no sound on the highly polished tiled floor.

'Oh, Rebecca, it's so good to see you awake,' Meg James said, sounding genuinely relieved. 'You scared us half to death. Whatever made you run away like that? No, don't try to talk too much for now. You've still got a long way to go. I know what happened at school and at the Dickinsons' but you should have spoken to me about it, not rushed off like that. You could have died. In fact, you almost did – and what a tragedy that would have been. You haven't even started to live yet.'

'Will I have to go back to them?' Rebecca asked flatly.

'No, of course you won't if you were unhappy there. But don't start to worry about that for now. Just concentrate on getting better, eh?'

Rebecca yawned widely. She'd only just woken up but suddenly she was very tired again, and before she knew it she was fast asleep once more.

Rebecca stayed in hospital for another seven days and each day she grew a little stronger although she didn't really care much one way or the other. What did she have to look forward to anyway? Another foster-care placement? Another set of people who didn't really want her?

She was sitting in a chair by the window staring out across the hospital grounds on the day Miss James was due to fetch her. She was in a very melancholy mood when she heard the door to her room open. Assuming it would be Miss James come to take her, she looked towards it and was shocked to see Pat standing there.

Her first feeling was one of joy but it quickly turned to distress as she realised that she might be staring at the mother who had once abandoned her.

Pat shuffled from foot to foot with tears in her tears. Rebecca had dark circles under her eyes and although she was on the mend now, she still looked far from well.

Forcing a smile to her face, the woman said, 'Well, miss, you certainly know how to put the wind up us, don't yer?'

Rebecca averted her eyes as Pat moved closer. She desperately wanted to lay her head on Pat's chest and cry her eyes out at the injustice of it all. After all, Pat was the only one who had ever seemed to genuinely like her, but she could never do that now. Not now she had figured out who she might be. No doubt she was only here because she was feeling guilty.

'I've phoned every day since they found you and brought you here,' Pat informed her. 'So how are you feeling now?'

'What do *you* care?' Rebecca shot back scathingly.

Pat looked bewildered. 'What you on about, girl? Of *course* I care. You should know that by now. What's up with you?'

Thankfully, Rebecca was saved from having to answer when Meg James entered, bearing magazines and a bag full of chocolate bars.

'Oh, hello Pat,' she said brightly, after nodding towards the patient.

'Thanks for letting me know where she was, love,' Pat answered, hiding her confusion behind a smile. 'I were worried sick the whole time she was missing. The nurse informed me that she's well on the mend now, although I can't say her temper's improved any.'

Miss James chuckled. Both she and Pat were well used to Rebecca's stand-offish attitude by now and yet they both still had a great affection for her, if only Rebecca could have known it.

'So where are you bundling me off to now?' Rebecca asked ungraciously as she rose and started to pack her few measly possessions into her holdall.

'You're going to live in Warwick with a lovely family – the Wigleys. I'm sure you'll like it there. They have another girl in placement about the same age as you, so you'll have someone to talk to. And they also have a son. Ben is nine and a real little football fanatic.'

Rebecca didn't much care where she went any more. What did it matter? One place was much the same as another.

'We might as well go then,' she said sulkily, and she waltzed past the two women without a glance as they stood there not quite knowing what to say.

Chapter Thirty-One

14 June 2004

'I'm telling you, if you don't get her out of my house – *today* – I won't be responsible for my actions,' the irate woman fumed as Meg looked on. Meg James had married a couple of years ago and was now Mrs Daley; she was also the proud mother of a one-year-old boy who her mother now looked after since she had returned to her job after maternity leave. Another social worker had taken over her cases whilst she'd been away, but she'd had little more success with Rebecca than Meg had, so at least she knew now that it wasn't something she was doing wrong. Rebecca was a law unto herself and wasn't going to conform for anyone. Meg had lost count of the number of placements Rebecca had had, each ending in disaster when she refused to abide by any rules. Right now she was suspended from her latest school again. She'd also lost count of how many times Rebecca had run away only to be caught by the police and hauled back. But she was fast approaching her sixteenth birthday now, and after that she could go it alone, although Meg had grave misgivings about how the girl would cope. She'd gone from school to school, which had done nothing at all for her education, not that Rebecca had much interest in learning. The biggest problem now was, where was Meg going to place her next?

'Has she been shoplifting again?' she asked Pru Devonshire, Rebecca's latest foster-mum.

Pru nodded. 'Yes, she has, but why she does it is a mystery to me. I mean, she steals the most unlikely things – things that she's never going to use. It's as if she does it just to prove that she can.'

Meg had to agree with her, although she was at a loss as to what she was going to do about it. Nothing she had tried so far had worked, and Pru was such an easygoing person – if Rebecca couldn't get on with her, then what chance was there?

Pru and her husband Derek lived in a huge Georgian terraced house in Leamington Spa that was something of a Tardis. It just seemed to go on forever. It even had a cellar that the couple had converted into a music and play room for the children. There was something in there to suit children and young people of all ages. There was even a table tennis table, but Rebecca had scarcely set foot in it, preferring to stay in her own room and keep herself to herself. Pru was a very experienced carer and had a huge success rate with the children she had fostered over the years, but she was big enough to accept that nothing she did was going to suit Rebecca; now that the girl's behaviour was beginning to have an impact on the other children in the household, she knew that she had no choice but to bring the placement to an end.

'I'm sorry, Meg,' she said regretfully, 'but I think we both have to accept that there are some children who we can't help. Thinking back over the few months Rebecca's been with us I can only remember one occasion when she really seemed to enjoy herself, and that was the other evening when I took all the kids to the circus. Usually Rebecca won't come anywhere with us, but when I offered to take her there she got quite excited about it. It was like watching a different person then, and believe it or not she can look quite attractive when she smiles, although I have to say it's a very rare occurrence.'

Meg patted her hand. 'It's all right. You've done your best, but now I ought to speak to Rebecca and then I'd better get back to the office and see what the boss has to say. Placements are like gold dust at present. We seem to have more children coming into care than we can cope with. It's quite frightening really and I'm afraid Rebecca's reputation is going before her now, so please bear with me. It could be quite late before I manage to locate another place for her.'

'Of course,' Pru sighed as she too rose.

Outside the door, which was slightly ajar, Rebecca had listened to every word, and now she stole away to the privacy of her room, fuming silently. She had just managed to reach her room when Pru's voice wafted faintly up the first set of stairs and then even more faintly up the second set.

'Rebecca . . . could you come down here for a moment, please?'

Rebecca appeared, her face innocent. It wouldn't do to let them know that she had been eavesdropping.

'Meg needs a word in there.' Pru gestured towards the lounge door before skittering away with a guilty expression on her face.

Rebecca walked in to find Meg staring out at the steady flow of traffic on the busy street beyond the enormous bay window.

'Rebecca,' she began. 'I'm afraid I have some bad news for you—'

The words went over the girl's head and thankfully at last she was allowed to go back to her room.

So Pru was going to dump her too now, was she? That would mean yet another move, but she had had enough now. In a little while she would be sixteen years old and then no one would be able to tell her what to do. Why wait until then? If she went now and kept her head down they might not find her until it was too late to drag her back into care. Her thoughts instantly flew to Harvey Brand's Circus on the outskirts of the town and her spirits rose. She had hardly been able to believe it when Pru had told her the circus was there, particularly *that* circus. And Miss Gina had still been a part of it with her dancing dogs, looking exactly as Rebecca had remembered her all those years ago when she had first seen her in the Pingles Fields in Nuneaton.

A quiver of excitement rippled through Rebecca. If only she could find her way back there, surely they would find a job for her to do? She didn't care what it was. She would cook, clean, wash floors if need be, but at last she would be able to live her dream.

Crossing to the pine dressing-table set against one wall, she studied her reflection in the mirror. She was tall and slim now, although no one could have said what shape she was beneath the baggy clothes she still insisted on wearing. Her hair had grown and thickened, and now she wore it in one very long unbecoming plait that dangled down her back. It was still a mousy colour but she knew that she could have made it look nice if she had tried; however, since the terrible encounters with her uncle she had no wish to appear attractive. It was so much safer to hide behind her plainness. She knew that her best feature was still her eyes. A deep striking blue, they could appear almost black when she was angry and they were thickly fringed with dark lashes. But there was nothing she could do to disguise them.

Snatching the drawer open, she took out a tin that she kept hidden beneath her underwear, and as she tipped it onto the bed a quantity of notes floated across the duvet. Each placement she had been to had given her regular pocket-money and she had never spent a penny of it. What was there to spend it on? She had no interest in clothes, make-up or music as other girls her age did, so she had saved, and saved, and now she knew that she must have well over a hundred pounds, which seemed like a fortune to her.

Gathering it together, she zipped it into the back pocket of her baggy jeans then, grabbing a bag from the bottom of the wardrobe, she began to pack her clothes into it. Once she was sure that she had everything she needed, she crossed to the window just in time to see Meg Daley drive away in her small Peugeot. Now all she had to do was wait. Derek was at work and Pru would be leaving later this afternoon to meet the two younger children from school. That would be the perfect time to escape. Sinking onto the edge of her bed she waited impatiently as she watched the hands of her alarm clock tick the minutes away.

At lunchtime a very subdued Pru called her down to eat. There was a selection of cold meats, salad and garlic bread steaming hot and fresh from the oven, but Rebecca wasn't hungry. She noticed that Pru did little more than pick at her own food too, and as soon as she could, the girl went up to her room again. It seemed they had nothing left to say to each other: it had all been said and the situation was beyond salvaging.

Rebecca hovered by her bedroom window and at last, just before three o'clock, she saw Pru set off to get the children from school. Picking up her bag, she ran down the two steep flights of stairs. But then, just as she made for the front door, it suddenly opened again and Pru appeared. 'Goodness, I'd forget my head if it was loose. I forgot my . . .' Pru's voice trailed away as she noticed the loaded bag slung across Rebecca's shoulder. 'And where were *you* planning on going?' she asked. 'I hope you weren't thinking of running away.'

She was level with Rebecca now and the girl felt as if she had been backed into a corner as she heard the sound of the heavy traffic whizz past on the road outside.

'What if I was? Who'd care?' she spat back defiantly.

'I would, for a start.' Pru reached out to take the bag from her but Rebecca hung on to it for grim life as temper flowed through her. Just who did Pru think she was anyway? The woman didn't want her, so why should she care?

They were tugging the bag between them and suddenly Rebecca lashed out. Taken unawares, Pru stumbled and fell, and as she went down she banged her head hard against the hall table and lay very still. Rebecca watched in horror as blood began to pool onto the wooden floor from the back of her head . . . and then to her further horror the door opened and Pru's husband appeared. He had finished work early because of a bad headache, and as he stared at his wife lying there he could hardly believe his eyes.

'*Jesus Christ*, girl! What have you done to her? I reckon she's dead!' he shouted as he dropped to his knees and felt for a pulse.

Not waiting to hear any more, Rebecca raced towards the front door and fled with tears streaming down her cheeks. Now on top of everything else she was a murderer and she knew that at all costs, she had to get away.

'*Oy!* Come back here, you!'

Rebecca glanced behind to see Derek standing on the steps dialling a number on his mobile phone. No doubt he would be phoning for an ambulance and she guessed that the police would not be far behind. She *had* to get away now! Taking off in the opposite direction, she didn't stop for breath until she was passing the Royal Pump Rooms and Baths. Knowing that there was little chance of being seen now, she slowed down then and headed for the banks of the River Leam. *Please don't let her be dead*, she repeated to herself over and over again, for although she had never been very nice to Pru, she knew that the woman had tried her best for her. Rebecca had done some terrible things in her time, but never anything as awful as this and she didn't know how she was going to live with herself.

She wasn't far from the circus now and her heart began to thump with a mixture of fear and excitement. If Gina would only take her in, no one would ever think of looking for her there and she would be safe. Soon she was on the outskirts of the town looking eagerly for the turrets of the Big Top which had been erected in a large field just ahead, but there was nothing to be seen. Quickening her pace, she shoved her way through a hedge and then gasped with disappointment when she was confronted with an empty field. The circus had moved on. She was too late.

Sinking onto the grass, she buried her head in her hands. Once again it seemed that the gods were against her. But then Rebecca sat up straight. The circus might have moved on, but there was nothing to stop her going to find it. They couldn't have gone that far, after all. And she hadn't meant to hurt Pru. If the silly cow hadn't forgotten her bag . . .

Rebecca began to kick about the bits of litter that were blowing around the field in the warm June breeze and eventually was rewarded when she came to part of a poster. HARVEY BRAND'S CIRCUS NEXT SHOWING IN HINCKLEY LEICS, she read.

She had no idea where Hinckley was but guessed that it couldn't be too far away, so she turned back towards the town and headed for the railway station. Perhaps she could get a train to Hinckley from there. Surely the police wouldn't be looking for her yet?

A sleepy-eyed man behind a desk informed her that she would have to get a train into Nuneaton and then a bus into

Hinckley, so she quickly paid for a one-way ticket and hurried onto the platform to wait. She was on her way to fulfil a dream and nothing had ever felt so right. She felt as if she had been waiting for this moment all her life, and now she could hardly wait for it to begin – although she wished that it had been under happier circumstances.

It was late afternoon by the time she stepped onto the platform of the Trent Valley railway station in Nuneaton. She looked about fearfully, but no one seemed to be watching her, or taking any notice of her at all, in fact. Thankfully, after enquiring she discovered that the bus station was just across the road and she boarded a bus to Hinckley within minutes. Of course she had no idea whereabouts in Hinckley the circus was, but she was feeling more optimistic by the minute and sure that she would find it.

The bus turned into a long road called Hinckley Road and Rebecca saw a large college on her left. She had paid for a ticket into Hinckley bus station, but as the bus turned at some traffic-lights onto the A5 she saw the turrets of the Big Top ahead on her right and she quickly scrambled to the front of the bus so that she could get off at the next stop. It had been much easier to find than she had expected, and she wondered if this was a good omen.

Hastily glancing about to make sure that there were no policemen on watch, she entered the field where workers were scurrying about like ants preparing for the evening performance. And then she saw it – Gina's trailer. There were three or four dogs tethered on long leads outside and she could hear more yapping from within. She stood there, suddenly uncertain of what she should do. If the dogs were outside it stood to reason that Gina was sure to appear before long, and she had all the time in the world now that she was finally where she wanted to be. Unless the police found her, that was. She chewed nervously on her lip as she pictured Pru lying in a pool of blood then miserably tried to blink the image away.

Sure enough, ten minutes later a blonde woman appeared carrying metal dishes full of what Rebecca presumed was dog food. She placed them down and petted the dogs, then as she turned to enter the trailer again, she spotted Rebecca watching her and paused. There was something about the girl that looked vaguely familiar. But then Gina saw so many faces on her travels. As she turned away, about to enter the trailer again, Rebecca seized her chance.

Grabbing her bag, she raced towards her.

'Do I know you?' Gina frowned.

'You might remember me,' Rebecca said breathlessly, her face alight with hope. 'I talked to you once when I was a kid and you were in Nuneaton. I told you about my mum dumping me when I was born and that I was in care. Then last week I came to see you again when you were in Leamington, but I couldn't stay behind to talk to you after the show because I was with my latest foster-mum.'

A memory began to stir and Gina peered at her more closely. Yes, she could vaguely remember it now, although the girl in front of her was much older now. But she would never forget those bluebell-coloured eyes. They were quite breathtaking.

'So what can I do for you?' she asked pleasantly in her broad Yorkshire accent.

'You told me back then that I had to be eighteen before I could join the circus and I am now, so I've come to see if there's a job going,' Rebecca gabbled.

If this girl was eighteen then she was a monkey's uncle, but Gina didn't want to hurt her feelings.

'I thought you said you came to see me last week with your foster-mum?'

'Ah, well I did . . . but I wasn't eighteen then.' Rebecca dropped her eyes as Gina raised hers.

'Hmm, well . . . if you're after a job you'd best go and see the ringmaster. He's the one who does all the hiring and firing,' Gina advised. 'And to be honest I'm not sure that there are any jobs going.'

'Oh, but I don't want just *any* job.' Rebecca looked desperate now. 'I want to work for *you*. It's all I've ever wanted to do ever since the first time I saw you with your dogs.'

Gina frowned. The poor kid looked worn out and very unhappy – desperate almost. 'Then I'm sorry to disappoint you but I'm a one-woman show,' she said kindly. 'I don't need anyone to work for me. Now why don't you just go home?'

'But I haven't *got* a home.' Rebecca's shoulders sagged and despair gripped her as she saw her dream slipping away from her. 'I've never had a proper home since my adopted mum died. I've just been shunted from one place to another.'

'Look, why don't I get us both a nice cold drink, eh? I'm sure things can't be as bad as you say.'

Gina disappeared into the trailer and returned holding two tall glasses of lemonade. She passed one to Rebecca and then sat down beside her on the trailer steps.

'Right, now how about we start again? And I want the truth this time. Like how old you *really* are for a start-off 'cos no way are you eighteen, my lass!'

Rebecca almost choked on a mouthful of lemonade at Gina's tone. There was going to be no pulling the wool over this one's eyes, so she supposed she might as well come clean.

'Well, I'm sixteen really – at least I will be soon – and I've been living with carers in Leamington. But I've never been able to settle with anybody and they decided today that I'd got to be moved on again. The thought of yet another foster-placement was too much, so I decided that it was time to set out on my own. I can do that legally when I'm sixteen anyway, so I thought seeing as I'm almost there I might as well do it now. And I hoped . . . that you'd have a job for me.' Again she tried to shunt away the thought of what she had done to Pru, but the woman's face kept popping up behind her eyes and she was terrified that Gina would see the guilt she was suffering.

She was staring at Gina so intently now that the woman looked away. There was something about this kid that tugged at her heartstrings. From what she could make of it she'd had a raw deal. But even so, the last thing she needed was the coppers knocking on the door, which they well might do if the girl was still under age.

'Look,' she said eventually. 'I'd love to help you, I really would. But the thing is . . . the circus has a reputation to maintain. It's not like it used to be in days gone by when gypsies and circuses were supposed to nick children along the way. We're respectable hard-working people, so I'm afraid the best thing you could do is to go back to your foster-mum and try and stick it out. I'm sorry, kid.'

Rebecca rarely cried, but today she couldn't seem to help it. She was just so tired of feeling that she didn't belong anywhere, and she had hoped that this would be the start of better times. But who had she been trying to fool? There would never be better times now, after what she had done to Pru. She could run away from the police but she would never be able to run away from herself.

'Please won't you reconsider?' she implored. 'I wouldn't expect to be paid much and I'd do anything. And I'd work really hard, I promise!'

'I'm sure you would. But I daren't risk it. Now off you

go. Come back when you're old enough and we'll talk again, eh?'

'But—'

Gina held her hand up. 'Sorry, pet. No can do,' she said firmly, and with that she re-entered the trailer and closed the door with finality on Rebecca's dreams.

Chapter Thirty-Two

Rebecca had spent the next few hours dejectedly skulking about the circus field but now it was dark and the field was almost deserted.

She'd watched the whole place come to life as the circus troupe prepared for the performance and she had sat on the perimeter of the field listening to the roar of the audience as the show progressed. It was like being in another world, and now more than ever she knew that she wanted to be a part of it. But what could she do if Gina wasn't prepared to help her? It had all seemed so straightforward when she'd run away from Leamington, but now she realised that she was in a mess with nowhere to go. Earlier in the evening she had passed a brightly painted caravan. The doors were wide open in the warm June breeze and she'd been shocked to see the bearded lady inside, carefully gluing her beard to her chin; she'd realised then that there was a lot more to circus life than she'd anticipated. Nothing was quite as it seemed, which was, of course, part of the attraction.

She knew that Gina had seen her before the performance as she ushered the dogs into the Big Top, but the woman had studiously ignored her. She had done the same after the performance and now Rebecca's spirits were just about as low as they could get. The only thing in her favour was that it was a lovely evening so she could sleep beneath the hedgerow bordering the field. It wouldn't be the first time she'd had to

do it, although the last time had brought about dire conse-
quences. Still, she comforted herself, it had been mid-winter
then. At least now the weather was in her favour. Slinging
her bag under the hedge she lay down and got as comfortable
as she could before dropping into a deep sleep.

It must have been the early hours of the morning when the
rain started. The first gentle drops brought her springing awake,
but within minutes it was lashing down as she crouched miserably beneath the hedge. She'd been there for some time when
she saw the lights in Gina's trailer snap on and then the door
opened and Gina was running towards her beneath the shelter
of a huge umbrella. She was dressed in a large terry towelling
dressing-gown, and by the time she reached Rebecca she was
none too happy.

'Just what the hell do you think you're still doing here?'
she said crossly. 'You'll catch your bloody death of cold.
Didn't I tell you to get your arse back home?'

'I'm not going back . . . not ever!' Rebecca said stubbornly,
the rain dripping off her face, – and suddenly Gina chuckled.

'Well, you've got spirit, I'll give you that. In fact, you remind
me of myself when I was your age. Come on, I don't suppose
it would hurt if I let you shelter in the trailer for the rest of
the night. But it's only for the *one* night, mind.'

Her face suddenly animated, Rebecca scrambled to her feet.
Then, keeping close to Gina, she followed her back to the
trailer. Once she had clambered up the steps and stepped
inside, her mouth fell open with astonishment. It was nothing
like she had expected it to be! The front part of the trailer
was fitted out as a luxurious lounge, with all mod cons
including a television in one corner which was hooked to a
small generator beneath the trailer. Next to that was a spacious
kitchen sporting a fridge-freezer, a cooker and a microwave.
Velvet drapes in a warm pink colour hung at the windows in

the lounge and the fitted seats were covered in the same fabric. There was also a table and chairs and expensive rugs on the floor. A number of dogs lay here and there, and they eyed Rebecca curiously although not one of them offered to bark.

'Wow!' Rebecca said appreciatively. 'It's like walking into a little palace.'

Gina smiled with pride. 'What you have to remember is this is my home, so I've tried to make it as comfortable as possible. But come along, take off your shoes and I'll show you the rest of it.'

Rebecca followed her through a door that led off the kitchen and into a narrow hallway. Throwing the first door open, Gina told her, 'This is my room.'

Rebecca peeped past her and once again she was suitably impressed. A double bed with built-in wardrobes on either side of it took up most of the room, but there was also a dressing-table and a chest of drawers in there in matching pine. The colour scheme in this room was a pale blue and it looked fresh and inviting. The second door revealed a compact but very functional shower room with a toilet, a sink and a shower cubicle. The fittings were all in chrome and a number of fluffy green towels were draped across a heated towel rail. It was very modern and Rebecca found it hard to believe that she was actually in a trailer. The next door revealed yet another bedroom with two single beds in it. There was also a single wardrobe and a chest of drawers, and it looked cosy and inviting. The last door led into a small space that was fitted from floor to ceiling with cages. Inside each one was a warm blanket.

'The dogs travel in these when we're on the road,' Gina explained. 'It's safer for them than letting them wander about the trailer. But now I think you ought to take a shower and I'll find you a nightie and a dressing-gown. You're soaked to the skin and I dare say a cuppa and something to eat wouldn't go amiss.'

Rebecca's first instinct was to refuse everything, but her stomach was rumbling ominously now and she realised with a start that she hadn't eaten a thing since lunchtime the day before.

'Perhaps a drink and something to eat but I don't need a shower,' Rebecca replied.

'Oh yes you bloody well do if you're going to be sleeping in my bed,' Gina shot back in a no-nonsense voice. Rebecca sulkily followed her to the shower room and seconds later, Gina passed her some clean nightclothes.

Ten minutes later she emerged, her long hair wrapped in a towel, wearing Gina's borrowed clothes.

There was a pile of hot buttered toast and a pot of tea waiting for her on the table and she tucked in gratefully as Gina sank onto the settee and curled her feet beneath her. She then lit a cigarette and after drawing on it she watched Rebecca curiously.

'How did you know I was outside?' Rebecca asked through a mouthful of hot buttered toast.

'Oh, I knew you were there all right.' Gina blew a smoke ring into the air. 'I've been keeping my eye on you all night, and when it started to rain I took pity on you. No one deserves to sleep under a hedge, especially a kid.'

'I'm not a kid! I'm almost sixteen and well able to take care of myself.'

'Well, you weren't doing a very good job of it tonight, were you?'

Rebecca helped herself to another cup of tea, muttering, 'I would have been all right.' She knew that she was being ungrateful, but she had never been good at speaking to people.

A silence settled between them that seemed to stretch on

for a long time until Gina finally said, 'I don't know about you, but I'm all in. How about we go to bed and try to get some sleep?'

A glimmer of a smile was her answer, so she rose and showed Rebecca along the passage to the second bedroom. 'Sleep tight, pet,' she said at the doorway and Rebecca nodded, not knowing what to say or do. Once she heard Gina's bedroom door close she slipped the towelling dressing-gown off and caught sight of herself in the mirror. She suspected that the nightdress Gina had loaned her was real silk, and it clung to her skin seductively, showing off the curves that she usually went to such great lengths to hide. Her damp hair was loose about her shoulders now and she hardly recognised herself. But old habits die hard, and snatching her elastic band from her wrist she hastily bundled her hair back into its customary unflattering ponytail and clambered between the crisp white sheets. Tonight, she felt as if she had been given a reprieve, but what about tomorrow? Would Gina really tip her out with nowhere to go? Or would the police find her? How was Derek managing with the children back in Leamington? But she was too tired to worry about it any more for now, and before she knew it she was sound asleep.

She woke the next morning to the appetising smell of bacon frying and stretched lazily. She had slept like a log and couldn't remember a time when she had felt so happy – until she remembered what she had done to Pru, that was. She slipped the dressing-gown on that Gina had loaned her, and went through to the kitchen, where Gina was expertly flipping bacon and eggs in a large frying pan. She nodded towards the table.

'Sit yourself down. This will be ready in a minute.'

Rebecca did as she was told, glancing through the open

door as she went. The rain had died away again and it looked set to be another glorious day. There was a line strung between the large van that towed the trailer and the front of the trailer, and Rebecca could see the wet clothes she had been wearing the night before flapping in the early-morning breeze. Gina must have washed them and hung them out to dry for her. Now at least she would have an excuse to wait here until they were dry. She was about to sit down when a number of warm little bodies seemed to come at her from all directions, and laughing she dropped to the floor as they pranced all over her.

'Like dogs, do you?' Gina asked, watching her closely.

'Oh yes.' Rebecca giggled as they licked her with their warm little tongues. 'I used to have a dog when I lived with my aunt and uncle. He was called Casper, but—' She stopped abruptly, unable to go on, and Gina could see that she must have loved him dearly. It was a point in the girl's favour and Gina proudly began to introduce her own pets before saying after a while, 'Now come and get this breakfast while it's hot.'

Gina had just placed a plateful of food in front of her when the light from the doorway was blocked by a large man who stared at Rebecca inquisitively. He looked to be in his mid-forties and he was tall and muscular, with piercing dark eyes. Rebecca guessed that his hair must have been black once upon a time but now it was a salt and pepper colour that gave him a distinguished look. Aware that she was staring, she lowered her eyes.

'Sorry, Gina,' he said. 'I didn't know you had company.'

Looking slightly flummoxed, Gina told him, 'Oh, this is my niece, Harvey. Her name is . . . Bex. She er . . . she's come to stay with me for a few days.'

'Oh, I didn't realise you had a niece.' He stared at Rebecca again. But then thankfully he smiled and turned away. 'Well,

I won't keep you if you're just about to have breakfast,' he said. 'I'll see you later, Gina. Goodbye for now, Bex.'

When he had gone, Gina let out a long sigh of relief.

'Does this mean you're going to let me stay?' Rebecca's voice was so full of hope that Gina's heart sank like a stone. The kid had only been there for a few hours and already she was having to lie for her.

'I didn't say that, did I?' she said, more sharply than she had intended to, then she explained, 'Look, Rebecca, that was Harvey. He's the ringmaster and he owns the whole circus lock, stock and barrel. If he were to find out that I was harbouring a runaway he'd have both of us out of here, pronto. I had to say *something*, didn't I?'

'Yes, but now that you have, couldn't I stay for just a little while longer?' the girl pleaded. 'He obviously believed what you told him. And I'd do anything you said – *anything*!'

'Hmm.' Gina tapped her chin thoughtfully. And then, to Rebecca's great embarrassment, she reached over and tugged the band from the girl's hair, allowing it to flow freely down her back.

'If I did – and I'm only saying *if*, mind – we'd have to change your looks a little and you'd have to answer to Bex . . . it's short for Rebecca anyway and it isn't such a mouthful.'

When Rebecca looked slightly confused, Gina hurried on, 'We could start with your hair. We could cut it to shoulder-length and I could put some blonde highlights through it for you. And then of course we'd need to get you some more modern clothes. There's no room for plain people in a circus and you could actually be quite pretty if you'd make a bit of an effort.' Rebecca's eyes were her best feature, she thought, and a quite striking shade of blue, almost lavender, or like bluebells. 'So what do you say then?' she went on. 'Are you ready for a completely new look, for a completely new start?'

Rebecca fingered her hair doubtfully. She couldn't even remember the last time she'd had it cut, and the thought of suddenly being trendy was a little daunting. She'd hidden behind her dreary hair do and baggy clothes for so long she wasn't sure how she would cope with being halfway attractive. But then if she did what Gina was suggesting, she wouldn't be Rebecca any more, would she? She would be Bex, with a whole new life in front of her.

'The thing is,' Gina went on, sensing the girl's hesitation, 'I have been thinking of taking someone on to help out a bit. The dogs need regular exercise and grooming, and I could teach you how to train them. But don't go running away with the idea that this life will be easy. It's damned hard work, especially on the days we're moving on. We'll be up at five in the morning, earlier than that sometimes if we have a long way to go – and then when we reach our destination we have to get all set up again, ready for the evening performance. Everyone pitches in to help and you could be doing any number of jobs in all sorts of weather.'

'I wouldn't mind that,' Rebecca said hastily, her eyes great pools of hope.

'And there's no such thing as a day off in this life,' Gina went on sternly. 'The only time you get to rest is when we overwinter in Hertfordshire or King's Lynn. Even then we still have to care for the animals and continue with the training. This job is non-stop. Does it still sound so attractive?'

'Oh, yes!' Rebecca breathed without hesitation. 'It's all I've ever wanted since the first time I saw you when I was just a little girl, and I've . . . well, I've never really belonged anywhere before.'

Gina sighed. 'In that case I suppose it won't hurt to give you a trial. But it will be only a trial, mind! Say one month? And then we'll see how we both feel and how it's working out. And if Social Services or the cops come sniffing around, you'll tell them that you'd told me you were eighteen. Is it a deal?'

'It's a deal,' Rebecca said ecstatically, and suddenly the world was a brighter place.

Chapter Thirty-Three

Rebecca's elation lasted for a whole hour and then it began to fade – fast!

By then she was sitting at the table with a towel wrapped around her shoulders and Gina was hacking away at her hair as if she was some sort of demented sheep-shearer. Locks were tumbling to the floor at an alarming rate, and all the while Gina spoke to her encouragingly.

'Don't look so worried, you'll love it when I've finished.'

Rebecca, or Bex as she must now get used to being called, wasn't so sure and hoped that Gina knew what she was doing. At last, Gina stood back and eyed her critically before smiling broadly.

'*That's* better. Now just stay there while I go and get the bleach.' She hurried away as Rebecca tentatively reached up to finger her shorn hair. Gina returned within seconds and after mixing the bleach in a small plastic bowl she began to cut silver foil into long strips. 'Now I'm going to put you some highlights in,' she explained as she lifted strands of hair and started to plaster the purple mixture onto them with a small brush.

Half an hour later, when Rebecca dared to peep into the mirror she could have mistaken herself for an alien. Long metallic strips sprouted out randomly all over her head and she felt colour burn into her cheeks. All this and for what? True, Gina had said she would give her a month's trial, but what then? No one had ever truly wanted her for long, so why should Gina be any different? Happy endings only happened in some of the books she had read, not to real people like herself, especially not after what she had done, albeit accidentally, to Pru.

Gina had shot off into her bedroom now and Rebecca could hear her dragging drawers open as if there was no tomorrow. When she finally returned, her arms were full of clothes.

'We're going to have to go shopping for you and get you some decent gear,' she commented. 'But until then some of these should fit you. Anything has to be better than what you were wearing.'

Rebecca eyed with mounting horror the strappy T-shirts, jeans, jogging bottoms and lacy underwear. None of them were anything at all like what she was used to wearing.

'Now don't get turning your nose up until you've tried them on,' Gina said, seeing Rebecca's horrified expression. 'Right – let's see how these highlights are doing.' Deftly unwrapping one of the silver foils, she smiled with satisfaction before hauling Rebecca off to the bathroom. There, Gina shoved her head over the sink and washed and conditioned her hair before leading her back to the dining area. After plonking the girl back down on the chair she then brandished a hairdryer.

'Won't be long now and you'll be able to see the new you,' she told her.

Eventually she stood back and, satisfied with her efforts, handed some clothes to Rebecca.

'Go and try those on,' she ordered. 'And then we'll put a bit of slappy on you. It's amazing how much more grown-up it can make you look.'

Rebecca eyed the orange T-shirt and tight jeans doubtfully, but did as she was told all the same. As she had already discovered, she had met her match in Gina and there would be no point in arguing. But then she *really* wanted this, more than she had ever wanted anything in her whole life, so it was up to her to make an effort. The lifestyle that Gina was offering would be worth it. She emerged from the bathroom feeling very self-conscious. The jeans were a little big around the waist and the lacy bra was a little loose too, but the T-shirt fitted perfectly and showed off her cleavage. Rebecca felt sure she would curl up and die with embarrassment, but she tried to look enthusiastic, knowing that she had no other choice.

'Right then! Now for the finishing touches. You've got wonderful eyes so I'm going to emphasise them. Luckily your skin is flawless too, so you won't need too much.' Gina opened her make-up bag and got to work. Eventually she said: 'Have a look in the mirror now and tell me what you think.'

She took Rebecca's's hand and led her into the bedroom, and as she looked at herself in the full-length mirror on the wardrobe door, she gasped with disbelief. That girl staring back at her couldn't be *her*, surely? Her hair was now shoulder-length and the highlights in it gleamed a warm golden colour. A little mascara had made her lashes appear longer and thicker, and framed her deep blue eyes to perfection. And suddenly she had a shape! The clothes she was wearing flattered her figure and made her look young and trendy, and for now she was utterly speechless although not at all sure that she would ever dare to venture out of the trailer looking like this.

'What do you think then? Do you like your new look?'

Rebecca shook her head in amazement. 'I'm not quite sure,' she admitted in a small voice. 'I look so . . . different.'

Gina chuckled. 'That was the general idea. But come on now. We've work to do and it won't do itself. You can start by taking all of the dogs for a walk around the field. Four at a time. I'm going to clean up in here and then I have to work on some new tricks with them. Chop-chop now. And don't forget, from this moment on you are Bex.'

After fetching some leads from the cupboard that Gina pointed to, the new Bex fastened them on to the four dogs closest to her and took a deep breath before ushering them ahead of her down the trailer steps. She was painfully aware of the low-cut top she was wearing and before she had gone fifty yards was convinced that the whole world and his mother were staring at her. Keeping close to the hedge, she watched the preparations for the evening performance. The Big Top seemed to be bulging with people all practising their acts. The acrobats and the trapeze artists were dressed in gaudy leotards, and she noticed Harvey in a far corner lifting weights as if they weighed no more than a feather. That must be why he was so muscular, she thought. Later she was to discover that he was also the circus's Strong Man. It seemed that everyone there was multi-tasking in some way or another, and already she was realising that this life wasn't as easy or glamorous as she had imagined – just as Gina had warned her.

An hour later, while Gina put some of the dogs through their paces, she set Bex to work on grooming the rest of them. Gina was very proud of her animals and insisted that they looked their best at all times.

At lunchtime she cooked them both delicious spaghetti bolognaise, and when they had eaten she left Bex to wash up while she stood outside in the warm sunshine chatting to Harvey. They seemed to be close and Bex wondered if there was something between them, but that theory flew out of the window later that afternoon when Gina informed her, 'I'm going over to Harvey's trailer now to help him bath his wife, Maura. Poor soul, she has a muscle-wasting illness and needs round-the-clock care, so I help out as much as I can.'

Bex was surprised. 'If she's that ill, why isn't she in a nursing home?' she asked.

Gina tugged a brush through her long blonde hair and slicked some lipstick on. 'Harvey would never let that happen. He and Maura were married when they were both in their teens and he's of the old school. Believes you stick together in sickness and in health.'

Once Gina had gone, Bex went to the mirror again and surveyed her new image. She had already received a wolf whistle – her first ever – from the young clown, Ricky, who also doubled as one of the acrobats, and she didn't quite know how to handle it. Ricky was actually quite handsome when he wasn't in his ridiculous clown costume. He was the son of Sheila, the so-called Bearded Lady. Bex had also met Mickey the Midget, and had been amused when he had bowed solemnly and kissed her hand. He might be small but it seemed he was a bit of a ladies' man and never short of a girlfriend. In fact, Gina chuckled to her later that day, he usually left behind at least one broken heart in every venue they visited.

That evening, Bex stayed behind the curtains as Gina swept into the ring with her Amazing Dancing Dogs to thunderous applause, and once again the magic of the circus took over as she watched Gina's performance enthralled. During the interval Bex sold candy floss and ice creams to excited children, and she knew that she had done right. Harvey looked handsome in his ringmaster's outfit and held the audience in the palm of his hand, and Bex wondered if she would ever tire of watching him. The trapeze artists and the acrobats were now dressed in exotic tight-fitting costumes, and as they performed she found herself smiling at the gasps from the audience. The performers made everything look so easy but already she knew just how much work went into making their performances so flawless. She was sad when the music heralded the end of the show and the children filed past her with sticky mouths and animated expressions on their faces, clutching the hands of their doting parents.

Rebecca felt a sharp pang of regret. She could never remember anyone looking at her as these mums and dads looked at their kids, and she knew that she had missed out on a lot – and this was all down to Pat. And yet . . . she still felt regret when she thought of her, and although she would never allow herself to admit it, she was missing her. A long time ago, Pat had let her down badly when she abandoned her – *if* she was her mother, of course – but perhaps there had been a good reason?

Rebecca shook herself mentally. I must be going soft, she thought, and hardened her heart again. As far as she was concerned, Pat was part of her past now and that was the way it would stay. This would be a brand new start. Just as Gina had said, she was Bex now. Rebecca was gone. She just wished with all her heart that the change could have begun without having Pru's accident on her conscience.

It was gone eleven o'clock before Bex finally fell into bed exhausted. Once the last of the audience had left, everyone pitched in to tidy the Big Top for the next day and it was hard work. Bex went between the rows of seats collecting rubbish in a large black binliner whilst the men swept the ring and threw down fresh sawdust. Then the animals had to be fed and bedded down.

She was aching with fatigue by then and sighed contentedly as she nestled down in her little bedroom. She was lying there reliving her first day when she heard low voices: they seemed to be coming from just outside her bedroom window. Tweaking the curtain aside, she peeped out to see Harvey and Gina with their heads close together whispering. She dropped the curtain hastily. It wouldn't do to be seen. They might think she was spying on them, but it did seem strange at this time of night. But then she decided that they were probably only discussing what had happened earlier in the day. One of the circus girls had been raped the night before, and Harvey had managed the whole incident with great sensitivity. He had called in the police and a doctor to examine her before driving her back to her family in Hull to recover. The girl, who was training to join the acrobats, had met the chap at the evening performance and foolishly gone to a nightclub with him before he attacked her. However, it seemed from what Gina had confided to Bex that she wasn't quite so sympathetic to the girl's plight.

'It was always on the cards with Tania,' she'd said sadly. 'Between you and me she was a hot-arsed little madam, always off with some bloke or another.' So now Bex put them from her mind, and in no time at all had drifted into a dreamless sleep.

The next day, Bex had a go at making breakfast. She'd never really had much cause to cook before and Gina laughed at the undercooked sausages and the burned toast. 'Let's hope you make a better trainer than you do a chef,' she teased, and although she felt herself flushing, Bex smiled with her. Gina was remarkably easy to get along with, although she knew exactly how she wanted things done when it came to her dogs. It appeared there was a right way to bath them, and a right way to groom them – and Gina would settle for no half-measures.

'People pay a lot of money to see them appear looking their best,' she scolded as she rinsed some excess shampoo from Tallulah's coat. 'If this had been left in, it would have irritated her skin and her coat wouldn't have dried properly.'

'Sorry,' Rebecca muttered. There was a lot to learn but she was determined to get it right. The alternative was to find herself alone again – and that was unthinkable.

Chapter Thirty-Four

The following week, the circus packed up and went to Mablethorpe in Lincolnshire.

'We stay there for twelve weeks during the peak holiday period,' Gina informed the girl as she drove, keeping her eyes tightly on the road. 'It saves a lot of work, not having to pack up every couple of weeks. You might even find time to get a few walks along the beach.'

Bex doubted it. They'd been up since four o'clock in the morning and hadn't even stopped for breakfast. Gina was right – being a part of a circus was backbreaking hard work. She was up every morning at first light and when she finally dropped back into bed again, she was so exhausted that even getting undressed was an effort. But for all that she was still enjoying her new life and Gina was more than fair to her. Ricky was nice too and always went out of his way to speak to her, a fact that made her feel funny inside. He was such a kind young man and nothing was ever too much trouble for him.

'So when will the next performance be?' she now asked innocently.

Gina chuckled. 'This evening. Just because we're moving camp it doesn't mean that we can afford to lose money. What we earn in season has to keep us through the winter, so every penny counts. As soon as we get to the new site everyone will pitch in again getting the Big Top up and everything ready for this evening's performance – so if you're tired I suggest you try and snatch a nap on the way, because I promise you're not going to get another chance before late tonight.'

Yawning, Rebecca closed her eyes and did just that.

It seemed no time at all before the slamming of the van door brought her springing awake. She rubbed her eyes and saw that they were in a large field quite close to the sea-front.

'Come on,' Gina shouted. 'We're here, so you get the dogs out and give them all a walk around the field to stretch their legs. Oh, and don't forget to give them a drink too.'

Rebecca slid out of the van and went around to the back of the trailer to release the dogs from their cages. They were getting used to her now and they wagged their tails enthusiastically when they saw her. First she hammered the large stake that Gina used for tethering them into the ground, then she put them all onto long leads and fetched some dishes of water for them. Another thing she had discovered was that the animals always came first and the needs of the people came second. She walked them around the perimeter of the field four at a time, and by then the men were busily unloading the Big Top and everywhere was a hive of activity – although Ricky took time to come and chat to her, and as always the sight of him set her heart fluttering. It was a totally alien feeling for Bex. No other boy had ever singled her out before and she found she liked speaking to him. The task of erecting the Big Top then began in earnest, and Rebecca watched in fascination as the bare field was transformed into a circus ground.

Once the dogs had all been exercised and were resting happily in the shade of the van, she set to and helped Gina get the trailer into the right position. All the trailers and caravans were parked in neat rows along the edge of the field close to the hedge behind the Big Top, and Rebecca quite liked the idea of staying there for a few weeks. She had had very few holidays and intended to make the most of every second of being at the seaside – when she wasn't working, that was.

By mid-afternoon the Big Top was erected and the box office was in place. The flags had been hoisted too and now they flapped lazily in the breeze blowing in from the sea. Everyone then set to getting the seats in place within, and then the ring was put in position and the sawdust was thrown down whilst others were busily fixing the trapezes into the roof of the great tent. Already a queue of people was forming at the box office for tickets for the evening performance. Ricky was busily serving them and as Rebecca walked by with an enormous broom to level the sawdust in the ring, he winked cheekily at her.

She hastily lowered her eyes and hurried past. With his thatch of thick dark hair and his deep brown eyes, she was struggling to understand what he might see in her. He was so handsome that she was sure he could have had his pick of any girl he wanted, but unlike some of the other circus men, she had never seen him so much as flirt with a girl. But then she was Bex now – she had left Rebecca behind, which was still taking some getting used to – and perhaps Ricky was just trying to help her settle in? In fact, most of the circus folk were beginning to accept her, and Bex liked the feeling of belonging. It was something she had never experienced before and she dreaded anything going wrong. But always underneath was the niggling fear when she thought of Pru. Had the woman survived, or was she guilty of murder?

The first week flew by and the Big Top was full to capacity each night with holidaymakers. Rebecca was thoroughly enjoying herself, and with each day that passed she began to feel more relaxed and safe. After all, who would even think of looking for her here, miles away from the Midlands? If anyone had bothered to, that was. Sometimes of an evening she would take a stroll along the beach and when he was able to, Ricky began to join her. She found that they actually had quite a lot in common, and the more time she spent with him, the more she liked him. They enjoyed the same music and she discovered that he had a great sense of humour. He could make her laugh, something the old Rebecca had rarely done, but as if he sensed that she needed time to settle he never attempted to be anything more than a friend for now and she was grateful for that.

Before she knew it, they were late into September. Her birthday had come and gone, and now at least she had no fear of being dragged back into care should she be found. She knew that it would be a different story if the police were to track her down, however, and she still worried constantly about what had happened with her foster-mum. So much so that her heart fluttered each time she saw a police car. On a few occasions she would suddenly get the feeling that she was being watched, usually of an evening following Gina's performance, but whenever she spun about to check, there was no one there and she would scold herself for being so nervous.

It was one evening as Rebecca was busily selling programmes for the evening performance that a young man standing in the queue at the box office caught her eye. He was tall and dark-haired, and something about him was disturbingly familiar. She tried to study him more closely, but it was difficult from a distance. Inching her way through the throngs of people who were all laughing and chatting, she managed to get a little nearer. The young man was with another chap about his own age, and as she approached them, Bex's heart began to beat faster. It was a long time since she had last seen him and he had grown up, but there could be no mistaking him. It was her brother, Joshua.

Rebecca's heart was hammering against her ribs now and she backed away into the shadow of the enormous marquee as colour flamed in her cheeks. What was she going to do? Just when she had begun to think she was safe, Joshua had appeared like a bad penny. If he were to spot her, everything could be ruined. She had no doubt he would have read what she had done to Pru in the newspapers. But there was no way she could hide. Gina would soon give her what-for, if she didn't pull her weight for the evening's performance.

Composing herself with a great effort, she turned and tried to lose herself in the crowd, hoping that Josh wouldn't spot her. When the audience was finally seated for the performance, Bex heaved a great sigh of relief. So far, so good. Josh and his friend had ringside seats, and up to now had been so engrossed in the performance that they hadn't even glanced in her direction. She could only pray that it would continue. During the interval she felt sick with dread as she served a queue of people with ice creams and popcorn. All the time she kept a wary eye on her brother, but thankfully he and his friend stayed in their seats chatting and her spirits began to rise a little. One thing she hadn't considered until now was the fact that she looked vastly different to the girl that Josh would remember, and chances were that even if he did glance her way he wouldn't recognise her.

As soon as the show was over she would be busy taking the dogs back to the trailer, and hopefully that would be the end of it. It was highly unlikely that Josh would come to another performance, but just the sight of him had awakened a lot of painful memories and she knew that it would take time before she could feel safe again. Once more, her thoughts drifted back to Pru and guilt, sharp as a knife, stabbed at her. If only she knew what had happened to her! But the only way to find out was to go back – and sadly, she knew that she would never have the guts to do that.

The night seemed to stretch on and on, but at last the acrobats came on to do the finale and the show ended to thunderous applause as the whole of the troupe began to circle the ring, taking their bows.

Bex waited beyond the enormous curtains as Gina ushered the dogs towards her and bent to put the first four on their leads. Gina seemed preoccupied and was deep in conversation with Harvey, so Bex quietly led the excited animals towards the rear entrance of the Big Top.

The car park at the front of the tent had been full to over-flowing, and before the show Ricky had directed some of the cars to the back of the tent. Now the holidaymakers were heading towards them and Bex had to lead the dogs through the crowds. It was a warm and balmy night, and after being confined to the Big Top and the overpowering smell of grease-paint and sawdust, she welcomed the scent of the sea and the cool breeze on her face. However, halfway to the trailer she had the sensation of being observed again – and she paused to look over her shoulder as the dogs frolicked at her feet.

Her heart sank into her shoes as she saw Josh staring at her with a puzzled expression on his face. He was standing at the side of a very expensive-looking Range Rover and Bex quickly averted her eyes and hurried on. Once at the trailer she yanked the door open and, pushing the dogs ahead of her, she stumbled inside, slamming the door behind her. She was shocked to find that she was trembling as she cautiously crept towards the window and tweaked the net curtain aside.

The Range Rover was pulling away now. Perhaps it was only a coincidence that Josh had been looking towards her? Or better still, perhaps he had been looking at the dogs? She could only hope so, and pray that this would be an end to it. After all, not many people would visit the circus twice during their holiday, so she was probably panicking for nothing.

With her heart settling back into a steadier rhythm she turned her attention back to the dogs, and got on with her job.

By the time she had settled them all and tidied up outside, it was dark and she was feeling tired. She had been up since early that morning, and now all she wanted was to drop into her comfy little bed and sleep. But as she approached the door to the trailer, which was open, she heard the murmur of voices and glancing inside, she saw Harvey sitting and Gina talking. She had grown used to the amount of time Harvey spent with Gina now; it was hardly surprising as she gave him a lot of help with Maura, his invalid wife. Bex had met Maura, who was a gentle soul, and she felt sorry for her, for despite her illness the woman's eyes were still vibrant with life. It must be so awful, to have an active mind trapped within a body that could no longer do the things it had once done. Most nights Bex would hear Gina and Harvey talking once she had gone to her room. Now, not wishing to disturb them, she turned away and headed towards the gate to the field. Many of the circus performers were still about doing last-minute jobs before they retired for the night, and some of them called out a greeting as she passed them. Ricky was amongst them, and when he saw her he quickly stopped what he was doing and approached her.

'Off for a stroll then, are you?' he asked with a smile.

Bex nodded. 'Yes, I thought I'd take a stroll along the beach. It's a lovely night, isn't it?'

'In that case I reckon I'll join you – if you don't mind, that is?'

'Of course I don't mind,' Bex told him, glad of the darkness that would hide her blushes, and they fell into step as they headed for the sea-front.

They passed the funfair where owners were busily shutting down the rides and turning off lights and soon they reached the beach.

Bex removed her sandals and set off towards the sea, which was gently lapping onto the beach. They began to walk along the shoreline in the direction of Skegness and Bex was acutely aware of the handsome young man at her side. She had never had a boyfriend, or felt the inclination to have one, but Ricky could make her pulses race and she didn't quite know how to handle the feelings he awakened in her.

'So how are you enjoying circus life then?' he asked after a time.

Bex smiled, enjoying the feel of the soft sand sifting through her toes and the sea breeze cool on her face.

'I love it actually,' she admitted after a while.

'Good, I was hoping you'd say that.' Ricky looked slightly embarrassed. 'The thing is, I've sort of been hoping you'd stick around, see.'

A tingle crept up her spine. And then he stopped her and, tilting her chin, he gently kissed her on the mouth – at which a thousand fireworks exploded behind her eyes. For a moment she gave herself up to the pleasure of the kiss, but then she suddenly stepped away from him.

'W-we shouldn't be doing this,' she mumbled, heading back the way they had come.

'But why not?' Ricky sounded confused as he struggled to keep up with her. 'We aren't hurting anyone, are we?'

Bex screwed her eyes shut. It would be so easy to allow

herself to be swept away, but she knew that she mustn't let that happen. Ricky was drawn to Bex, the image that Gina had created, not the *real* Rebecca: the girl who had run away from her past and for whom the police might still be looking – right now.

'I – I've got a lot of baggage,' she went on, feeling that she owed him some sort of explanation. 'And I don't really want to get into a relationship with anyone . . . not ever.'

Ricky looked hurt. 'Most people who run away to join the circus have baggage, but I don't want to know about your past. Why can't we just start from here? I thought . . . Well, I thought you liked me.'

Bex felt tears sting in her eyes. No one had ever really wanted her before, and the temptation to fall into Ricky's arms was strong. But she liked him too much for that. Ricky was a genuinely nice young man. How would he feel if she were to tell him about her past? That her uncle had abused her – that she was soiled goods. That she had violently attacked her last foster-mum. No, she had been rejected too many times before and had no intentions of letting it happen again. Things were just right as they were. The most Ricky, or anyone else for that matter, could ever be was a friend.

'I *do* like you and I'm sorry.' She stopped to put her sandals back on, avoiding his eyes. 'I just don't feel that way about you, Ricky.' The lie slipped easily from her lips as she left him standing there, staring after her.

Chapter Thirty-Five

She was halfway across the field when once again she got the feeling that someone was watching her. She spun about just in time to see a shadow disappear around the side of the Big Top.

'Is anyone there?' she called nervously, but only silence greeted her. Deciding that she was letting her imagination run away with her again, she quickened her steps and moved on.

Relieved to find that the trailer was in darkness when she got back, she hurried inside and went to her room, glad that she wouldn't have to face Gina. Perching on the end of her bed, she stared miserably off into space as she remembered the way Ricky's lips had felt on hers. He had awakened feelings that she had never known she had, but she knew that she had done right by stopping it from going any further. Ricky deserved someone better than her. Someone pure and unspoiled.

Her feelings were in a complete turmoil, and later, her thoughts went back to Josh. Although he had always stuck up for her as a child, deep down she had resented him – possibly because she knew that he was their parents' favourite. Was that why she had always found it so easy to be horrible to him? He was her older brother, but that part of her life was best forgotten now.

The sound of the generator humming softly outside her bedroom window was soothing, but as she sat there she became aware of another noise. Kneeling up, she tweaked the net curtain aside.

Gina was standing in the deep shadows with Harvey, but even in the darkness Rebecca could see that the couple were locked in a passionate embrace. Hastily dropping the curtain she jumped back as if she had been burned.

What could Gina be thinking of? Harvey was a married man, and to make things even worse his wife was an invalid. How could they do this to Maura?

Bex suddenly saw Gina through different eyes. She had thought of her as being kind and generous. Now she realised why the woman never bothered with any of the admirers who flocked around her like bees to honey. Gina was having an affair with Harvey.

As she sat there, she heard the trailer door open and seconds later Gina tapped at her door.

'Are you in safe, pet?'

Bex swallowed her disgust. 'Yes, I'm in.' Normally she would join Gina for a cup of hot chocolate before they retired to bed, but tonight she didn't feel that she could face her. The woman was no better than her own mother had been! But then she knew that what Gina did was none of her business, so she should keep her opinions to herself.

Shrugging out of her clothes, she pulled a nightdress over her head and climbed into bed. After all the excitement of that day, she was sure that she would never sleep, but she was tired out and within seconds was sound asleep.

Gina tapped on Bex's door at the crack of dawn.

'Are you awake, luvvie?' she called gently.

Bex yawned and stretched before answering, 'Yes, I am. I'll be out in a minute.'

'Then don't be too long. Breakfast is nearly ready.'

She heard Gina's footsteps fade away, sprang out of bed and headed for the shower.

When she sat down at the compact table ten minutes later, the girl noticed that Gina looked pale and strained. She was lifting sausages from under the grill onto a plate and she smiled at Bex before asking, 'Sleep well, did you?'

Bex nodded as she buttered herself a slice of toast.

'Good, now get some of this down you before you start work. My mum always used to say a good breakfast was the key to a good day.'

Once she had joined Bex at the table the girl noticed that despite what she had said, Gina was merely picking at her food and was unusually quiet.

It's probably her guilty conscience, Bex thought but she wisely said nothing.

She was on her second cup of tea when Gina blurted out: 'I ought to tell you before you hear it from someone else. Maura . . . Well, she's deteriorating so fast now that it's getting harder for Harvey to care for her in the trailer, so he has decided it will be better for her if she was to go into a nursing home. I've told him I'll go with him to look at some today. Will you be able to manage here on your own?'

Rebecca's lip curled with contempt. *Nursing home indeed!* No doubt he wanted the poor woman out of the way so that he could continue his affair with Gina. Hadn't Gina once told her that Harvey would not even contemplate the idea?

'Bex – did you hear me? I asked if you could cope with the dogs on your own for a while!'

Pulling her thoughts back to the present with an effort, Bex nodded. 'Of course. I'll be just fine here.'

'Good, then I'll go and get ready.' Gina sadly shook her head. 'It's going to be very hard on Harvey, especially when we move on. It will mean him travelling backwards and forwards all the time to see her, but he doesn't have much choice any more. The poor lamb can't do anything at all for herself now.'

As Gina hurried away to get dressed, Bex suppressed a sneer. She had put Gina on a pedestal, but now she had to accept that she was no better than some of the women with whom her aunt had associated: women who would jump into bed with their best friend's husband for the price of a packet of fags or a can of lager. It was a bitter pill to swallow, and as she waited for Gina to finish in the small bathroom, the girl's thoughts were troubled.

Twenty minutes later, Gina set off for Harvey's trailer just as she did each morning to help him get Maura dressed whilst Bex began to give the dogs their morning treats. They frolicked around her feet and despite her sombre thoughts, she began to feel a little better. After all, it was really no business of hers what Gina and Harvey got up to.

She had already walked four of the dogs around the perimeter of the field when Gina and Harvey emerged from his trailer.

Harvey strode over to her and Bex had to grudgingly admit that she could see why Gina was attracted to him. He was still a remarkably handsome man despite the fact that he appeared very old to her. He must be forty at least, she thought to herself.

'Thanks for agreeing to hold the fort for Gina.' He smiled at her as she shuffled uncomfortably from foot to foot. 'I know it's a huge imposition to ask, but do you think you could just pop in and check on Maura too, from time to time? She shouldn't need anything – but just in case?'

Bex nodded, and watched as he and Gina clambered into his old Land Rover and set off. The sun was high in the sky by now and the mist that had blown in from the sea was clearing. It looked set to be a fine day so she quickly put the leads on the next four dogs and exercised them too. They would all need grooming, so all in all it was going to be a very busy day.

At eleven o'clock she stuck her head into Harvey's trailer to check on Maura. The woman was sitting in an easy chair with her feet propped on a low stool, and she had a warm blanket tucked across her legs. She was staring sightlessly out of the trailer window towards the sand dunes and Bex felt a stab of sympathy for her. She guessed that Maura must have been very pretty once, but her illness had robbed her of her beauty and she now resembled an empty shell, crippled and bowed with pain. Even so, it was obvious that Harvey still tried to keep her looking nice. He had brushed her long hair into a ponytail and tied it with a bright ribbon, and she looked clean and respectable.

'Is there anything you need?' Bex asked softly.

The woman's head turned towards her and the smile she gave lit up her emaciated face. 'N-no, thanks, love. But th-thanks for asking.'

Talking was obviously a great effort for her, but in that instant Bex realised that even now her brain must be functioning properly. And again she could only imagine how awful it must be to have a normal brain trapped in a crippled body.

'Are you quite sure? I mean, I could make you a cup of tea or a cold drink.'

With difficulty, Maura waved towards a tray set on a small table at the side of her, and Bex saw that Harvey had left everything she might possibly need within her grasp. But if he cared about his wife, why was he carrying on with Gina? It was all very confusing.

'I'd better get on then,' she said now. 'I'll pop back in a while, and meantime if you need anything, just shout. I'll leave the door open now that it's warmed up and someone should hear you.'

'Th-thanks, love.'

It was late afternoon by the time Gina and Harvey returned. Bex was grooming one of the dogs and Gina came towards her looking very preoccupied as she asked, 'Is everything all right?'

Bex nodded. 'Yes, all the dogs have been exercised and bathed ready for tonight's show, and I'm grooming them now.'

'Thank you.' Gina only appeared to be half-listening as she stared towards Harvey's trailer, and she suddenly blurted out, 'Some of the places we looked at today were awful. There were people just left sitting in chairs with nothing to entertain them, although we did see a couple of homes that might be suitable.' She shook her head. 'I can't believe that it's come to this, but what else can Harvey do now? Maura needs more care and medical attention as her condition deteriorates than he is able to provide while we're travelling, but it's going to be very hard for both of them.'

Had Bex not seen Harvey and Gina in a clinch the night before she would have felt sympathetic to Harvey's plight, but now she couldn't help but wonder if this wasn't just the excuse he needed to get shot of his wife so that he could continue his affair with Gina. But of course, she knew that she couldn't voice this opinion so she remained tight-lipped as Gina wearily made her way into the trailer to put the kettle on. She looked worn out but Bex knew that by the time the evening performance rolled around, she would be her usual bubbly self. Gina was a performer, and as she was fond of saying: 'The show must go on.'

As the crowds began to pour into the Big Top later that night for the evening performance, Bex stood peeping through the curtains. The jugglers and the clowns bustled past them as they did the last-minute preparations and the band began to tune up for the start of the show. This was the time that Bex enjoyed best. She loved to watch the children's faces as they gazed about in awe, and found herself smiling – until she saw

Ricky, that was, and then she quickly looked away. She'd managed to avoid him all day, but now she was forced to stand there with the dogs on their leashes until it was time for Gina to lead them all into the ring and put them through their tricks.

'All right?' He nodded curtly at her, and despite the fact that she had told him she wanted nothing to do with him, his cold attitude hurt. She forced herself to concentrate on what she was doing as the final visitors took their seats. Very soon the show was under way and she watched the magic unfold as one act after another entered the ring.

At last it was time for the finale, and the show ended to rapturous applause. Bex had studied the crowd from her hiding-place all night and was grateful to see that there was no sign of Josh. She could only assume that he hadn't spotted her, and for that she was infinitely grateful. Perhaps now she could start to settle down again?

'Right, you take these four over to the trailer first,' Gina ordered when the encore was finally over. Nodding, Bex slipped the leads onto them and set off through the rear exit. It was another balmy night and as she stepped through the enormous canvas doors she breathed in deeply, enjoying the feel of the cool air on her cheeks.

She had gone no more than a few steps when a young man stepped out of the shadows and into the artificial lights that had been erected all around the Big Top.

'Hello, Rebecca.'

Joshua's familiar voice, slightly deeper now, wrapped itself around her like sea mist. She stared back at him as if she had been hypnotised.

'What are *you* doing here?' She knew that she was being rude but could think of nothing else to say.

'That's hardly a nice way to greet me after all this time.'

He grinned, but finding no answering smile from her, he went on, 'I thought it was you last night but I couldn't be sure. You look so . . . Oh, I don't know. Grown up and different, I suppose. Anyway, I couldn't rest until I came back to make sure. How are you?'

'I'm fine,' she mumbled as she dropped her eyes from his. 'But I'm afraid I don't have time to stand about talking. I have work to do.'

'So when *can* we talk then?' he asked, and she shook her head.

'I don't think we have anything to say really,' she replied in a small voice. 'We haven't been in touch for years, so why start again now?'

'I've been looking for you, as it happens, and I'll tell you now, Rebecca, I don't intend to leave until we have talked – so it's up to you.'

She sighed. He obviously meant what he said, but if she stayed here for much longer she would have Gina screaming for her.

'Look, I have to take all the dogs back to the trailer and get them fed and settled,' she told him. 'But I could meet you in, shall we say, one hour?'

'I'll be waiting here,' he answered, and she hurried away with her heart in her mouth. Things seemed to be going from bad to worse again, but then she should be used to that by now. After all, when had life ever run smoothly for her?

Chapter Thirty-Six

It was gone ten o'clock when Bex returned to the rear of the Big Top, and there was Josh standing exactly where she had left him. Aware that they were attracting curious glances from various circus folk who were still busily flitting about, she suggested, 'Should we go for a walk along the beach?'

He nodded eagerly as he fell into step beside her, but they had gone no more than a few paces when Ricky suddenly appeared from around the corner. He looked from Bex to Joshua before turning hurriedly and going back the way he had come – but not before she saw the pain that flared briefly in his eyes. She chewed on her lip in consternation. She had no doubt that Ricky would think Joshua was some young chap she had picked up, but there was nothing she could do about it now, so she forced herself to move on, amazed at how much the sight of his hurt had affected her.

They walked in silence until they came to the beach and then took off their shoes and paddled along the shoreline.

'So why did you need to see me?' she asked.

Joshua frowned. 'We were brought up together,' he answered, 'and when I was told you'd disappeared I was worried sick.' He inched a little closer to her and Bex deliberately stepped away, putting some distance between them again.

He looked upset but made no comment as they moved on.

'That was a long time ago when we were children,' Bex said quietly.

'Yes, it was,' he agreed. 'But I've never stopped worrying about you. I know how hard it must have been for you, having to live with Aunt Alison and Uncle Ken, and I felt useless because I couldn't do anything to help you. And then when you decided you didn't want to see me again . . . Well, it hurt but I always thought that when we were grown up we could get in touch again, so it was a shock when I heard that you'd run away. I never guessed you were the sort to join a circus.'

Bex shrugged. 'Who knows what we might decide to do as we get older? And I don't really want to have to think back to the time when Dad dumped me at Aunt Alison's.'

'Bad as that, was it?'

She could hear the sympathy in his voice but it didn't touch her. He was like a stranger now, someone from a past she would rather forget.

'I've seen Uncle Ken a couple of times, as it happens,' Joshua said. 'He doesn't change, from what I hear. He's still the biggest rogue on two legs. And did you know that he and Aunt Alison split up? She's got herself a toyboy, by all accounts.'

'I'm *really* not interested,' she said, wishing he would shut up, and his stomach flipped as he stared back at her. He could hardly believe that this strikingly pretty young woman was plain little Rebecca – and had it not been for those glorious bluebell eyes, he doubted he would ever have recognised her.

'What are you doing now?' Bex asked Joshua. She wasn't really interested but felt that she ought to ask.

'I'm at uni studying Law.'

His answer came as no surprise. He was following in their late adoptive father's footsteps.

'I've come into my inheritance now and I've been trying to find you because I feel that it wasn't fair for our dad to leave nearly all of it to me. I want to share it with you, Rebecca. After all, we were both his children.'

'But we weren't, not really, were we?' she said. 'We were both adopted. We're not even blood-related.'

'I'm glad you said that.' He grabbed her hand and pulled her to a standstill. 'You see, I've . . . Well, I suppose I'm a bit shocked, seeing how you've turned out. And we're not *really* brother and sister, are we? What I'm saying is, I . . . I . . . find you very attractive.'

Bex stared at him in horror.

'You m-must be stark staring mad,' she stuttered as she snatched her hand from his and backed away, but he just came towards her again with his hands outstretched.

'Don't say that,' he implored. 'I can't help how I feel, Rebecca. When you were a kid, everyone said how plain you were, but you've certainly changed. You were just my little sister back then, but if we're not related there's no reason why we can't . . . get close. I know this must have come as a shock to you – it has to me too – but now that I've found you again I don't think I could bear to lose you. I came here by chance with a friend for a holiday, but don't you see? It was meant to be. You've just blown me away and I can honestly say I've never met a girl who can hold a candle to you.'

'Get away from me!' Bex said, looking around nervously.

'Is this because of that boy I saw you with on the beach last night?' Joshua demanded now, his face contorted with anger, and the first flickers of fear began to stir in her stomach. 'Is he your boyfriend?'

'Who . . . Ricky? Were you following me then?'

'Well, I wanted to make sure whether it was you or not – but I wasn't actually *following* you.'

'For your information, although it's absolutely none of your business, Ricky is just a friend,' Bex informed him scathingly. 'I don't have a boyfriend, and what's more I don't want one.'

'Oh, Rebecca, I'm so sorry.' His shoulders sagged. 'I've frightened you, haven't I? And I've gone about this all wrong.'

'Just go away and we'll forget we ever met up again,' she advised as she turned to retrace her steps, but again his hand shot out and he gripped her arm.

'But the money! I want to share it with you.'

'I don't want it, or anything off you.' She stared coolly into his eyes. 'Our dad never made a secret of the fact that you were his favourite.' The words hurt but she knew that they were true. 'And if truth be told, I don't think Mum ever really loved me either. I was never what she imagined a little girl should be. She so wanted a daughter but I was a Plain Jane, so she tried to compensate for that with frills. But it didn't work, did it?'

'But just look at you now.' He eyed her up and down appreciatively, making her squirm. 'They always say it's the ugly ducklings that turn into swans, and in your case it's true.'

Suddenly very aware that there was no one in sight, Bex began to stride through the sand. This whole episode was making her feel very uncomfortable, and now she deeply regretted coming with him – not that she'd had much choice. The last thing she needed was for Gina to see her with Josh and start asking questions. Suddenly the past looked in grave danger of catching up with her, and the fear of being found was back. If she should take the money Josh was offering, she had no doubt that solicitors would be involved – and she couldn't afford that to happen whilst she was on the run from the police. A picture of her foster-mum lying in a pool of blood suddenly swam before her eyes again. It was an image that haunted her day and night, and she had to blink to hold back tears.

They came to the concrete ramp that led up to the small pleasure beach and Bex hurried her steps, but it was no good, Josh stayed right at her side.

'Look, couldn't we meet up again somewhere when you've had time to think this through?' he pleaded. 'Even if you don't want to see me again, at least let me make sure that you're comfortable financially.'

Feeling slightly safer now that they were back in a lighted area, Bex stopped and faced him.

'I appreciate the offer, but as I've already said, I don't want anything from you. We were so young when we last lived together as brother and sister, and that's the only way I'll ever be able to think of you. I've moved on now, and so should you. Goodbye, Joshua.'

With her head held high she crossed the street and entered the circus boundary again, but she could feel his eyes boring into her back and it took all her willpower to stop herself from running. But where would she run to? Josh knew where she was now, and if he chose to, he could make things very difficult for her. It was a terrifying thought. To Josh she would always be Rebecca – but she was Bex now and she wanted it to stay that way. As far as she was concerned, Rebecca was dead and buried.

In the shadow of the Big Top she gave way to something she still very rarely did and allowed herself to cry. For a short time she had finally felt as if she belonged somewhere, but now it was all ruined. Josh's declaration of his newfound feelings for her had sickened her to the core and she could scarcely believe that in two short days two different men had told her that they cared for her. Thoughts of Ricky made the tears fall faster. He *was* someone she could have cared for, had she not been running away from her past. Now she wondered if she would shortly have to leave the circus too. Only time would tell. Eventually she swiped the tears from her cheeks and headed for the trailer as eyes watched her progress from the shadows of the deep hedge that surrounded the field. Thankfully she was unaware of them as she prepared herself to face Gina.

Bex found her sitting at the table with her head in her hands. As she entered, Gina looked up and Bex saw that she too had been crying.

'There's tea in the pot if you fancy a cup,' Gina said chokily, and without a word Bex fetched a mug and poured some out. She then joined Gina at the table and the woman said, 'Harvey told Maura what he intended to do tonight – about the nursing home, I mean.'

She looked so tired without her heavy make-up on, and despite herself, Bex felt sorry for her. It was all very confusing. Gina appeared to care deeply for Maura, but how could she if she was carrying on with her husband behind her back?

'How did she take it?' she asked softly.

'She's all for the idea.' Gina gave a sob. 'That's what makes it so much worse. She's so unselfish and she knows how hard it is for Harvey to cope. She's told him to arrange a place for her as soon as possible.'

'I see.' Bex was unsure what to say.

'But anyway, where have you been? For a walk along the beach?'

When she nodded, Gina smiled shakily. 'And did Ricky go with you?'

When Bex shook her head she looked surprised. 'Oh, well I'm sure you know he has a huge soft spot for you. You've got yourself an admirer there and you could do far worse than Ricky. He's a good lad.'

'I don't *want* an admirer!' Bex snapped. Without another word, she slammed her mug onto the table and stalked off. Gina watched her go with a worried frown on her face. Bex was good at her job and Gina had no regrets about employing her, but there were times – like now – when she wished she would open up a bit more. Whenever she tried to find out a little more about her past, Bex would close up like a clam and Gina had given up asking her personal questions now. But then, wasn't she herself guilty of keeping her own past a closely guarded secret?

Sighing, she crossed to the window and stared over at the soft light spilling from Harvey's trailer, wondering why life had to be so complicated.

For the rest of that week, Josh hovered about the grounds of the circus like a shadow and Bex began to dread having to walk out of the door. But he always kept his distance and didn't attempt to approach her, for which she was grateful.

'Have you seen those two chaps that have been loitering about all this week?' Bex overheard Harvey ask Gina one evening, and her heart sank.

'Can't say that I have,' Gina answered as Bex walked past them. She had no idea who the second chap might be but thankfully, Josh was causing no trouble and Harvey was so taken up with scouring the area for a suitable nursing home for his wife that he left Josh alone. It wasn't unusual for certain people who had a love of the circus to make a slight nuisance of themselves while they were camped in one place for a time.

And then one evening, Joshua was once more waiting for Bex at the rear of the Big Top after the show.

'I have to go home tomorrow. Can't we just talk?' he implored her.

'I don't think we have anything more to say,' she told him solemnly. The things he had said to her still made her flesh crawl, and she didn't even want to be near him.

'But the money—'

'I told you – I don't *want* the money.' Her face softened then; he was only trying to do the right thing, after all. 'Look, Josh, I appreciate the offer, but you're going to have to accept the fact that we're nothing to each other any more. If you care about me as you say you do, you have to let me get on with my life. For the first time I can remember I'm happy and I want to forget the past. Or try to, at least.'

She knew that her words had struck home as she saw the resigned stoop of his shoulders, and now, lifting one of the dogs, she told him, 'Goodbye, Josh. I hope you'll be happy.' With that she walked away. There was no sense in prolonging the parting, as far as she was concerned.

When she reached Gina's trailer, she glanced over her shoulder just in time to see Josh disappear around the corner of the Big Top. She felt as if an enormous weight had been shifted from her shoulders and prayed that this would be the last time she would ever have to set eyes on him.

Gina noticed immediately that the girl was in a better frame of mind that evening. As she sat at the table removing her heavy stage make-up she asked cautiously, 'I take it you've had a good day then?' Bex had been so stroppy before that she had barely dared talk to her.

'I have, as it so happens. And now if there's nothing else you want me to do, I think I'll go for a stroll along the beach.'

It was becoming a habit and Gina smiled indulgently. 'Off you go then, but don't get talking to anyone you don't know.'

It was well after eleven o'clock as Bex set off and she had gone no more than a few steps when she passed Harvey, who was clearly heading for Gina's trailer.

'Night,' he said as he passed her, and Rebecca answered him civilly as she made for the sea-front.

The streets were quiet now. Most of the families had gone back to their holiday homes to put their children to bed, and only the odd group of young people who were moving from one pub to another were still about.

Once her feet sank into the soft sand she smiled with pleasure and began to stroll along. The wind had got up in the last hour or so and it was decidedly colder than it had been for days, but she enjoyed the feeling of freedom all the same.

Instead of walking along the shoreline as she normally did, she kept close to the sand dunes to give her some protection from the wind, and soon she had left the lights of the town far behind. Far out at sea she could see a ship's lights reflecting on the water, but other than that she felt as if she might be the only person on earth and it was a good feeling. She had walked much further than she ever had before as she tried to put her thoughts into some sort of order, and had just turned and started heading back when a shadow coming towards her made her start. It was pitch black now and a thin drizzle had begun to fall; the moon was hidden behind scudding dark clouds.

Bex gulped but then assured herself that it was probably just someone taking a late-night stroll along the beach the same as herself. She began to hurry all the same, but it appeared that the other person was coming closer.

Panic set in and she started to jog as best she could. The sand slowed her progress, however, and soon she was breathless, but at least she could see the lights of the town now in the distance. Whoever was behind her was breathing heavily, and she tried to go faster. And then suddenly an arm came about her throat and she was lifted bodily from the ground. She opened her mouth to scream but a hand landed across her mouth and she felt herself being dragged into the sand dunes. And then despair paralysed her as she realised that, even if she could have screamed, there was no one there to hear her.

Chapter Thirty-Seven

In her mind now she was back in the small bedroom in Bedworth. She could feel her uncle's hands crawling across her body as the man pawed at her viciously.

She kicked and struggled as she tried to see her attacker's face. She desperately needed to know who was doing this dreadful thing to her, but it was too dark to see his features and he was just a large shadow looming over her. Somehow she managed to free one of her hands as he threw her onto the wet sand, and she had the satisfaction of feeling her fingernails rake down his cheek before the wind was knocked out of her. And then she could only lie there, struggling to catch her breath as he tore at her clothes. She felt her jeans being forced down over her legs and then the cold rain like needles on her bare skin. The man was making deep guttural noises in his throat now, and it came to her then who he must be.

'Josh,' she managed to choke out. 'Please don't do this.' The only answer was the sound of her knickers tearing as he ripped them apart. And now she began to kick and lash out like someone possessed, but her strength was no match for his and she felt his weight shift on top of her, effectively pinning her to the ground. The rain was falling faster now and it mingled with the tears that were coursing down her face. Her hand reached up to scratch at his eyes, but he smacked it away and then pain ripped through her as he entered her roughly. She opened her mouth to scream but the pain was so great that all that came out was a stifled whimper. He raped her mercilessly as she lay helplessly beneath him, wishing that she could just die there and then. It seemed to go on and on, with no end to the torture and humiliation, but then at last he gave a great sigh and his heavy weight dropped onto her again as a welcoming darkness claimed her.

Bex blinked and slowly opened her eyes. She was wet and cold and had no idea where she was, but then the memories flooded back and she managed to roll over and drag herself up onto her knees. She had been raped. She could feel the rain lashing against her legs and her bare backside, but for a moment she had no strength to do anything about it. She knelt there until it suddenly came to her that the man might come back and do it again, and the realisation lent her strength. Somehow she got herself into a sitting position and felt around on the sand until her hands came to rest on her sodden jeans. She rose shakily and dragged them on, then without giving herself time to think, she stumbled off in the direction of the lights. Somehow she must get back to the trailer and safety.

The sea was crashing onto the beach now and the wind was bitingly cold. Her teeth were chattering and she was sure that she would never feel warm or clean again, but she went doggedly on, knowing that she must not risk this happening again. By the time she staggered up the concrete ramp that led to the pleasure beach and safety, she was sobbing uncontrollably. She had left her shoes behind and the pebbles and stones that were scattered on the cold concrete bit cruelly into the tender soles of her feet, but she kept going. And then at last, there in the distance was the Big Top and she knew that she was almost home. She realised that she must have lain unconscious on the beach for much longer than she had thought, because everywhere was deserted. She was glad of the fact, for she knew that she would have died of shame had anyone seen her in this condition.

When she finally reached the trailer she tentatively climbed the steps and opened the door. The dogs wagged their tails when they saw her but thankfully there was no sign of Gina.

Creeping along the corridor, she heard the woman's gentle snores through her bedroom door. There would be no fear of waking Gina. She had always told Bex that once she was asleep, she slept like the dead. Stripping off her sodden clothes, Bex stepped beneath the shower. Looking down at herself, she was horrified to see that bruises were appearing all over her, and there was blood caked between her legs. Shuddering, she snatched up the sponge and began to scrub herself brutally. But deep down she knew that it was more than soap and water that would be needed before she could feel clean again. The sand from her body puddled in the shower tray before gurgling away down the drain as she relived the attack in her mind, shaking like a leaf. *Why?* she asked herself over and over. Why did it always have to happen to her? What had she ever done that was so very bad? But she knew of old that self-pity would solve nothing, so at last she turned off the shower and wrapped herself in a large bath-sheet.

Once in her room she slid into bed, too tired even to put her nightie on, and lay curled in a ball. Josh had told her that he loved her, so why would he have done this to her? She had no doubt that it was Josh, even though she hadn't managed to see his face. Who else would take the trouble to follow her? And what was she going to do about it? She knew before she even asked herself the question that there was little she *could* do. If the police were to become involved they would discover that she was on the run and then she really would be in trouble. She might even be sent to prison, and she knew that she wouldn't be able to bear that.

Her thoughts raced on. As things were, she wouldn't even dare to confide in Gina because the woman was sure to want the incident to be investigated. She must somehow try to forget it had ever happened – just as she had all those years ago when her uncle had abused her. Who would believe her anyway? They would probably just say that she had agreed to go for a walk with a feller and things had gone a little further than she had reckoned on. She could still recall this happening to one of the circus girls a few weeks ago, and in this particular case they had probably been right. Tania had been well known as a terrible flirt and unfortunately most circus people were tarred with the same brush. And would Gina think the same of her, once she discovered what had happened? Bex would hate that, because despite trying to keep the barriers up, she was now forced to admit that she had come to love Gina like a daughter loves her mum.

Fretting and gnawing her lip, she lay staring at the flimsy curtains and watched as the dawn broke.

'Come on, sleepy-head, rise and shine.' Gina's voice brought Bex waking from a horrible nightmare. She was shocked that she had managed to fall asleep and felt absolutely awful. And now she would have to face Gina. Would the woman realise what had happened when she saw her? Bex felt as if it must be written in large letters all over her. SOILED GOODS! – *AGAIN!*

Pushing herself to the edge of the mattress, she groaned. She felt as if every single part of her had been hit with a hammer and she had a raging headache. Nausea threatened to overcome her, but she forced herself to get up and go to the bathroom. Peering into the mirror suspended over the sink, she saw that her eyes had dark circles beneath them and she was pale, but thankfully there was only one bruise on her cheek, and that she would be able to explain away. Her arms, legs and body, however, were a different matter entirely and she was horrified to see that she was covered in deep purple and blue bruises. No wonder she ached everywhere.

After pulling a large dressing-gown on, she padded into the kitchen hoping that Gina wouldn't look at her too closely. Gina was sitting at the table reading a newspaper and she glanced up with a smile which died instantly as her eyes settled on Bex.

'Phew!' she whistled through her teeth. 'What's happened to you?' Then without waiting for an answer, she quipped: 'And what does the other guy look like?'

'It wasn't anything like that,' Bex lied as she slid onto a seat. 'I went for a walk on the beach and it was so dark I tripped over a rock and hurt my face.'

'Hmm.' Gina clearly didn't believe her but she said nothing as she lifted the tea pot and poured tea into a mug.

'I just hope you don't feel as bad as you look,' she commented.

Bex shook her head. 'I'm fine,' she insisted, and an awkward silence settled between them. Bex forced herself to eat a slice of toast, not wishing to give Gina anything else to concern herself about, but it tasted like cardboard and stuck in her throat. She took swallows of tea to wash it down and was greatly relieved when Gina stood up and pottered away to get dressed.

Now that she was alone she stared around at the little trailer where she had briefly known contentment. But could she stay here, now that Josh knew where she was? It would be so easy for him to trace the whereabouts of the circus even when they moved on, and she didn't know if she dare risk it. She went to her room and began to rummage through her clothes, and half an hour later, Gina's eyebrows rose into her hairline when the girl reappeared dressed in the old jeans and the baggy jumper that she had arrived in. Her hair was scraped unbecomingly back into a ponytail and her face was without make-up.

'What's this then?' she enquired, looking her up and down.

Bex shrugged, nodding towards the grey drizzly weather beyond the trailer window. 'I just fancied wearing something a bit warmer seeing as the weather's changed for the worst,' she lied.

'Mmm, then we'd best get you some new warm clothes.' Gina tutted. 'I can't have you walking about looking like a tramp.'

Bex's cheeks flamed but she didn't reply. The last thing she wanted today was to get into an argument, so she simply leaned down to start putting the leads on the dogs without a word.

She traipsed around the perimeter of the field feeling just as cold and miserable as the weather, with the dogs playfully leaping ahead of her, and it was as she was heading back to the trailer that Ricky suddenly appeared. For a moment it seemed that he was going to pass her without speaking, but then when he spotted the bruise on her cheek he became still and frowned, before saying, 'I bet you won't go walking off along the beach with *him* again.'

'With whom?' Rebecca retorted indignantly.

'That chap you passed me over for and who you went off with the other night.'

'As it so happens, *that chap*, as you refer to him, happened to be my . . .' Bex stopped herself from going any further. The less Ricky knew about Josh the better, so let him think what he liked.

She could see the different emotions flitting across his face as he looked at her drab outfit: anger, hurt and perhaps a measure of satisfaction? He no doubt thought it served her right for telling him she didn't want to go out with him. And strangely, it stung. She had a feeling that she could have been happy with Ricky if things had been different – not that there was any point in dwelling on it. Happy endings were not for the likes of her. And then a horrible thought occurred to her. Could it have been Ricky who had raped her? He had turned and was walking away now, and she watched him go thoughtfully. Better than anyone, he knew that she went for a stroll along the beach most nights. And like Josh, she had rejected him. She shuddered at the thought. Now more than ever she knew that she couldn't stay here any longer – but where would she go?

Her thoughts were gloomy as she ushered the dogs back into the trailer, where Harvey and Gina were sitting talking.

'Oh there you are, Bex.' Gina looked harassed. 'Harvey and I are going to look at some more care homes for Maura today. Will you cope here alone?'

'Of course,' Bex said ungraciously, and she went about her business as Gina hurried away to get ready and Harvey returned to his own trailer.

The day passed painfully slowly as Bex relived in her mind what had happened the evening before, and by the time Gina and Harvey returned that afternoon her mood was darker than ever.

'I think we've found somewhere just right,' Gina told her as she threw her bag onto a chair and kicked her shoes off. It had been a long stressful day and she was glad to be home.

311

She just wished she didn't have the evening performance to get through.

Bex curled her lip at the hypocrisy of it all, wondering how Gina could pretend to be so caring towards Maura when all the while she was carrying on with the poor woman's husband behind her back.

Catching the expression on the girl's face, Gina asked, 'And what was that look for, miss?'

'I *know*,' Bex shot back; she had nothing to lose now if she wasn't going to be staying.

'You know what?'

'About you and Harvey. I saw you together one night outside the trailer. How *could* you carry on like that with her husband when Maura is so ill?'

Gina's lip trembled and she patted the seat at the side of her. 'Come and sit down, I think I should explain,' she said quietly, and Bex did as she was told, folding her arms tightly across her chest.

Gina seemed to struggle for the right words for a while but then she began, 'I know how it must look to you and I'm not going to deny that I love Harvey. When I first joined the circus, I was a mess. He and Maura helped me a lot. I'd . . . Well, let's just say that I'd been in a lot of trouble and they helped sort me out. Then after a time Maura became ill, so it seemed natural that I should help Harvey with her. I know it might not look like it, but I actually love them *both*. Anyway, I gradually began to realise that I loved Harvey and I was ashamed of how I felt. I don't know when it was that Maura realised it too, but one day she asked me straight out if I had feelings for him and I had to confess that I had. But she didn't condemn me, she seemed to understand. Maura accepts that she's dying and she told me in a round-about way that once she's gone, she wants me to look after him. What Harvey and I have between us sort of grew naturally, but we've never . . . you know, we've never . . . We wouldn't do that whilst Maura is still alive. It wouldn't feel right.' Gina took a shuddering breath before going on, 'We agreed that God forbid, when Maura dies we'll wait for a respectful time before we come together, although I think a lot of the circus folk, just like you, have come to see the way it is.'

When Bex frowned, Gina took her hand. 'I know it seems disloyal,' she told her, 'but sometimes things happen beyond our control. One day you'll understand.'

'I doubt it,' the girl said spitefully, and wrenching her hand away, she stormed off to her bedroom. She had so much of her own to contend with, and Gina's confession on top was just too much.

Bex was in no mood at all for the evening performance, but as usual she took her place behind the enormous curtain and waited with the dogs until it was time for Gina to enter the ring. It was then that she saw Ricky standing at a distance, watching her, and she quickly turned her head away. Could it have been Ricky who had raped her, or was her first instinct right – that it was Josh? She had no way of knowing. It had been so dark on the beach that her attacker could have been anyone – but could she risk staying here now, knowing that it might have been Ricky? The answer came immediately. No, she couldn't. She would have to leave, and the sooner the better.

The evening stretched on interminably, and tonight there was no pleasure in it for Bex. She just wanted some time alone to put her thoughts together. As usual when the performers had taken their final bow she ushered the dogs back to the trailer and disappeared off into her bedroom as soon as was possible. There would be no walks along the beach tonight, or any other night for that matter after what had happened.

'Do you want any supper, Bex?' Gina called some time later.

Bex could hear her pottering about the trailer but she remained silent, hoping that Gina would think she was asleep. After a time she heard the door close and rightly guessed that Gina had gone to help Harvey settle Maura down for the night as she did each evening. It was then that she took the bag she had arrived with from the bottom of the wardrobe and began to pack her clothes into it, but only the ones that she had come with. She would have no need of the fancy clothes Gina had bought her any more. They belonged to Bex, and soon she would be Rebecca again. She also quickly counted the money she had earned and was shocked to see that it amounted to almost three hundred pounds. There had been no need to spend anything since living with Gina as the woman had bought all her clothes and fed her too, besides paying her a reasonable wage. It would be enough to keep her going for a couple of weeks at least, until she found alternative work, and she was grateful for that. Now all she had to do was wait until Gina was back and asleep, and then she would leave this very night. There seemed no point in delaying; there was nothing here for her any more. Although where she would go to was a mystery for now. She would face that problem when the time came.

Sometime later she heard Gina come back and she lay there listening to her moving about the trailer as she turned off the lights and locked the doors. Slowly the circus ground became silent, and eventually the sound of Gina's gentle snores reached her through the thin adjoining wall.

Quietly sliding off the bed, Bex put on her trainers and lifting her bag, she padded silently towards the door. As she

314

entered the lounge she looked around regretfully, knowing that she would never see it again. The trailer and this way of life had been a haven for a while, but once again life had dealt her a cruel blow and it was time to move on again.

Picking up the pad and pen that Gina always kept on the side, she hesitated, then slowly wrote: *Goodbye, I'm so sorry x.*

It was cold and windy outside and Bex shuddered as she zipped up her jacket and moved past the Big Top. She had given little thought as to where she might go, but now she realised that wherever she went there would be no buses at this time of night.

As she walked through the town she saw the owners of the arcades closing the machines down and switching off lights; the streets were deserted and she rightly guessed that it must be well after midnight. Soon she found herself walking along the dark lanes towards Chapel St Leonards, and now she began to feel nervous again. There were no streetlights here and everything looked very scary at night. Trees bent towards her as she hurried beneath them, and the sound of the wind whistling through the branches set her nerves on edge. After a while she became aware of car headlights coming up behind her and without giving herself time to think, she stuck out her thumb. Surely it was better to risk a lift with a stranger than risk being raped again in the dark deserted lane.

The car drew closer and then to her relief it drew into the side of the road. As she ran towards it, she was thankful to see that there was a young couple inside rather than a man on his own. 'Where are you going?' she asked.

'Into Skegness. Is that any good to you?' The young man at the wheel, who looked scarcely old enough to be driving, seemed friendly and she felt herself relax a little. Both he and the girl in the passenger seat looked harmless enough.

'That would be great. Thanks.' Rebecca scrambled into the

315

back seat and sank back gratefully as the warmth met her. The car moved on again and she saw the young man watching her in the mirror as he asked, 'On holiday, are you?'

'Er, yes,' she lied. 'Just backpacking about – you know. Staying in hostels and whatnot.'

'Isn't that a bit dangerous on your own?' The girl who had said nothing up to now turned and looked at Rebecca through the seats.

'Not really, I'm more than capable of looking after myself.'

Hearing the surly tone in her voice the girl seemed to realise that she didn't wish to talk, so she then continued the conversation she had been having with her boyfriend as Rebecca stared out at the dark countryside scudding past the window.

Every now and again, the headlights of the car behind them reflected in the rear-view mirror and blinded Rebecca, so she inched along the seat and settled back, glad that the young couple were no longer questioning her.

Twenty minutes later, they were travelling along the front in Skegness and the young man announced, 'We're almost at our hotel now. Would it be all right to drop you off here?'

'Yes, fine – thanks,' Rebecca said, and as the car drew to a halt, she clambered out onto the pavement. 'Bye then, and thanks again,' she called, then slammed the car door and watched the couple drive away.

She stood, looking about. What should she do now? It was too late to knock on B&B doors asking if there were any rooms available. She would have irate landladies shouting at her if she tried that, and she had no idea if there were any hostels about. It was as she was standing there that she saw a police car cruising towards her and quickly scuttled down the steps onto the beach until it had passed. The pier lay up ahead and she reluctantly headed towards it. She didn't relish the thought of sleeping rough – not that it would be the first time. Once beneath it she peered into the darkness cautiously but was relieved to see that she appeared to be alone. The sound of the sea crashing against the huge metal girders was louder here but at least they offered some shelter from the wind. She crouched down behind one of them and hugged her knees. It looked set to be a long night, but at first light she would go and find a café and have a good breakfast, then she would start to look around for a job and somewhere to stay. Suddenly the brief happy time she had spent with Gina seemed a million miles away, and once again loneliness filled her as she tried not to think of Ricky and Bex, the girl that she had almost become, and all she had left behind.

Chapter Thirty-Eight

At six o'clock the next morning, Rebecca stumbled up the path from the beach onto the sea-front. She felt cold, hungry and dirty and was in so much pain that she could barely walk. Spotting some public toilets up ahead she hobbled inside and washed as best she could at the sink before brushing her hair and trying to make herself look respectable. She then set off in search of a café and was soon rewarded by lights spilling onto the pavement from a window in a little back street.

On entering, she was pleased to see that she was the only one there. An elderly lady appeared from a door behind the counter, her expression harassed. The woman was so tiny she looked as if a good puff of wind would blow her away and there were more lines on her face than on a map, but she smiled a welcome.

'My, you're an early bird,' she said. 'I've only just got here meself.' She yawned. 'I don't mind admittin', these early mornin's are killin' me. Me husband's ill see, so I'm havin' to run this place meself. But that's enough about me. You ain't come here to listen to my troubles, have you? What can I be gettin' you, dearie?'

Rebecca ordered a full English breakfast although she knew that she should be very careful with her money. But then she supposed that she could afford to push the boat out just this once. Hopefully by the end of the day she would have found a job and somewhere to stay, and she wouldn't have to panic then. She certainly didn't relish the thought of another night beneath the pier.

As she sat waiting for her meal people began to trickle in and she was surprised to see how many were up and about. Most were men on their way to work. A young man with startlingly red hair grinned at Rebecca as he queued at the counter, but turning her head, she pointedly ignored him. The last thing she needed in her life was yet more complications; she just wanted to keep herself to herself. Soon she was tucking into surprisingly good bacon and eggs, and as she sipped at the mug of hot tea she felt warmth begin to flow through her again.

She made her food last for as long as she dared, then hoisting her bag onto her shoulder, she left the café.

It was still cold and damp but she was in better spirits with a good meal inside her. She still ached all over, but then she supposed that was only to be expected so soon after the attack. As she stood there considering which way she should go, the red-haired young man emerged from the café and paused to ask, 'Are you looking for somewhere?'

She thought of ignoring him again but he seemed friendly enough, so she answered cautiously, 'Actually, I'm after a job and somewhere to stay.'

He scratched his head. 'Phew, you might be on a sticky wicket there. Trouble is, most of the work hereabouts is seasonal and it's almost the end of the season now. I shall be looking for winter work myself in another couple of weeks. Through the summer I work in one of the big arcades along the front, but once everywhere shuts down, jobs are like gold dust round here.'

'Oh well, thanks anyway.' Rebecca hoisted her bag more comfortably onto her shoulder and set off for the front, not entirely believing him. Surely not everything shut down for the winter? There was bound to be a job going somewhere.

Five hours later she was beginning to wonder. She had been into almost every shop and arcade she passed, but the answer was always the same. 'Sorry, we'll be closing for the winter soon.'

Now she headed for the front once more and dropped miserably onto a bench. It had started raining and she could feel it dripping down the back of her collar. Her hair was plastered to her head and she was hungry again now after all the walking about. It looked as if another night under the pier might be on the cards and she didn't relish the thought at all. She briefly thought of going into a restaurant and treating herself to a meal but quickly decided against it. If her money was going to last her any length of time at all, she would have to make every penny count. Heaving herself to her feet, she made her way back to the small café where she had had her breakfast that morning. It was cheap and cheerful there and they might sell sandwiches which would tide her over.

The café was half-full when she entered, and the same elderly lady who had served her that morning looked up from the chips she was frying and smiled. 'Back again, are you?' she asked. 'I must be a better cook than I thought.'

'Actually, I was wondering if you sold sandwiches,' Rebecca said quietly.

'I can sell you whatever you fancy so long as I've got it in,' the woman assured her. 'Just let me finish this order and then I'll be with you.'

Taking a seat at the same table she had sat at earlier in the day Rebecca waited patiently until the woman beckoned her to the counter.

'Now then, it was a sandwich you were after, weren't

it? How about a bit of ham, or I've got cheese if you'd prefer?'

'Ham would be fine,' Rebecca answered. 'And could I have a large mug of tea, please?'

Within minutes the woman had served her and Rebecca savoured the warmth of the large mug as she wrapped her cold hands around it. The café was slowly emptying now and soon there was only herself and a family left in there. The woman began to clear the tables and as she passed Rebecca she asked curiously, 'Here on holiday, are you?'

'No, I . . . Well, actually I'm looking for a job,' she told her. 'Trouble is, it seems most of the places round here close down for the winter and up to now I've had no luck at all.'

'Hm, well, that's about the long and short of it.' The woman eyed her thoughtfully before asking, 'Ever worked in a café before, have you?'

Rebecca almost choked on a mouthful of tea as she hastily shook her head. 'No, I haven't to be honest, but I wouldn't mind trying it.'

'It's long hours and I could only pay minimum wage,' the woman warned, and she was shocked to see how different the girl looked when she smiled. 'And of course, if I took you on – and it's a big *if* – it would only be as a trial, mind. Not wishin' to be rude, but I don't know you from Adam an' you could be out to rob me.'

'Oh, but I'd never do that,' Rebecca hastily assured her. 'I'm very trustworthy.'

'That remains to be seen, but I'll tell you now – the first time I find you with your hands in the till, you'll be out o' that door so quick your feet won't touch the floor. This is a tough job. You'd be workin' from early in the mornin' till late at night.' The woman continued to stare at her until Rebecca felt colour burn into her cheeks.

'I wouldn't mind that, really I wouldn't,' she promised.

'And just sayin' I *do* decide to give you a trial, when would you be prepared to start?'

'I could start right now,' Rebecca said enthusiastically, looking around at the tables full of dirty pots.

The woman followed her gaze and was tempted. She hadn't sat down since opening up that morning at six o'clock and her feet felt as if they were about to drop off. But the girl looked awfully young. What if she was a runaway?

Rebecca held her breath as the woman pondered, but then to her relief she said, 'Right then, the sink's over there.' She pointed to a large Belfast sink behind the counter, full of hot soapy water. 'You can put your coat an' your bag through that door there, an' then you can clear the tables and wash up. The main rush for dinners is over now and it should be steady this afternoon – just folks poppin' in for a cuppa an' a piece o' my homemade cakes. We won't be too busy again now until teatime. Do you think you're up to it?'

'Oh *yes*.' Rebecca's eyes were shining as she stood up and went round to the door the woman had pointed to. Once through it she found herself in a small room that boasted two mismatched comfy chairs, a coat-rack and little else. She hastily hung up her sodden coat and dropped her bag onto the floor, then, rolling up her sleeves she marched back into the café and began to collect up all the dirty pots. The old woman sat and watched her with her feet resting on a chair and a large mug of tea in front of her, rising only to serve anyone that came in, and within an hour the tables were cleared and wiped, the pots washed, dried and put away, and everywhere was spick and span again.

'What would you like me to do now?' Rebecca asked.

'You could sweep up.'

Again Rebecca willingly did as she was told and the old

woman was impressed. The girl didn't look too well but she obviously wasn't afraid of hard work, which was half the battle if you ran a café. She seemed polite enough too, even if she was a bit quiet. Each time a customer left the café, Rebecca would instantly clear the table and wipe it down before washing the pots up, and as teatime approached the woman began to relax a little. She wasn't as young as she had used to be, and if the girl turned out to be any good she could prove to be a godsend.

'So what shall I call you then?' the woman asked as she and Rebecca began to prepare the vegetables for the evening rush.

'Just Rebecca,' the girl replied cagily.

'Fair enough. Rebecca it is, an' I'm Margie Bennet by the way, but you can call me Margie.'

Rebecca nodded as she continued to peel the carrots, and all was silent until Margie asked, 'So where are you stayin'? You ain't from around these parts, are you?'

'No, I'm not, and actually I don't have anywhere to stay yet,' Rebecca confessed. 'You wouldn't happen to know of anywhere, would you? It would have to be very cheap.'

'As it so happens I just might, or what I should say is, I may know someone who might.' Margie grinned. 'Young Red, that's the red-haired young chap that came in while you were here this mornin', lodges in a place a few streets back. It's a big old house that's been turned into bedsits. Now from what he tells me they ain't up to much – you know, not very clean – but you could soon spruce the place up a bit if there were one goin'. He'll no doubt be in for his evenin' meal once his work's done so I could have a word with him if you like?'

'Oh, yes please,' Rebecca said. Anywhere would be better than having to spend another night under the pier.

Sure enough, at about half past six that evening the café

door opened and the same young man who had spoken to her that morning appeared. He looked slightly surprised to see Rebecca waiting on tables, but he made no comment as he headed for the counter. From the corner of her eye, Rebecca saw Margie having a word with him, and later the woman told her, 'Red here reckons there could be a bedsit goin' if you're interested.'

'Oh, I am,' Rebecca assured her.

'In that case you'd best go back with him then when he's eaten. The worst o' the rush is over now an' I can manage on me own till eight o'clock.' Margie opened the till and passed Rebecca a twenty-pound note. 'That's for what you've done today,' she told her. 'An' if you still want to give the job a go, be here at six in the mornin' to help me open up.'

When Rebecca looked dubiously at the young man known as Red, who was now sitting at a table waiting for his roast chicken meal, Margie chuckled. 'Don't get worryin' about him, he's as safe as houses.'

Knowing that if she wanted a roof over her head that night she would have to trust him, Rebecca went through into the back room and collected her things. Half an hour later, with promises to Margie that she would be there the next morning, Rebecca followed Red from the café and they began to walk through a labyrinth of back streets.

'I ought to warn you not to expect too much,' he said, with his hands thrust deep in his pockets. 'Mr Kaine who owns the bedsits has let them run right down, that's why they're so cheap.'

'I won't mind that,' Rebecca said, and they moved on in silence until Red stopped in front of a huge old townhouse that seemed to disappear into the darkening sky.

'This is it.' Fumbling in his pocket he produced a key. 'Mr

Kaine lives in the downstairs flat. I'll give him a knock for you, so you can have a word.'

Inside was an enormous, dimly lit hallway with a number of doors leading off from which various smells were escaping. Indian takeaways and stale urine seemed to be vying for first place. She wrinkled her nose up and looked around apprehensively at the threadbare carpet and the graffiti on the walls.

Red rapped on a door. Almost instantly it was flung open and a very old man appeared, clad in carpet slippers and the dirtiest waistcoat Rebecca had ever seen. His wispy grey hair stood out around his head like snakes, and he smelled so bad that she had to make a valiant attempt not to step back and appear rude.

'Whaddaya want?' he snapped unceremoniously, peering at Rebecca from bushy eyebrows that seemed to have a life of their own.

Obviously well-used to the man's behaviour, Red motioned towards Rebecca. 'This young lady is looking to rent a bedsit,' he told him. 'Is that one on the top floor still empty?'

'It is that.' The man peered at Rebecca through thick-lensed spectacles. 'It's fifty quid a week up front an' I don't want no trouble bringin' back. If yer don't pay yer rent on time, yer out an' that's an end to it.'

'That will be quite acceptable. May I see it, please?' Rebecca replied politely.

The man's eyebrows rose before he turned and stomped away without a word, then came back clutching a key.

'It's on the top floor an' yer share a bathroom wi' three others,' the man wheezed as he climbed the stairs ahead of her. 'An' there ain't no fancy lifts here.'

Rebecca was mentally calculating. If Margie paid her the minimum wage, she would be able to pay the rent here and buy food, so all in all, things were looking up.

By the time they reached the top landing the old fellow looked seriously in danger of having a heart attack, but after leaning heavily on the banisters for a while he pushed himself away and unlocked a door. 'This is it,' he told her as he clicked on a bare light bulb that was dangling from the centre of a stained ceiling. 'Yer can't be expectin' the Ritz fer fifty quid a week. Take it or leave it. An' the bathroom's just down there.' He waved a nicotine-stained finger along the landing as Rebecca looked around in horror. The place was absolutely filthy, but even so she knew that it was the best she was going to get for the money he was asking, so she hastily told him, 'I'll take it, thank you.'

'That's two weeks' rent up front then,' he said, eyeing her suspiciously.

Dropping her bag onto a small table that was leaning drunkenly against one wall, Rebecca hastily withdrew her purse and counted five twenty-pound notes into his grubby hand.

They disappeared into the pocket of his grubby trousers at the speed of light and he handed her a front door key and a room key before turning and shuffling away.

'I did warn you that the bedsits weren't posh,' Red apologised. 'But you'd be surprised what you can do with them if you give them a good clean.'

'It will be fine,' Rebecca told him gratefully. 'And it was good of you to help me.'

He shrugged. 'It was nothing. Are you sure you're going to be all right?' She nodded and he went on, 'There's a one-stop shop on the corner where you could get some cleaning stuff. And I'm down on the next floor in number ten, so if you need anything, just give me a knock.'

'I will, and thanks,' she whispered as he closed the door softly behind him.

Once she was alone, she stared around at her new home.

The room was so small there was scarcely room to swing a cat, and it didn't smell too good either. Crossing to the window, she threw it open to let in some fresh air. This place was a million miles away from the comfortable room she'd had in Gina's trailer, and misery swamped her. Gina must have felt so hurt after finding her note and after all she had done for her – but what choice had she had but to leave? Loud music was throbbing in the room below her and it sounded as if someone was having a party in another room further along the landing. Rebecca pulled herself together. Even this was preferable to sleeping rough, so she might as well make the best of it.

A small divan bed stood against one wall; the mattress was stained and she dreaded to think what bugs might be lurking in it – but then she supposed she could always shop about for a cheap second-hand one. A threadbare curtain closed off one corner of the room, and when she swished it aside she found a small kitchenette that contained a greasy little cooker and a sink with lopsided shelves screwed onto the walls above it. Next to the sink stood a refrigerator. It was so old that she was sure it must be an antique – and when she opened it, she almost gagged. It was full of rotting food that had obviously been there some time. Her first job would be to chuck it away and clean the fridge thoroughly. There were also a number of mismatched pots and pans which she decided would be usable, once they'd had a good scrub. Her savings certainly wouldn't stretch to new ones. Other than that, the only furniture the room contained was a very old-fashioned wardrobe which stood at the end of the bed, an equally old-fashioned chest of drawers, and the table she had spotted when she entered the room, with a wooden chair beside it.

Snatching up her handbag, she set off to find the shop that Red had told her about. There was no time like the present.

By eleven o'clock that evening the small room was looking much better. Rebecca had cleaned it from top to bottom, and although she could do nothing about the threadbare carpets and curtains, at least it looked and smelled a lot fresher. I'll go out tomorrow and buy some new cheap bedding and towels, she promised herself, and she finally fell asleep in a slightly happier frame of mind.

Chapter Thirty-Nine

When Margie turned up at the café the next morning at six o'clock sharp she found Rebecca waiting outside, and smiling to herself, she commented, 'So you decided to come then?'

'I said I would,' Rebecca retorted indignantly.

'Well, you're punctual – I'll say that for you,' Margie conceded. 'Now let's get this show on the road, shall we? The breakfast rush-hour will be on us afore we know it.'

Within an hour the café was full and Rebecca had no time to think as she rushed about taking orders, clearing tables and washing up. Red came in at one point to ask, 'How did your first night go at Kaine Towers then?'

There was a twinkle of mischief in his eyes and Rebecca laughed. 'It wasn't too bad. I found that shop you told me about and got some cleaning stuff, then I blitzed the place, so at least it's clean now.' She then rushed off to serve someone else and when she next looked around, he had gone – she assumed to his job in the arcade.

During the quiet period after the lunchtime rush, Margie gave her an hour off and pointed her in the direction of a shop in town where she would be able to buy some cheap bedding and towels. Once again she had the uneasy sensation that someone was following her, but a glance about her assured her that no one was there, and she knew that she must be imagining things as part of the after-effects of the rape. She came back loaded down with a duvet, pillows and towels, which she put in the small room at the back of the café. Instead of bothering with a new mattress, she had found something called a mattress-protector, which was much cheaper, but would still be a great help.

'There's a launderette just around the corner when you need to do any washing,' Margie informed her, and Rebecca was pleased. The rest of the day passed in a blur but at last Margie put the Closed sign on the café door.

'You've worked hard, my lass,' she told Rebecca. 'Do you think you'll stick the job? I know it ain't the most exciting job in the world to be doin' for a young girl, but I dare say a job is a job at the end of the day.'

'It will suit me just fine,' Rebecca told her, then she set off for her new home hoping she would find it in the maze of back streets. Again she stopped more than once to look over her shoulder, unable to shake off the feeling that someone was following her, but there was never anyone there and after scolding herself, she hurried on. She had eaten at the café, so when she finally got back she unpacked her shopping, took her new towels and went to have a much-needed bath. She stared in dismay at the dirty ring that circled the tub before going back to her room to collect her cleaning things. Obviously whoever she was sharing it with didn't believe in hygiene – but that came as no surprise. The place seemed to be full of down and outs – but then what was she herself?

Rebecca had been working at the café for almost a month when she woke up one morning feeling queasy and unwell. The weather had turned bitterly cold and she hoped that she wasn't coming down with one of the many bugs that were flying about. She certainly couldn't afford to stay off work, so she dragged herself out of bed at 5 a.m. and made for the bathroom where she was violently sick.

'Good grief, I've seen corpses with more colour in their cheeks than yours,' Margie said when Rebecca walked into the café. 'Sit yourself down and have a hot drink before the rush starts. You look like you could do with it. An' why do yer keep glancin' at the window? Are you expectin' someone?'

'Oh, it's nothing really. I just keep getting the feeling that someone is following me.'

The woman grunted. She had grown quite fond of Rebecca during the time she had worked for her, and had quickly discovered that although the lass was young she had a good head on her shoulders, although she was very close about her personal life and nervy too, jumping at her own shadow half of the time. So much so that Margie had stopped asking her questions now, which suited Rebecca just fine.

Rebecca had now taken over some of the cooking duties from Margie and found that she quite enjoyed it. The woman was also now trusting her to take the money from the customers and use the till, but that morning the smell of frying bacon made her feel nauseous again and she had to force herself to stand over the frying pan whilst her stomach revolted. By dinnertime, however, she was feeling much better and obviously looking better, because Margie commented on the fact.

'You've got a bit o' colour back now,' she said as they worked together to clear the tables.

'I feel fine now,' Rebecca agreed as she went about her duties. Margie had a horrible suspicion in her mind but as yet it was too early to voice it.

Over the last two or three weeks, Rebecca had become quite friendly with Red, although she still didn't know anything about him or what his real name was. Like her, he kept himself very much to himself and avoided telling her anything about his personal life. He had never shown any inclination to be anything other than friends with Rebecca, and now they regularly walked together to the café each morning where he would have his breakfast before going off to work.

All in all, she was settling well into her new life, but it didn't stop her missing Gina and the circus desperately. She missed Ricky too, but tried not to think of him as she remembered that awful night on the beach when she had been raped. She wondered if the circus folk ever missed her too but wouldn't allow herself to dwell on it. That was in the past now and once again she knew that she must move on.

That night, she set off for home with her head bent against the wind that was blowing in from the sea. She had gone some way into the back streets when a large figure suddenly loomed out of the shadows to stand in front of her.

'So how yer doin' then?'

The voice catapulted her back into the past.

'Uncle Ken! What are *you* doing here?' she demanded. 'And how did you find me?' Even as she asked the question she was thinking of the car headlights that had blinded her in the rearview mirror of the car she had got a lift in, the night she ran away from the circus.

'Oh, let's just say I've been keepin' me eye on you for a while now,' he said. 'Yer didn't really think I'd forget yer after what yer did to me, did yer?'

'The way I remember things, it was what *you* did to *me* that was the problem,' Rebecca retorted with a bravery she was far from feeling. 'Now why don't you just go away and leave me in peace!'

He smiled – an evil smile that made her blood run cold.

'Oh, I won't be doin' that fer a while,' he sneered. 'Not till you've paid.'

'And what's that supposed to mean?' But he was already walking away as she reeled with shock. All those times she had felt that someone was following her or watching her – could it have been him? And what had he meant by *Not till you've paid?*

She glanced along the deserted streets. He could be waiting somewhere to leap out on her. But she couldn't just stand there all night, so she fled with her heart thumping so painfully that it was like a drumbeat in her ears. Once again, just when she thought she was getting her life back on track, the past had come back to haunt her. She wondered how much more she could take.

Once back at the house, her hands were shaking so badly that she had trouble getting the key into the lock, and then just as she did so the door opened and Red appeared. 'Whoa there, where's the fire?' he asked as she almost fell into his arms.

'I was just keen to get in out of the cold,' she choked.

'Hmm.' Clearly not believing her, Red glanced up and down the empty pavements. 'Well, I was just off out to the chip shop to get some supper. Do you want me to bring you anything?'

'No, thanks.' She elbowed past him and then took the stairs two at a time as he stared after her in bewilderment. She was a strange girl, there was no doubt about it. But then she was in the right place. All the odd-bods ended up here, himself included. Shrugging, he went on his way.

Once in the tiny bedsit, Rebecca locked the door before placing the chair beneath the handle just to be on the safe side. Somehow she knew that her uncle would know where she was living, and if he came here she wanted to make sure that the room was as secure as possible. She fetched the milk out of the tiny refrigerator, which only seemed to work spasmodically, and after making herself a cup of tea she sat cross-legged on the bed, trying to think what she should do next.

The following morning, after a restless night where every little sound seemed to be magnified, Rebecca fell out of bed feeling dreadful again. It's probably because I haven't slept very well, she tried to reassure herself, but inside, panic was beginning to build. Her period was late and normally she was as regular as clockwork. Fighting nausea, she made her way to the bathroom and had a hasty wash before setting off for work. Red was waiting in the hallway for her as he tended to do each morning now, and she was grateful for his company. A hasty glance each way down the street revealed that her uncle wasn't loitering about, and as they walked along, Red asked, 'Are you not feeling very well? You're as white as a ghost.'

'It's just these early mornings,' she lied, and forced a smile.

She had been in the café for almost an hour when she had to make a run for the toilet in the yard at the back of the shop, where she was once again violently sick. When she returned, Margie suggested cautiously, 'Why don't you go an' see the doctor in your lunch-break? There's one a couple of streets away as would take you on, and you look as if a tonic of some kind would do you good. Is this job turnin' out to be too much for you?'

'Oh no,' Rebecca said hastily. 'I like working here but I think I've caught a bug.' The last thing she needed was to lose her job.

'Have it your own way,' Margie sighed to herself, then they both got on with clearing the pots into the sink.

It was early that afternoon when Rebecca turned from taking an order from a table at the back of the shop that she saw her uncle sitting in the windowseat. For a moment her knees threatened to buckle beneath her, but then forcing herself to stay composed she approached him and asked politely, 'What can I get for you?'

He grinned at her lasciviously. 'Now that would be tellin,' wouldn't it?'

'If you've come to order food I'm willing to take you order, but if you haven't I suggest you leave,' she told him.

He chuckled. 'Make it steak pie an' chips then.' He winked at her, making her stomach turn over with disgust. 'We can always have the dessert another time, eh?'

Margie watched her walk back to the counter, her face as white as chalk, and whispered, 'Is that feller botherin' you, love?'

'No, he's nothing I can't handle. He's just one of those creeps who think they're God's gift to women.' Rebecca busied herself as best she could whilst Margie prepared the orders.

When her uncle finally left, half an hour later, Rebecca let out a huge sigh of relief. He'd gone for now, but how long would it be before he was back – and where was it going to end? He not only knew where she lived but also where she worked now, and the thought filled her with dread. Once again she thought longingly of the trailer she had shared with Gina. She had felt protected there – until the night of the rape, that was – but there was no one to watch over her now. The circus would have moved on to overwinter in King's Lynn, and the knowledge made her feel lonelier and more vulnerable than ever. Perhaps she could ask Red if he would walk her home each night after work? She felt safe with him. He would often knock on her door when he went to the shop to see if there was anything she needed, and for the last couple of weekends they had been taking it in turns to do each other's washing at the launderette. He'd also invited her down to his bedsit for a meal more than once. She had always declined the invitation up to now, but if he asked her again, she decided she would go. It wasn't as if she had anything better to do each evening. She was too afraid to venture out onto the streets on her own, and as she didn't have a television she usually spent her time reading the books that Red fetched for her from the local library.

'Red, I know this is an awful imposition, but I was wondering, would you mind coming to meet me after work each night?'

They were heading for the café the following morning, and when he looked at her curiously she hurried on, 'It's just that it's a bit spooky round here now that most of the holiday-makers have gone, and I get a bit nervous. But you don't *have* to, of course,' she finished.

Red shrugged. 'It won't be a problem, if that's what you want me to do.'

'Thanks.' Rebecca self-consciously shoved her hands into her pockets. She'd never been one for asking favours from anyone and it went against the grain. They walked the rest of the way in a companionable silence and soon Rebecca was hard at work and, as ever, she had no time to brood.

Her uncle came into the café again mid-morning, and Rebecca made sure that she was washing up at the sink, so that Margie would have to take his order. The mere sight of him made her stomach churn, especially when she glanced up to see him leering at her.

The new arrangement with Red walking her home worked well, and it was on Saturday night as they were heading back to the bedsit that he offered, 'I'm going to cook a curry tonight. Do you fancy joining me?'

Rebecca nodded. 'Yes, thanks, that would be nice. Do you want me to bring anything?'

'I suppose another bottle of wine wouldn't go amiss,' he answered, and so Rebecca called into the corner shop and got one on the way back.

She arrived at Red's bedsit smack on time at seven-thirty, and when she entered her eyes stretched wide with amazement.

'Why, this is really lovely!' she gasped.

Red grinned. The bedsit was no larger than hers but it was decorated beautifully. He had painted all the walls in a soft cream colour, and bright canvases hung here and there, adding a splash of colour. He'd gone to great pains to strip the floorboards right back before varnishing them, and rugs that complemented the colours in the canvases were scattered about, giving the place a homely feel.

'I used to work in interior design with my partner before I came here,' he told her, and now her eyes stretched even wider, although why she should have been surprised that Red had once had a partner she couldn't imagine. He was certainly attractive enough. Perhaps they'd split up and he was suffering from a broken heart? That would explain why she'd never seen him with any girls.

'So how come you're here now and working in an arcade?' she asked in her usual forthright manner. 'Did you and your partner split up?'

Red looked decidedly embarrassed and Rebecca wished that she hadn't questioned him.

'It was something like that.' He clearly didn't want to talk about it. 'But now, I hope you like hot curry,' he said in an effort to change the subject and Rebecca nodded as she sank down into the only comfortable chair in the tiny room. The longer she lived here, the more she realised that most of the people in the bedsits were running away from something or someone, and she promised herself that she wouldn't ask him any more personal questions.

At the moment, Red was just about the only friend she had in the whole world.

Chapter Forty

It was early December, and as Rebecca made her way to work she shivered. The frost was thick on the pavements and she felt dreadful. She had now missed two periods and knew that she would soon have to visit a doctor – but she was so afraid of what he or she might tell her that she kept putting it off. It didn't help that she was having to walk home alone, but she had little choice since poor Red was confined to bed with a bad case of the flu. He seemed to catch every bug and virus that was going, and Rebecca felt sorry for him. Thankfully, her uncle was no longer visiting the café on a daily basis. Sometimes he might not show his face for days and she would begin to hope that he had tired of tormenting her, but then he would suddenly turn up again like a bad penny. He never spoke to her now but his eyes would follow her about until she was so sick with fear that her hands would begin to shake.

One day Margie had actually commented on the fact. 'Who's that bloke that keeps comin' in?' she asked with a frown. 'I reckon he's got his eye on you an' I don't like the look of him at all. He might be one o' them dirty old men that prey on young girls, so you just watch your step, eh?'

Rebecca had merely nodded, and now each time he entered the café Margie would watch him suspiciously.

This morning when she arrived at the café Margie looked

at her with concern as she peeled her layers of clothing off and put her apron on.

'You look peaky again,' she said bluntly. 'There ain't somethin' as you ain't tellin' me, is there?'

Rebecca flushed to the roots of her hair. 'No,' she said hastily. 'I think I just might be coming down with this flu bug that Red's got.'

'In that case, put yer coat on an' get yourself back home an' into bed. I can manage here fer a couple o' days till you're feelin' better,' Margie said kindly.

'Are you sure?' This might just be the opportunity Rebecca needed to get herself off to the doctor's. She knew that she couldn't avoid it for much longer. If what she dreaded was true, she would start to show soon and then there would be no hiding it from anyone. When Margie nodded, she put her coat back on again and within minutes was hurrying back to the bedsit. She was almost halfway there when her uncle suddenly appeared, as if thoughts of him had conjured him from thin air.

'Fancied a day off, did we?' he asked with a cheesy grin. 'I were just goin' to call in an' let yer cook me a nice breakfast when I saw you comin' back out again. Never mind, we could always go for a nice stroll along the beach. You used to like strollin' along the beach of a night when you were wi' the circus, didn't you?'

'What's that supposed to mean?' she choked.

He sniggered. 'I would have thought that were obvious. I certainly enjoyed the last stroll along the beach you took . . .'

'It was *you*!' she gasped, as the implications of what he was saying registered.

'Hmm. But should yer tell anyone, I'll just say as you came wi' me willingly – an' it'll be your word against mine.'

Rebecca felt the bottom drop out of her world as her hand flew to her stomach.

'But why?' she demanded. 'What have I ever done to you?'

His face twisted with hatred. 'You cost me me wife, that's what yer did,' he spat.

'H-how did I do that?' Rebecca stammered.

'She knew what were goin' on between us, *that's* how!'

Rebecca felt as if she was caught in the grip of a nightmare. 'But I never told her anything.'

'No, but yer told Pat as yer didn't want to stay in on yer own wi' me, an' she told Ali – an' that were enough to plant the seed. Then when I went away she pissed off wi' a bloke almost 'alf 'er age, meanin' I come out o' the nick to nothin'! No 'ome, no wife, no family – an' all because o' you, yer malicious little cow.'

Rebecca replied with a bravery she was far from feeling. 'Have you ever stopped to think that what you did to me when I was a child was wrong?' she dared to say, and he snorted.

'Huh! Don't come that wi' me. Yer were beggin' fer it, yer know yer were. Though I 'ave to say I enjoyed it a lot more, the last time. Yer've filled out nicely now.'

Rebecca stared at him with contempt shining from her eyes. He was worse than an animal but she felt powerless to do anything about it. If she *was* pregnant, it would be her uncle's child growing inside her – and she knew that she wouldn't be able to bear it.

'Anyway, I'm sure you'll be heartbroken to know that I'll be leavin' today,' he went on. 'I got some seasonal work up here once I found out where you were, but that's finished now, so I'm headin' back to the Midlands tonight on the seven o'clock train. Will yer miss me, darlin'? It were kind o' yer brother to tell me he'd seen yer, weren't it? An' a chance in a million that I should bump into him like that, fresh back off his holidays. Seems we have the same solicitor. The chap that defended me in court also handled Josh's inheritance. Anyway, I had to pop back to tie up a few loose ends an' there were Josh, large as life, just comin' out of his office. It's a small world, ain't it?'

Anger was replacing the horror now and she clenched her hands into fists as she ground out, 'You *bastard*!'

Clearly pleased with how his news had been received, he chuckled. He had had his revenge and now he could move on.

'Be seein' yer,' he laughed as he strolled away without a backward glance, and Rebecca stood there in a daze. Why hadn't she ever realised that it might have been him? She had always been convinced that it was either Josh or Ricky who had raped her, but in her wildest imaginings she had never dreamed it might be *him*. It was her very worst nightmare come true. Eventually she forced herself to walk on, but her thoughts were racing around in her head. If she was pregnant, there was no way she could keep this baby now. The very thought of it was repugnant to her. But then if she got rid of it, she would be just as bad as the mother who had abandoned her at birth so long ago.

By the time she got back to the bedsit, tears were coursing down her frozen cheeks. She was stumbling past Red's door, weeping, when it suddenly opened and he stood there looking at her in amazement.

'Oh, you're up and about,' she said thickly as she tried to swipe the tears away.

'Yes, I'm feeling a bit better today and I was just going to the shop to get myself a newspaper. But why aren't you at work? And why are you crying?'

She wanted to walk past him and tell him to mind his own business, but the need to talk to someone was so strong that she fell into his arms and began to sob.

'Come on.' Gently, he took her arm and led her into his room. 'You need a hot cuppa, by the look of it. My mum always used to say it was the cure for all ills. And then while you're drinking it you can tell me all about it. You know what they say, there's not a problem been invented yet that can't be solved.'

Five minutes later, he pushed a steaming mug into her cold hands as she sat huddled in the chair by the table, and then he sat down opposite and waited for the sobs to subside before saying kindly, 'Now why don't you tell me all about it?'

Different emotions played through her. All her life she had avoided becoming close to anyone, but right now she desperately needed a confidant and Red was there, so taking a deep breath she began falteringly, 'It . . . it all started soon after my birth. My mum didn't want me and so she abandoned me amongst the rubbish bins at the back of a big hospital in Coventry . . .'

Suddenly, it was as if floodgates had opened and the whole sorry tale came pouring out. By the time she was done, Rebecca was weeping bitterly and Red was temporarily speechless. Then he ran his hand through his thick thatch of startlingly red hair and said, 'So what you're telling me is, you think you may be pregnant by the uncle who raped you when you were a child?'

Rebecca nodded miserably as she rocked backwards and forwards in the chair with her arms wrapped tightly about herself.

'Right, then, now we have to figure out what you're going to do about it. I think the first thing would be to do a pregnancy test. There's bound to be a chemist open so I'll go and buy one right now. And then when I get back you're going to give me a description of your uncle, and the police can pick him up for questioning.' Even as he spoke he was shrugging his long arms into the sleeves of a heavy coat but Rebecca clutched at his arm and told him frantically, 'I don't want the police involved, *please!*'

He looked bemused for a moment but once at the door he told her, 'First things first. Let me get this test and then we'll talk about it. You wait there. I shouldn't be long.'

Rebecca stared at the door for what seemed like an eternity as the full horror of the situation dawned on her. Tempting as it was, the thought of having her uncle arrested, she knew that she couldn't go through with it. If the police became involved, they would realise that it was she who had killed her foster-mum and then she would be sent to prison too.

She sat rocking to and fro in an agony of wretchedness, but at last the door opened again and Red appeared, his face pinched and cold. Coughing, he handed her a small packet and told her, 'Go along to the bathroom and do a urine sample. It's best done first thing in the morning apparently, but you don't have time to mess about – and anyway, if you're as far on as you think you might be, it will show up. All the instructions are on there and you can use this.'

She stared at the plastic jug he fetched from beneath the sink before stumbling away to do as she was told. He was right – there was no point in delaying any longer. In this situation, ignorance was definitely not bliss. Minutes later, she stood in the bathroom and stared at the strip in her hand as a thin blue line slowly formed along it. There was no doubt now, her uncle's child was growing inside her.

She walked back to Red's room like an automation, and one look at her pallid face told him all he needed to know.

'OK, now don't look so terrified. Now that we know for sure, you have to decide what to do about it. What do you think you'd want to do?'

'I . . . I want to get rid of it,' she whispered. 'But if I

do that I'll be as bad as the mother who abandoned me, won't I?'

He shook his head. 'Perhaps your real mum had a good reason to do what she did,' he said sensibly. 'Sometimes things happen beyond our control, like this thing that has happened to you. I should know – nothing I had planned has worked out as I thought.'

Seeing her staring at him curiously, he shrugged. He had never confided his past to anyone since leaving his hometown, but seeing as Rebecca had opened up to him he didn't see why he shouldn't be honest with her too.

'The thing is, Rebecca . . .' He paused, wondering how she would take what he was about to confide to her. 'I'm gay.'

Rebecca's mouth dropped open. She had never met a gay man before and suddenly she understood why she had never seen Red with a girl.

'I had a partner,' he went on as pain flared in his eyes. 'And we had an interior design shop in Nottingham. We were happy, but then Rob found out he had AIDS and insisted I get tested too, which is when I discovered that I was HIV positive.'

'Oh no!' Rebecca's hand flew to her mouth.

'He went into a hospice at the end,' Red said quietly as his mind raced back to that terrible time. 'And then when he was gone I knew I had to get away. I had never told my parents that I was gay or that I am HIV positive, and I was worried about how they would react. They're lovely people, but rather intolerant of anyone who is different. So to cut a long story short, I told them I was going to backpack round the world, sold the shop and here I am.'

'I'm so sorry,' she said sincerely.

He smiled sadly. 'Don't be. It's like I told you – sometimes things happen that are beyond our control. But now we have to figure out what you want to do about this pregnancy and your uncle.'

'Perhaps I could find someone who would get rid of it for me,' she suggested tremulously.

Red's mouth set in a grim line. 'If you're talking about a backstreet abortion you can forget it,' he ground out. 'One of the girls from the bedsit downstairs tried that last year and she ended up in hospital and nearly died from septicaemia. No, if that's what you want we'll get it done through the proper channels.'

'But won't they ask who the father is?' The shame of having to tell someone else her terrible secret filled her with terror.

'No, they won't,' he said gently. 'Lots of women choose not to go through with a pregnancy for many different reasons. Luckily you're not too far on so it should be a very simple procedure and then you can start to put all this behind you.'

Rebecca's tongue raced across her dry lips but then she slowly nodded. 'All right then. Will you come with me in the morning?'

'Of course I will.' He took her hand and squeezed it gently. 'Now how about we have another cuppa, eh? There's not much more we can do tonight.' Somehow he sensed that she wasn't ready yet to discuss what she wanted to do about her uncle, so wisely, he didn't ask.

For the rest of the night they chatted easily, as if they had known each other all their lives, and by the time she left to return to her own bedsit Rebecca felt that she had found a true friend.

Ten days later, Red stood gripping her hand on the steps of a small clinic. He had arranged everything for her and she didn't know how she would have coped without him.

'Are you sure you don't want me to come in with you?'

She shook her head. 'No, really, I'll be fine. I just want it to be over now, but I'd be grateful if you'd come and fetch me this evening.'

'I'll be here,' he promised, then turning about he marched away as she squared her shoulders and pushed the door to the clinic open.

Rebecca lay on the bed in a back room of the clinic staring at the ceiling. She still felt slightly woozy from the anaesthetic, and she had a stomach ache, but it was no worse than period pains and she knew that the baby was gone now. Most of her rejoiced at the fact, but a niggling doubt now kept reminding her of the mother who had abandoned her when she was born. Abortion, abandonment – it was all the same thing. For years she had hated the woman who had got rid of her, but now she had done the exact same thing to her own child.

For the first time in a long while, Rebecca allowed herself to think of Pat; she was still convinced that the woman was her mother. Why else would she have shown her such kindness all those years ago when she had lived with her aunt? Rebecca knew that she had come very close to loving the woman, but resentment at the way she had left her had stopped her from opening her heart to her. It had stopped her from opening her heart to anyone, if it came to that, and she had carried a chip as big as a house brick around on her shoulder all her life.

As she thought of the kindly foster-mum who she had left lying in a pool of blood, her heart broke afresh. She had told Red about her too, and the reason why she had run away to join Gina. Oh Gina! She remembered too how cruel and judgemental she had been to her when she had discovered that Gina loved Harvey. Gina was right when she'd told her, *one day you'll understand*. And she *did* understand now – but it was too late to do anything about it. Then there was Ricky. Even now, just the thought of him could bring tears to her eyes. She realised that, had she stayed with the circus, they might have had a future together, but her bitterness and fear had made her hold everyone at arm's length and then run away again – just as she always did when she felt herself getting close to anyone.

At that moment her thoughts were interrupted when a nurse entered the room and lifted a chart that was hooked over the end of the bed.

'How are you feeling, dear?' she asked pleasantly.

'I'm fine.'

'Good, then in that case I'll just check your blood pressure and if that's all right you can go home.'

Half an hour later Rebecca walked unsteadily into the reception room where she found Red waiting for her.

He stood up instantly and took her small bag from her. She smiled at him shakily. 'It's all over,' she said, and he nodded before he rang to get a taxi to take them home.

On the way back to the bedsit he asked, 'How did it go?'

'It was no harder than going to the dentist's,' she said quietly. 'I just hope I've done the right thing and that I'll be able to live with myself.'

'Of course you will.' He slid his arm around her shoulders. 'And I've got some good news to tell you when we get home. You're having dinner with me tonight. Until you're properly well, I intend to keep a close eye on you.' She smiled at him gratefully, thinking how lucky she was to have such a good friend. To Red himself, Rebecca had appeared so grown up when he first met her, but now she had let her guard down he saw how vulnerable and young she was and he felt protective towards her. She didn't appear to have anyone else who cared for her.

It was when she was settled in a chair with a plate of spaghetti bolognaise on her lap that he asked, 'So do you want to hear the good news then?'

Rebecca nodded so he went on, 'I've been thinking about that foster-mum you told me about – the one you ran away from after the scuffle – and I realised that if I went to the library I could check back through the old newspapers and on the internet to find out what happened to her. Luckily, you'd told me the approximate date it occurred and where you were living, so it was quite easy to find the story. And guess what?'

Rebecca suddenly couldn't breathe as she stared at him open-mouthed.

'There was the smallest piece you could ever imagine in one of the local Leamington papers about it, saying that you'd run away after your foster-mum had tried to detain you and that she'd suffered a cut to her head and a slight concussion after a scuffle.'

'*What*? You mean she isn't dead? I'm not a murderer?'

Red laughed. 'You most certainly are not, and furthermore she blamed herself, saying that she'd just given up on you and was going to move you on to another placement. She felt very guilty about you being on the run, apparently.'

'Oh!' Rebecca could think of nothing else to say. Words seemed so inadequate. 'I . . . I don't know how I'll ever be able to thank you for all you've done for me,' she stuttered, tears pouring down her face.

'I haven't done that much,' Red objected. 'But the rest is up to you now.'

'What do you mean?'

'I mean I think it's time you laid a few ghosts to rest now,' he said. 'For a start-off, you should report what your uncle has done to you to the police. If you don't, he could do the same to some other girl – and you wouldn't want that on your conscience, would you?'

Rebecca slowly shook her head. No, she certainly wouldn't want any other young child to suffer at his hands as she had, but would the police believe her?

She voiced her fears to Red, but he said gently, 'Of course they will. I'll speak up and tell them what I know, and if your aunt had her suspicions about what was going on, she'll probably back your story up too. But you have to be brave. Then you must go back and visit the woman you think is your mother and talk to her. Next, find Gina and ask her to give you another chance. It shouldn't be that hard to trace her, and it seems to me that being with the circus was the happiest time of your life, from what you've told me. And finally, you should see Ricky. I've got a sneaky feeling you love him, and if he loves you too – who knows what might happen? We just might end up with a happy-ever-after ending, after all. All these years you've been running away from yourself, but if you'd just open your eyes and cut yourself a bit of slack you'll realise that you're not such a bad person, after all. You've just had a raw deal.'

'B–but what will happen to you if I go?' Rebecca asked.

Red's head swayed from side to side. 'I can't go back. I'm ill. I don't know how to face my family. And I've lost the person I loved most in the world,' he said. 'You're different, though. You've got your whole life ahead of you – and if you do the right thing now, it could be a happy one.'

But now Rebecca sat up in the chair and some of her old spirit flared in her eyes. 'I don't agree,' she told him sternly. 'With the right medication people with HIV can live for years and years – right into old age. I read a pamphlet in the clinic. One day you will find someone too. And your parents sound like decent people. Don't you think they deserve to know the truth and be allowed to make their own decision on whether or not they want to stand by you? It will probably come as a shock to them, but perhaps when they've had time to come to terms with it, they'll understand.'

He stared at her for a moment before saying emotionally, 'Seems like we both have a lot to decide, doesn't it?'

She nodded and they both lapsed into deep thought.

Chapter Forty-One

On a cold January day, Rebecca and Red stood outside the bedsits on the pavement to say goodbye. Red had already lifted the new suitcase she had bought into the taxi that would take her to the station, and now they stared at each other, suddenly tongue-tied.

'So, this is it then.' Rebecca bit back tears as she blinked up at Red.

He nodded with a wide smile on his face. He seemed to have come down with every cough and cold that was going the rounds throughout the winter, but Rebecca knew now that this was because his immune system was low. Even so, they had shared a peaceful Christmas together and she knew that she was going to miss him.

'It certainly is. I want you to think of it as the first day of the rest of your life. And by the way, girl – you look great!'

Rebecca flushed prettily. She'd treated herself to a smart black trouser suit and a new red coat, and with her hair trimmed into a becoming bob that danced on her slim shoulders, and her eyes shining, she looked very lovely.

'Just remember, you have nothing to be ashamed of,' he urged her. 'You always thought of yourself as a misfit, but no one would say that of you now. Go and knock 'em dead – for me, eh?'

'I'm going to really miss you,' she told him softly.

'You won't even have time to think of me.' There was a

twinkle in his eye as he bent to kiss her gently on the cheek. 'Now be off with you or you'll miss your train. And Rebecca? Good luck and keep in touch – you've got my parents' address.'

He was due to leave for Nottingham the very next day and she knew that he was nervous about seeing his parents again but hoped that all would go well for him.

She returned his kiss then slid into the rear seat of the taxi and waved until he was gone from sight. And strangely she felt as if she had left a little part of her behind. In the months that she had known him, Red had taught her so much. He was one of the kindest, most sensible people she had ever met, and they had gone through a lot together.

It was he who had taken her to the police station to report what her uncle had done to her, shortly after her abortion, and he had been a tower of strength throughout the whole proceedings. The police had picked her uncle up in Bedworth within days of her making her statement, and thankfully when questioned he had admitted everything. When they found him, he was buying sweets for a seven-year-old boy who had been walking home alone from school. Rebecca shuddered when she heard this. Now she just had the court case to get through the following month, but she had been told it was a forgone conclusion that he would be sent to prison for a very long time. Rebecca knew that paedophiles got a rough time of it in prison – but she could find no room for pity in her heart for her uncle. He was a wicked predator who needed to be locked away, preferably forever.

She still often thought of the child she had aborted and suffered all manner of guilt, but deep down she knew that it had been the right thing to do. And now she would have to learn to live with it, just as her mother must have had to, so long ago when she had abandoned her newborn babe.

On the train that would take her to Nuneaton, Rebecca

stared from the window and her stomach churned. Red had told her she must face her past and that was exactly what she intended to do, beginning with Pat. But what if the woman had chosen to forget her or no longer wished to see her? Rebecca decided to cross each bridge as she came to it, and settling herself back into her seat, she tried to calm herself.

Once in Nuneaton, she caught a bus to Bedworth and soon she was standing at the end of the road where she had once lived with her aunt and uncle. The place held no happy memories for her, but even so she lifted her case and strode resolutely along until she came to the gate outside Pat's house. There was a light on in the front-room window, so without giving herself time to think, she walked up the path and rang the doorbell. Almost instantly she heard the sound of footsteps in the hallway and then suddenly the door opened and there was Pat.

'Hello, can I help yer, love?' she asked in the voice that Rebecca remembered so well, and then as recognition dawned, her mouth dropped open and tears sprang to her eyes. 'Well, I'll go to the foot of our stairs,' she gasped. 'Is it really you, Rebecca?'

Rebecca nodded as Pat's hand shot out and yanked her into the hall, and then the woman had her arms tight about her and was crying with delight. 'Well, I never thought I'd live to see this day – an' just look at you! You're all grown up – an' lovely.'

Rebecca beamed as she returned the hug. Pat didn't seem to have changed at all, apart from looking a little older, and she was surprised at how pleased she felt to see her.

'I don't know – where's me manners,' Pat choked then. 'Come on in, pet. I'll make yer a nice hot drink an' then yer can tell me what you've been doin' with yourself all this time. I'll tell yer now I've been worried sick ever since yer ran away from that place in Leamington. But never mind that for now.'

Soon Rebecca was seated in Pat's homely kitchen and as they faced each other across the table over steaming mugs of tea, Pat asked, 'So what brings you back here then? I'm afraid yer aunt don't live along the road any more. She got herself a fancy chap while yer uncle were in nick an' she cleared off wi' him some time ago.'

'Actually, I didn't come to see Aunt Alison, although I intend to,' Rebecca explained, and then she took a deep breath. This was the moment she had been dreading. 'I came to see you. After I ran away from Leamington I joined a circus, but then something happened and I lived in Skegness for a time.' Her thoughts raced back to Margie, who had been so sorry to see her go, and of course Red, but then she forced her mind back to the present and she went on, 'As you know, I was always a bit of a loner when I was a child.'

'Huh! You can say that again,' Pat chortled.

'Well, I think the reason for that was because I'd always felt so alone because my real mum had abandoned me after I was born.'

Pat's face fell into solemn lines now and she stared down at the table, unable to meet Rebecca's eyes.

'I always resented my real mum and couldn't forgive her for leaving me,' Rebecca said quietly. It was the time for honesty now. 'But then whilst I was living in Skegness I met a wonderful person who showed me that things aren't always what they seem, that we sometimes have to do things we don't want to do. And it got me thinking. Perhaps my mum didn't have a choice. Perhaps there were good reasons why she couldn't keep me.'

She waited for an eternity for Pat to answer her, and when she didn't she finally asked, 'Are *you* my real mum, Pat?'

Pat's head snapped up, and when she stared back at her, all the love she had always felt for her was reflected there.

'Yes, I am,' she whispered as tears streamed down her cheeks. 'Can you ever forgive me for what I did to yer?'

'I already have,' Rebecca answered, as tears trickled down her own cheeks. 'And now we have a lot of catching up to do, don't we?'

And then suddenly they were in each other's arms and Rebecca's heart swelled.

Eventually they drew apart and Pat's hand snaked across the table to take hers. It was then that a thought occurred to Rebecca and she said, 'So if you really *are* my mum, this means that Caz must be my grandma?'

'Yes, she is.' Pat nodded solemnly.

Rebecca's eyes were wide with excitement. She was discovering her real family at last.

'I'm goin' to make a phone call to tell her you're here,' Pat said, looking as if all her birthdays and Christmases had come at once. 'An' then yer can tell me all about what you've been doin' with yourself.'

And she hurried away with a spring in her step to do just that. After she had made the phone call they sat catching up on all that had happened to them since they had last seen each other, and when Pat heard all that Rebecca had endured, she wept.

'It's all right,' Rebecca told her. 'I've come through it all now and I'm ready to make the best of my life. I just hope you'll be a part of it now.'

'Always,' Pat said, and she sounded so genuine that Rebecca's heart swelled with love for her.

Pat had never dared to hope that this day would ever come, and now that it had she hoped that things would work out for the best. Eventually she said to Rebecca: 'Now that I've told me mam you're here, she can't wait to see yer. Shall I call us a taxi?'

'Yes, please.'

The sky was darkening when they drew up outside the high-rise flats in Coventry, and Rebecca peered from the windows as memories rushed back.

'Fancy finding your mum and your grandma all in one day, eh!' Rebecca rejoiced. 'It can't get much better than this.' She could clearly remember the way the kindly woman would fuss over her and treat her each time she and Pat had visited.

Pat smiled. 'Your gran's got a heart of pure gold. When I realised who you were, soon after you moved in with yer aunt, we tried to keep an eye out for you. I don't mind tellin' you she were heartbroken when you ran away.'

Rebecca nodded numbly as Pat rubbed her arm before walking into the high-rise block and heading for the lift. Before she had time to think about it, they were standing outside Caz's door and the girl gulped deep in her throat as sweat broke out on her forehead. But then she thought of Red's words: *you've got to face your past*. It was as if the woman had been hovering behind the door because it opened instantly – and as they faced each other, Rebecca realised with a shock that Caz's eyes were very much the same colour as her own. Admittedly, they had faded now, but even so the resemblance was there for all to see.

Holding out her arms, she choked, 'Come here, pet,' and then they were in each other's arms.

Soon they were sitting face-to-face in Caz's little flat and now her expression was sad as she looked at her granddaughter. 'You must hate us,' she said.

'I did for a long time,' Rebecca admitted. 'But then I got to accept that perhaps there was a very good reason why none of you could keep me.'

Caz sighed. 'There was. But our Pat didn't even tell me she were pregnant or what she'd done till she'd left you at the hospital – an' by then there was nothin' I could do about it. An' so we had to learn to live with it and pray that your new mum an' dad would be good to you. I don't mind admittin' it almost broke me heart to know I had another granddaughter I'd never be allowed to see. An' your mam here never really got over it. It's as if there's always been a little part of her missin'.'

'It's all right, it's over now,' Rebecca said, and she realised with a little shock that it was true. How could she despise her mother now when she had just aborted a child herself?

'I suppose I should start at the beginning for you to really understand.' Pat rubbed her head as memories flooded back. 'I was very young when I met my 'usband, barely out of school, but he was a charmer back then an' he swept me off my feet. I remember me mum 'ere tellin' me "you'll rue the day if you take up wi' that one". But I thought I knew best, so within months we were married. Huh! The charm soon flew out of the window, an' before I knew it I had two little 'uns to care for. He was into all sorts o' dodgy dealin's, an' when he'd had a drink he'd knock me from pillar to post. I left him more than once an' went back to me mum. But she were the old school an' she told me "you made yer bed an' now you'll have to lie on it".'

Caz hung her head but Pat went on, 'So I did. My kids were all that kept me going, and more than once I took them into a hostel for battered wives because I was scared he'd turn his temper on them.' She gulped deep in her throat now as Rebecca waited, but then she forced herself to go on. 'Eventually he got caught doin' an armed burglary by the police and they sent him to jail. It was a relief for a start but then it got that I didn't know which way to turn for money.

The children needed clothes and food on the table, so God forgive me – I earned it the only way I knew how.'

She glanced at Rebecca, her voice low with shame as she continued: 'Time passed and soon it was only a year till he was due to be released. That's when I found out I was carrying you. I didn't know what to do. My husband was a very violent man and I knew that if he came home to find me nursin' a baby that wasn't his, he'd kill me. I thought of havin' an abortion but I left it too late – and then one night I went into labour all on me own. The children were in bed and I delivered you meself somehow. I don't mind tellin' you, I felt as if I was bein' torn in two. I so wanted to keep you but I was too afraid of what he'd do, so I managed to get to the hospital and I . . .'

She began to weep. 'You know the rest. I did what I did out of desperation, but as me mam said, I never stopped worrying about you and wondering where you were. Social Services somehow traced you back to me, since one of the neighbours had smelled a rat when I suddenly lost weight, and it was in the papers about you being found. But I explained the position to them and they agreed that they'd have you adopted. All I knew was that you'd gone to a couple in Nottingham. Then some years later you came to live with Alison and Ken. Alison told me that the little girl had been adopted and was from Nottingham and when I found out your birthdate and the circumstances, I just knew it had to be you.'

Pat paused to wipe her eyes. 'There were times when I came so close to telling you who I was. But you'd been brought up so differently to my kids, and I knew that I could never give you what your adoptive parents had, I couldn't even tell you who your real dad was. I watched from afar till they sent you away again – and that really broke my heart.

All I could do then was keep an eye on what was happening, and then you suddenly disappeared and I've not had a day's peace of mind since – and that's the truth. I was a fool, I should have told you who I was years ago and tried to get you back, but with my track record I knew I'd stand no chance. An' . . . well, I was afraid that you'd be ashamed of me. I'm so sorry, pet.'

'It's all right, really,' the girl told her again, her own beautiful blue eyes wet with tears. 'But where do we go from here?'

'Well, you could always stay with me for a while if you don't have to rush off,' Pat suggested, with hope in her voice. 'We've got a lot of catching up to do, and of course, you've got to meet your half-brothers and sisters an' all. I told them all about you when their dad died, and I know they'd welcome you – especially Joe. He's never forgotten you though you'll barely recognise him now. He's engaged to a lovely young lass from Collycroft but he'll be so pleased to see you. What do you think?'

'I think I'd like that . . . Mum.' Then suddenly they were all in each other's arms again as their tears mingled, and for the first time in her whole life Rebecca felt a measure of peace settle in her heart.

Chapter Forty-Two

Taking a deep breath, Rebecca lifted her hand and knocked firmly on the door of the small semi-detached house in Wootton Street.

Pat had spent the entire morning trying to persuade her not to come, but Rebecca knew that she had to. Once she had faced this last ghost from her past, she could move on.

For a moment she thought that no one was in and her resolve began to falter, but then she heard footsteps in the hallway and the door was opened by a good-looking young man. She realised instantly that this must be Casey, considerably grown now, but he obviously didn't recognise her.

'Is your mother in?' Rebecca asked calmly although her stomach was churning. It was late afternoon and the birds were singing in a cherry blossom tree that was in full bloom in the next garden.

'Mam!' His voice echoed along the hallway and when a door opened Alison appeared. But it was not the Alison that Rebecca remembered. This woman looked considerably older and was very conservatively dressed in a neat black skirt and a clean white blouse with a supermarket's logo emblazoned on the top pocket.

She was holding a mug of tea, and as she approached the door she raised her eyebrows questioningly at the smart young woman at the door. 'Yes?'

And then she suddenly looked into Rebecca's unforgettable

bluebell-coloured eyes, and as recognition dawned her face paled and a small amount of tea sloshed over the side of her cup onto the hall floor.

'You'd better come in,' she said shakily as Casey disappeared off up the stairs.

Rebecca followed her into a surprisingly tidy lounge at the back of the house. It could not have been classed as luxurious by any stretch of the imagination, but it was a huge improvement on the house that Rebecca had once shared with her. Her aunt placed her mug down on a small table before hastily lighting a cigarette then went to stare out of the window.

It was obvious that the visit was not going to be anywhere near as easy as the one Rebecca had paid to Pru, her former foster-mum, some days ago. She had caught the train to Leamington and when Pru saw her standing on the doorstep she had been ecstatic. They had talked all afternoon and parted on good terms, promising to keep in touch – but now that she was here, Rebecca was struggling to think of something to say.

It was Alison who finally broke the awkward silence when she said, 'I suppose you've come to see me about what's goin' on with Ken?'

'No, I haven't actually,' Rebecca answered. 'I just came to see how you are.'

'Oh, well I couldn't tell the police much when they come to see me,' Alison said lamely. 'But I'll tell you now – I might 'ave been a bad person but I wouldn't 'ave put up wi' that if I'd known what he was doin' to yer.'

Alison then eyed Rebecca up and down before commenting, 'You're lookin' good, girl.'

'So are you.'

'Thanks. I'm tryin' to put me life back together.' There was a world of regret in her aunt's voice and Rebecca almost felt sorry for her.

'I'm workin' now, only on the checkouts, but it keeps the wolf from the door. An' I dare say you've heard I've got a new bloke.' She grinned then, and just for a moment Rebecca caught a glimpse of the happy-go-lucky woman she remembered.

'Folks round here 'ave had a field day about it,' Alison went on. ''Cos he's younger than me, see? But do yer know what – I don't care what they say. At least he treats me decent. But how are you?'

'I'm OK now.'

Alison stared at her and Rebecca could have sworn she saw a glimmer of regret in her eyes but it was gone in a flash.

Another awkward silence followed until Alison asked, 'Would yer like a cuppa?'

'No thanks. I just wanted to see how you were, but now I have, I won't keep you.' The girl knew that they would never be easy in each other's company, but at least now they could part on good terms.

Alison followed her to the door and opened it for her, but just as Rebecca was passing through it she suddenly caught her arm and said softly, 'I'm sorry, kid.'

Rebecca smiled before walking away from her for the very last time.

'I'm going to miss you so much,' Pat said chokily as she held Rebecca to her. It was now early in April and for the last few months they had been almost inseparable. Rebecca had met and gotten to know her half-siblings during that time, and they had welcomed her into the family. She knew now that she would always have a home to come back to should she wish to. If truth be told, Pat had made it more than clear that she was welcome to stay there forever, but Rebecca knew that it was time to live her own life. There was just one more thing she had to do.

'I'll keep in touch and I'll come back and visit you often,' she promised with tears in her eyes.

Pat stroked the girl's hair back from her face – the face that was so like her own had been at that age. Instinct told her that to keep this beloved girl, she must let her go. She just counted herself very lucky that Lilli – Rebecca – had come back into her life.

'Well, you just be careful, an' if things don't pan out the way you want, you just come straight back here, do yer hear me?'

'Loud and clear!' Rebecca grinned as she hugged her mum. She knew now that she loved the woman – *really* loved her – and it gave her a warm feeling inside.

'Goodbye then. Take care of yourself – and Mum? I love you.'

Pat's heart swelled. 'An' I love you too. More than you'll ever know. Now get yourself off else I might lock you away an' change me mind about lettin' you go.'

Rebecca laughed as she skipped towards the gate and got into the waiting taxi that would take her to the bus station.

When she got down from the coach in Nuneaton she looked around at the familiar sights. Nothing seemed to have changed much, but she scarcely noticed, since for now she had but one purpose in mind.

Walking towards the town centre, she entered the gates into Riversley Park with her heart pounding in her ears. She passed the museum and the bandstand, and in no time at all was walking through the tunnel that would lead her into the Pingles Fields. And then there it was: the circus Big Top, rearing up in front of her just as she'd known it would be. She headed for the trailers spread around the perimeter of the field, and people shouted a greeting as they recognised her. 'Hey there, Bex! Long time no see! How you doing?'

She smiled at them as she moved on, and then there was Gina with the dogs outside the trailer; she was putting them through their paces before the afternoon performance began. It suddenly felt to Rebecca as if she had never been away, but even so she was nervous as she approached. And then Gina looked up and saw her, and her mouth gaped.

'Bex, I thought we'd seen the last of you! What brings you back here? Do you have any idea how worried I was when you disappeared off like that . . .'

Her voice trailed away as she realised how she must sound, and then she smiled – and dropping her case, Rebecca ran into her arms.

'I'm so sorry,' she sobbed. 'For everything. I got it all so very wrong. But I promise I'll explain everything if you'll give me another chance.'

Gina ushered her into the trailer and put the kettle on, giving Rebecca time to compose herself, then she joined her at the table and said gently, 'Was it because you found out about Harvey and me loving each other?'

'Partly,' Rebecca admitted. 'But it was lots of other things too. For you to understand, I suppose I should begin at the beginning.' And that's exactly what she did as Gina listened wide-eyed.

'My God!' she exclaimed when Rebecca had finished. 'You *have* been through the mill. No wonder you were always such a solemn little thing, but now I understand why.'

'And what about Maura? How is she?' Rebecca asked now. 'Did she go into a home?'

'She was about to, when she took a serious turn for the

worse.' Gina's eyes welled with tears now as she remembered. 'Harvey rang for an ambulance but she died in his arms with me holding her hand before it could get there. It was awful – but truthfully I think that's what she would have wanted. We miss her very much.'

'I'm so sorry,' Rebecca said sadly. 'How has Harvey taken it?'

'Pretty badly, to be honest. He's grieving, but one day when he's over it . . . well, who knows. I'll be here for him and we'll take it from there.'

Rebecca chewed on her lip. Life could be cruel. And then she asked tentatively, 'And how is Ricky?'

Gina grinned. 'Let's just say I think he'll be a lot happier when he sees you again. He's been wandering about like a lost soul ever since you left. Didn't you realise how much he loved you?'

Rebecca shrugged. 'Perhaps I didn't want to see it because I didn't think that someone like him could love someone like me.'

'You silly goose,' Gina scolded. 'Everyone needs someone to love and I don't think he'll need much persuading to welcome you back again.'

'But *am* I welcome? I mean, would you be willing to give me another try?'

Gina dropped her eyes. 'You'll find all your clothes where you left them,' she told her, so quietly that Rebecca had to strain to hear her. 'You see, I came to look upon you as the daughter I once gave up for adoption many years ago. She would have been a little older than you, and I think about her every single day. Just like your mum with you, I had no choice but to let her go. I was young and I had nothing to offer, and when it was done I ran away from an abusive father and joined the circus. Maura and Harvey helped me put my life back together and that's why I loved them so much. So, you see, you're not the only one with secrets. We've all done things we're ashamed of. That's what makes us human. But now if you're planning on staying, I suggest you go and get changed. We have a performance in less than two hours, young lady.'

'*Yes, ma'am*!' Rebecca giggled as she hurried away to the little bedroom she remembered so well – and as Gina had said, when she opened the door it was just as she'd left it. It seemed so long ago now and so much had happened since then, but now Rebecca was determined to look to the future.

When she emerged in jeans and a pretty T-shirt a short time later, Rebecca set about her duties as if she had never been away.

She saw Ricky briefly as she led the dogs towards the Big Top and beamed as his mouth dropped open in amazement. He rubbed his eyes as if he couldn't believe what he was seeing, but Rebecca merely waved at him before hurrying on her way. What she needed to say to him could wait until later.

It was, in fact, much later that evening, as the crowd was surging out of the tent following the evening's performance, that he approached her. She had felt his eyes on her all night.

'I didn't expect to see you again,' he said cautiously, not at all sure how she would react to him.

The dogs were capering around her legs and she asked him, 'Do you fancy a stroll around the park when I've got these all settled?'

'I er . . . yes, if you like.' He scratched his head in bewilderment as she led the dogs away. She didn't seem at all like the girl he remembered. She seemed more . . . light-hearted – yes, that was it, as if she'd had an enormous weight lifted off her shoulders. Yet she'd told him in no uncertain terms, that night on the beach, that she didn't want him – and now here she was asking him to go for a walk with her. Women were funny creatures, that was a fact, and he doubted he'd understand them if he lived to be a hundred!

An hour later found them strolling side by side along the banks of the River Anker as the weeping willow trees gently swayed in the breeze and dipped their branches into the water. Spring had arrived and everything was slowly coming back to life after the long, cold winter.

Ricky walked a safe distance away, afraid of being rebuked again until Rebecca suddenly caught his hand and drew him to a halt.

'So?' she said, giving him a tentative smile. 'Are you pleased to see me then?'

'Well, I er . . . yes, of course I am.'

'Then why don't you show it?'

'What? And have you snap my head off again?' he retorted. 'You made it more than clear that night on the beach that you didn't care about me, and I'm not going to risk that again.' Thrusting his hands firmly into his pockets, he lowered his head.

'A lot has happened since then,' Rebecca told him gently. 'When I went away it made me realise just how much I did care about you. Back then, I didn't think I was worthy of a man like you, but now . . . Well, let's just say I've done a lot of growing up. You see, I've spent years running away from different situations, until someone finally made me realise that I was actually running away from myself. I was blaming everyone else for the barriers I'd put up because I didn't feel that I belonged anywhere.' She paused and took a breath.

'Bad things happened to me when I was just a kid,' she went on as he listened intently, 'and after that, as soon as

367

anyone tried to get close to me, I backed off. But I don't want to run away any more, Ricky. I want to belong . . . What I'm saying is, we were getting on really well before I left and I'd always thought – well, I suppose I thought that we'd become a couple. That there was something special growing between us.'

His head snapped up now and his face was brighter than the moon shining down on them.

'I've never stopped wanting you,' he said huskily. 'And I meant every word I said that night. I *do* love you.'

'Then how about we go back to where we left off and try again?' she suggested as she studied his face anxiously.

He reached out and took her hand, and it felt right, and as they began to wander along, Rebecca suddenly knew that she would never know another lonely moment or ever run away again. It had been a long, heartbreaking journey but she felt she had finally come home to where she belonged.

Epilogue

August 2006

The tiny church on the east coast was full of the scent of roses and lily of the valley as Rebecca floated down the aisle on Harvey's arm in a froth of silk and lace. Pat had had large vases full of the flowers placed strategically here and there, to match the blooms in her daughter's bridal bouquet. The pews were full to capacity with the circus folk all dressed in their very best, and they smiled at the bride as she passed them. Red was there looking well and happy, with his new partner, a nice chap called Ben who seemed to have eyes only for Red. Rebecca had met him briefly the day before and was thrilled to find that Red was now living back at home with his parents, who were ensuring that he received the best medical treatment that money could buy. And Joe was there too, sitting in the front pew with his pretty fiancée next to Pat and Caz, her mother and grandmother, both looking splendid in hats that would not have looked out of place at Ascot. But then her eyes rested on Ricky, standing in front of the altar looking handsome in his smart morning suit, and everything and everyone else faded away and there might only have been the two of them in the church.

'We are gathered here today in the sight of God to join together this man and woman in Holy Matrimony . . .'

Rebecca blinked back happy tears as the vicar began the

marriage service, and then Gina stepped forward and lifted the gauzy veil that covered her face. Rebecca stole a glance at Ricky and her heart swelled with happiness. He looked so proud.

In the front pew, Pat was smiling radiantly and dabbing at her tears, looking every inch the bride's mother in her new two-piece suit. They had had such fun choosing it together. Pat had also shopped for every item of Rebecca's wedding outfit with her and gone to great pains to make sure that everything was just perfect, right down to the very last detail.

Gina had now gone to take her place at Pat's side and she too smiled fondly as she gazed at the happy couple. She and Harvey had been married in a quiet register office ceremony the year before, and she looked contented as she sedately folded her hands in her lap.

It was almost two years since Rebecca had rejoined the circus and she was scarcely recognisable as the troubled girl that Gina had first taken in. Now her eyes shone and she had become a favourite amongst the circus folk, totally accepted as one of their own. She could feel their love coming off them in waves as they all looked on, beaming their approval.

Following the wedding, she and Ricky would be living in a new trailer that they had chosen and furnished together, and Rebecca could hardly wait for her new life to begin.

She tried to concentrate on what the vicar was saying, but felt as if she was floating. She had never realised that such happiness could exist! The sad little misfit that she had once been had grown into a woman who belonged.

Don't miss Rosie Goodwin's new novel:

The Empty Cradle

Rosie Goodwin

To the outside world, Charlotte is the privileged daughter of the local vicar. Behind closed doors, however, her life is cruelly controlled by her father's cold power. As she grows up, Charlotte longs for freedom, but her captivating innocence leads her into trouble. Sent to Ireland to hide a shameful pregnancy, she discovers that once again her father has deceived her. She is forced into a convent's harsh and humiliating regime, where she must eventually give up the one thing that makes her life worthwile.

When Charlotte returns to England, older than her years, she chooses to forget the past. Becoming a London midwife, she longs only to help bring other women at this hardest and most joyful moment in their lives. But her deep compassion, and desire to prevent anyone else suffering the same horror she did, leads her into a darker and more dangerous place.

Available now from Headline

978 0 7553 8575 1

headline

Whispers

Rosie Goodwin

The old manor house has stood empty for years, left to rot since the last master of the Fenton family died. Until Jess Beddows steps inside, and feels she has come home. Against her family's wishes, she buys the house, promising to bring it back to life.

In an attic room untouched for a century or more, she finds a journal. It holds the heartbreaking tale of Martha, and of the cruel, entangled lives of the house's servants and masters nearly two hundred years before. As Jess is drawn into their tragedy, the whispers begin. Before long, everything she loves will be threatened by violent emotion and long-kept secrets. Can she survive the echoes from the past?

Praise for Rosie Goodwin's novels:

'A touching and powerful novel from a wonderful writer' *Bookseller*

'The tear-jerker of the season . . . [a] heart-rending tale' *Western Mail*

'The all-too-rare skills of a true storyteller shine through Rosie Goodwin's writing' Gilda O'Neill

978 0 7553 5394 1

headline

You can buy any of these bestselling books
by **Rosie Goodwin** from your bookshop
or *direct from her publisher*.

FREE P&P AND UK DELIVERY
(Overseas and Ireland £3.50 per book)

The Bad Apple	£8.99
No One's Girl	£8.99
Dancing Till Midnight	£8.99
Moonlight and Ashes	£8.99
Forsaken	£8.99
Our Little Secret	£8.99
Crying Shame	£6.99
Yesterday's Shadows	£5.99
The Boy from Nowhere	£5.99
A Rose Among Thorns	£6.99
The Lost Soul	£8.99
The Ribbon Weaver	£5.99
A Band of Steel	£5.99
Tilly Trotter's Legacy	£8.99
The Mallen Secret	£8.99
The Sand Dancer	£8.99
A Band of Steel	£5.99
Whispers	£5.99

TO ORDER SIMPLY CALL THIS NUMBER

01235 400 414

or visit our website: www.headline.co.uk

Prices and availability subject to change without notice.